A BLAST FROM THE FUTURE—
INTO THE PAST...

As soon as Lu went to the bathroom, Dumfries popped up out of his booth and headed straight for me.

"Jim, we don't have much time," he said, and slid into Lu's place across from me.

And I had no script. All I could hope for was to keep him going without blowing the illusion until Salvador got wise and arranged another blackout. "Who are you?" I said, sure I wasn't getting the tone right. *Who* are you? Who *are* you? Who are *you*?

"Jim," he said, "look into my eyes. You must recognize me. I'm *you* from the future, an old man. I've traveled through time to see you. You must do what I tell you. Everything depends on it."

THE BRIGHT SPOT

Robert Sydney

BANTAM BOOKS

THE BRIGHT SPOT
A Bantam Spectra Book / July 2005

Published by
Bantam Dell
A Division of Random House, Inc.
New York, New York

All rights reserved
Copyright © 2005 by Dennis Danvers
Cover illustration copyright © 2005 by Dave Johnson
Book design by Carol Russo
Cover design by Jamie S. Warren Youll

If you purchased this book without a cover, you should be aware that this book is stolen property. It was reported as "unsold and destroyed" to the publisher, and neither the author nor the publisher has received any payment for this "stripped book."

Bantam Books, the rooster colophon, Spectra, and the portrayal of a boxed "s" are trademarks of Random House, Inc.

ISBN 0-553-58759-5

Printed in the United States of America
Published simultaneously in Canada

www.bantamdell.com

OPM 10 9 8 7 6 5 4 3 2 1

FOR MY DAD, BECAUSE
HE WOULD'VE LIKED IT BEST

Contents

1 NICHOLAS BAINBRIDGE
2 THE LAPDOG GENE
3 MEAN STREETS AND HAPPY TEARS
4 MINVIRT
5 WHAT DID WHO SAY?
6 ANY VICES, MR. BAINBRIDGE?
7 OH
8 JUST A NAME
9 A DOLL'S HOUSE
10 DADDY NEEDS A NEW PAIR OF SHOES
11 CERTAINTY AGAIN
12 HERE THEY COME
13 THE BRIDEGROOM'S RETURN
14 WHERE'S THE ART?
15 TOO LATE
16 JUST DOWN THE ROAD

17 DRINKS ON TREY

18 A FINAL MESSAGE

19 THE SNOWMAN RULE

20 THE RIME OF THE ALDEBRIAN MARINER

21 COMMUNION

22 STEER CLEAR OF THE CONGO

23 RISE AND SHINE

ACKNOWLEDGMENTS

I would like to thank those who read *The Bright Spot* in progress and offered invaluable suggestions and criticism—Shawna McCarthy, Juliet Ulman, Christopher Schelling, and Sarah Weisiger. I would also like to thank Liz Darhansoff for many years of wise counsel. Finally, thanks to Judy Howlett for the loan of her dog Dice in the creation of Buck.

OEDIPUS: Where are you, children?
Come, come to your brother's hands—

—SOPHOCLES, *Oedipus the King*

HAMLET: What's Hecuba to him, or he to Hecuba,
That he should weep for her?

—SHAKESPEARE, *Hamlet*

NICHOLAS BAINBRIDGE

1

At this time a slight sleep relieved me from the pain of reflection, which was disturbed by the approach of a beautiful child, who came running into the recess I had chosen, with all the sportiveness of infancy. Suddenly, as I gazed on him, an idea seized me that this little creature was unprejudiced and had lived too short a time to have imbibed a horror of deformity. If, therefore, I could seize him and educate him as my companion and friend, I should not be so desolate in this peopled earth.

—MARY SHELLEY, *Frankenstein*

THEY CALLED THEMSELVES RECREATION, DESCRIBED themselves as sort of educational, sort of artsy. The pay was lousy, but I needed work. They never touched anything that wasn't a classic—a term they took to mean old enough so that even all the translators' rights had run out a century ago. They didn't want to share the carcass with other scavengers. They thought themselves cutting edge when they screwed around with *Heart of Darkness*, like they'd never heard of Coppola. Come to think of it, they probably hadn't. *Heart of Darkness* either, for that matter, except as a test question or two, long, long ago. They were into literature for the money.

They monitored the feedback from high school kids responding to the standard dose of virtual classics and identified the plot forks that didn't sit quite so well with the modern sixteen-year-old in a VR box as they had with the original audience reading them off the page. Sufficient youthful dissatisfaction made any classic a candidate for a ReCreation makeover. The idea was the kids would get more *involved* if the story wasn't just cut and dry, always the same, if their roles weren't so passive, and they had *choices* to make. As the promotional propaganda cooed: "Young minds will be empowered by shaping the literature they experience, just as it is shaping them!"

As if it wasn't obvious what they were really up to. They, and a dozen others just like them at the time, were trying to reproduce the success of *Lucky Lucifer's Pair-o'-Dice,* an immensely popular adaptation of Milton's *Paradise Lost* based on the none-too-surprising finding that most sixteen-year-olds liked Lucifer a *whole* lot better than the boring, conceited Lord God of Hosts. *Lucky* started out as an educational alternative virtual, quickly broke into mainstream, then became an enduring media phenomenon (if "enduring" means more than a couple of years). The Midwest educational programmer who dreamed it up and financed the whole thing with do-good educational grants from Coca-Cola and Philip Morris (or whatever they were calling themselves that week) was now a good deal richer than God. Who says there's no justice in the universe? Not Lucifer, certainly.

THE BRIGHT SPOT

ReCreation hoped to follow in his digital footsteps with a clear business plan: (1) create educational alternative virtuals—grant-funded and tax-incentived and available on demand 24/7 to kids who want their learning to be fun and engaging; (2) hope like hell the little bastards choose *your* fun and engaging garbage out of the landfill on offer; and then (3) watch their folks follow like lemmings, dragging everybody else over the abyss with them.

What choice did we have? Being a single, childless person over thirty-five wasn't yet illegal—which was very tolerant of the society at large, considering what selfish, immature, shallow, un-American, unnatural deviants we all were.

Yeah. The kids were where the money was in those days, and ReCreation was hoping this classics angle might pay off and they too would become richer than God. Unfortunately, until that noble goal was reached, hiring actors like me was a necessary inconvenience.

"We're trying to save this stuff from extinction," Wally the writer—Gary the director's brother-in-law—said in my interview. I think he actually believed it. That's what they called the literature they ReCreated—*stuff*, even when they were being pious. Wally said a lot of stupid things, often to himself, and no one ever contradicted him. I gathered from this he was the one with the lion's share of the venture capital. As for Gary and the others, they pretended to care about the words, pretended they were all about empowering hapless youth who had to learn all this old stuff, but all they really cared about were the numbers.

ReCreation itself was little more than a big loft over

some dead retail, furnished with folding chairs, a slumpy sofa, and tables made from old doors and sawhorses. One end of the room was filled with secondhand recording equipment with the logos of several defunct production companies still painted on it. Wally and Gary didn't care. ReCreation, as far as I know, didn't even have a logo. They had a vision. They were either going to make it big, or pack it up when the money ran out. Who needed a logo? What they needed was an instant classic.

Wally typically sat at the other end of the loft from the hardware and the crew, and wrote his heart out. I suspected that the whole enterprise might really be about Wally's writing aspirations, and he secretly didn't care about the money. Of course, if they didn't make any money, his writing career would be very brief.

The rest of us, under Gary's direction, brought Wally's words to life on the other end. There were a half-dozen others in various capacities doing all the real work, as well as playing bit parts as needed.

In my first role for them, I was cast as Marlow in *Heart of Darkness II*, in which Marlow, after telling his mates *Heart of Darkness* in one incredibly long-winded evening, decides next morning, in a fit of implausible feminism, that he must make his way to Brussels and tell Kurtz's nameless Intended nothing less than the Truth, even if she is a woman. I asked Gary if he didn't mean lowercase truth, but he insisted he wanted all caps, bold and italics for good measure, extra mayo and pickles. All of which told me he'd never read any Conrad and wasn't about to start now.

"Fine," I said. That's what I always said to directors. Which is one reason I'm not an actor anymore.

HD2 starts with me hitting the mean streets of Brussels, and before you know it, the Intended and I are floating down the Congo having a torrid affair—*African Queen* meets *Last Tango in Paris*, but without the butter and leeches. This got us immediately filtered out of all but the most progressive educational feeds, but Wally didn't seem to mind dumping our target audience before we laid a finger on them. He was making art. He was inspired. He was nuts. Meanwhile, back in *HD2*, the object of our river cruise and our sexual marathon grew increasingly muddled and complex. Something to do with redemption and missed opportunities and looking up Kurtz's African lover for a possible ménage à trois, according to my undeliverable lines.

For me, this was yet another career-ending opportunity. If *HD2* broke out as the latest dreadful, I'd never live it down. Fortunately, I was heavily made up to accommodate Gary's idea of ruddy sailor, and I was using a stage name, Nicholas Bainbridge. Everyone called me Nick. Including my costar, the Intended, whose real name, she swore, was Luella Anthony.

No one knew my real name.

No one even nibbled at the *HD2* feed but the porn crowd, and Luella and I weren't good enough to hold them for long, especially since we had to stop now and again and muse about what it all *meant* in Wally's bad prose. Though, increasingly, Luella and I wandered from the script in self-defense or out of boredom. Once, when we were going at it in a pretzel-like position Wally must've cribbed from the Kama Sutra, Luella cried out, "The horror! The horror!" and I cracked up laughing.

I think that's when I started falling for Luella, the

real one, not the Intended, whose name (we had to give her a name) was Tiffany. "Tiffany isn't Belgian, is it?" I asked and everyone gave me a blank look but Luella, who stifled a smile. She reads, I thought then. I wonder what her story is. And I determined to find out.

So far, I hadn't had much luck. She was younger than my around forty, but not by that much. She rode the bus. I didn't know which one. But I'd seen her at the stop up the street. Her street clothes, like mine, were strictly thrift store. She never talked about her life outside that loft. But then, I didn't either. There wasn't that much to talk about. My place was about the size of this sentence. Furnished. After dinner you could hear cans hitting the pile at the bottom of the air shaft. I added mine to the clatter, beans usually. When the cans reached the windowsill, I planned to walk across the shaft and visit my neighbors, trade recipes or something.

Heart of Darkness II faded as quickly as a neutrino. But ReCreation liked my work, which is to say they suspected I was desperate enough to make another one of their turkeys, and they had yet to exhaust their funds. Dead grandfather money, I believe it was. Anyway, we did a meeting.

"Have you ever read *Frankenstein*?" Gary asked me.

"Yes," I said. They nodded at each other—the flock of them—impressed I was such a reader. I'd discovered they were all related to one another in some way or other—cousins, nieces, step-something-or-others—except for Brenda, the researcher, who, as implausible as it seemed, used to be Wally's girlfriend. These days, they scarcely gave each other a glance.

"Why do you ask?" I said.

THE BRIGHT SPOT

"We want you to play Victor Frankenstein."

"What's the gimmick?" I'd learned from the ReCreation bunch that *gimmick* wasn't a pejorative term, but the thing to be sought after in any potentially lucrative work of art. Mary Shelley and I waited with trepidation to hear Gary and Wally's take on her novel.

"Well, you know the part in the novel where the monster runs into William, Victor's kid brother, and the monster tries to befriend him, but the kid's a little shit, and the monster kills him?" Gary, who never encumbered himself with the classic he was ReCreating, made a quick look around to make sure he'd gotten the scene right, and got the nod from Brenda. After they saw all that feedback, she would've been the one to check it out, maybe even reading the scene itself. She was holding the pages in her hands—not the scene from the novel, but the numbers on the feedback—the breakdown on how all these kids across the nation felt the scene should go, if it was up to them, which, with ReCreation's help, it was.

"Yes. I know the scene. The whole novel hinges on it."

"Oh yeah? Pretty good, then, huh? 'Cause we've got a negative feedback wave there like you wouldn't believe. Kids *really* like the monster. They figure he gets a bad deal. Everybody treats him like shit, apparently. They identify with him. You know what I mean? Here's the gimmick: The kid's *nice*. The monster and the kid become friends. Like, like—I don't know—Rocky and Bullwinkle, Lucky and Beebub."

The ReCreation catalogue was filled with stupid ideas, but this was the stupidest yet. It just might have a chance to make it big. "Sure, I'll do it. You should get Luella for Elizabeth, Victor's fiancée."

"There's no fiancée," Gary said. "Luella's the female creature. Right?"

Brenda nodded.

"There is no female creature," I said. "That's only in the movies. Victor destroys it before he brings it to life."

"Tell that to Wally."

Wally, as usual, was sitting at his card table, at the other end of the loft, in another universe, writing up a storm. Everybody looked at him. "When do we start?" I asked.

"We'll call you when we cast the monster and the kid. A couple of days maybe."

I caught up with Luella waiting for her bus. "I understand we're going to be working together again," I said, still a little breathless. I hadn't run three blocks in a while. The blurry wall of moving cars behind her made me slightly dizzy. At this time of day, the streets were a single, slithering snake of machinery.

We hadn't talked much about anything except whatever scene we were working on, though often we traded wisecracks and eye rolls behind Gary's back, and ad libs designed more for each other than an audience neither of us believed would ever exist. Standing there at the bus stop, she smiled at me like we were still trading some inside joke. "Is that a good thing?" she asked.

"Yes, certainly. Definitely a good thing. The best. You want to go have a drink or something? To...to celebrate?"

THE BRIGHT SPOT

Her smile widened. "Celebrate your certainty? Sure. But do you do that—go out for drinks?"

"Not usually." She knew what kind of money I made. She made the same.

"You don't have to spend a lot of money to celebrate. Just bus fare. There's a place in my neighborhood. Very affordable. My treat."

The bus pulled up, like part of a torrential river just stopped and became this bus. The cars flowed around it. I followed her on before I remembered I didn't have any cash. I rode on her pass, or because she was friends with the friendly driver, I wasn't sure which, but my mind was on other things. The bus was packed. Luella and I rode standing, hanging from the same loop, our bodies pressed up against each other, jostling together with the ceaseless motion of the bus.

Lots of people think we actually fuck making virtuals, thinking that's the only way it could be so incredibly real. If that were true, canned laughter would make any joke funny. Somebody has to fuck, it's true, but it's not us. We assume the positions, we deliver the lines. We don't experience the fuck unless we pay to play, like anybody else.

But here I was, riding in a real bus plastered up against the flesh-and-blood Luella, as the bus weaved and bounced down the street, the driver swerving back and forth to miss the potholes that were everywhere once we left the smart grid. Or maybe he was aiming for them. The effect was about the same. It was a rough-and-tumble ride, and I loved every minute of it.

THE LAPDOG GENE 2

> ELWOOD: *Years ago my mother used to say to me, she'd say, "In this world, Elwood, you must be"—she always called me Elwood—"In this world, you must be oh so smart or oh so pleasant." Well, for years I was smart. I recommend pleasant. And you may quote me.*
>
> —MARY CHASE, *Harvey*

Luella lived in a neighborhood on its way up. She was one of the folks being left behind—the ones who didn't have bars on their windows, stockade fences around their backyards, and licensed cars parked out front on their freshly paved streets. We passed all that and headed down a street where the only car on the block hadn't gone anywhere in so long it had cats living in it. She stopped in front of a small run-down house on the corner. It was dark, and the front porch drooped. There were voices and laughter coming from somewhere close by. "We're here," she said.

"Is this where you live?" I asked.

THE BRIGHT SPOT

"No, this is the place I was telling you about. You know—to celebrate." She hooked her arm through mine and led me around the side of the house to the backyard. We entered through a ramshackle chain-link gate. "You've heard of sidewalk cafes?" she said. "This is an alley cafe."

It was called Murphy's because the house belonged to a Clarence Murphy, who didn't happen to be there that evening. An assortment of kitchen tables, plastic tables, picnic tables, card tables, with every sort of chair, filled the backyard. There were Christmas lights strung everywhere, candles on the tables, people in most of the chairs. A big old refrigerator sat next to the back door that went into the kitchen—off-limits—and the bathroom beyond that—flush only when necessary. You bought beers out of the fridge, putting your money in a lidless rectangle of Tupperware, or if you didn't have any money, you brought something when you could—beer, food, whatever—to keep the place going. Murphy, Luella told me, had started the place with two cases of Icehouse twenty years earlier, when he found the perfectly good refrigerator sitting abandoned in an alley, the victim of remodeling, and it was too big to fit through his back door. Folks brought furniture, mostly from alleys as well.

It had never once run dry or gone broke, the story went, though the new neighbors were on the case. It was an eyesore, they said, clearly visible from their cars rushing by, closer and closer all the time—as relentless as the rising tax assessments on these mostly-paid-for dumps. Pretty soon their owners couldn't afford to live here anymore. In the meantime, they had Murphy's.

This night, there looked to be about twenty dollars in the Tupperware, and about six cases of assorted beers packed into the fridge. There was a box of white wine, and Luella had some of that in a coffee cup she got out of the kitchen—even as she was telling me it was off-limits. I had an Icehouse, not my usual choice, in honor of those founding cases Luella told me about.

There was a big TV on top of the fridge, another alley refugee that wouldn't fit through Murphy's back door. Ancient DVDs played continuously. A blue tarp was strung over it to protect it from the elements, making it look like it was wearing a glowing blue bonnet. Sometimes everybody watched—Luella said—sometimes nobody did. This was one of those nobody nights. Everybody was too interested in who Luella'd brought home to the neighborhood.

"This is Nick," she said. "We work together."

"Is he the one you're always talking about?" one of the women said, laughing, shaking her shoulders.

"Yes," Luella said. "If you must know—he plays Marlow."

There were several whoops and cheers, and the whole crowd toasted me. When the hubbub died down and we took a table in the back corner by ourselves, I asked Luella, "You tell everybody about our work?"

"Tell them? I'm worse than that. I smuggle out copies. They pass it around. There's a couple of bootleg boxes in the neighborhood, one at the library, when it works. Why not?" she said. "It's fun. They like hearing about it. They think it's glamorous. They don't care how bad it is. They know somebody making virtuals. Beats the hell out of some workware job, doesn't it?"

THE BRIGHT SPOT

"I wouldn't know." I was having trouble adjusting to all these people smiling at us who'd virtually experienced Luella and I doing something I only hoped to do.

"I didn't think so," she said.

"I'm sorry. What?"

"You've never done a workware job."

"True. I've managed to avoid them. You going to hold that against me?"

"Only if you're defensive about it. Nobody *wants* to do them. And if some rich kid like you manages to end up poor, why should I have a problem with that? I've been poor all my life."

"You've caught me at my most affluent—no debt, no possessions. I thought all you poor kids wanted to be rich."

"We do. I'm just not very good at it." She laughed, and our eyes met, and we were content with that for a while. I was used to looking at her in character—looking like Luella, but chiseled into some state of refinement through acting and makeup Gary thought suited Tiffany. The real Luella was altogether different. Like the difference between a cut rose and an oak tree.

Then Clarence's wife, Sylvia, came to our table and welcomed me to the place, told me I could come back anytime, with or without Luella. "Unless you're a cop."

"Not guilty," I said. "Cops and I don't get along." That was all I wanted to say on that subject. "Where do you get your old DVDs?" I asked, nodding toward the antique set playing *Signs*. No wonder nobody was watching. Aliens invade Earth so Mel Gibson can get right with God. Didn't aliens have better things to do with their time? Even totally implausible ones?

"Clarence has a big box of old movies his boss gave him when he cleaned out his garage—back before everything was 'ware, when Clarence had a job. Folks bring them in now and then. We make do. Like everything else."

"I'll bring some next time. I'm a collector. I have lots of dupes."

Sylvia smiled. "What's your name again?"

"Nicholas."

"What do they call you, Nicholas?"

"Ted."

Sylvia laughed big at that. "All right, *Ted*. We'll see you around. Luella, I like your boyfriend."

Luella said, "He's not my boyfriend, yet."

Sylvia winked at me. "Honey, this is your lucky night." Then she was gone to another table to thank them for bringing the wheel of cheese and can of crackers that was the hors d'oeuvre for the evening.

Lots of people stopped by our table. It was an older crowd mostly. They'd known Luella since she was a kid in the neighborhood, known her mother, Bea, who'd passed a few years back. That's how they put it. They were old-fashioned that way. They spoke fondly of Bea and Li'l Lu beside me, told me stories, and checked me out.

The younger ones asked Luella if she'd heard about Mike, who turned up dead the other night, and she had. They shook their heads. Nobody seemed surprised. They'd all gone to school together. He dealt. He was dead.

What I kept noticing was how everybody talked to Li'l Lu with a touch of deference. They'd liked her mother. They liked her. They wanted to like me—

THE BRIGHT SPOT

because she did—but I *better* not fuck up and hurt a single hair on her head. I couldn't imagine anywhere on the planet I could take Luella where my friends would do the same for me, nor would there be nearly so many. We'd be lucky to have enough for poker. No one had to tell me I was a lucky man, I felt it like a warm glow, like an alien invasion.

Some older folks called her Bea's Lu, apparently coined to distinguish her from some other Lu who had been around sometime or other. It came out as one word. It took me a minute to figure out what they were saying.

"What is that?" I asked, "the hive bathroom?"

"Be nice," she said.

"Gladly. Maybe it's an archaic verb. Beslew. As in 'Ye have beslew my heart.'"

"Do you always talk so pretty?"

"I can talk any way you like."

"I just bet you can."

"It's true, you know—I'm completely beslewed."

"Keep talking," she said. "You're doing all right."

Luella stuck with wine. Sylvia unearthed a hidden Guinness for my third beer. I was deeply flattered.

"So, you want to walk me home?" Luella asked. "I'll make you an omelet."

"I'd love to." Neither one of us had had anything to eat but cheese and crackers since a takeout Chinese lunch.

"We can take the alley. I'll introduce you to Buck. He'll take to you quicker if you come in the back door. Through the front, he might think you're the postman." Home turned out to be four doors down. Buck turned out to be her dog, a Pekingese-chow mix, who raced around deliriously, bringing me his toys, hoping I knew what to do with them. He fetched, he tugged, he sat up and begged. "Pick him up," Luella said. We were sitting on the sofa. She was rolling a joint.

I wrapped my hands around his rib cage, lifted him up facing me, and looked into his dark, wild eyes. He went still and serene, with a look of supreme delight on his smashed-in mug, his black tongue peeking out the corners of his mouth. He was lighter than he looked. He was mostly fur.

"It's the lapdog gene," Luella said, licking the paper's edge with the tip of her tongue in a slow, steady motion. "Pick him up, and he's all blissful submission. Put him down, and he's all play. Go ahead. Put him in your lap. He'll be your friend for life."

I put my knees together and placed him like a lion at rest. He sat there as still as a statue in front of a Chinese restaurant. I scratched the top of his head, and he closed his eyes in doggy nirvana, groaning with delight. Luella lit the joint and handed it to me.

It was my lucky night. No matter how things turned out later. That was one incredibly lucky night, even if the omelet didn't get made till late the next morning.

By the end of the week, as promised, ReCreation called us back in to work. We were, by then, an item, but we decided to keep it to ourselves. We were actors. Pretending we were something we weren't came naturally.

The monster and the kid had been predictably cast. The monster topped out at nearly seven feet and had hands like hams. He was very soft-spoken, however, and painfully polite. The kid was another matter. He looked like a mad scientist's kid brother—very Aryan, eyes like circles of cloudless sky, skin like a bucket of cream, too beautiful for his own good. He looked ten and was actually thirty-one. He was a professional (he told us every few minutes) who'd been in the business over twenty years. He'd made *sacrifices,* he said pointedly.

By this I gathered he'd had genetic modifications some years ago to keep his fading career as a kid actor going, and now, without the money to reverse the procedure, he was stuck with looking like a kid for the rest of his life. When he wasn't telling us all what a pro he was, rattling off credits, quoting reviews, dropping names, he was hitting on Brenda and Luella, reassuring them that some things hadn't been modified in the least. Surely if the kids who didn't like William's fate in the original *Frankenstein* met this William, they'd be begging the monster to wring his arrogant little neck. His little prick while he was at it.

"Let's talk concept," Gary said, getting things started. Gary believed in bottom-up intelligence, by which he meant he wanted our ideas since he rarely had any of his own, and he didn't entirely trust Wally's.

I groaned and stared at the ceiling, longing to will myself back in bed with Luella, but it didn't work. William, I missed his real name, jumped right in. "My character's the one with the issues here, right? The real struggle. The whole tolerance thing. Overcoming fear and prejudice."

"Oh brother," I said.

"Let him finish," Gary said. "How do you see the other characters?"

He placed his perfect little fingertips together. "Fixated on me. My big brother Victor there couldn't get along with the big guy, and now he's my best bud. Got to hurt. And the female creature's got to be disappointed, hooked up with a monster. *Great* idea: She makes a play for me behind the monster's back, and I take pity on her."

Gary looked momentarily impressed.

"Wally!" Luella surprised everyone by shouting down to the other end of the loft. Wally raised his head above the fog of composition.

"Wally," she said, "do you know the story of *Pygmalion*?"

He shook his head.

"Let me tell it to you." She left the meeting and sat down with Wally. A few minutes later, they summoned Gary, who argued with them for a while, but soon relented. Luella and Gary returned, and Gary delivered the word from the oracle:

"Victor brings the female creature to life and falls passionately, obsessively in love with her. She returns his love. The monster consoles himself with his pal, William—who, like I said before is, well, *nice*."

"What is this 'nice' shit?" William demanded. "Am I playing a damn queer or what?"

"Be tolerant," I suggested.

"I wasn't talking to you," William snarled. "I was talking to him." He pointed a menacing tiny perfect finger at Gary.

"Nice is just *nice*," Gary snapped. "You want the job or not?"

Since he put it that way, yes, of course he did, but William hated me and Luella forever after. He probably

THE BRIGHT SPOT

hated Wally and Gary too, but Wally would never notice and Gary didn't care, so what did it matter?

As Luella and I rode the bus back to her place, which had also been my place for the past week, we were both in a funk imagining working on this idiot project for the next several months. God knew what Wally and Gary would have us doing next, and that insufferable William... We commiserated for a while as the bus jostled along.

Then out of the blue Luella asked me if I was interested in taking on a one-time job some weekend. "It's a real-time interactive. You ever do that?"

"Once or twice. A murder dinner-theater thing. It's like busking in a box. Is it a better gig than this ReCreation nonsense? I'm more than half ready to dump them altogether."

"It's more interesting. It's historical—right after the war. It's very tightly scripted, but you're such a quick study, you won't have any trouble with that. You also have to be ready to think on your feet, ad-lib if necessary. I think you'd be perfect. The pay's good. Interested?"

"Definitely. What's not to like?"

"It's probably illegal."

"Does anyone die?"

"No. They're just deceived."

"Do they want to be deceived?"

"Oh yes."

"Then I'm your man."

"I'll set it up, then. It might be a few weeks."

MEAN STREETS AND HAPPY TEARS

3

Be all that you can be, in the A-a-army.

—U.S. Army recruiting jingle

Some weeks later I was all settled into the neighborhood. The street alongside Murphy's was being repaved to accommodate the increase in car traffic brought on by the new neighbors. The buses could navigate the old roads okay, but cars and their owners were more delicate, more in need of a helping hand from the state. Where the rich folks went, the latest in pavement technology soon followed. Isn't that why we all pay taxes?

A workware crew, naturally, was doing the job. Every evening they got a little closer to Murphy's, until finally they were working right alongside the place, just the other side of the chain link, under the big lights they use, brighter than daylight, but colder and whiter. Nobody even bothered to put a DVD in the set. Everybody just sat there watching them, talking about them. Not them, exactly. The life.

THE BRIGHT SPOT

The smell drove a lot of people away, including Lu, but I stuck around. They said it was the smell, but it was a lot of things. It was one thing to watch a workware crew if you never thought you'd be in their number, but if you had been or even thought you might, it was painful to watch. Masochistic, you might say.

Lu had struck a nerve when she asked me if I'd ever done a workware job. Each year as I got a little older, and my earnings as a professional actor got a little smaller and jobs harder to find, I imagined myself being one of those guys someday. That one there, duck-walking around like it was perfectly natural to walk that way for twelve hours at a stretch, plugging components into the roadway without a real inkling of what he was doing, as gray as a goose, his eyes as dead as a camera lens. What had he been in his younger days? Singer? Stockbroker? What failure had put him out there? Birth or bad investments or bad reviews? No, it was the good reviews that did you in, that kept you hanging around, hoping for a break, so you never got it together in what everyone else called the real world, and then all that was left was workware. That's one thing about workware, you didn't waste any time hoping. Not one little bit.

"They can't hear nothing we're saying," Dell said, watching them squirt the road with plastic paving, implanting the sensors, aiming the lights, dancing around the guck and the stench like a ballet in double time. The street ballet. Without the workware they couldn't stand the heat, the smell, the chemicals in their lungs. They wouldn't know the simple color code that told them which one was the thingamajig and which one was a gizmo, which wire would fry you to a crisp and which one wouldn't. Without the 'ware they'd be lying dead in the street. With it, they worked so fast it was like watching a shell game in twelve-hour shifts. Under all those shells, a human was hidden.

"They hear just fine," Amber said. "They don't *understand* nothing."

"Same difference," Dell said. "If you're not understanding it, you're not hearing it. You don't *remember* it, anyway."

"They don't need to understand anything but what they're doing," Lyndon said. "No distractions. It channels your energies."

"Channel, my ass. Everybody needs to understand more than work. 'Less they wanta be a fucking machine." Dell glared at us fiercely.

Lyndon wasn't cowed. "Maybe they're safer being machines. They'd be dead without the 'ware. That's why soldiers and firefighters got it. My daddy was a fireman, twenty-five years...."

"Screw soldiers and firefighters. Screw your daddy too. They can have it. Fighting fires and wars and shit is one thing. Making roads for rich people to drive their cars on—what's that shit anyway? Let 'em pour their own damn roads."

"You tell 'em, Dell."

"It eats your brain, I'm telling you. They say it shut *down* at the end of your shift, but it don't. I'm telling you, I know what I'm talking about." He eyed us all defiantly, hoping someone would argue with him. Lyndon was thinking about it. He might be a peaceable fellow, but he didn't appreciate that crack about his daddy.

Sylvia's shadow fell over the discussion. "Dell done

THE BRIGHT SPOT

laid himself too many roads, roofed too many houses, hacked up too many hogs and chickens, cleaned up too much shit—ain't that right, Dell?" As she spoke, she set down a rum and Coca-Cola—Dell's preferred poison when he could get it—on a little napkin in front of him. There were even a few ice cubes floating in it. Veterans Day at Murphy's.

"Damn right," Dell said, toasting us all.

By this time the road crew was out of sight, and the new road looked ready for traffic. They wouldn't waste any time. The bus we took to work now was driverless. I went home and crawled into bed with Lu, holding her close.

"Tomorrow's the big day," she said.

"Right," I said, but I couldn't get the image of the workers dancing out of my mind. Dell's voice insisting: *I'm telling you, I know what I'm talking about.*

I smelled coffee. I felt Lu's lips at my ear. She whispered softly, "Ted...Oh, Te-ed."

I was lying in bed on my back, my eyes closed, Buck on one side of me in pretty much the same position, snoring softly, Luella on the other, whispering in my ear.

"Why're you calling me Ted?" I mumbled groggily. "You mixing me up with some other guy?"

"You told Sylvia people call you Ted." She kissed my neck. She was good at it, accomplished even. I stirred to life.

"Mmm. People call me lots of things. I was kidding with her." I opened my eyes. Lu looked back at me with her big brown eyes, climbed on top of me, resting her chin on her folded hands, settling her body on mine like a cat on a sofa back. God, she felt good.

"You don't seem like a Nicholas to me."

I propped up my head and met her gaze, shifted my position, trying to make her as comfortable as possible. "How about Nick, then?"

She smiled. "Did you say 'dick'?"

"If you like."

She kissed my mouth. Buck groaned and snorted as he found himself being evicted from the bed with a rude shove.

Lu and I had originally had this conversation some weeks before and had repeated it several times since, so that it wasn't about anything but getting to the same blissful conclusion.

But while usually on a Saturday we would fall back to sleep to the sounds of Buck crunching dry food in the kitchen, waking only when he demanded his walk, this morning Lu whispered in my ear again.

"Come on, Nick. Wake up."

"Mmm?"

"Drink your coffee. We need to get going. Today's the day." She kissed my cheek and went into the bathroom. I opened my eyes to get a glimpse of her retreat, a sight I never tired of.

It was the day of the special, one-day, mysterious job—a bit of a journey, I'd been told—and we mustn't be late. "My coffee will be cold," I grumbled in mock protest.

"Is that a complaint?" She turned in the doorway, framed and beautiful.

"I have no complaints. Not a single one in the universe, in the multiverse. I can't even *imagine* a single complaint." She smiled at my lustful excess and disappeared into the bathroom. I groped for my coffee where I knew it would be on the bedside table. It was still warm. Lu had covered the cup with the saucer when she set it down, knowing she would call me Ted, and we'd make love, and here I'd be, listening to her shower, living in paradise, drinking warm coffee. Lu always seemed to know what she was going to do two, three, four steps down the road. I wasn't like that. But I didn't mind following her. I didn't mind it one bit.

Even the ReCreation gig wasn't turning out as badly as I'd imagined. The *Frankenstein* alternative was now entitled *Billy and the Big Guy* and was drawing pretty decent numbers—on their way up for three weeks running. The plots were always the same: The sickly sweet Billy gets himself in trouble by being so good that evildoers everywhere come looking for a piece of him, just to have a shot at bringing down such perfect goodness. On the brink of certain death for our little Billy, the gentle giant monster—Big Guy, as Billy calls him, BG for short—shows up from whatever contrivance has delayed his arrival, and, after all attempts at reason fail in a couple of minutes or less, reluctantly lays the evildoers to waste with spectacular carnage, ripping hapless villains limb from limb, head from trunk. The gore drenches the audience like a shattered watermelon.

Lu and I are the Boris and Natasha, the Gomez and Morticia, of the tale, the vaguely sexual recurring evil, bumbling after our heroes, recruiting new enemies to the cause along the way, never actually suffering BG's wrath ourselves. Not too far below the surface—in these shallow plots nothing went very deep—our sexuality was, in fact, the real enemy. Certain financial realities had finally impressed themselves on Wally's horny muse—namely, that any number of villains might die a gruesome death, but no lovers were to fuck. So Lu and I never did the deed, but we always acted like we just had or wanted to in the worst way. It was our sexuality that put us in the mood for some evil fun, just like the fallen Adam and Eve. The sustained lust wasn't much of a stretch for me and Lu. Just why all this puritanism was proving popular with the young, I won't speculate. Adolescence was hard on everyone, Mary Shelley included. Course, she turned hers into art. We came along and turned her art into schlock.

William turned out to be an even bigger asshole than he first seemed to be, but the monster, whose real name was Stanton Wetherell, was as nice a guy as you ever want to meet. All of us got in the habit of calling him BG, and he didn't seem to mind. He endured his thankless action sequences, tearing apart thin air—the victims were pasted in later—with patient good humor, but I couldn't imagine him tearing apart a fried chicken wing, much less separating an evildoer's head from his worthless body. His most recent career had been wrestling, but he couldn't cut it there. "Nobody loved me, nobody hated me," he said of his failure. I knew how he felt.

But now, things were better in my life, spectacularly better, like in a movie or in a story, about the time it ends, if you choose wisely. I was in happily-ever-after territory here, and as far as I could tell, there were chapters and chapters left. Thanks mostly to Lu, I was happier than I could remember ever being. Sometimes it was hard to believe this was my life, and I didn't want to change a thing in it. Nicholas Bainbridge had done all right for himself. Mr. and Mrs. Bainbridge hadn't raised any stupid children.

But before I realized all this, I'd said yes to a weekend job, a job that had grown increasingly mysterious in the weeks since. I think Lu knew it was the mystery that interested me, and so she kept me in the dark. I didn't know the story. I didn't know the gimmick. All I knew was the contact's name—Mr. Salvador—and the money. Too much. Way too much. Whatever it was had to be way illegal at those prices.

"What's the crime?" I finally asked.

Lu stopped and thought about it. "Lying to an old man," she said. "What is that, fraud?"

"But he *wants* to be lied to?"

"That's right."

But I couldn't get anything else out of her. Mr. Salvador would explain. In the limo. On the way to the job. Today.

Buck reminded me he needed his morning walk by jumping back up on the bed and standing on my chest. Sometimes his chowish body was a little heavy for his Pekingese ways, but he'd won me over completely. I'd just about taken over the dog-walking duty. I liked doing it. I'd never had a dog before. I found I liked wandering around the neighborhood first thing in the morning. A boy and his dog.

I stuffed my hip pocket with plastic bags and headed

out the door. It was a fine Saturday morning, still early in a way. Everybody who worked Saturdays—which on our block was pretty much everybody with a job but me and Lu—had already gone to work. Everybody else was still inside, except the dogs and their people.

Buck had quickly introduced me to every dog in the neighborhood—those he liked and those he didn't, those who walked themselves and those who came with people attached. One of the solo acts, a blond chow I suspected of being Buck's daddy, was a particular favorite of mine. Most of the ones with people lived in the gentrified blocks and came with pedigrees, the very latest gear to accomplish the difficult task of hooking a person and a dog together, and sweaters. Houndstooth seemed to be in this season. You could always tell a lot about a dog from how he dressed.

"What kind is he?" a woman once inquired of Buck, as the two dogs sniffed each other's butts, circling this way and then that. Her own dog, Kyle—trussed up in something like a violet parachute harness over his salmon mohair—was a variety with a name like someone sneezing. I didn't quite catch it the first time, and didn't want to hear it repeated. *Gesundheit* lurked on the tip of my smartass tongue.

"Buck's an Ipso Facto," I said proudly. "Very rare."

"Is that so?" she said. "He sure is a handsome one. Such a lovely coat."

I didn't have the heart to tell her it was just a mutt on a rope getting so friendly with her Ah-choo, and he did have a lovely coat at that—splotches of rust and tan like a pinto pony.

Buck, the little social climber, strongly preferred the

THE BRIGHT SPOT

gentrified alleys, and, if left to his own devices, would always choose the turns that took us there. I suppose the garbage smells were more promising—the remains of crab dip or goose livers—the stockade fences more satisfying to piss on than chain link, the pampered cats more easily intimidated and less diseased. That morning, I headed directly for one of his favorite alleys. I wasn't trying to rush him exactly, but I wanted to get back and take a shower myself. If we did our usual aimless meander wherever his nose led him, there might not be time.

My strategy worked, and he did the job right away. I bagged it up, and he was doing his little victory dance, a stiff-legged kicking routine Ipso Factos do, when the gate in the stockade fence beside us flew open like a saloon door, at the exact moment I dropped the shit in the trashcan and let the lid fall closed.

"Good morning," I said pleasantly. That's how I was brought up.

"Take that out of there this minute," a sour-faced man snapped at me. He was nicely dressed in expensive casual clothes. I don't know if I could feel casual in anything that cost quite so much as those, and maybe he couldn't either. He looked awfully young for the look on his face. It usually takes years to get a look like that. Maybe he was bred for it.

Buck didn't like his tone and snorted back at him.

"Get him away from me," the man said, though Buck was all bluster and nowhere near him.

"Calm down, would you? You're scaring my dog. You have a nice day now."

I gave him a little wave with all my fingers, avoiding the obvious temptation, and started dragging Buck—

who was apparently ready to stay and make a fight of it—down the alley. But Mr. Casual was itching for a fight too and hollered after me. "I *told* you to get that creature's *shit* out of my trashcan!"

Now *I* didn't like his tone. I should've kept walking. Instead, I walked back, stopping just where Buck reached the end of his tether a foot from Mr. Casual's Italian loafers. I pointed at the can. "It says 'Property of the City' on it. The city doesn't have much left. But it's still got the garbage cans. And this alley we're standing in, for that matter. This is what they call public property."

"That's *my* can." He pointed to his house number painted rather amateurishly on the side.

I gave it a critical appraisal. "I hope you didn't pay anybody to do that. Rather shoddy work. Why don't you just piss on it? That's what Buck does. Me, I plan on putting *all* his shit in it from now on."

"We'll see about that."

"You going to call the trashcan police? Nine-one-one? Wouldn't want to let some crazed nut who picks up after his dog and throws it away in a city trashcan run loose in the public alleyways! Oh my! Oh my! I'll tell you what, *neighbor*. I'll make it easy for you...." That's right. I gave him my address. Can you believe it? I don't know what I was trying to prove. If I was too stupid not to just walk away, I probably should've just beaten the crap out of him and been done with it. He would've sued me for everything I was worth—he might've cleared a dollar ninety-eight—and that would've been that. But no, I had to get cute. Live and never learn.

I hurried Buck home like he'd been the problem,

THE BRIGHT SPOT

feeling more pissed off about the whole business than I knew I should. But by the time I emerged from the shower, I'd put Mr. Casual and his trashcan in perspective.

What did I care? I had a limo to catch with the woman I loved. I told Lu that, telling her the story of Mr. Casual as I was getting dressed. It wasn't the first time I told her I loved her. But it's the time I remember most often. Our eyes met in the mirror, and there were tears in hers. Happy tears, she said. Like most people, I guess, I had a whole lot more experience with the other kind.

MiNViRT

4

> FATHER: *A character, sir, may always ask a man who he is. Because a character has a life which is truly his, marked with his own special characteristics.... And as a result he is always somebody! Whilst a man... And I'm not speaking of you personally at the moment...Man in general...Can quite well be nobody.*
>
> —LUIGI PIRANDELLO, *Six Characters in Search of an Author*

i confess i was like a little kid standing on the curb waiting for the limo to show, childishly impressed by the size of the thing when it hove into view. I'd never been in one outside of once or twice in virtuals, though I thought of them more as movie cars. In the movies from a century ago, back when everybody and their dog drove Hummers and RVs bigger than Lu's house, and middle schoolers hired regular limos for the homecoming dance, something like this is what it took to impress. Now, in this neighborhood, it was only

THE BRIGHT SPOT

slightly less noticeable than a flying saucer stopping off at Murphy's for a cold one. Forget what the thing must've *cost*—one of those prices rounded off to the nearest point million. Just the annual fees on it would keep the whole Murphy's crowd in beer and pizza for a year, with plenty left over for the limo driver.

He sat up front reading a newspaper and was the only one around not paying attention to the car's arrival. He made a show of perusing the headlines and finishing off a Danish. They still called them drivers, though this one seemed largely ornamental, or maybe he was supposed to be security. The car, of course, drove itself, unless the whole grid collapsed, and what good would he be then? He didn't look particularly entertaining. Whatever his purpose, he gave us only a brief glance as we climbed inside, but his eyes gave him away. In that brief glance, he'd taken in all the neighbors watching through cracked blinds. I recognized the paper he pretended to read. It was two or three days old.

As we nestled into the curved seats, the limo closed up around us like a black velvet case for a dinosaur egg. The windows too went black. I looked for some way to open them, but there wasn't any. We weren't supposed to know where we were going. Maybe we weren't going anywhere. There was a box in the middle, no one and nothing else, though there was room for a three-piece band and a dance floor. I got it. We were meeting our host in the box.

"You've been dealing with a virtual Mr. Salvador," I guessed. "You've never actually met the guy."

"That's right," said Lu.

"Lu, he could be anybody."

"I think that was sort of the idea, Nick."

We lurched into motion. I could feel the turns. Right, left, right. I would've thought it'd be smoother. I hadn't been in a car in a long time. The only light came from the box, glowing sky blue, waiting. Lu and I traded a glance. She was leaving it up to me.

What the hell—I touched it, and she did too, and we were in Mr. Salvador's virtual. The box seemed to morph into a handsome deco building about a meter high. A hotel? Pretty standard opening. We seemed to shrink down to its size, and I was immediately disappointed. This thing wasn't near as ambitious as the limo it was playing in. The illusion was clearly bounded, stopping at the curb with a gray wall of emptiness. Cute. Craning my neck back, I saw cloudless sky. Not so much as a pigeon. And I wouldn't trust the elevators. It was clean, though. Cleanest building you ever saw.

This was a strictly no-frills illusion. What they called *minvirt*—short for *minimum virtual*—"they" being people who talked like that. How little can one manage and still deliver the illusion of reality? they wanted to know. They gave me a pain. I could imagine the gang who did this thing spending hours deciding on just the right shade of gray for nothing. That would get bogged down in a discussion of just what sort of nothing they were after this time. Like last time? Oh no. Something new. A *new* nothing. And so on and on and on until you wanted to murder them all. I'd worked for these guys, and that was the part they liked—talking it to death. That's why there were always so many of them, so it wasn't as obvious they were just talking to themselves. That's why the more min the minvirt was, the more max

THE BRIGHT SPOT

the budget. All those espressos started adding up to real money.

There was a row of shiny, new newspaper machines alongside the building. Besides the stuff that could have been anywhere—*Apartment Guide, Fifty Plus,* and *USA Today*—there was a *Washington Post,* so this must be DC. Forty years ago. The headlines were all about the soldiers coming home, the wonders of workware, though they were still calling it Freedomware back then.

We entered the diner at the corner of the building. In a booth in the back was a man with silver hair, tanned and fit, dressed in a knit shirt and slacks like he'd just come off the golf course.

"Jesse Salvador," he introduced himself. He pointed to an old-fashioned clock on the wall, the second hand whirling around. "We don't have much time." He dealt photos on the table like a fortune-teller. The first one was an old man, well up in his eighties I'd say, sitting in a rocking chair a couple of sizes too big for him, on a porch somewhere. In the background, a blurry woman in a bonnet looked on. My guess?—a nurse or visitor took the picture on visitors' day. The old guy may or may not have noticed.

Then there were a series of grainy shots that looked like the diner we were sitting in, the very booth, blown up from old video, the time and date in the corner. I checked the sight angle, and there was a camera up above the counter looking right at us like the eye of God. I hadn't seen one of those big, bulky things in a while. Cameras had become more discreet as they had become ubiquitous. What good was a spy you knew was watching? In the very booth where Lu and I sat across from

Salvador, the photos showed a man and a woman across from each other. If you used your imagination, you could believe the man in them was the old man in the first photo but quite a bit younger.

The next photo, a passport shot of the same vintage, confirmed the suspicion—the eyes, the nose, the mouth, the ears. He was also a dead ringer for me, except he wore a beard. There was a separate shot of the woman in the booth as well. She might've been sitting at a bus stop. I don't think she knew anybody was taking her picture. She looked a lot like Lu, but way too pale. Even her hair was white. But that was easy to change.

"This is James Dumfries today," Salvador said, pointing to the old man. "This is James Dumfries and Galatea Ritsa forty years ago," he said, pointing to the couple in the booth and in the other two shots. He tapped his fingernail on the old man's forehead for emphasis as he told their story. "Here's the deal: The old man is *loaded*, with nobody in the world to leave it to. But he'd pay *anything*, he says, *anything* to see himself with this woman again." He smiled like someone changing a diaper. "He *loved* her, you see. You two will play the lovers for him. Make the poor old fart happy before he kicks off. I believe we have agreed on terms."

Terms aren't everything. I don't like to be rushed, and his story didn't hold together. "I don't get it. He could hire us to play anybody he wants three times a day and tuck him into bed every night with milk and cookies for this much money—and, no offense, he wouldn't have to go through you."

"But it wouldn't be real."

"Neither is this."

THE BRIGHT SPOT

Tap, tap on the forehead again. "He doesn't know that."

"What? How could he not know? Is he senile?"

"Perhaps. He's also taking quite a few medications. You know how those side effects can affect a man's judgment. Or maybe I'm just persuasive. I've got him believing he won't be seeing a mere performance by actors, oh no, he'll be time-traveling to have a look at himself as a younger man. That is why he's willing to pay so handsomely, and it's that illusion we must deliver. Don't worry. He's a babe in the woods. If we didn't take him, someone else would. Basically, I've got him convinced a box is a time machine. He's never used a box before. He doesn't believe in it." Salvador chuckled, finding it laughable that anyone believed or disbelieved in anything. Maybe he was right.

"But even if he believes he's traveling back in time," I said, "how can we hope to fool him? Chances are if it's a woman he wants to see again so badly, he has some pretty vivid memories of her. It's not enough just to look right. What are we supposed to say?"

"And do," Mr. Salvador added. "The slightest touch might be important. But we're not going blindly into the past. We haven't chosen the time at random. We not only have a video of their meeting, we also have a recording of their conversation. Mr. Dumfries understands that because of the tremendous energies involved in time travel, this is a one-time trip of short duration limited to a specific place. Fifteen minutes in this diner. That's it. He gets a front-row seat in the booth across the way there. We have more than enough video to string him along so he gets his money's worth. You in or out?"

"Show me first," I said. "Play the recordings."

"All right." He pointed to the TV hanging up over the counter. He showed it there. The surveillance camera showed a couple talking intently, the date and time ticking off in the corner. The audio wasn't perfectly synchronized, so their lips moved before they spoke. I didn't listen that closely to what they were saying. It was one of those scenes you knew what was going on even if you couldn't hear the exact words. She was dumping him. I'd played his role enough times not to need to listen to some other guy playing it. He was going down in flames, and he knew it. But why, I had to ask myself, was there a sound recording in the first place? Who would want to record these two and their troubles? Then I noticed—each time she moved in the video, a rustle followed in the audio. She was the one recording their conversation. The recording device was probably in her jacket pocket. There was no telling how Mr. Salvador came into possession of the recording, and I didn't expect he would tell me.

After twelve minutes, the video showed Galatea leaving the table, and the sound followed her into the bathroom. Dumfries sat staring into space like his heart just fell out of his chest, and he was trying to decide whether to drive a stake through it or not. The audio was a woman sobbing in a stall. The echoes overwhelmed whatever tiny microphone had recorded her, so the sound was badly distorted, but there was no doubting her agony. If it felt this bad to dump the guy, I wondered, why was she doing it? When she returned, they wordlessly exited to the street. For a few seconds, the sound followed them into the traffic that wasn't there in

THE BRIGHT SPOT

Salvador's virtual, then went abruptly silent. The video lingered on the empty booth for a moment, then went blank.

"What's on the rest of the audio?"

"We don't have it."

Right. "This Galatea Ritsa, why doesn't the old guy just look her up now?"

"Because she's dead."

"When?"

"A long time ago."

"Can you be more specific?"

"What does it matter?"

"When?"

"The day after, according to the papers. Hit by an SUV while jogging. She was a big jogger, apparently. We're a little late for the funeral. When I cooked this thing up, the first thing I did was look her up to make sure she wouldn't present a problem. Look. We're almost there. We're good to go, today. You in or not?"

"In."

"What about you?" he asked Lu.

She started. "In," she said. She'd been watching me and Salvador with rapt attention. She said later she saw a side of me she'd never seen before. That's me. Multi-faceted.

The limo stopped, and we stepped out into a big empty warehouse, somewhere on Planet Earth. The windows were all painted over. The diner set was built in the middle of the place. The clock on the wall was running, the second hand sweeping around.

They weren't taking any chances. Lu and I looked like the people we were impersonating, and we were shooting on a set that was an exact match of the place in the video, shooting action and place together. We use mostly stock locales on the show, but even the best virtual can distort sometimes, go wonky, so the Eiffel Tower flickers or the ocean skips a roar. This way, Dumfries would still be looking at what he wanted to see. If he was like most guys, he'd see what he wanted to see anyway. For his part, Dumfries would be inserted into the virtual remotely, along with digital extras like the waitress and the other customers. Lu and I would go virtual during the performance so we could track it all. There was a box under the table, the contacts in the tabletop.

We watched the video half a dozen times. Then we had a couple of hours to get it down. There wasn't much to it. They were breaking up. He was trying to talk her out of it and getting nowhere. When she started crying, he took her face, kissed her tears, but she broke away and split for the bathroom. She came back, they left. The hard part was not rushing the lines. They didn't say that much, saying things like "I know, I know" in the midst of silence, as if half their conversation was telepathic. Even when they did speak, they were hard to hear.

The "Is there someone else?" part came out loud and clear, however. Once she said, "Yes, there is someone else," there was no stopping him. That's what got her tears going. He had a particularly bad moment where he started naming what sounded like every guy they knew, trying to find out the *one*. "It's Gus, isn't it? Carl. Terry. Arthur. It's Alan, isn't it? Don't lie to me. It must be

George...." Jesus, man, let it go. She never would say who it was. Maybe it wasn't any of them. Maybe it was all of them. Maybe it was some other guy altogether. A woman maybe. But the thing was, it wasn't him. Not anymore. Not ever again.

As we worked on the scene, I kept imagining a virtual James Dumfries in the booth across from us, watching, listening, reliving, thinking he was watching himself forty years ago. What was the point? If you wanted to relive a moment of your life, why this one? Why this heartbreaking pathetic fifteen minutes? But then, he hadn't picked the time, I reminded myself. Salvador had. Dumfries had only picked the person he wanted to see. The crew ignored us. The driver watched us rehearsing for a while, then went and sat in the limo, still looking through old news.

I thought of a thousand questions I should've asked Salvador, but there wasn't time. We kept rehearsing while we made ourselves up. Lu looked pretty hot as a blonde. With a phony beard, I looked exactly like Dumfries.

"Try to look more scared," she coached me.

"What am I scared of?"

"I don't know. But he looks scared to me."

"The truth probably."

The old guy had nothing to be scared of today. Whatever he got from us, it wouldn't be the truth. This was how it worked supposedly: Somewhere else, with Salvador at his side most likely, the drugged old man believed a box was the controls for a time machine, and when he switched it on, he blacked out for a moment— one of the side effects of time travel—and then he woke up to our charade in virtual space. All the extras—the counter waitress filling catsup bottles, a guy eating stew in a corner booth, a woman on the phone—had been worked up earlier and were inserted into the virtual. We'd be sunk if he tried to get the waitress's attention.

We found the box contacts in the tabletop. We got the cue and went virtual. The extras seemed to appear out of thin air.

Dumfries made his appearance in our shared virtual reality, woke up, and we played the scene. Though like anyone in a virtual he could have the illusion of moving around while sitting on his duff, this was supposedly time travel, and he'd been cautioned that even stirring from his seat could tear the very fabric of the space-time continuum, or some such hokum, and for most of the time he watched our dead-on performance with tears streaming down his face like a baby without moving a muscle.

But as soon as Lu went to the bathroom, he popped up out of his booth and headed straight for me.

"Jim, we don't have much time," he said, and slid into Lu's place across from me.

And I had no script. All I could hope for was to keep him going without blowing the illusion until Salvador got wise and arranged another blackout. "Who are you?" I said, sure I wasn't getting the tone right. *Who* are you? Who *are* you? Who are *you*?

"Jim," he said, "look into my eyes. You must recognize me. I'm *you* from the future, an old man. I've traveled through time to see you. You must do what I tell you. Everything depends on it."

Of course. In spite of what he might've told

THE BRIGHT SPOT

Salvador, he didn't want to just *visit* the past. He wanted to change the future. That's what time travel was all about. He wasn't a mere tourist passing through. He wanted to give the space-time continuum a swift kick in the butt. Unfortunately, instead of a time machine, he was stuck with a couple of actors pulling a cheap scam to bilk some poor old man out of his money.

I wondered how he came by it, who the hell he was. There was something about him that looked familiar. Something in the eyes, like he said. But it wasn't me I saw there. It was his intelligence, his genius. I'd seen his picture somewhere, and you could see it even in an image, even in this aged man. A certain fire.

"Why should I believe you?" I said. "I mean, if you were me in the future, you would *remember* me, right? You would *remember* meeting yourself because it would've already happened. Do you have such a memory?"

I'd read a story like that once and was stalling with this bit of sophistry, but he nodded at the justice of my argument, then smiled apologetically. "These days, I don't know which memories are real and which aren't. That I can't remember something doesn't mean it never happened. Maybe paradoxical memories are the first to go. It doesn't matter. Because one thing I do know, and you will find out too soon yourself if you ignore me, is that Galatea will be killed tomorrow. You must stop it. Forget maintaining silence. Go to Kennemeyer. He'll know what to do."

"Can't I just tell her to be more careful? Or why don't you tell her yourself? She'll be out soon, I'm sure."

"Yes, she will, and you will leave and say nothing

further to each other, just as you've arranged. But things won't work out as you've planned. You will never see her again. You must do something different. You must change things. She mustn't know we've spoken. She must never know. She can't see us together. Find Kennemeyer. Will you do it?" He glanced nervously toward the bathroom, poised to leave once I agreed to the impossible.

"Yes," I said. The show must go on. I had to stay in character. If I was who I said I was, how could I say no to myself?

He scuttled back to his booth as Lu emerged from the bathroom, clueless everything wasn't going according to script. I may have rushed my exit a bit, springing up from the booth like we were going on a picnic instead of trudging out into oblivion. James Dumfries watched us hit the doors like some sad story coming to an end, tears still streaming down his cheeks, obviously totally taken in. His eyes burned with hope. Then he winked out of sight—his time travel over.

Lu and I returned to reality, but since we were in the set, it looked just like the virtual, sans extras. I wondered what reality Dumfries was waking up to, with all his newfound hope that I—he—would change the past and save a woman long dead.

Now I've done it, I thought. Now I've totally fucking done it.

WHAT DID WHO SAY?

5

"Who's on first?"
"That's what I just said. Who's on first."

—BUD ABBOTT AND LOU COSTELLO

"WHAT DID HE SAY?" THE LIMO DRIVER WANTED TO know.

The tech people were already packing the equipment, striking the set. In a few hours, this place would once again look like it did a hundred years ago when it went belly-up. This whole thing seemed like an awful lot of trouble to go to for what amounted to a simple shell game.

"I asked you a question," the driver said.

"I'm sorry. What did who say?"

"The old guy. He talked to you. I was watching on the monitor." He pointed to where a monitor had been. It was already packed away. These guys were fast.

The monitor pulled together the visuals. Only the crew listened to the audio. You can't have amplified sound drifting into the illusion—Lu and I would've sounded like a couple of gods having a reverberant chitchat. The driver couldn't have heard my low conversation with Dumfries from where he stood, and even if he had, he would've only heard my half. "He lost it. He begged me to patch it up with the girl someway. I told him there was no hope."

The driver gave a quick little shake of his head as he tilted it back, frowning. "Isn't that always the way? Pathetic, isn't it? I couldn't listen to that damn recording of the two of them. Breaks your heart. A thing like that. The way I see it, if the bitch was two-timing him, he's better off without her, and that's the truth. But tell a guy that. Just try. She was probably fucking all those guys." The driver talked to me as if Lu wasn't even there. I could feel her doing a slow burn beside me.

Maybe she wanted me to defend womanhood, but I just wanted to get going. The way I saw it, you don't piss off the ride home, especially when you don't even know where you are. I thought he was wrong about Galatea, though. I didn't know what was right, but I didn't like his theory.

"Dumfries spoke to you?" Lu asked me when we were inside the limo.

"Yeah."

"What did he say?" She still seemed angry. Was this all about the loutish driver? *Try to look more scared*, she'd told me. What would I have told her? Look angrier. But what were Galatea and Lu so pissed about? Surely, it couldn't just be the exasperating stupidity of tactless men.

THE BRIGHT SPOT

"Like I told the driver: 'Don't let her go'—he said—'you'll regret it for the rest of your life.' What could I say? I told him I didn't know that there was a whole lot I could do about it."

"And he just took that and let it go?"

"He saw you coming and skedaddled. Maybe he was afraid of being dumped twice." I laughed at my weak joke, but it sailed right by her. She was lost in her own thoughts. Something in all this was confusing her, and she was trying to figure it out. I was plenty confused myself, but I knew I didn't know enough to figure it out, so I didn't even bother, and I knew more than she did, or at least I thought I did. Does she know something I don't, I wondered, or am I only thinking that because I just lied to her? Guilt does funny things, I reminded myself.

I'm not sure why the lie came so readily. Sure, the driver might've been listening. That's probably why he was there in the first place, a backup to electronic surveillance, which this little space buggy probably had in abundance if anyone was interested in our conversation. But that wasn't why I lied. I didn't tell Lu the truth even when limo and driver were long gone. The old guy had said Galatea must be kept in the dark, and somehow I thought it was a good idea to apply that to Lu. Something about this whole thing was seriously not right. Did I not trust her? Was I trying to protect her? Hell, I don't know. Nicholas Bainbridge didn't either. But he was a careful sort, was Nick.

"I should tell Salvador," I said, pointing to the box.

She nodded, looking at me funny. She knew I was lying to her. Maybe she could've told me why. "I doubt if he's plugged in, but you can try. I'll sit this one out. I'm in no mood for Salvador." I didn't ask what a Salvador mood might be. Greedy? Foolish? Once was enough for me, and she'd met the guy a couple of times before today.

I touched the box, returned to its last locale, but this time, as Lu predicted, it was sans Salvador. I even hollered out his name like I was calling an order into the kitchen, but he was nowhere to be found. I wasn't surprised. He was as much a fiction, I was guessing, as Lu and I impersonating Jim and Galatea, as big a phony as his time machine. I called up the photos he'd laid out on the table from the box's memory, and sent copies to myself. But the most important images I already had burned into my brain, those eyes looking into me, pleading with me. *You must do something different.* That's what I like, I thought. Clear direction.

I was dead tired. We'd been at this all day. I checked the time on the wall clock, but in this saved reality, the second hand had halted its sweep about the time Jim and Galatea hit the mean streets. It was a lot later than that. We probably wouldn't get home till after dark.

"What did Salvador have to say?" Lu asked when I returned from the box.

I shrugged. "He wasn't there." No reason to lie about that.

She nodded. "Did you notice the crew?"

"What about them? Efficient as hell."

"Of course they were *efficient*. They were workware. I can't believe you didn't notice. Totally zoned out." It wasn't clear whether she meant me or them—accurate in either case, I suppose. "Have you ever seen that before? A workware crew?"

"No, never."

"Next thing you know they won't need us actors anymore. They'll just load up the roles and turn them loose."

"*I* need *you*," I said, putting my arm around her shoulders.

She nestled against me. "Me too." After a while, she said, "They won't remember a thing. They did it as much as we did, but they won't remember."

It took me a moment to realize she was still talking about the crew. "It doesn't *always* block the memory, does it?"

She cocked an eyebrow at me.

"Okay, stupid question. This wouldn't have been one of those times." I remembered hearing that the soldiers guarding top secret installations now were all workware. It saved the army a ton of money on security clearances. You didn't need them if you could wipe their minds clean at the end of the day like a pane of glass, shatter it if necessary.

We made it home just before dark and spent the evening down at Murphy's watching *Chinatown,* one of my donations to the collection. But even Polanski couldn't get my mind off James Dumfries and Galatea Ritsa. This wasn't just about a lost love. It was about her death. A murder, most likely. But I was just as late to the crime as I was to the funeral. Forty years. I should just forget it, I told myself repeatedly, which only helped it burrow deeper and deeper into my brain. *Everything depends on it. Everything. Everything.* Who wrote this dialogue? I wanted to know. Just what "everything" are we talking about here? Give me nothing anytime. Much easier to play against nothing than everything, much easier to play a complete Nobody than Everyman.

Sunday, we took the bus to the park, with Buck sitting in my lap. It was like holding a sack of hams, a little too heavy but not too bad. The lapdog gene did its job, and he didn't squirm. Some people gave us dirty looks. Technically, dogs weren't allowed. Technically, lots of things weren't allowed. But this was a driverless route, so there was no one to enforce the rules, and just as many people wanted to scratch his cute little head as wanted to toss him out the window. The two camps could fight it out if they wanted. By the time they settled it, we'd be there.

I usually loved the park, but not that day. I kept imagining Galatea struck by some speeding vehicle, bouncing from the hood, dead on impact. As I watched her cartwheel through space like a broken rag doll, I felt a panicky urgency to change the past. All I had to do was figure out what to do. *Something different*, of course. *Find Kennemeyer*. Whoever the hell he was. And he only knew what to do *then*. Chances are, I thought, he'd be as clueless as I am *now*—the only time that really matters, according to all the deepest thinkers. It was over. It was done. There was nothing that could be done about it now.

Then *Bam!* There went Galatea again, and I was off to the races. I must've been great company, my mind caught in an endless loop.

"Lu," I finally asked her, "do you know anything

about this James Dumfries guy?" We were lying under some pine trees watching kids feeding geese in the pond down below. Buck snored on his back, having just delved the eternal now with a tennis ball for a half hour.

"So that's what's been bothering you."

"What do you mean?"

"Oh, come on, Nick. You've been on another planet since we did that job. Do you feel guilty? Is that it?"

"Don't you? Here's this broken-down old guy, and we spend our Saturday helping him relive the worst fifteen minutes of his life, so that Salvador can pick his pocket and split the take with us. We could've been here instead. We *should've* been here."

She propped herself up on one elbow and looked at me. "What can we do about it now?"

"Nothing, I guess. I just feel bad about it."

She touched my cheek. "You're so sensitive. You didn't even know who he was, and you're all worried about him. I can't believe I know something you don't for a change. James Dumfries invented workware."

Of course. That's where I'd seen him before. In school. One of the Famous Men one learned to recognize in an endless lineup of Famous Men. Of course, he was much younger when he was famous than the man I saw yesterday. But he just did the science, if I remembered right, the thing they called the DNA computer, though it wasn't exactly either one. The workware came later, an application of his work, I guess you'd call it. I said as much to Lu.

"He still ended up rich, apparently."

"Not after Salvador gets through with him."

"What're you saying? You want to give your share back to Dumfries? Would that make you feel better?"

I thought about it. "If I could find him."

She studied me, trying to figure my angle. I didn't know if I had one, except to buy my conscience off, which I'd never known to be quite so noisy and persistent before.

"It shouldn't be too hard," she said. "If you find him, you can give him my share too." She pushed me back in the shadows under the pine boughs and climbed on top of me, pinning my arms above my head. "You're some kind of guy, Ted."

"Who're you calling Ted? You mixing me up with some other guy?"

"No. I know exactly who you are."

"And who is that?"

She didn't answer at first, not with words anyway. "Here he comes now," she whispered in my ear, and nibbled at the lobe. "I think he's put on some weight."

"It's broad daylight, Lu."

"Don't worry. Buck will bark if anybody gets too close."

"That's what I'm afraid of."

"I don't think you're as afraid as all that."

She kissed my mouth and unzipped my pants, and I was in no position to disagree.

Talk of giving Dumfries his money back came cheap, since we weren't about to be paid tomorrow. We had some time to talk ourselves out of anything too noble.

Maybe we were stupid, but we'd agreed to wait for

THE BRIGHT SPOT

the big money transfer until it was certain everything had gone according to plan. We got a small cash advance—about the equivalent of a week's ReCreation wages—and the rest was just a promise. If the deal went sour, Salvador said, this would protect us. As long as no electronic money changed hands, nobody could connect us with him and the crime. That's why he got the big take, he said, because he was taking the big risk.

It also occurred to me that Salvador might not get his dough right away either, and that was what the delay was really all about. Maybe the old guy had to die first. Salvador might have forgotten to mention that part of the plan. To protect us, no doubt.

So when a month went by and the money hadn't shown, I thought what Lu thought, that Salvador had screwed us. But I also thought what I said out loud: "Maybe the old guy didn't die like he was supposed to."

"What do you mean?"

"When Salvador explained the deal, he said Dumfries was loaded, but had nobody to leave it to. Maybe meaning that Salvador got the old guy to leave it to him, name him in his will—as payment for his time travel."

"So Salvador wouldn't get anything until the guy died."

"Salvador strikes me as someone who would have that angle covered. He wouldn't like too much uncertainty."

"So you're saying..."

"That Salvador planned on killing off Dumfries—maybe one of those side effects would get out of hand—but it didn't work or he lost his nerve. Or maybe he just plain screwed us and is rolling in dough." Which is why,

I was tempted to say, you don't do business with someone on a strictly virtual basis in the first place, but I managed to keep that opinion to myself. That was as easy to change now as Galatea Ritsa's rendezvous with a speeding automobile.

Whatever had gone wrong, we could hardly complain to the authorities that we'd been cheated out of our share of the take, so we tried to be philosophical about it. Instead of easy come, easy go, it was never came, never went. It was a day's work well done. Art for art's sake. The end of our short-lived career in crime.

Meanwhile, *Billy and the Big Guy* kept us busy. It was starting to inch into the getting-noticed category. There wasn't exactly a buzz, but there were murmurs here and there, and the demand for episodes was a gradually steepening curve. We didn't lose our artistic integrity. Wally banged them out as fast as we could make them.

If the only consideration was money, Lu and I would've told ReCreation to take a flying leap at the moon for the pittance they were paying us, but fame was another matter. You couldn't *buy* fame. Not with the amount of money we'd attempted to scam off Dumfries anyway. If all you had was money, it had to be a bundle, or you had to spend it on incredibly stupid things. And rich-guy fame wasn't the right kind anyway. We were actors. We wanted to be famous for pretending to be other people. Go figure. So just so long as *Billy and the Big Guy* looked like it *might* possibly become a hit—no matter how lousy the pay, no matter what kind of stinker it was—we weren't about to quit.

THE BRIGHT SPOT

And to tell you the truth, it was starting to grow on us. The roles of Victor and the She-Creature were fun to play—smoldering slapstick and repartee we mostly ad-libbed, though Wally's writing skills were definitely improving. It wasn't often you got to be funny and sexy at the same time—in virtuals anyway. Even William was getting into his character, so that he was the noblest little shit you ever met in your life. And Stan's earnest monster made even the mayhem poignant. It was like Gandhi finally being pushed too far and dismembering a few bad guys for the good of us all. You could almost believe it hurt him more than it hurt them. At least their misery didn't last as long. Stan did this soulful misunderstood look to the heavens at least once an episode—a look that must've had every middle school girl who ever took in a stray bawling her eyes out.

Without the Salvador money, we didn't have to think twice about whether we were going to stick with ReCreation. We just wished we had better contracts. *Billy and the Big Guy* would have to hang on for at least a year before we made any real money—fix-the-roof money, as Lu called it—and the chances of that were slim indeed. Not that it bothered me. I was used to not being rich, hanging out in the upper crust of poverty, knowing it was a long way down from here, and it went all the way to the bottom. Lu knew all this too, but it bothered her more. She wanted to know what had become of Salvador. She didn't like being cheated.

Me, I kept thinking about Kennemeyer. Whoever the hell he was. And then I had to go and ask somebody who he was, and somebody had to go and tell me, and that's when the real trouble started.

• • •

It was a late night at Murphy's. Dell was at it again. This time his son Clinton showed up to take him home.

"Come on, Pop. It's time," Clinton said to his father.

It looked past time to me. Dell hadn't made any sense in over an hour and wasn't likely to get up out of his chair on his own. He'd chemically bonded with the plastic. Then there was the little matter of the two-block walk home. Dell wasn't that big, but he was bigger than Clinton, who was a wiry kid, a college sophomore, the only one of those in the neighborhood.

"I'll give you a hand with him," I said.

We got on either side of him, draping his arms over our shoulders, and walked him down the alley. Dell even managed to take a few steps, and the accomplishment went to his head. He started trying to talk again.

"Clinton's a *serious* boy," he told me. "Into poli-*tics*. Demonstrations and shit. Very, very serious. Don't he look serious to you, Mr. Bainbridge? What kinda name's Bainbridge anyway?"

"Theatrical," I said. That gave him something to think about, and he wasn't quite up to it. His feet gave up the effort of pretending to walk and got all tangled up together.

I didn't have to ask what Clinton demonstrated against. I'd seen his *Workware Is Slaveware* T-shirts. I didn't have to ask why either. We were carrying plenty of reason down the alley, and he was getting heavier with each step.

"Fucking shit," Dell shouted, his final thought for the evening, and lapsed into silence. By the time we got

THE BRIGHT SPOT

him home, he was out cold. We flopped him onto his bed in his painstakingly neat room off the kitchen and started getting him out of his clothes. "I can get him from here, Mr. Bainbridge. Thanks for helping me with him."

"Call me Nick. We're just getting to the hard part. He's dead weight. I'll help you finish the job, so one of you doesn't get hurt."

The only injuries were mine, cracking my head a couple of times on the sloped ceiling. When Dell was all tucked in, Clinton thanked me again and offered me a cup of coffee for my trouble. I surprised him by taking him up on it. We sat at the kitchen table and made small talk about me and Lu and about his schoolwork. He was the one who pushed it into serious territory.

"Why do you hang out with that burned-out bunch at Murphy's, Mr. Bainbridge... Nick? You seem like an intelligent man."

"There's plenty of intelligent folks at Murphy's."

"Who think life comes down to two choices: workware or drinking your life away in some junkman's backyard."

"What're the other choices? Know-it-all student? Underpaid actor? Suspected dissident? A little time at Murphy's might do you some good, Clinton—loosen you up a little. You never know."

He started to take offense, but shrugged it off. He wasn't mad at me. He wasn't even mad at his dad. "Maybe you're right. I just get so crazy when I see him like this. Bitter and used up. I remember what he used to be like. Things shouldn't be this way."

"So you're looking to change them. Good for you. Have you studied on it much? Workware?"

He gave a humorless laugh. "You might say that. It's kind of an obsession with me."

"What do you know about James Dumfries?"

"What everybody knows."

I had to laugh. "Everybody usually doesn't know everything they should. Take me. I'm a smart guy. I was a straight-A student for a while, but I don't know much. Most of what I learned, I learned for some test. Once the tests were over, I was glad to let it all go, to make room for whatever I was interested in that week, usually a woman. I only really learned what I wanted to. I liked stories, novels, plays—anything made up—so I read those, watched a hell of a lot of movies. I remember those. Makes me seem smart. But science? I don't know a Krebs cycle from a motorcycle, a neutrino from a cappuccino. And I'm even worse with history, politics, and geography. I learned all that stuff, but I don't know any of it. So tell me, what is it everybody knows about James Dumfries but me?"

I was flattering him in a roundabout way, and he didn't seem to mind it much. I suspected Clinton wanted to be famous too, but not for pretending to be anything he wasn't, and one thing he was, was smart. He told me what I wanted to know like we were in a senior seminar—and him only a sophomore:

"James Dumfries headed the research that led to Freedomware back during the war. They were trying to make better desert soldiers, mountain soldiers, swamp soldiers, space soldiers. It was supposed to retune their bodies and minds for optimal performance in these harsh environments, increasing their chances for survival. He imagined postwar applications like firefighters

THE BRIGHT SPOT

and stuff like that, but he had no idea. He thought he was doing a good thing, helping boys make it out of the war alive. He wasn't looking to make workers who never got tired, never got bored, never got interested, couldn't steal, couldn't talk back, couldn't remember what the fuck they'd been doing all day, day in and day out. And he certainly didn't mean to create the illegal perfect whores, perfect boxers, perfect killers workware makes possible. I don't know what planet he was living on, but he had neglected to consider the commercial applications. He spoke out against it when workware was first introduced, but nobody cared. Workware was going to create all these jobs, you see. That was the big promise. What machines had once done, man could do again, they said. It was cheaper even. Machines were expensive and complicated. Potential 'ware workers grew in ghettoes around the world at no expense whatsoever. Workware was their opportunity to *make something of themselves*."

His bitter grin gave you chills. Clinton didn't pull any punches. He and his dad weren't so different after all. But Clinton had the good sense to stay sober. For now at least. It was a long hard fight, taking on the Man, with many opportunities to fall. That's what I'd heard anyway. I prided myself on staying out of His way.

"Had Dumfries always been a good soldier before that?"

"All that's still classified, but according to several sources, he fought with the military all the time."

"What about?"

"Command issues mostly. They wanted a more

centralized military command structure. He wanted it more localized."

"Is that the answer I give on the test?"

"Sorry. You see, the way workware is now—because it still works exactly like the old Freedomware—is that there's a chain of command you can't see. A crew is transmitted a specific set of instructions by a central command, and these instructions can't be changed by anyone in the crew. The military brass were afraid their control might be compromised somehow. Changes could only come from above. So like if that paving crew runs into a problem, a pipe where it's not supposed to be or something, they suspend operations and send a signal to their company headquarters in Florida or wherever, they assess the problem through the workers' senses, then send the new orders to the crew. You don't even notice it. Takes seconds. Dumfries wanted more localized control, so that an officer in the field could reprogram his troops even if the central command was destroyed."

"How big is a crew?"

"Any size, depending on the task. One or two, thousands. Whatever's needed."

"Yeah. I can see why he lost that debate. What happened to Dumfries after he spoke out against workware?"

"I don't know. He dropped out of sight. He was idolized for something he hated doing. That must've been pretty awful. There were lots of rumors that he lost his mind. He'd be close to ninety by now."

"Ever hear of someone named Galatea Ritsa?"

"No. I don't think so."

"What about Kennemeyer?"

THE BRIGHT SPOT

"Edmund Kennemeyer?"

"If you like. I only caught the last name. Who's Edmund?"

"He was big in the early anti-workware movement, when they actually thought they could stop it by appealing to people's conscience. He was a philosopher, I think. An ethicist. He wrote a couple of books. I think he's still alive."

I tried to remember if I knew words like *ethicist* when I was a sophomore. I didn't think so. "Did Dumfries and Kennemeyer know each other?"

"I don't know. Maybe. I could try to find out." He seemed eager to get right on it. He was a born student. That would probably be his best shot—keep going to school forever. But he struck me as the type who didn't know when he had a good thing, who'd think maybe the world could use a little of what he'd learned and would find out the hard way the world didn't want to hear about it. Because change always meant trouble. Whatever else it meant, you could count on that. And most people had too much trouble already.

"I've been trying to find out more about them, for a part I'm playing. I've got some old photos of Jim and Galatea. I'll send them to you. Would you mind seeing what you can dig up? If you have the time."

"I'd love to." He looked like I'd just offered to buy him a steak dinner.

"You must be pretty good at tests yourself," I said.

"Yeah. That's how I got the scholarship. It was a national test."

"They still have those?"

"A few."

"Well, good luck with it." He was going to need it. There was probably already a fat file on him that would keep him out of work for years to come. Scholarship student, suspected dissident, known radical, possible terrorist. Anything's *possible*, right? In the land of the free. He'd be better off with a record as a convicted child molester. You can go to classes for that, take the cure. Mere possibilities resisted treatment. That was the beauty of them. They could haunt you forever.

ANY VICES, MR. BAINBRIDGE?

6

> *Idle Valley was a perfect place to live. Perfect. Nice people with nice homes, nice cars, nice horses, nice dogs, possibly even nice children.*
>
> *But all a man named Marlowe wanted from it was out. And fast.*
>
> —RAYMOND CHANDLER, *The Long Goodbye*

CLINTON COULDN'T FIND ANYTHING OUT ABOUT Galatea Ritsa except what Salvador had already told us—a piece in the paper about her death. He found no clear evidence that Edmund Kennemeyer and James Dumfries knew each other during the war either, but a lot of those records were destroyed or never kept. People who knew each other often pretended they didn't in those days. Get friendly with the wrong person, and the next thing you knew you were a conspirator.

Now, however, Kennemeyer was just another old man, and I didn't have to be a detective to track him down. He lived in the area. I looked him up and called him the first weekend Lu was busy.

She was doing a benefit in Philly for veterans. Someone on the programming committee had called up Gary and asked him if the She-Creature was available. Just what the war-ravaged boys needed—an evil nymphomaniac willing to fly to Philly. They regretted they couldn't afford the both of us, a sentiment I understood—even though they could've had the both of us for what they were paying her.

I told Kennemeyer I was a writer working on a biography of James Dumfries—would he mind talking to me about him? I thought dropping Dumfries' name set him back a moment, but maybe he was just old.

"Why not?" he said. "Got nothing better to do. Come around back. Don't go to the big house. They think they have to interrogate anyone who visits me. Ignore the warning signs. The perimeter security's on the blink again. Do you have any vices, Mr. Bainbridge?"

"One or two."

"Bring them along, will you?"

I rolled a couple of skinny joints and filled an empty water bottle with box wine. Lu had some pills, but I didn't know what they were, so I let them lie. I wore my best jeans, a clean shirt, and a jacket I thought looked writerly. I had two pairs of shoes, old and older. I chose old for the occasion.

Clinton had found some of Kennemeyer's old speeches from the big anti-'ware demonstrations. The guy had roused some serious rabble in his day. If he said shit like that now, he'd find himself on a road crew in no time. It wasn't just what he said that made it so powerful, it was the rumble of the crowd behind him, *lots* of people, flesh-and-blood people, not just stock mob sounds.

THE BRIGHT SPOT

Even when it was silent, it was a big silence, like a dragon sleeping in a cave. But now he was old and nobody cared anymore. People were even nostalgic about them, the old radicals. Like cute dinosaurs.

Whatever his radical glory days, Kennemeyer was now living with his nephew in a place called The Lakes at Llewellyn, way the heck out, inside the walls at Llewellyn. I hated those places. Going to the "communities"—as they liked to call themselves, as if there was anything communal about them except the love of money—was like wading through sewage without the 'ware, but I was willing to do it to get Jim Dumfries' pathetic mug off my mind.

Will you do it? Will you do it? Will you do it?

Yes! Yes! Yes! Just leave me the fuck alone!

It didn't make sense to me why I couldn't just let it go. I'd taken part in swindling an old man. I didn't feel great about that, but I didn't have any money to give back to him. That wasn't the part that drove me crazy anyway. It was the other, the telling him, *promising* him, as I now put it to myself, that I would change things. And him believing me. What a dope. The both of us, me and James Dumfries—a pair of dopes.

I thought I allowed plenty of time for the trip, but everything that could go wrong, did. All the schedules had been updated, and the new schedules were not yet posted. The ones I'd printed up planning this little trek were all for last year's buses. Last year's routes too. Half the stops had been moved. Outmoded stops were clearly labeled: THIS IS NOT A BUS STOP. But no word was forthcoming where the new one might be found. Over that way, across six lanes of traffic? Up there, beside the tunnel? Excuse me, sir, does the bus come through here? The whole thing ran on rumor. I asked my fellow passengers what they knew, and they passed on tips, advice, warnings, in a variety of languages. I didn't always understand what they were saying, but I studied their hand movements. An actor can't have too many of those in his toolbox.

I changed buses four times—the bigger the homes got, the smaller the buses. A few more million per ostentatious barn, and we'd be riding around in salvaged Volkswagens. The last bus, the Llewellyn Connector, while not quite that small, was definitely trying for cute. It was an orbiter around the walls, for schools, churches, athletic fields, and recreational shopping. It took me only marginally closer to my destination inside the walls, where only those with cars usually ventured, but I thought it might be worth it to ride through these parking lots instead of walk through them.

When I got on the Llewellyn Connector, it was half filled with nannies with kids in tow who were somewhat less well behaved than Buck on a bad day. The nannies were all wearing their nice white uniforms. Domestics around here were always suited up. The kids too wore uniforms. They'd just come from the uplifting experience of competitive team sports, building their little characters, growing future leaders. You can't start them too young was the current thinking, had to get those fangs sharpened in time for the future. I gathered the game was over, and they were on their way to claim some booty. They didn't think too much of me.

THE BRIGHT SPOT

As possibly the first adult male without a service uniform ever to have ridden in this little buslet, I was the object of immediate suspicion and a flurry of hushed commentary as I slumped up the aisle to the back. If only I'd worn ratty (but once expensive) sweats, I could've passed myself off as a spent, rich jogger, soaked in good, healthy sweat from honest leisure activity. Dressed as I was, who knew what I was? I clearly wasn't from around here.

To hell with them. I was a spent, impoverished actor, and I was in no mood. I slumped down in my seat and tried to interest myself in the landscape outside that repeated itself like a wallpaper pattern. Tree, tree, shrub. Tree, tree, shrub. Just blend, I thought, just blend.

But then one of the children—in a voice that cut through the hushed chatter and filled the cute little bus right up to the roof—inquired of her hapless keeper whether I was one of those *deviants* she'd heard so much about. She pronounced it perfectly, quite the precocious little scholar. Hell, she could probably spell it. During the ruckus that ensued, she stole a smug little glance at me. I'd made her day for her. A deviant sighting was apparently no end of fun. I didn't hear the keeper's speech, low and discreet. A bribe of some sort, I'm guessing— *Keep your yap shut, and there's some serious chocolate in it for you, honey.* Anyway, it worked, and the little phony lost all interest in me in a matter of seconds and sank back into the warm, safe ooze she called home, like a crocodile in a zoo.

There wasn't a back door in this toy bus, so when I got off, I *had* to pass right by the kid whether I wanted to or not. How could I pass up the opportunity to teach her not to mess with a professional actor? I stopped in the aisle, bent at the waist so that my face was inches from hers, and gave her a look worthy of Victor at his evil best. I handed her and her keeper *Billy and the Big Guy* cards, then let loose a superb maniacal laugh that must've given every kid on that buslet nightmares for a week or more. And all for free. Gratis. They should've thanked me. Most of the women were shocked, or pretended to be, and I was cursed in a half-dozen languages, but I saw a few smiling, including the little monster's keeper.

Deviants of the world, unite!

The closest I could get to The Lakes at Llewellyn was Llewellyn Commons—little shoppes 'n' things for your shopping pleasure. It was in the lease that anything sold here had to have no utility whatsoever and cost at least a month's rent in my neighborhood. I couldn't even window-shop. The sticker shock would kill me before I got from the knicks to the knacks, so I cut across the parking lot.

The main entrance to the Lakes was there, a wide road with a pile of artfully arranged bricks beside it, letters bolted into the brick, humming in the wind, big enough to be read from speeding cars: THE LAKES AT LLEWELLYN. From here I only had a mile-and-a-half walk to the guardhouse through the same wallpaper design I just rode past. There were no sidewalks on either side, so I trudged up the heavily mulched median. When they built this place, they must've ground up the whole forest that used to be here and piled it into these medians— miniature rolling hills of dead wood, punctuated by

THE BRIGHT SPOT

perfectly spaced trees whose lowest limbs were about chest height. Down and up, duck and waddle, down and up...

At the end of this stroll was a guardhouse where a toy cop sat on his throne, a little office chair on rollers. Toy cops are even worse than real ones, in my experience. This one got right to the point, rolling up to the window designed for people in cars, looking up at me like a mean dog peeking out from under a porch, teeth bared, snarling, "This is a private community, buddy. Move along. Back the way you came."

If I had anything to contribute to the discussion, I was supposed to bend over, so he wouldn't have to get a crick in his neck looking up at me. For that reason, I stood up straight and tall like my mother taught me. "I'm here to visit a private person in your private community, buddy, and how are you today?"

"Don't get smart with me."

"Don't worry. I wouldn't want you to fall behind. I'm here to see Edmund Kennemeyer. Here's his number." I took the slip of paper where I'd written Kennemeyer's number and slapped it against the glass in front of toy cop's face so he could read it, assuming he could read. He jumped a foot like I was actually going to smack him, a nice guy like me.

"I *know* his number. What business you got with Mr. Kennemeyer?"

I left a nice big handprint on the glass. "None of yours." I leaned forward confidentially. "Maybe I should warn you: I'm going to sell him some automatic weapons so he can take over the place. Don't worry. I'll put in a good word for you."

He scowled at me. I was supposed to be scared, intimidated, *something*. He had a badge and a gun, and he might roll over me with his little chair. "You mind if I look in that bag of yours?" A metal tray slid out of the side of the guardhouse into my crotch. He pointed at my little backpack. It contained two water bottles (one with wine), a poncho, a candy wrapper (empty), a folder of photographs of Jim and Galatea, several bus schedules that had no relationship to reality, and a compass I hoped did.

I took off the bag, put it on the tray, and watched it disappear into his lair, talking the whole time. "Of course I *mind*. Do you mind if I look in your wallet? What you got in the desk there? How about those pants pockets? Body cavities? Can't forget those."

He grabbed my bag and zipped it open. He dug though it twice, threw it back in the tray, and shot it back out to me.

"You going to call Mr. Kennemeyer now, or should I take my shoes off? Or maybe you're into underwear? You look like the type...."

Eventually he let me in. If he'd wanted to, I suppose, he could've come out of his guardhouse and shot me, or at least beaten me with that big stick on the desk. But he'd have to lift himself out of his chair to do that, so I wasn't really worried. He could've rolled over to the desk and called the real cops, but that would've been embarrassing for a toy cop like himself, who no doubt told his employers he could handle any situation a real cop could and probably got paid more. And here I was, a mere pedestrian. What kind of a situation was that? *Did you hear about Barney? He couldn't even handle a pedestrian!*

Besides, the real cops would've taken at least a half hour to get there on a good day, and we were already sick of each other's company.

I finally made it to Kennemeyer's and started around to the back like he said, ignoring all the signs warning me off in no uncertain terms, making it clear I shouldn't rule out death as a possibility should security measures be required. Required by whom? I didn't need any security, and I was the only one out here wandering the flagstones. The stone walkways might have made an interesting pattern viewed from above, but they weren't too good at going anywhere.

The house itself was built by somebody who thought you bought class by the ton. It wasn't just big, it was massive, built out of stone blocks the size of Murphy's refrigerator. What wasn't stone was glass, big massive panes of thick glass, and I saw through one of them on the second floor, twenty feet off the ground, a woman I guessed to be the nephew's wife, running on a treadmill in the gym, lost in some runner's virtual, naked and beautiful and drenched with sweat. I watched her for a while. She had a nice slender build, a nice stride. She was making great time.

Kennemeyer lived in a pool house beside a pool that looked like a set for a Hawaiian musical. The waterfall was shut off, and a crew of three in Pool Concepts uniforms were working on it, standing in a couple of feet of water. They paid no attention to me, and I figured them for workware.

Kennemeyer was standing on his plank porch,

under a thatched roof, waiting for me. He was dressed in jeans and a T-shirt, and his head was shaved. He still looked white, though, the roots maybe. With his big dark eyes and bushy white brows, he looked like a white owl. He was old, at least as old as James Dumfries, but he wasn't letting that get to him. He paced quickly back and forth, still light on his feet. If immortality was intensity, this guy could've pulled it off if anyone could. He was a little guy, and he had a posture like a pencil. I felt like a slumping hulk beside him.

"Get in here," he said. "Don't let them see you." He pointed up at the many windows overlooking the pool. All I could see was the reflection of the waterfall under repair, and the repairmen like three white herons working the shallows. I knew some workware jobs tuned your nutritional needs. I wondered if these guys subsisted on a diet of algae and goldfish.

I hurried in after Kennemeyer. He slid the door shut, latched it, and yanked a heavy curtain across the glass. The curtain hadn't been made for the door, and it dragged along the floor. It was heavy brocade, totally out of place. Kennemeyer had probably scavenged it from somewhere in the big pile up front. There had to be rooms up there where no one ever went, where they just parked the airplane or grazed the elephants.

His pool house place had a certain charm. A pingpong table with all manner of stuff piled on it, a pool table and a set of weights that both looked like they saw a lot of use, an acoustic guitar on a stand, a bunch of wicker, including a bar with no bottles, and a bed where Kennemeyer clearly did most of his living. There was about a month of newspapers on one side, and the im-

THE BRIGHT SPOT

print of a body on the other, a couple of pillows leaking down. There was no box, no TV, not even a radio. There was a single bookcase crammed full of the usual radical activist stuff. Probably some collectors' items there, but he hurried me past it to the bar and the barstools.

"Do I need some glasses?" he asked hopefully.

I pulled the bottle of wine out of my backpack. He sniffed it and smiled in satisfaction. He poured us both a glass and downed half of his immediately.

"Need a light?" he inquired.

I pulled one of the joints out of my pocket.

"Excellent."

He lit the joint and sucked most of it down in one hit. "Any tobacco?" he inquired wistfully, still holding the pot in his lungs.

I shook my head, and he exhaled, shrugging philosophically. "Just as well. That stuff'll kill you."

"You got a spoon?" I asked him.

He looked hopeful.

"Just kidding," I said.

"Funny guy. So how can I help you, Mr. Bainbridge?"

"Nick. Like I said over the phone, I'm writing a biography of James Dumfries, and I was hoping you could tell me about your friendship with him."

He took another long hit, which left little of the joint to hold. Naturally, he handed it to me. I popped it into my mouth to put it out, then swallowed it.

"Never met the man in my life," Kennemeyer said deadpan, leaking smoke.

This couldn't be true. I'd just spent a major, unpleasant portion of my life getting out to this godforsaken place, and he didn't even *know* the man? "But the two of you were actively campaigning against workware at the same time. Surely—"

"Surely nothing. I didn't know him. Besides, that's all settled now. It's a free country, right? We're all free as fucking birds. Nobody has to work any stinking workware job if he don't want to. There's plenty of other jobs. Like executive vice president or theoretical physicist or artist-in-residence or only-son-and-heir. What is it you do, *Nick*?" He took another big swallow of wine and eyed me with his big owl eyes.

"I told you. I'm a writer."

"And I'm a starting quarterback. What have you written?"

"Nothing you would've heard of."

He laughed. "My hearing's fine. Open your jacket. I'll prove it to you. Go on. Just open it up."

I held open my jacket.

"See there. Not even a pen. You're not a writer. Why should I talk to you, if you won't even level with me?"

I couldn't believe I'd forgotten a pen like some dumb amateur. I hadn't thought it through. I'd thought it would be easy to take in some old man. Never underestimate your audience. He had me, so I retreated to the truth. "Okay. I'm an actor."

"They don't have workware for that yet?"

"So I don't smell the bad lines?"

"What workware's always been for, Mr. Bainbridge—so you don't ask too many questions. Like 'Why do you pay me so little when you make so much?' and 'Why do I take all the risks?'" Another healthy swallow of wine. "Like 'What did you know and when did you know it, Mr.

THE BRIGHT SPOT

Kennemeyer?'" He was trying to be funny, but he was also scared, which meant he knew something.

"You're forgetting, questions are part of an actor's job. 'To be or not to be?' 'Which way did they go?' 'Wherefore art thou Romeo?'"

"That's Juliet's line."

"I went to an all-boys school. Look, Mr. Kennemeyer. I've just got one question. If you didn't know James Dumfries, what do we have to talk about? You wouldn't have let me come all the way out here just to get you blitzed, would you?"

He smiled, he brought his glass to his lips—*yes*, he wanted me to believe, I'd been conned by one sly, old fox—but I wasn't having any of it. "Maybe we could talk about Galatea Ritsa instead," I said.

That blew his cover. He almost dropped his wineglass. He could try to tell me he never met the woman, but there was no way either one of us would believe it. "Who the hell are you?" he said.

"I met James Dumfries in a virtual a couple of months ago. He sent me to you. He said you'd know what to do."

"About what?"

"I'm not sure. Galatea Ritsa, I guess you might say. I was hoping you could tell me."

He winced when I said the name, like even saying it out loud was risky. "So you're not writing a book, and whatever I say is strictly between the two of us?"

"That's right."

"But how do I know Jim sent you to me? You might just be nuts. You might . . . have some hidden agenda. Talking to you doesn't sound very safe to me."

That iced it. Safe. What the hell was I doing here anyway? "You're right. You don't know. I could be the psycho bus killer who spends half the day riding the bus out to otherwise safe communities, offing the first old man I find living in the pool house. The toy cop out front pays me to do it so there'll be some reason for his pointless existence other than harassing anyone stupid enough to show up on foot. Safe. You can have it." I tossed back my wine, picked up my bottle, and stuck out my hand. "Thanks for your time, Mr. Kennemeyer. Enjoy the buzz. Safely, of course."

"Don't get sore. You don't have to rush off." He gestured toward my abandoned wicker stool with one hand and clutched his empty glass with the other. Thin, little, old-man hands, even if they were corded with muscle. I guess I'm a soft touch.

I poured some more wine in his glass, pulled the other joint out of my pocket. "I don't know why I should light this if you won't level with me."

"Okay, okay. But first you have to tell me why you're so interested in Jim."

"Fair enough."

"Not here. They listen to me. They call it looking after me. I call it spying. God, I hate this place. Follow me."

We slipped out of the pool house and took a gravel path to a garage at the back of the property. Inside the garage was a fleet of vintage cars. We climbed into a monster SUV that was new about the time Galatea Ritsa died. Hell, it might've been one like this that hit her. The garage opened onto a two-lane blacktop.

"Do you know how to drive?" I asked Kennemeyer as we whipped onto the ancient asphalt, tires squealing,

THE BRIGHT SPOT

and he only laughed at me. What did it matter if he knew how to drive? There was no way this old behemoth was licensed to be on the road no matter who was behind the wheel.

"Where's that other joint?" he asked, and I reluctantly lit it for him.

I started to tell him my story, but he shushed me again. "Not now. I want to drive. Besides"—he gestured at the old radio—"they might be listening."

He couldn't be serious, but I didn't have much choice. He took me on a tour of bucolic countryside, and I kept waiting for the cops to swoop down on us. After a while, I finally rolled down my window and got into it. I could worry just so much. Whatever kind of radical nut Kennemeyer was, he had one rich nephew, and I imagined Ed Kennemeyer could only get in just so much trouble, this side of killing somebody richer than he was.

On both sides of the road, horses posed behind white plastic fences—the horses at Llewellyn. They frolicked, they gamboled, they arranged themselves in touching tableaus. There was probably a calendar for sale down at the Commons autographed by them all.

Kennemeyer turned down a dirt road, and we bounced down it, raising a plume of dust behind us that must've been visible for miles, but Kennemeyer was having too much fun to care. When we reached the end of the road, he slammed on the brakes and slid sideways to a stop, raining the forest with dirt and rocks, grinning from ear to ear. "God, I love to drive!" he said, and hopped out, beating his chest and breathing deeply of the dust-filled air redolent with exhaust fumes.

An abandoned house sat alone in the woods, all boarded up, someone's prewar dream palace in the wilderness. We went around to the back porch that overlooked a wooded ravine and sat on a half-rotten, mossy bench.

I told him my story, showed him the pictures. He listened intently. The whole thing was agony for him, as if he too was haunted by murdered Galatea. He sat staring at the picture of old Dumfries in his rocker for a long time. His eyes filled with tears. He traced a fingertip across the old, wrinkled face, then put it down, staring into the ravine, wiping the tears from his eyes. I wasn't even sure he remembered I was there. Finally, he said, "I'm afraid I can't help you, Mr. Bainbridge."

This wasn't the answer I was expecting. An audience that cries usually applauds, tells their friends, comes back for more. Not Mr. Kennemeyer. He wanted to remain safe. Maybe I should've let him. Maybe it was too late for that already.

"Thanks for nothing, Mr. Kennemeyer. You must have some idea what this is about. And obviously it's about *something*, or you wouldn't look like that, wouldn't make such a big secret of it. I guess Jim Dumfries didn't know you as well as he thought he did. He could've sent me to anybody. He sent me to you. And all you know is dance steps."

"He didn't send *you*. He thought he was sending himself."

"Well, I'm all he's got. And I'm beginning to wonder what I'm doing here, if even his best friend doesn't care what's happened to him." I was guessing with the best friend line. Who else would you send yourself to when

THE BRIGHT SPOT

the world's falling apart? I thought about the way he'd touched the photo. Maybe they'd been more than friends.

"What do you want from me? You admit you were trying to swindle him, and now you're all righteous? About what? Helping? Helping's over, Jack. This was *forty* years ago. It's over. It's done. You can't change what's already happened."

"You can always change something. Otherwise things wouldn't keep changing. What was it Jim Dumfries wanted to change?"

"Why don't you ask him?"

"I don't know where he is. I don't even know if he's still alive."

He caught my tone and stared into the ravine again. "Do you have some reason to think . . ."

He couldn't even say it. "That two plus two equals four? No. No reason in the world. I'm sure Jesse Salvador is propping Jim up in bed right now, feeding him milk shakes, discussing the wonders of time travel."

Kennemeyer surveyed the woods. There could be a dozen people out there listening to every word we were saying—or one drone, it was all the same. "What do you want? I draw you a picture of where he is?"

"I've got pictures."

"Then you don't need me," he said. Kennemeyer looked into my eyes and held them, then looked pointedly at the picture of the old man that lay on the bench between us. *Exactly*, he seemed to be saying: *You've got a picture of where he is, and that's all I'll say.*

So that was that. There wasn't anything else to say. And the more I thought about it, the more I thought there just might be people in the bushes, hanging from the trees, passing over in balloons, or piloting little drones, all listening to every word we said. And they probably all had a better idea what it meant than I did.

We were pretty quiet driving back. There didn't seem to be anything else to talk about. When we reached the turnoff to his place, he slowed.

"You want to have sex?" he asked. "I know I'm old, but I'm in pretty good shape."

"No thanks. Age doesn't enter into it."

"You straight or faithful?"

"Both."

"That's too bad. I thought all you actors were queer and easy."

"A common misconception. It's philosophers you're thinking of."

He chuckled softly. "You're all right, Nick."

"You're kind of cute yourself, Mr. Kennemeyer." He dropped me off at the bus stop and saved me another mile-and-a-half mulch hike. I left the half bottle of box wine on the seat.

"You look just like him, you know. Way back then."

"Yeah, I know. That's why I got the part."

"Do you think you'll see Jimmy again?" he asked.

"I suppose anything is possible."

"Well, if you do, tell him Ed said hello, though he may not want to hear it."

"Will do. You've got my number in case you think of anything more you want to tell me about all this."

"I wouldn't count on it, Mr. Bainbridge. I'd leave it alone if I were you."

He drove off toward the guardhouse, accelerating

rapidly. The toy cop probably screwed his chair into the floor when he saw that thing roaring down on him. I *bet* he knew Ed Kennemeyer's number. I bet he knew it by heart. I imagined the nephew's wife probably had to interrupt her jog through China to throw on some clothes and come bail the old geezer out again. And people think rich people have it easy.

OH

7

"Who was that masked man?"
"Why, that was the Lone Ranger!"

—*The Lone Ranger*

KNOWING THE BUSES WERE CONFUSING DIDN'T spare me any hassles getting back. There were ways to mess up I hadn't tried yet. I caught the 27E instead of the 27N and ended up miles out of my way, walking the last leg through the neighborhood. By the time I got to my street, there was already an early crowd at Murphy's, and Sylvia called me over to the fence to give me the heads-up.

"You got company, Ted. They been there almost an hour." She pointed to a police cruiser parked on the nice upgraded road.

"Is Lu back?"

"Oh yeah. She must be serving them tea."

There were two of them, both plainclothes, which I took to be a good sign. Perhaps they didn't plan on making any arrests today, though cops working Sunday was

THE BRIGHT SPOT

never a good sign. They looked alike in that played-on-the-same-football-team kind of way. One was black and one was white. But they were the same age, the same build—now crumbling and sagging, but still big. You wouldn't want either one of them to fall on you. They wore the same cheap suit—one blue, one brown, in a fabric that wasn't supposed to wrinkle, and it didn't. They were named Murphy and Johnson, or maybe the second one was Lawson. I couldn't hear too well on account of Buck barking his head off at the intruders for a second time, showing off for my benefit, to let me know he was on the job. I stumbled into the living room, trying to look surprised the cops had come calling. Always look surprised when cops show up out of the blue. They don't like to be expected—it means you're guilty or they're predictable, both of which are probably true.

I finally shut Buck up by scooping him off the floor and plopping him onto my lap as I sat in my usual chair. The lapdog gene kicked in, and he lapsed into a low growl that sounded more erotic than threatening. The cops sat on either side of me. Lu was straight across from me in a chair she'd brought in from the kitchen. I didn't know where to look. Every face was questioning but Buck's, whose eyes were now closed.

"You and the dog are awfully close, aren't you?" Lawson asked, or maybe it was Johnson.

"You might say that," I said, scratching Buck's head.

"Do you have any idea why we're here, Mr. Bainbridge?" Murphy asked.

For anybody out there who doesn't know, the correct answer to that question is always, always, always "No." "No, Officer," if you can pull it off, which I thought I delivered with just the right amount of servility for a man with a clear conscience.

"A neighbor of yours has sworn out a complaint against you. He says you threatened him and mounted a"—he held up a paper to read—"'unrelenting campaign of harassment and intimidation' against him that's gone on for a couple of months. Would you know anything about that, Mr. Bainbridge?"

I didn't have to lie. I didn't have a clue what he was talking about and told him so.

"Do you mind?" he asked, taking out a little sound player and setting it on the coffee table.

What was I supposed to say? *I'd rather hear Beethoven? Oh no, I don't mind—I love to hear evidence against me?*

"Go ahead," I said pleasantly.

And so the cop played it, and there was my voice clear as a bell, threatening poor Mr. Casual with a shit shrine behind his house. Definitely a threatening tone. A real sick individual. You could hear Buck in the background, growling and snarling and egging me on in the vilest street talk of Ipso Factos. We were a couple of dangerous customers, all right. The audio was great. The video was probably equally impressive. Mr. Casual spared no expense on security.

All the latest systems recorded everything that went on around the perimeter of your property. Evidence, you know. It helped keep the country safe for everyone, the pitch went. Evidently Mr. Casual had one of those and found a use for it. A real patriot, a real little helper. I felt safer just having him in the neighborhood.

I didn't know what to say. No line came to me but the

truth. I'd been harassed for stupid shit before, but this was *literally* stupid shit. "Come on. I was kidding the guy. I was walking my dog. He was an asshole. That's it."

"Is it?" Johnson or Lawson wanted to know. "Your neighbor has recorded you depositing canine feces in his trashcan on twelve separate occasions since then. He has also salvaged the physical evidence, so there's no doubt it came from your dog. Would you like the dates?"

"The physical evidence? He's saving Buck's shit? And you guys are calling on *me*? What is that—two months ago, now? Buck shits twice a day like clockwork. That's one hundred and twenty shits. I'm sorry that ten percent ended up in Mr. Casual's can, but it's not a conspiracy, I'm not trying to harass the man, and it's not *his* can anyway—it's the city's." I thought this argument might appeal to public employees like the police, but it sailed right by them. They knew who they worked for.

"'Mr. Casual'?" Murphy asked.

"That's what I call him."

"You have a *name* for him?"

"He didn't exactly introduce himself. I was telling the story to Lu. I gave him a name. He had on nice casual clothes. Mr. Casual." I glanced at Lu and smiled, but she wasn't smiling back. This wasn't just about shit. Not Buck's shit anyway.

As if he could read my mind, Murphy said, "And then there's the question of just who *you* are, Mr. Bainbridge. That's your name, Nicholas Bainbridge?"

You'd think cops would learn some subtlety, some acting skill for just such moments as this, and you'd be wrong. They were so excited to have discovered that Nicholas Bainbridge wasn't my real name, they could hardly contain themselves. They were forgetting that their knowing my name was a fake was only useful to them if I didn't know they knew. I was tempted to tell the hoped-for lie, defend my false identity with tooth and claw, make the cops' work easy for them, and get the whole business over with, but I wasn't ready for that. I'd probably have to come clean to somebody, Lu sprang to mind, but not these assholes. Who I was was none of their business. They were just cops.

I gave them a big, condescending smile. "Oh *no*, of course not. Nicholas Bainbridge is a *stage* name. My real name's Richard Tedowski. With an *i* on the end."

"Do you have any identification?"

"It was stolen—had my pocket picked at the Oktoberfest. I reported it to the police at the time and filled out the form for a new ID, but I never received it. They said there was a backlog."

"Do you have the tracking number of your complaint?"

"I carried it around for a while, but I lost it. I tried calling three or four times, but the wait was always so long I gave up, and then I sort of forgot about it. I never had much need for it."

"Do you have any other identification—anything with your name on it?"

"Not here. We just sort of moved in together not so long ago. Everything like that is at my old place. Do you need it?" Without actually getting up, I tried to look reluctantly willing to rise from my chair and make the journey if I absolutely had to. I wanted to be a law-abiding citizen, but it was also Sunday, and I wanted to take my shoes off.

THE BRIGHT SPOT

They traded a look. I had no doubt what I'd just told the cops was perfectly plausible to them. Maybe too perfectly. But they'd had enough for today, especially since their next move would be to ride over to some loser's room and read his mail for evidence of the great dog-shit conspiracy.

"How about you just stay away from that particular trashcan in the future, Mr. . . . ?"

"Tedowski. Okay. Be glad to." I gave them a now-wasn't-that-easy? smile. Pushing my luck again. They'd gotten interested because I was sporting a phony name. Just because I'd tossed them a new one to chew on didn't mean I was out of the woods yet. There was still the parting question, the Columbo move, though I never met a cop yet half as smart as Peter Falk. You could see Murphy waiting to pop it like an after-dinner mint.

We all stood up. I kept Buck tucked under my arm. If the question turned out to be a tough one, I could always put him down and buy myself a moment or two to come up with an answer.

But the parting question didn't turn out to be for me, but for Lu. Murphy turned to her. "What about you, L'il Lu? You have any light to shed on this business?"

Of course. I should've known. *Everybody* knew L'il Lu around here—went to school with her, ran with somebody she dated, knew her mama, *something*. Murphy was probably one of a long line of guys who'd dated her and carried a torch. She looked him right in the eye. "Dick never told me anything about it. Other than the day it happened. We just laughed about it. I walk the dog sometimes too, you know. I could've put some of the shit in that can."

Murphy didn't care about shit. What was it Kennemeyer said?—*What did you know and when did you know it?* "So you *knew* his name wasn't Nicholas Bainbridge?"

"Of course. Dick Tedowski. Sometimes I call him Ted. That's what his mother called him and his father—Big Ted and Little Ted."

"Is that right. Everybody down at the corner seems to think his name is Nick."

"The stage name's good publicity for the virtual we're in. *Billy and the Big Guy.* You should check it out."

"I'll do that."

"You got any more of those cards, Dick?" she asked me, and I passed them out as we shuffled toward the door.

Everybody seemed to know everybody was lying in some way or other, but nobody minded it particularly, not yet. As long as Mr. Casual was happy and L'il Lu wasn't going to rat me out.

When the two cops finally squeezed their fat butts out the door, Lu and I went back to the kitchen. I started making coffee, and she sat down at the table. We made a little small talk about her gig in Philly as I worked. "Is there something I should know about you?" she asked when I turned on the machine and sat down. She didn't seem as mad as I'd thought she'd be.

"I wouldn't say that. It's nothing bad. It's nothing you need to know. Thanks for the help. You were great. I'd like to stick with the name Nicholas Bainbridge, if you don't mind."

THE BRIGHT SPOT

I figured she would mind, but she thought about it. She could think of a dozen good reasons why someone might want to lose an old name, take on a new one. It happened all the time. She believed in live-and-let-live. It was the neighborhood religion. "All right. But no more cops, Nick. Okay?"

"Okay."

She laughed. "Dick Tedowski. Jesus, Nick, is that all you could come up with? I had trouble playing it straight."

"'Big Ted and Little Ted'? I just about lost it. You should've seen the look on Lawson's face when I handed him a card."

"Who's Lawson?"

"The white guy?"

"His name's Jackson."

"Lawson must be a stage name."

We laughed and laughed. We were hilarious. We brought the house down. We could hardly stop laughing. But when we did, the coffee machine's dying gurgles filled the silence, and Lu jumped up, busying herself getting the cups, waiting, pouring. She was thinking what I was thinking, I'm sure: This keeping secrets thing wasn't going to work.

"Where did you go today anyway?" she asked when she sat back down.

"I rode out to Llewellyn to see a guy named Edmund Kennemeyer, who used to know James Dumfries."

"You're still hung up on that?"

"He interests me."

"What did you find out?"

"Not a whole lot. He turned cagey on me. Scared.

Which makes me think there's a whole lot more to this than somebody wanting to see his old girlfriend dump him again."

"Of course there is." She gave me a look. She wasn't just stating an opinion. She knew something. More importantly, she might be persuaded to tell.

"You finally going to tell me what it is?" I asked.

"You finally going to tell me your name? You finally going to tell me what the old man said to you that's got you hauling out to *Llewellyn* on your day off? How the hell did you get there anyway?"

"I rode the bus."

"I thought they killed all those routes."

"They tried. They chopped them up into little pieces, but they're still crawling around looking for a place to die. Since we're putting all our questions on the table, Lu, I've got one we can start with. How'd I come to get chosen for this job in the first place? You look enough like Galatea Ritsa to be her sister, and maybe that's a coincidence. But I look enough like James Dumfries to *be* him. So how did we conveniently come to be working at the same shop?"

She nodded, a little smile on her face. Lu liked to bargain. "How about I tell you what you want to know, and you tell me what I want to know—starting with your name, for example?"

"I thought you were okay with not knowing."

"I am. That doesn't mean I don't *want* to know. How badly do you want to know about the Salvador job?"

"They're totally different things."

"I'm not denying that. But that's not really relevant here. I'm proposing a swap—your confession for mine."

There was something sad and scared around the corners of that smile. It was time. She was telling me in so many words she wanted to confess, and I suppose I did too.

But I added a clause of my own: "You have to promise never to tell my name to *anyone,* and never, *ever* use it yourself, even joking around, even if we're alone. I never want to hear it, okay?"

She was a little stunned at my intensity. I was too. I'd never even considered the possibility of telling anyone my real name since I sent it to its final reward a few years back. "Okay," she said. "I promise. So what is it? What's the big secret?"

"You first."

She shrugged, took a deep breath. I had the idea she *had* thought about what she was going to say. Plenty of times. "We were at the same shop because I came looking for you. You were the reason I took a job there. You'd registered your photo with the Guild under the name of Nicholas Bainbridge. Salvador found you in a look-alike search, same way he found me. You'd just started with ReCreation. Salvador hired me first, and I was sent to check you out, to see if you were right for the job. Salvador said he knew one of the ReCreation backers and could call in a favor to get me hired, but Wally took a shine to me, and I didn't need his help. You know the rest. I checked you out. I thought you were perfect for the job."

"And why did Salvador trust you so much?"

She took a deep breath and let it out. "I was sleeping with him."

• • •

"Oh," I said.

"Yeah. Oh. I didn't even *know* you, Nick. I thought... Hell, it doesn't matter what I thought. I was doing this job, going to make some big money, get out of here. There's only one thing that didn't go the way it was supposed to go. I was supposed to recruit you, get you on board, and when the job was over, split with Salvador. I told him that part was off, that I'd fallen for you, and I was sticking with you. That's why we didn't get any money, Nick. He was pissed. He was supposed to get the money and the girl, and all he got was the money, so he kept it all for himself."

"And I get the girl."

"If you want her."

"Course I *want* her. You told me you'd never met with the real Salvador, that it was all virtual."

"I lied. I didn't want to go into it. I didn't think it mattered. It was over. The minute you and me got together, it was over."

"Were you ever going to tell me?"

"I don't know. When were you going to tell me your real name?"

"Never."

"You promised."

"I know. I know." I pointed to the terminal. "I'll spell it for you. Do a Guild search on it."

She gave me a puzzled look but complied. I spelled it. It's not that hard to spell, but people get it wrong all the time. She hit Search. When the results came up, it took her a moment, then a light dawned.

"You understand?" I asked her.

"Perfectly."

THE BRIGHT SPOT

Here's what she understood:

There were my credits, one flop after another. Not just flops. "Disastrous" was the overall theme. I, however, was always the "one bright spot," the consummate professional who didn't seem to know what a stinker he was in and acted his little heart out. This never got me anywhere because even if a virtual was okay, if I was in it, it went down. It got worse in the details. Even the ones with big names and hype died if my name was in the credits. Careers ended wherever I went. Good writers wrote garbage. Big companies went bust. A brilliant editor went into rehab mid-edit. And there I was, still standing through it all, the story hacked to pieces all around me, the bright spot.

The one truly good thing I was ever in was sued for copyright infringement after running one week. All copies were ordered destroyed. You should read the reviews. The best week you've ever read in your life, my life anyway. I was the *brightest* spot, the next whoever who'd *finally* broken an endless run of bad luck. Reviewers yucked it up so big that when the suit was filed, they had to yuck it up again about what a bright spot I was. More like a black hole. A blight spot. I was the kiss of death. Don't you see a light when you die? That was me. The Bright Spot.

Nobody would hire somebody with a resumé like that, unless they *wanted* to lose money, and *The Producers* had already ruined that gag for anybody else. My only hope as an actor was to change my name and make sure that no one—and I mean *no one*—would ever guess I was the same guy who cursed everything he touched. Still doubt it? I didn't just doom virtuals. I once played Puck in a Shakespeare-in-the-Park gig in its *centennial* year. Its last year, as it turned out. Big surprise. Even the Bard couldn't dodge the Bright Spot. The reviewer called me magical.

There was an old movie actor named Kevin Bacon, a favorite of mine, famous for being in everything with everybody. I was like that, only the opposite. I was famous for being the nobody whose competent, professional, even brilliant work always came to nothing and went nowhere.

Nicholas Bainbridge, however—I hear that boy's a rising star.

Call me Nick.

"It says here you're dead," Lu said.

"And still walking. Imagine."

"Oh, baby," she said, and put her arms around me. Nothing ever felt so good.

We held each other for a while, relieved of the lies we'd been lugging around, as if our wonderful life couldn't survive setting them down. I wasn't crazy about revealing my glorious past. I wasn't crazy about knowing she'd screwed Salvador. I *was* crazy about getting the girl though. I was crazy about her. And I didn't doubt for a minute she believed her love for me cost us the payoff—which told me she must be pretty crazy about me too. You might be thinking, *It's only money*, but that only tells me you've never been poor.

But I doubted she had it right. I had a hunch we didn't get paid because the deal went bad, and that James Dumfries, dead or alive, was the one who could tell us how. But we didn't talk about any of that yet. We made love instead, until it was good and dark, and we were about as contented as two humans could be.

JUST A NAME

8

I never saw any of them again—except the cops. No way has yet been invented to say goodbye to them.

—Raymond Chandler, *The Long Goodbye*

About the time the moon came up, we sat up in bed and finished telling each other the rest of the story, with none of the pieces held back, and for the first time we tried to make sense of it together. What was it Jim and Galatea were up to? What happened when we played them? What was supposed to happen? What was it the old man wanted me to do? Buck woke up, said nuts to both of us, and went into the kitchen to sleep.

Lu was pretty sure there was more to it on Salvador's end than just stealing the old man's money. Sometimes Salvador acted like it wasn't about money Dumfries had but something valuable Salvador was going to get out of the deal. She overheard what sounded like negotiations, like he planned on having something to sell. But what? She never could figure it out.

I told her about my weird conversation with

Kennemeyer, and we spread the photos out on the bed and pored over them. "What's that woman in the background?" Lu asked. "What's that thing she's got on?" There was an out-of-focus woman, bent slightly at the waist, holding or pushing something outside the frame. She had some sort of blurry white hat or scarf on her head.

"A nurse or something. It's some kind of home, I'm guessing. There must be a million of them. He doesn't look too good, does he?"

She studied the old man's face. "He looks like Dell on a long night. You think that's the meds?"

"Got to be. If he was going to go for a scam like this, he'd have to be well lubricated. He looked different, though, when he came up to me. Smart. A bit nuts. But he wasn't doped up, more like the opposite. Bright-eyed as could be. And spontaneous. Now, something I've been wondering—if he's trying to change history, and that's the whole reason he's doing this, you'd think he would know what he was going to say, that he'd have a little speech all ready. But it wasn't like that. It seemed to be something he just decided to do on the spot."

"Maybe he's senile, like Jesse said."

"Maybe. Could you do me a favor? Could you not call Salvador *Jesse*?"

She searched my eyes. "Sure, I can do that. Would it help if I called him 'that fucking asshole'?"

"No. Too personal. Just stick with Salvador."

"Okay."

We looked back at the old man's picture. The bleary-eyed fellow there was a dead end. Lu pointed at the diner shots. "Salvador was real proud of the bullshit he'd fed

THE BRIGHT SPOT

Dumfries, the little touches that made it convincing. He wouldn't tell me anything about where and how he'd met up with Dumfries to feed him this line, or how he'd gotten those tapes, but he couldn't resist talking about the line itself, how well he'd played the old guy, and how clever he was for creating such a beautiful scam out of a couple of crummy recordings and a little bit of information—like the woman's name. He got the old guy into a series of conversations about time travel and what he'd do if he had a second chance, and when the time was right, he dropped Galatea's name, and Dumfries practically did all the work himself, told him things he shouldn't have told him, and he wasn't about to tell me. Once, Je—Salvador—sorry—said, 'When I found the *place*, it all came together, like a *flash of inspiration*.'"

She hammed up the line a little to show me what an arrogant jerk Salvador was, but I didn't encourage the show-and-tell. "So what's your point?"

"Forget about Salvador, okay? That's my mistake. My *point* is that the diner—the real one—must be where Salvador took Dumfries to do the time-travel routine. It mattered *where* they did it—the place in the recordings. He arranged for the old man to take a car trip too. He was taking him somewhere. My guess is this diner still exists—the real one—and *that's* where Dumfries thought he was using a time machine."

"Right. Salvador took him to the right *place*, so the time travel wouldn't be such a stretch. So we're looking for a diner in DC that was also there forty years ago?"

"That's my guess. But it wouldn't even have to be a diner anymore."

"That'll make it easy to find. Even if we can find it,

all we'll know is where Jim and Galatea were forty years ago, without knowing what they were doing there. And maybe we'll know where Salvador and Dumfries were a couple of months ago, but that doesn't put us any closer to where they are now. What I can't figure out is how he got the old man to believe any of this stuff. How was he supposed to know about Galatea Ritsa? *And* have access to a time machine? The old guy didn't seem that far gone."

"Salvador told him he was a spook—Homeland Security. James Dumfries would be no stranger to spooks. Sometimes I wonder if the old man actually believed him or was just playing along because he was bored or crazy or something. I hate to sound like our beloved Billy, but I keep thinking my character is the key to the whole thing. We know who these two guys are—Kennemeyer and Dumfries. But who is Galatea Ritsa?"

"Clinton never heard of her. I haven't been able to find out anything about her except the same thing Salvador apparently saw—struck by a car while jogging. It's like she didn't exist before that or after. Just saying her name made Kennemeyer jumpy as a cat."

"Maybe they weren't doing what it looked like they were doing. Maybe this whole breakup scene was smoke. Because if that was all it was about, what's Kennemeyer got to do with anything? Was he driving the car that hit her? Was he the other man? Why not just tell the woman to skip tomorrow's jog? It doesn't make any sense."

"I don't think Kennemeyer was Galatea's other man, unless she was a cross-dresser."

"He might be bi."

"They might bring back welfare. Anything's possible. Maybe Salvador really is a spook with a time machine, and he's living in the future. What about Salvador anyway? Have you looked for him?" I tried to keep any accusation out of my voice. It came out like a cold wind.

"When he stiffed us? You bet. Nobody's seen him since before the deal. He's not any of the places he talked about us going afterward. Naturally. I didn't ever really think we'd be going there anyway. He could be anywhere. He's a dead end."

"Meaning there's nothing there, or we should steer clear of him?"

"Both, I guess. He's really bad news, Nick. I'm sorry I got you hooked up with him."

"Are you kidding? If it weren't for him, we never would've met. He fixed us up. I should thank the guy. He can have the money, if there is any."

"Do you mean that?"

"Thanking him? No, I guess not. You're the one I ought to thank. I mean *that*."

"You trying to make me cry?"

"You're a professional. You don't need my help."

"Yes I do, Nick. I really, really do."

"Me too."

We cuddled for a while, still talking about the whole thing. Altogether, we chased it around the room for a couple of hours at least but never caught up with it. We fell asleep happier souls, however. We might be dumb, but we were honest, and whatever Galatea and Jim's troubles had been so long ago, there was nothing we could do about them now—a couple of dummies like us, a couple of actors—cattle, like Hitchcock said.

Moo.

• • •

Lu wanted to walk Buck in the morning, in case Mr. Casual was on the prowl. I didn't argue. After yesterday—the haul out to Llewellyn, toy cops, real cops, giving and taking confessions, some truly spectacular sex—I was totally exhausted. But it was a good tired. This Dumfries nonsense had been weighing me down for too long, and it was time to move on. I rose from my bed a new man. I gulped coffee and showered. Life was good.

I was looking forward to getting back to work, returning to something I was good at—pretending to be someone else inside the tiny, manageable reality of a story. Like this mirror, I thought. I ran through Victor's leers, sneers, and smirks as I shaved. Victor's a very clean-shaven fellow, only a blade will do—the She-Creature likes a smooth cheek to caress with her long, talon-tipped fingers.

"Ain't you pretty, though?"

I shifted my focus, and there were two extra faces in the mirror that didn't belong to me. The cops were back.

"Good morning, Mr. Dickowski, or whatever your name is. Get dressed. You're coming with us. We have a few questions we'd like to ask you." Jackson. His name was Jackson, as in son of a jackass. I liked him better as Lawson.

I appealed to Murphy. "Oh, come on, guys. I've got work today. I'll buy the man a new can if he wants, have it monogrammed for him."

"This isn't about dog shit this time, pretty boy." Jackson smirked.

"Then what's it about, ugly cop?" I was kind of hop-

THE BRIGHT SPOT

ing he'd try to hit me. I'm a good ducker, I am. Very quick. The mirror was behind me, seven years' bad luck with Jackson's name on it. I was grinning at him. *Go ahead. Try it.*

Murphy cut in. It was his turn to dance. "Knock it off, you two. Nick, did you happen to know an Edmund Kennemeyer?"

"Not well. I just met him yesterday."

"Ain't that a coincidence?" Jackson said. "The same day he turns up dead. You got five minutes to get dressed."

"Where's Lu?" Murphy asked.

"She's out walking the dog. Kennemeyer's *dead*?"

"Yeah," Murphy said. "If you move it, we can leave Lu out of this. Know what I'm saying?"

I got dressed in three minutes while Jackson pawed the place and Murphy browsed the books. He found my detective fiction and complimented my taste. He was certainly the politest cop I'd ever met. I used my remaining two minutes to leave Lu a note telling her where I was and not to worry. At least that's what I tried to do. It came out, *Gone to jail, see you soon! Love, Little Ted.*

The police cruiser had a better ride than the limo, and we were going a whole lot faster. You could look out these windows, but I found it better not to. This thing had someplace to be and had no use whatsoever for where we were. We zipped along at top priority, the fastest bullet out of the barrel. Murphy and Jackson didn't look out either. They kept their eyes on the suspect, to see if he was about to crack. It took me a moment to realize we were heading away from the city, away from the jail. "Where are we going?"

"Llewellyn," Jackson said. "Isn't that what killers do, return to the scene of the crime?"

"You guys don't really think I killed the guy, do you?"

"Why should we think that?" Jackson said. "Apparently, you're the last one to see him alive. He had your phone number on him. We got some nice prints off a bottle of wine. Before that, we got you on the local bus terrorizing some little kid half out of her mind. Lawsuit in that one, for sure. Great laugh, by the way. We got you at the gate threatening the security officer. Some really crazy stuff—with possible domestic security issues. I'm no expert, but I listened to enough blowhards pretending to be—they'd peg you as a sociopath with homicidal tendencies at least. They got the heavy-duty 'ware for bad boys like you—once they put you on that stuff, you ain't never coming off. We got you peeping outside the mansion at the lady of the house, ignoring serious warnings signs everywhere that the property was secured by potentially lethal force, meaning either you're totally nuts—see the pattern here?—or you knew about the screwdriver someone drove into the security panel with a hammer approximately an hour before your arrival, or both. We got you joyriding with a stolen unlicensed antique vehicle with an eighty-five-year-old unlicensed driver at the wheel—you stop me when I get any of this wrong—after you got through plying the old queer with pot and wine. We got you trespassing on—"

Murphy held up his hand, and Jackson shut up.

Murphy said, "Since the DA here has seen fit to tell

THE BRIGHT SPOT

you our whole case, you got anything to say for yourself besides 'I didn't do it, Officer'?"

"I missed the motive and the method."

"Don't need a motive for a psycho. We got you cackling like a madman on a public conveyance—deliberately trying to terrify a child with a dozen shocked witnesses—each one trying to outdo the last one saying how crazy you were. You done pissed away motive when you pulled that one. Method's nothing too complicated—drowned in the pool in a few feet of water. Anybody strong enough to overpower an eighty-five-year-old man could've done it. He put up quite a fight, apparently."

"Is this after he came back with the stolen vehicle?"

"That's right."

"So you know I wasn't there. He had to go by the toy cop and his surveillance without me in the car. Meanwhile, I was getting on the wrong bus. The 27E instead of the 27N. It was a fucking nightmare. I'll have to tell you about it sometime. Point is, there must be surveillance on those buses that'll put me there. Have you talked to Pool Concepts? They had a crew at the pool."

"Yeah," Murphy said. "We checked with them. That's how we know you didn't come back to the house with the old man. With the exterior surveillance down, we pulled the visuals off the 'ware workers, on the off chance they might've picked up something. They tracked Kennemeyer coming back all by himself."

"Tracked. You mean they were watching him?"

"That's exactly what I mean."

"What were 'ware workers repairing a pool doing watching Kennemeyer?"

"Good question."

"Did they pick up the murder?"

"You might say that. Looks to us like the three of them did it. You know anything about that?"

"*Did* it? What do you mean—they were running 'ware when they killed him?"

"That's exactly what I mean."

"You're kidding."

"Wish I was. Course, if somebody *made* them do it somehow, then they'd just be the murder weapon, so to speak."

"Look. I'm an *actor*. I couldn't tell you how 'ware works, much less get pool guys to murder an old man."

"You say you're an actor," Jackson said. "How the hell do we know? You can't even get your *name* straight."

Murphy cut him a look. It was clear who was in charge. Jackson had interrupted his flow. "Anybody accuse you of murder?" Murphy asked me. "I don't remember that. I just thought you might know something. Kennemeyer being a friend and all."

Right. "He wasn't a friend. I was researching a role, an old buddy of Kennemeyer's named James Dumfries. I called him up, asked if he'd mind talking. He was bored, lonely, he wanted to get high, I helped him out. I mean—I *wanted* him to stroll down memory lane. Only, he ended up driving. The car thing was his idea. It was probably stupid to put my life in the old guy's hands, but he just wanted to have some fun. I gather it'd been a while."

"Driving? Nobody drives anymore."

"Not just that. Everything. He was a real robust guy with absolutely nothing to do. At least that's the impression I had."

"Did he indicate to you that his life might be in danger?"

It probably wasn't, I wanted to say, *until I showed up asking about Galatea Ritsa.* "No. Not unless he feared dying of boredom." I risked a glance at the blurred world out the window. We were already getting close. After this much time yesterday, I was still on the first bus, with the Llewellyn Connector a good hour and a half into my future.

"So, why is it we're taking this little ride out to Llewellyn?" I asked.

"The lady of the house wants to meet the peeper," Jackson said, making it sound just about as smutty as he could. I was a sicko, all right, watching that beautiful naked woman running twenty feet up in the air without going anywhere. No reason to give that a second glance. Happens every day. I guess I had Kennemeyer to thank for that opportunity. Normally, I would've needed an expensive telescope and the even more expensive house across the lakelet to see something like that. *The perimeter security's on the blink again.* It'll do that when you drive a screwdriver into it.

"If surveillance was down, how did you come up with this peeper fantasy of yours?" I asked Jackson.

He was hoping I'd ask. "She saw you. She's got a mirror. Big thing. To see the birds, she says. Leaves a window open in the virtual. Did you show her your bird, Dickowski? Birds in mirror may appear larger than they really are." He cracked himself up with that one. He'd be telling it for years. The Dickowski Story.

"What about the nephew," I asked Murphy, "the lady's husband?"

Murphy nodded wearily. "Yeah. Trey Kennemeyer. What about him? We're trying to track him down. He was supposed to be in Sri Lanka, but he wasn't there. They're checking in places I never heard of. Ever been to Sri Lanka, Nick?" I shook my head. "Me either. I never been fucking anywhere, except in this damn thing."

The cruiser slowed like a spent bullet and settled to the pavement in front of the big pile of stone. "Well, here we are," Murphy said. "Big thing, isn't it? The floor space is listed as over an acre—what is that?—four or five ordinary mansions? *Two* people live here, not counting the deceased they had stashed out in the pool house, and the servants, all of whom run on 'ware and live elsewhere. Under the circumstances, the lady's given them the day off while they get checked out. The workware folks are seriously upset, as you can imagine. They're afraid panic might set in. The economy would grind to a halt." Murphy jabbed a thumb at the big pile we were parked in front of as if it were the economy. "Ever do the 'ware, Nick?"

"I've never had the pleasure."

"Wish I could say the same."

"It's not so bad," Jackson said. "Riot 'ware saved my ass more than once. So why is it we're sitting here? The house is over there, in case you hadn't noticed."

"I've got a few more questions for Nick here, if you don't mind. Kennemeyer had something to do with the 'ware, didn't he?"

I didn't have any idea where Murphy was going with this, but I was curious enough to go along. "In a way. He was against it—one of the leaders of the movement. He was kind of a big deal at the time, but since he was on

THE BRIGHT SPOT

the losing side, I don't think too many people know who he was."

"Except young radicals like Clinton?"

"Who?"

"You're good, Mr. Actor, but everybody knows you helped take Dell home the other night. But you're right. No need to go there. He didn't have anything to do with this. No speech in it for him, no radical babe on his arm, telling him what a big *difference* he's making listening to himself talk. What about this other guy—the one who was Kennemeyer's friend, the one you came all this way to talk to him about? Did *he* have anything to do with 'ware?"

Murphy could look it up as well as I could, right there on the cruiser's terminal. I didn't see any reason not to tell him. "Basically, he invented it. During the war. But he was against all the uses it was put to afterwards. He made a fuss for a while, then just dropped out of sight."

"Good riddance," Jackson said. "Maybe these anti-'ware guys would like to spend their time cleaning sewers instead of demonstrating, so the poor, mistreated 'ware workers wouldn't have to. You through now?"

Murphy ignored him. "Nick, I've been checking. Do you know when the last time something like this happened—three persons running legal workware acting in concert to kill somebody they're not supposed to kill?"

"I have no idea."

"Never. Not once. Even a cop like Jackson here is brave and brutal and damn near invincible on the right shit. But these weren't soldiers or cops, they were pool repairmen. Drowning people wasn't part of their 'ware package. They tell me they had drowning-response treatment in that package, so they could've *saved* Kennemeyer's life if they hadn't drowned him first. They use 'ware in prison to keep bad guys from killing each other—the shit works. But then you come calling on a big anti-'ware activist to talk about the inventor of the shit, who also was against it, as it turns out. The next thing you know, pool repairmen on 'ware start acting like some assassin squad, and Kennemeyer's dead, and the poor fucks who did it don't even know what happened to them. There are some people who want to prosecute them, so the 'ware doesn't look bad. And do you know how the nephew made his fortune?"

"'Ware?"

"Give the boy a pizza. Come on, Nick. As far as I'm concerned, Lu says you're okay, you're okay. I don't care if you call yourself Peter Rabbit. What did you guys talk about? Do you have anything at *all* for me?"

I figured maybe he could find out something I couldn't. I gave him the only thing I had that didn't have to be self-incriminating. "Just a name. I can't find out much about her except she died forty years ago—hit by an SUV while jogging. Galatea Ritsa. She was James Dumfries' lover for a while, at least I think she was. You can't be sure of anything with this guy. Kennemeyer wouldn't really talk to me."

"Why not?"

"He was scared. I don't know of what. He was sure he was under surveillance."

"Probably was by somebody. Had good reason to be afraid, apparently. Spell the woman's name."

I did.

Murphy turned to Jackson. "*Now* I'm through."

A DOLL'S HOUSE

9

> DR. RANK: *At the next masquerade I'm going to be invisible.*
> HELMER: *That's a funny idea.*
> DR. RANK: *They say there's a hat—black, huge—haven't you heard of the hat that makes you invisible? You put it on, and then no one on earth can see you.*
>
> —HENRIK IBSEN, *A Doll's House*

We got out of the cruiser and walked up the front walk—more flagstones. They were six distinct pastels repeating a pattern in a sinuous line up to the door. I wondered where the quarries were for each color—each one pale and lovely and not from around here. It was a small world, after all, if you had the dough to dig it up and haul it around. And in all those quarries, wherever they might be, all the workers were running the same 'ware. It was almost inspiring, the progress of man. Murphy and I walked in front, Jackson behind us. The closer we got, the smaller we felt. If some guy with stone tablets and lightning bolts raved on the roof, I wouldn't have been surprised in the least.

"Watch yourself with this one," Murphy said to me as we approached the door. "She's the one who discovered the body. She takes a swim every morning at sunrise. Swam right into him apparently. Still a little..." He twirled his fingers around his temple. I think he was actually trying to help. A helpful cop. Life was full of surprises. Something in his voice reminded me of Sylvia.

"You wouldn't be any relation to Clarence and Sylvia Murphy, would you?" I asked, thinking there might be some distant connection.

"They're my parents," he said, then broke into a smile that verified he was his mother's son. "You might want to pick your jaw up off the ground before the lady comes to the door."

He was still chuckling when the door opened, and then we all got quiet. There she was on the ground with clothes on, and she did okay with those too. Probably because she didn't risk too many all at once—shorts and some part of what used to be a sweatshirt hacked down to size—an outfit to show off her fine runner's legs. I don't care about lovely women's legs the way lizards don't care about the afternoon sun. She was barefoot too, with painted toes on her dusty-rose threshold. I had trouble not staring. She had trouble minding. Fortunately, I figured, cops made pretty good chaperones, especially when one of them knows your girlfriend.

"How do you do," I said. "I'm Nick Bainbridge."

"Deena Kennemeyer. It was so nice of you to come on such short notice. I've been desperate to talk to you. You were the last person to see poor Ed alive." She didn't

THE BRIGHT SPOT

shake my hand. She took it. Her long fingers laced through mine, and there we were, hand in hand. The She-Creature couldn't have done it better. She was my height, a little over six foot, and smelled like she might've just stepped out of the shower. Her hair was rumpled, still damp at the roots. I wonder how many miles she'd run to get here.

She smiled a smile of dismissal at Murphy and Jackson, and they practically evaporated before I figured out they were leaving. They were just my ride. I was being summoned by a woman who used the police as a limo service. If she asked them, they'd probably do windows. With her running on the other side, there'd be no shortage of volunteer squeegees.

"Thank you so much, Officers. I'll see Mr. Bainbridge gets home safe and sound." Hand in hand, we ascended the remaining steps—six of them, big broad ones, one in each of the pastels. I wasn't even in the house yet, and I was already in over my head.

Murphy trudged back down to the cruiser, the soul of discretion. You had to admire him. He'd actually used his chauffeuring time to do a little police work. If his bosses found out, he'd probably be in a world of trouble. Didn't he know cops didn't bust people in this part of town—where they stole millions? That was on my side, his side, where thieves were lucky to get a hundred bucks out of a wallet and businesses went under before they were worth knocking over.

Jackson couldn't resist a parting wistful glance over his shoulder. I was living his dream: *The lady of the house wants to meet the peeper.* I'll have to tell him all about it, I thought, if I get out alive.

• • •

The place was so massive the big hexagonal foyer was built for indecision, with lots of room to mill around while you tried to figure out which doorway led where and why it was you cared. My hostess let go of my hand and stepped out into the foyer so I might have a better look at her. I halfway expected her to twirl around. She didn't really have to try so hard. Compared to her, there wasn't much to look at. There was a chrome hat rack without any hats, or maybe it was a sculpture. Big squatty plants. Chairs nobody ever sat in. A light fixture that hung down at all different lengths from a ceiling a few miles up there somewhere. Some big paintings worth a few million each by painters you've actually heard of. What was needed was a signpost to show you where in the hell you were going.

"Coffee, Mr. Bainbridge? Breakfast?"

"Coffee's fine. I haven't had breakfast in years."

"A diet?"

"A cost-cutting measure."

"We have everything."

"I'm sure you do. Just coffee. I really can't stay very long. I have to get to work. I'm a little puzzled why you asked me out here, Mrs. Kennemeyer. The cops didn't say."

"Dee. Everybody calls me Dee." She fixed me with a look to suggest that not just everybody could call her Dee the way I could if I took a notion.

"Nick," I said. "Everyone calls me En."

She laughed too hard at that. Nervous, I guess. Stage fright. I was a pretty good-looking guy, but I didn't buy

THE BRIGHT SPOT

her interest in me for a second. Even if she did run naked in front of a high window every day, she also threatened any audience with death. Either she was a nut, or she was putting me on. Or both. "Are you always like this?" she asked, seeming to mean witty and charming.

"Almost never."

She didn't know what to say to that, so she gave me what was supposed to be a vampish smile. I don't know why she was so bad at it. Maybe, looking like she did, she'd never had to play offense before. She went up on her tiptoes and pointed the way, a cheap but effective move. "There's coffee things in the solarium, is that okay?"

"If you say so."

She led the way down a corridor, and I followed. She made that about as enjoyable as she could without actually shimmying, bending over, or taking off the few clothes she had on. I wondered if she'd ever worked Vegas and thought it likely. That would explain her rushed performance. In Vegas you don't have to warm an audience up. They come that way straight off the plane, full of fantasies and liquor and credit cards. I, on the other hand, was a guy who'd had one cup of coffee and was already late for work. But she was relentless. By the time we were sitting on a loveseat in the solarium, drinking our coffee and looking out over the pool, she'd smiled and touched and bumped the point across that she was one hot, lonely woman, and I could have my way with her if I was so inclined.

I wasn't. I figured that, like the cops, she labored under the delusion I knew something. The coffee was good, though. Damn good.

The pool was still swarming with cops, feds by the look of them, with various tech types sprinkled in, but she hardly paid them any mind. "I've got it on one-way," she said of the window. "We can see them, but they can't see us."

"That's reassuring. I don't care much for the police. Have they been here all morning?"

"Not all of them. New ones keep showing up all the time. They've sealed off the pool house. They won't let me go anywhere near the place. I wanted to see to Ed's things, and they just chased me away, so I didn't know what to do. I thought you might help me sort this thing out."

"Like I told the police, I was just researching a role. I didn't really know Mr. Kennemeyer before yesterday."

Her eyes shone. "A *role*. That's right. The police officers *said* you were an actor in virtuals. Is that true?" She tried to sound breathless and starstruck, but she knew I was a nobody. With money like hers, she could have real stars for dinner. This whole routine was beginning to annoy me.

"I'm missing work right now, as a matter of fact. I play a deranged genius with an insatiable sexual appetite. You should check it out. Sounds like just your thing." I handed her a *Billy and the Big Guy* card. She gave it a puzzled once-over. "But I'm being insensitive. You didn't ask me out here to discuss my acting career, but poor old *Ed*. Were the two of you close?"

She froze for a moment. She hadn't considered that questions were a two-way affair. "Oh yes. Quite close."

"Bounced you on his knee when you were just a little girl, I bet."

THE BRIGHT SPOT

"Why, yes. He...he was very fond of me." Why didn't she just tell me the truth? An amateur's mistake—stuck in liar's mode, making up everything whether it needs it or not. If you want to create an effective illusion, it pays to hang on to as much reality as you can. Now I'd caught her out.

"I was under the impression he was your husband's uncle. Were you and your husband childhood friends, or did old Ed just live in the neighborhood? When you were a little girl, he would've been, what? Sixty-five? Seventy? Why don't you cut the crap, Dee? You're a beautiful woman, and you've got truly incredible legs, and I enjoyed the hell out of watching you run naked, but I'm missing work here, and I doubt if I know anything worth seducing me for anyway. I suppose I could let you seduce me first and tell you I don't know anything later, but that seems awfully low, and you seem like a nice enough person. So why don't you just tell me what you want to know, and I'll see if I know the answer?"

Her face pinched, then she gave it up, just like that. This acting thing was harder than it looked. "I don't know!" she wailed. "I don't even know what I want to know! He just up and dies! Murdered by the pool guys! My husband just vanishes! Nobody tells me anything! I'm just the *babe*, right? I don't need to *know* anything! Well, I know one thing—this is a big damn deal—Ed getting killed like this. Trey, that selfish bastard, didn't keep Uncle Ed around because he *loved* him so much, I can tell you. They hated each other. That's why Ed moved out to the pool house. They used to fight all the time—the little Trey was ever around. Now he's dead, and Trey's not even here to deal with it! The prick!"

She had to catch her breath after that, but she felt better for it, and it was the best move she'd made so far. I liked her better as herself. She'd dumped the perfume ad thing she'd been attempting with her voice, and when she got really mad a bit of a screech came out. A good, sincere screech.

"Did you tell the police all this?"

"Are you kidding me? Who do you think pays for this place? I don't want Trey in jail. I don't particularly care if he's *here,* but I don't want him in jail."

"What did Ed and your husband fight about?"

"Nothing. Everything. Stupid stuff. I don't think they ever fought about what really pissed them off. Trey kept Ed around to keep an eye on him. It was like Ed was in jail. He didn't even have a bank account. Ed used to say Trey kept him on a short leash, but neither one of them would talk about it to me. Trey told me to butt out. Ed was nice about it, said there were things it was better not to know, and I didn't have any problem with that. Until now. I mean, I'm stuck here in the middle of all these cops, and I don't know a damn thing. I was hoping to find out something from you. Some femme fatale, huh?"

"You don't do so bad. I just don't know much. Ever hear of Galatea Ritsa?"

"What's that?"

"It's not a what. It's a who. A woman Ed knew a long time ago." I rattled off the list of Galatea's suspected lovers, but Dee had never heard of any of them either. "What about another friend, James Dumfries—ever hear of him?"

"No. Wait a minute. Is that Jimmy?"

THE BRIGHT SPOT

"Ed called him that."

She got a faraway look. I think she'd been holding the fact that Ed was dead and gone at arm's length until then. She'd known for, what? Three, four hours. "Ed was all right, you know? We were both kind of stuck here. We used to have a few drinks, talk." She sighed, shook her head. "He didn't like girls either." She cut me a look, but I didn't rise to the bait. "It's no secret I married my husband for his money, and he married me because, well, I look like this. But it doesn't make any sense to me. I got what I wanted, I guess—there's certainly nothing this dump doesn't have—but Trey's never here, never *looks* at me. I don't even think he's got my *picture* with him. I thought, you know, after a while, he'd like me. I'd like him. It'd get like that. Stupid. Anyway, Ed and me used to cry on each other's shoulders. He had nice shoulders." Her voice caught, and her eyes glistened. "Anyway, one of those nights—we were really wasted—he told me Jimmy was 'the love of his life,' but it hadn't worked out. Later, Trey got super pissed. He told me not to drink with Ed anymore. I told him to fuck himself but did what he said like always. Ed didn't trust me after that, thought I'd told Trey what we talked about, but I never told Trey anything."

"How did Trey know? Was he in the house?"

She waved her hand over her head. "He listens. Remote surveillance."

"So he could be listening now."

She looked around the room. The cops might not be able to see us, but Trey apparently could. "Then maybe he'll get his sorry ass home and talk to the cops!" she shouted. She wiped her palms across her damp eyes and smiled, cheered by her last remark, hoping the bastard was listening, watching, recording.

I smiled vacantly into the air at my absent host, then back at Dee. There were tissues sitting on the table, so I plucked one and handed it to her. She acted like it was the nicest thing anyone had done for her in a while, not counting servants running on 'ware. "When you and Ed talked, did he say why things hadn't worked out with Jimmy?"

"He said Jimmy had a wife. She found out and made him choose. Turns out Jimmy and the wife got a divorce not too long after he broke things off with Ed, but there were too many hurt feelings to patch things up. Isn't that always the way? You have one of those?"

"A divorce?"

"A wife."

"As good as."

"At least as good as a bad wife like me, huh? How far do you think this as-good-as-a-wife would let you stray before you got into serious trouble?"

"We passed that point when you went running by through the air, and I didn't look the other way." I wasn't exactly sure how she'd gotten to be quite so close to me in the last few moments, but there she was, very close, and then she kissed me.

I confess I must've let it go on for a good ten or fifteen guilty seconds before breaking it off. The hot and lonely part was no act. But I didn't care much for my role. Maybe I was virtuous, maybe I felt the eyes of Trey upon me, but when our lips parted, I reluctantly removed her arms from around my neck. "I can hardly believe it myself, but I have to say no."

"Maybe we could just make out awhile?"

"A long while. But I really do need to get to work."

She studied me for a moment. "She's lucky."

"Who's that?"

"The as-good-as-a-wife."

"I'll tell her you said so."

"I'll bet. If you're an actor, you're probably broke, aren't you?"

"That's right."

"Why is it the nice guys are always broke?"

"I've often asked myself that question."

I stood up, and we made the trek back to the foyer with her in the lead. I gave myself a good talking-to the whole way and ignored the artwork I hadn't already ignored on the way in.

"I'll let you know if I find out anything about Ed," Dee said. "The cops haven't been through his apartment yet, though there's not much there but old stuff."

"His apartment?"

"In the house. He's only been living out by the pool for the last six months or so. It was his idea. He got tired of Trey spying on him, and I think he figured out how to mess with the surveillance in the pool house. At first he just hung out there a lot, then he moved in."

"Can I see Ed's apartment?"

"I thought you had to go to work."

"I can't tear myself away." It was supposed to be a joke, but it came out like there was something in it. There was certainly something in the smile it earned me.

"It's upstairs."

"You lead. I'll follow."

"You better watch yourself."

"Everybody keeps telling me that."

I added my own voice to the chorus while I was at it, but I was only half listening. I was too busy not noticing the stairs—stone slabs suspended in some kind of clear plastic that glowed like a desert sunset. I couldn't tell you how many flights. I was in good shape. I hardly noticed.

Ed's apartment was near the top of the pile. It was a self-contained unit with a bedroom, a living room–office thing built around a box and a terminal, a bachelor kitchen, and a bathroom. There wasn't much left of Ed Kennemeyer about the place at first glance. It looked like a suite at a resort waiting for somebody to check in.

We tried the living room–office first.

She pointed to the box. "He never saw anyone. He could've linked with anybody, but he was always on his keyboard doing e-mail. I guess he had his little friends around."

"Yeah, like Snow White. Mind if I have a look?" I pointed at the terminal. I don't know what I expected to find. Ed had erased all traces of himself from the terminal as far as I could tell. I suppose somewhere someone could sort through his e-mail if they worked in the right government agency or knew how to hack, but I couldn't get at it. After all, it was Ed's private information. It was nobody's business but the cops'.

We tried the bedroom next.

"The maids cleaned it out already," Dee said. "All his stuff's out of here except a few clothes and boxes of junk in the closet."

She stretched out on the bed while I searched the

THE BRIGHT SPOT

closet. I had no idea what to look for. The clothes looked old, so I searched through the pockets for a while, hoping to find Galatea's phone number on a matchbook for a seedy bar down by the docks where she sang the blues, or a key to a bus station locker containing a mysterious satchel filled with clues. No such luck.

The boxes had the heavy, dusty sag of old cardboard. They'd been packed a while. Hard-core nostalgia. There was a box of carefully wrapped World War I–vintage model airplanes. There was a collection of bar coasters. There were term papers, quaint little antiques in their own right, for every philosophy course ever conceived. Epistemological explorations. Hermeneutical circles. The Problem of Evil. The Cartesian Splits. It was all there. But no clues.

Meanwhile, a bored Dee posed on the bed. I tried not to look at her, but there were mirrors everywhere—no door was complete without one—and it seemed every time I stole a glance, her eyes were waiting for me, saying go ahead and look. I think that's why I found it, trying to look where those eyes weren't. I hopped up and down to catch a glimpse of the topmost shelves of the closet. Way back in the corner there was a shoe box wrapped in twine I had to stand on a chair to reach. It said THEATER on the side.

"You want me to hold you steady?" Dee asked.

"I'll manage," I said.

I slipped the twine and opened the box. Inside were memorabilia. An actor's memorabilia. The Bright Spot had a box like this before he tossed it off a bridge—too melodramatic by half. This one was very neat and tidy with old rubber bands around each bundle that looked like they'd snap if you just looked at them cross-eyed. There were programs, photos, and, of course, reviews. Right on top. Must be good ones. I moved those out of my way and took out one of the programs from the middle of the pack, like picking a card out of a magician's deck. Bits of rubber band clung to it.

It was a production of *A Doll's House* at the College of William and Mary. I checked the cast. Edmund Kennemeyer played Helmer, and James Allen Dumfries played Dr. Rank. I wasn't so lucky that Galatea played Nora. She was played by Constance Watkins, who I'm sure did a fine job of it. I checked the date. Ed and Jimmy were undergraduates together, acted together, were more than likely, given what Dee had just told me, lovers together. I riffled through the rest of the programs, and apparently Ed had stuck with the acting for a while, mostly community theater, some semiprofessional.

"What'd you find?" Dee asked. She was lying on the bed on her side, her head propped up on one arm, one bare leg bent at a similar angle. I was sitting on the chair in front of the closet. She'd been watching me.

I held up the theater program. "Ed used to act, apparently."

"Oh yeah. He wished he'd been an actor. That's probably one of the reasons why he took to you." She laughed, pointing at the program. "I know that play. Right after we read it in high school, I babysat this kid whose folks were going to see it and made the mistake of telling her the *name*. So she's like, 'I want to go see a dollhouse! I want to go see a dollhouse!' all screaming and crying and stuff, and there I was, stuck with her, trying to tell her she'd be bored to death by it, that it was

THE BRIGHT SPOT

just about some woman who wanted to be poor for the rest of her life, but I could never shut her up, never get her to believe me. She thought it was about dolls and dollhouses. That was the last time I ever babysat."

I laughed at her story, and our eyes met. I sprang to my feet, and held the shoe box in front of me. "Do you mind if I hang on to this for a while?"

She rolled over on her back, her hands behind her head, looking up at me, a dreamy smile on her face. "It's evidence, isn't it?"

"Probably."

"Then I guess you'd better take it with you, when you go."

"Thanks." That's all I could say. Anything else seemed too risky.

She gave me a moment longer to do the reasonable thing and get into bed with her, but I stood my ground. "You're just determined to leave, aren't you?"

"I'm afraid so."

She got up off the bed in one quick movement and took my arm. "Well, let's get it over with. I don't know how much more rejection I can take."

I started to say, *I don't know how much more I can dish out,* but I didn't. I was bucking for sainthood.

She took me to the car, nestled in its own cocoon off the foyer, and opened the door. "You know how to use one of these?"

"You enter your destination on the map thing, push Start to go, Return to send it back. I think I can handle it."

"I don't need the car back right away—I have

others—if you want to hang on to it for a while and send yourself back with it."

"I'll send it right back. Believe me. You don't want me to leave a car like this parked in my neighborhood."

"It's got a security system."

"I don't want to kill any of my neighbors either."

"It doesn't have to *kill* anyone. You just don't want to come back."

Only in my dreams, and I'd feel guilty about those. I got in the car, into a soft leather seat designed to put chiropractors out of business. She leaned inside and gave me a goodbye kiss, a mere peck compared to our last effort. Always leave them wanting more.

"I want that stuff back when you're through with it," she said, pointing to the shoe box in my lap.

"Of course. I have your address. Thanks for everything. It's been a pleasure meeting you. Sorry about Ed and your husband and all." I found home on the map screen with a few stabs of my finger, hit Start, and I was out of there. I didn't look back. There was no point. I was moving too fast.

I'd made it out alive—at least until Trey, wherever he was, checked out the hot kiss on his surveillance, but I decided not to tell Jackson about it. He wouldn't believe me if I told him. Nobody kisses the peeper. Jackson ought to know.

DADDY NEEDS A NEW PAIR OF SHOES

10

CUSTOMER: *Eumenides?*
TAILOR: *Euripides?*

—OLD JOKE

I picked up an escort before I was halfway home—Murphy in his cruiser. We pulled up on the new road next to what I now knew was his parents' place, now the closest point on the grid to Lu's place. I was still trying to process that one. Once you knew, it was obvious, even the same friendly, easygoing manner. He's still a *cop*, I reminded myself. I left the shoe box under the seat.

It was early yet, and no one was stirring on the other side of the chain link. The place just looked like a junkman's packed-dirt backyard in the daylight. It took people to make it anything else. The whole neighborhood looked quiet. There probably weren't more than a half-dozen folks watching out their windows, watching Nick talk to the cop.

"How was it?" Murphy asked, smirking.

I didn't ask what he meant by "it." "I think you've got her all wrong."

"Must've been pretty good, then." He gave me a hard look, thinking (hoping?) I'd done L'il Lu wrong.

"We had a nice conversation, under the circumstances."

"Uh-huh. Well, I checked out that name you gave me. Officially, she doesn't exist. There's a notice in the newspaper, probably pulled right off the crime report for that day—they do that sometimes. The report itself is now a 'corrupted file.' That's what happens to files you're not supposed to see anymore—they get 'corrupted.' Nobody bothered to corrupt the newspaper. Officially, the newspaper made a mistake, made it up, just pulled that name out of a hat. Before that, no Galatea Ritsa. After, the same. Looks like she was undercover and got killed in a hit-and-run accident. The newspaper report got out before anyone could kill it."

"If she was a spook, maybe it wasn't an accident."

"Those sorts of accidents don't show up in the papers, or even the crime reports. Knocking somebody into a tree with an SUV doesn't sound like spy versus spy. But whoever did the cleanup wasn't too thorough. I got to thinking that the newspaper said SUV even though it was a hit-and-run. How'd they know that? There must've been a witness. I checked the officers' logs who would've worked that area, would've been the ones to find the body, interview the witnesses. We're required to log all that, to account for our time. It's separate from the crime reports. Seems that an officer interviewed Edmund Kennemeyer that night around seven."

"So he was on the scene."

"That's a leap, but it makes sense. But you know what's got me curious, Nick? You said you didn't find out about this woman from Kennemeyer, so I got to ask you—where did you get the name?"

I should've had a story ready, but I didn't. I had to make it up on the spot. It wasn't exactly my best work. "It came up in a meeting about this role I'm considering I told you about—James Dumfries after the war, embroiled in controversy. I didn't even know if she was a real person. You wanted something from me, so I gave you all I had."

"And who, exactly, dropped the name?"

"I don't recall. One of the writers, I guess. Probably got it out of the newspaper files."

He gave me his little cop smile. "There's exactly one newspaper file, and there's nothing in it to connect her to Dumfries."

"Maybe one of the researchers has been in touch with the family," I suggested, as if we were brainstorming together. "I really have no idea. She was just another character to me."

"Do you have the script for this thing?"

"Oh, there's no *script*. It's still under development."

"What's the name of the company?"

"There's not really a company yet. Just some meetings."

"You rode the bus all the way out to Llewellyn on the strength of some meetings?"

"That's right. I was drawn to the role."

"Who was running these meetings?"

I gave him the names of a couple of producers I was

certain would never, ever return his calls. He took a little notebook out of his inside pocket and wrote them down.

"Why do they want you, if I may ask?"

"I look like Dumfries—when he was a younger man. They did a look-alike search. Anybody who's interested in a certain look can search the Guild files for any number of variables, including look-alike. It's done all the time for biographies, historicals, unless they've got the budget for a big name—and then nobody cares what the subject really looked like."

"I thought they did all that stuff with effects."

"Effects take time if they're done right. Actors are cheap."

Murphy took a glance around at where we were standing. He couldn't argue with me there.

"How about James Dumfries? Would you happen to know his present whereabouts?"

"I have no idea."

He opened up his little notebook. "I've been checking, naturally. His last known address is what they call a total living facility in Maryland. They specialize in old guys who have a bad habit of wandering off—at least that's their story. Seems he showed up missing a couple of months ago, and they still can't find him. Sounds like he snuck out with some help. They believe he's still alive. All the patients or guests or whatever they are have life monitors, and supposedly his hasn't checked out yet. What about a Jesse Salvador—you know him?"

That one was easy. "No. Doesn't ring any bells."

"Maybe he was using another name. It's been hard to sort out just who he was. He worked at the facility, some kind of shrink supposedly, but all his diplomas are phonies. He disappeared same time as Dumfries—after he'd been having regular sessions with the man for several months. Now he's turned up dead. Seems he was stuffed into a garbage truck by some 'ware workers around the time he disappeared. Some old buzzard claimed to have seen it happen out his alley window—there's a bunch of these total living facilities around there—but nobody took him seriously until they heard about Kennemeyer. The investigating officer there gave me a call, asked me if this 'ware killers story was the real thing, and I told him it looked that way to me. They've been sifting through the local surveillance as well as the waste disposal company's database ever since. The workware people too, naturally, have been all over this one. I talked to the officer a little while ago. They recovered the body this morning from a landfill in Charles City, Virginia. I got the exact lot number if you'd like it."

He flipped his little notebook closed. "We see everything. We hear everything. We even file our garbage. But most of the time we don't look, we don't listen. We don't know the garbage from the bodies."

His anger hung in the air. He wanted to be a good cop, the kind that catches the bad guys and makes the world safe. I knew the playground where he grew up. He must've been playing on one in his own head to come up with the good-cop fantasy. I almost felt sorry for him. "What was this phony shrink supposedly treating Dumfries for?"

He flipped open the notebook. "'Artificial memory,' they told me, some kind of technique for using 'ware with senile dementia patients to assist their memories. They wouldn't tell me much. I'm just a dumb cop, you understand. That's two people dead, Nick. And everywhere I turn, James Dumfries and the fellow who looks just like him keep showing up. Why is that, Nick? What do you know about this? Why is it I get the feeling you're not being completely straight with me?"

"Maybe you're psychic. Ever hear of the Fifth Amendment?"

"A time or two. We can deal unless you're the killer."

"No we can't, and you know it. 'Ware killers. Dead spooks in a landfill. It's too big for you. And even if we could, I don't want the press."

"You're an actor. I thought you thrived on publicity."

"Only the right kind."

"You afraid people will find out your real name?" he said casually. "Start that Bright Spot stuff up again?"

Check. And I was just starting to like the guy. That's what he was doing following me home. He had hold of an arm to twist now. "You know about that?"

"It wasn't that hard to track down—we've got our own look-alike searches. Once I thought to search the dead, adjust for age, there you were. Jackson has this theory you killed that other fellow and stole his identity, but he's not in love with it. I think you paid a guy to fix it for you. If he was a reputable crook, he might've even told you it wouldn't hold up if anybody really started checking, so you should keep your nose clean. I figure you were trying to start over. Is that about right?"

"Close enough."

"You must take this acting thing pretty seriously."

"Don't let it fool you. It's all an act."

He chuckled at that. "Maybe so. But I figure if I lean

THE BRIGHT SPOT

on you, it might not get me anywhere, so I got no reason to share this information with anyone unless I have to. I'd rather play it nice. Come on. Help me out here. You must have something."

"Find Dumfries."

"Thanks for nothing. You know anything that can *help* me find him?"

"I wish I could help you out. I really do. But I just know history book stuff. I understand he had a wife, kids. Have you tried tracking her down?"

He searched my eyes. "Oh yes. Wasn't too hard. She's still living in the house where she and her husband lived; her family was the one with the money, it seems. Interesting little detail: The house is about a half a mile from where Galatea Ritsa was hit forty years ago—if you can believe what you read in the papers." Murphy smiled. He'd been waiting to pull that one out of his hat. I take back what I said about cops never learning to act. Murphy must've gone to night school.

"And what does she have to say?"

"Don't know yet. I'm riding out there tonight. Say, I've got an idea. Why don't you come along? Use some of that charm with the ladies on this old gal? She didn't sound too cooperative on the phone. If you're going to play her husband, you must want to talk to her, right? You *did* say you really wanted to help."

Yeah. Right after he let it slip he knew my name. Check and mate. I walked right into that one. But I didn't want to pass it up either, like a role I had to play. I did want to talk to her. I wanted to talk to her very much. Jimmy's wife, the woman who never came up once in that diner, oddly enough.

"Okay, I'll ride along, but only if you leave Jackson back at the station."

"He's not so bad."

"Yeah, I know. He's just a cop. We should all try to understand."

"Watch yourself."

"You keep telling me that. Isn't that your job, watching all of us, making sure we do right?"

"Somebody's got to. See you at six. We can't be late. The woman tells me she goes to bed at eight."

I didn't want Murphy to see the shoe box, so I left the car sitting there and walked to the house as he drove away. I took the opportunity to freshen up and call Lu at work. While it was ringing, I walked out back with Buck so he could zoom around the tiny yard a few times and freshen up the bushes.

Wally answered in a talkative mood. The creative juices were flowing, erupting, spewing. He launched into telling me about a new plotline, something he was fond of doing in spite of all my attempts to stop him. He wanted to get the war into it, he said. That was part of *Billy and the Big Guy* from the beginning—our heroes could show up inexplicably, anytime, anywhere, with Victor and the She-Creature hot on their heels. It might be Mars in the future (Wally found a dog-eared Kim Stanley Robinson paperback at a flea market) or New Orleans in 1812 (he heard Johnny Horton singing in a documentary). Some reviewers thought it was art. It was really just that Wally was nuts. If he wanted something in the show, it went. It didn't matter whether it made any

THE BRIGHT SPOT

sense. It didn't matter what else was going on. Plotlines weren't *resolved* in *Billy and the Big Guy* as much as they gave up and went away. And now it was the war, as only Wally could do it, and he wouldn't stop *telling* me about it. I'd stood there too long. Buck was pissed out and was gathering his toys from around the yard, piling them at my feet for a major play session.

"Wally!" I shouted—cutting through his rambling synopsis involving a rabbi, a tank driver, and some sort of two-hankie deathbed conversion to I'm-not-sure-what religion—"I just wanted to tell you I'll be there just as soon as I can catch a bus." I hung up. I felt bad, I really did, but I could've been buried in squeaky toys by the time Wally won the war. It would've been better if I'd waited it out and talked to Lu, but she'd understand. She felt the same way: Give me the lines, not the notion. Talk's not the *script*. You can't act *talk*. *There's this guy, see,* doesn't cut it. Besides, the longer I talked to Wally, the longer it would be before I caught a bus. I scooped up Buck and tossed him on the bed with a couple of toys and told him to knock himself out.

When I came trotting out to the car, there were three young men gathered around it, discussing its merits.

"I'm telling you, the security shit's *not* turned on," one of them was observing to another as I came up.

"Hey, guys. Don't lean on the car. I've got to send it back."

"Nick! This is yours?"

"Just a ride from a nice lady. Pardon me. I need to get something out of it." I went inside and got the shoe box, punched Return, and closed the door. It warned everyone in a pleasant tone to get the hell out of the way, then shot back to Llewellyn.

"Aw, man, why'd you have to do that? We could've made a deal, Nick. You could've played a little scene: 'Some mean boys beat me up and took your car, nice lady. Come here, baby, and be nice to your poor busted-up man some more!'"

Everybody laughed. This was Vincente—he added that *e* on the end all by himself—the neighborhood comedian. "Nick, is it true you actors get all the pussy you ever want?"

"That's no way to speak of women. And yes, it's absolutely true."

"I guess that's supposed to make up for being a broke chump all the time, huh?"

"You got it."

André, who was more impressed to have a professional actor in the neighborhood, asked, "Is this the same lady sends that limo around?"

"No. That was just a gig Lu and I did a few months back."

"I thought I seen it a couple times."

"You *think* you see a lot of things," Vincente remarked. "What's in the box?" he asked me.

"Shoes."

He smirked at my old shoes. "'Bout time."

Another cheap laugh. I was tired of playing straight man and took my exit. I stashed the shoe box at the house, walked to the bus stop, and waited a long time for the bus. It was driverless, nearly deserted. I sat in the back with my feet in the aisle.

THE BRIGHT SPOT

It *was* time to get a new pair of shoes. I moved their purchase to the head of the line, next paycheck, right after Buck's monthly bag of food. Lost in this pitiful reflection, I almost didn't notice a limo emerging from the next street over from mine as the bus pulled away. But I soon talked myself out of it meaning anything. It shot away in traffic the opposite direction I was headed. I was a whole lot more worried about the cops than mysterious black limos. I was surprised the feds hadn't talked to me yet. Maybe they had no intention of solving this one. Maybe they already decided who did it, and I didn't fit in their frame. If I was lucky, maybe I could keep it that way.

CERTAINTY AGAIN   11

> *"Ah, but I believed in him more than any one on earth—more than his own mother, more than—himself. He needed me! Me! I would have treasured every sigh, every word, every sign, every glance."*
>
> —Joseph Conrad, *Heart of Darkness*

Murphy had shown up at Recreation, so Lu knew most of what I knew from him. Gary was still upset about a cop questioning one of his actors on his dime, but Wally was fascinated. Murphy, thinking Wally might be the imaginary writer who'd told me about Galatea Ritsa, proceeded to question him at length as well. I would've loved to have heard that conversation.

As soon as I arrived, Wally rushed up and asked what I thought of the name Galatea Ritsa for a character in the show, and I said I liked it just fine. "The policeman was looking for her," he said. "Do you know her?"

"We've never met. Are you going to fit her into your war story?"

He drew a blank for a moment until he recalled our

THE BRIGHT SPOT

conversation of an hour before. "Oh, no. Well, sort of. It's all cops now."

For now, I thought.

I played catch-up all day, getting myself pasted into the scenes I'd missed, so I never got a chance to talk to Lu about the whole business until we were riding the bus home. We had two seats together. Lu sat by the window. She liked to look out.

"What did Murphy want to know from you?" I asked.

"Whether I knew Jesse Salvador, Dumfries, Galatea. I just kept saying it was your gig, and I didn't know much about it. He wants to think I'm not involved, so he went for it well enough. Mostly, though, he was nosing around about you. You didn't tell him you knew Salvador, did you?"

"Course not."

"Do you think you going to see Kennemeyer had anything to do with him getting killed?"

"With Salvador turning up in a landfill? I'm sure of it."

"But how can something that happened forty years ago be worth killing somebody over now?"

"Whatever they didn't want known back then. So far I'm hoping we're just a couple of actors who did a job and aren't worth killing, but I can't seem to shake loose of this thing. Now Murphy's got me riding out to see Dumfries' ex with him tonight. Sooner or later the wrong cops are going to notice I'm everywhere I shouldn't be."

"Are you sure it's cops?"

"Of course it's cops. Who else can make dead women disappear, poof! Who else can take ordinary pool guys and garbage men and make them assassins? They could be corporate, government, secret—there's all kinds of cops—but it sure looks like cops to me."

"Murph says the Kennemeyer woman is really hot." She didn't act like she'd changed the subject at all.

"Murph?"

"He's always gone by Murph. Don't *ever* call him Clarence or Junior, and don't change the subject."

"Me? I don't remember we were talking about 'the Kennemeyer woman.'"

"I know. You've been trying to avoid the subject of what you did all morning. Like now. You won't even answer a simple question without getting all defensive about it."

"Okay. She's hot—very, very hot—but heat isn't everything. Let me guess. Murph said if that actor fellow don't do you right, L'il Lu, you can just come to me for solace, 'cause you know my love is true."

"He didn't sound like some singing cowboy, but something like that. What should I tell him?"

"Tell him to forget it. You're the only one for me, Lu."

"Good, because that's what I told him."

Then I told her what I'd learned from Dee, told her about the shoe box, Ed's acting career and his love life, and that bastard, Trey, wherever he might be. I was even stupid enough to tell her Dee's babysitting story. I thought she'd think it was cute.

"Sounds like you two really talked."

THE BRIGHT SPOT

"We tried pretending but found the real thing worked better."

"You know what I mean."

"Yeah. We really talked. She really liked me. She was bored and lonely and beautiful and thought I was cute and wanted to have her way with me. She asked me if I had a wife. I told her 'as good as.' And I stuck to that story."

She was quiet for a moment, staring at the world passing by, or her reflection in the glass, or maybe she was trying to get her own glimpse through time. Into the future. "Really? Is that how you feel?"

"Certainly."

She smiled. "Certainty again."

"I never lost it."

She turned back to me. "If I'm as good as a wife, does that mean we're as good as married?"

"We could get married and find out."

"You better watch yourself. That almost sounds like a proposal."

"Everybody keeps telling me to watch myself. I know what I'm doing. It was *supposed* to sound like a proposal. It was a proposal. So, what do you say? You want knees? I can do knees. There's a big aisle."

She broke into a smile and sprouted tears like a fountain. "Yes," she said, and we almost missed our stop, celebrating and snuffling and generally making a spectacle of ourselves for the entertainment of our fellow passengers, who applauded us as we got off the bus.

I hadn't really planned on proposing, but once it'd happened, I found I really liked the idea, that it was just about the best idea I'd had since my last really good idea—running to catch up with Luella at that bus stop three months earlier.

We walked Buck together, tried the idea out on him, and he went for it big-time. Ipso Factos like stability and closure. We would've all gone out for a pizza or something, but I had a date with a cop. I managed to wolf down a sandwich before Murphy showed up. Lu met him at the door with the news we were engaged. He took it well, I thought. At least he seemed to be walking okay. I lingered over my goodbye to tell Lu one more time I adored her, and where I'd stashed the shoe box in case she'd like a crack at it, then hurried after Murphy for another cruiser ride. This one was out to where the old money slumbered and cops showed up by invitation only. Murph even wore a hat for the occasion, so he could hold it, I guess.

Dusk was falling. Murph and I waited in the *drawing room*. It was that kind of place, the sort of new house old money built, nostalgic for the past even when it was new. I'd counted three rain forests' worth of mahogany getting here. Impeccably detailed but understated rain forests, mind. Nothing brash or showy.

It was quiet in the drawing room. Neither one of us spoke. We sat up straight. We didn't fidget. We breathed quietly through our noses. We were both good boys. My eyes roamed the room. There were three floor-to-ceiling windows, where the last of the light was making a stand. I didn't give it long. The gloom was already knee-deep. The bent curves of the furniture glinted darkly like crouching insects. I imagined Gregor Samsa in the wing-

THE BRIGHT SPOT

back, waiting with us, imagined the whole place scurrying down a hole if anyone were to switch on a light. There was a white marble fireplace that smelled like wet ashes, though it was hard to believe this hearth had ever been warm. It radiated a chill, like moonlight. There was a white grand piano parked massively in a corner like it had just taxied in, the open lid its folded wings. Music sat on the stand. I could almost make out the title in two-inch letters. *Nocturne in* something-something.

A high door opened—closed.

We rose.

She glided forward, all in black, with a pale head, floating toward me in the dusk. She clasped my hands, totally ignoring Murphy. "My God, you look exactly like him! It's remarkable."

I didn't know what to say. What was remarkable was that she could see me at all in this light. "Nicholas Bainbridge," I said, in case she was inclined to forget it. Murphy had told her I was an actor playing her ex and that I would be coming along for reasons he'd left vague.

"Delighted," she said. She squeezed my hands for a moment and let them go. She turned to Murphy. There was something wrong with her neck, so she had to turn her whole body. Part of the floating-head effect came from a white neck brace. "You must be the policeman," she said.

"Yes, ma'am," Murphy allowed.

The light was failing at such a rate Murphy would soon be invisible except for the whites of his eyes, or his teeth if he should smile. All the furniture had disappeared but the piano perched in the shadows like a fat white moth. The white fireplace was a cloud of smoke behind us, dissolving in the gloom.

Her head floated back to the door, and she flipped a switch. The room flooded with light. She was wearing black satin pajamas and slippers. Her hair was a tight gray frizz. Her face, a thick maze of lines stretched taut over her skull. Sharp, quick eyes looked out.

"Yoga," she said, gesturing at her clothes. "It keeps me young. You should try it," she added, as if she'd already judged what shape we were in.

It was Murphy's party, so he took the first dance. The old lady liked to lead. I felt like sitting down at the piano and playing a tango, but I just sat on my hands and watched them wear each other out.

"I hope this is important," she said.

Murphy smiled to allow he hoped so too.

"I don't know if you're aware, Mrs. Dumfries, but—"

"My name is no longer Dumfries. Mr. Dumfries and I have been divorced for almost forty years. My name is Jean Brand now."

"Yes, Ms. Brand. I don't know if you're aware, but your husband—your *ex*-husband—has been missing from the facility where he lives for over two months. Would you have any idea where he might be? Anyplace he might go? Have you heard from him, by any chance?"

She laughed out loud. It was like Katharine Hepburn. Hopelessly theatrical. It *might* be her real laugh, but you could never be sure. "I can only imagine what he would say to me!"

"So he hasn't contacted you?"

"Certainly not."

THE BRIGHT SPOT

"Are there hard feelings between you?"

She looked at him as if he were a hopeless idiot. "We *are* divorced. Why wouldn't there be hard feelings? Don't be ridiculous. I'd be the last person on Earth he would contact. You've wasted your time and mine coming out here, I'm afraid. Jim Dumfries, really. That was over and done with many years ago."

"Is that what you called him?" I piped up, since Murphy was getting nowhere. "Jim? Such details are helpful to me," I added, "playing my part."

She looked into my eyes. No matter what she did to tell herself otherwise, when she looked at me, she was half looking at him, way back when, when she used to love the guy. Still did, it seemed, in her memories. Her wrinkled eyes glinted with something that hadn't been there a moment before. "Jim," she said. "I called him Jim."

I smiled at her, and she smiled back. It wasn't easy for her. You could see traces of the pain, probably from whatever the brace was for, but still it made her look younger by a decade or so. "How did you two meet for the first time?"

"In college. William and Mary. We were in a play together. He was a scientist, but he had a passion for the theater. I was a theater major, but I wasn't very good. I found him and his work more fascinating. His dedication, his drive. He was already showing everyone what he could do even then."

"So you must've known his friend, Ed Kennemeyer. He was in theater too, I believe."

There was a silence that seemed to have something in it, as if I'd banged out a dramatic chord on the big grand and it was fading ever so slowly away. "Yes," she said icily. "I knew Ed. He and Jim were friends." She put a little extra weight on that word *friends*. She should've left it well enough alone.

"Ed Kennemeyer was murdered yesterday," Murphy cut in, and she swiveled his way.

"My God! How awful! You don't think Jim had anything to do with it, do you?"

"Why do you say that?" Murphy asked.

She fixed him with a deadly glance. "Oh, don't talk like a stupid policeman," she snapped.

The big Murph didn't have a ready answer for that one, so I stepped in. "The two men did seem to have been more than friends at one time," I suggested. "Perhaps—"

She turned on me, wincing for the workout her neck was getting. "If you're implying my husband was *homosexual*, Mr. Bainbridge, you are very much mistaken. My husband and I had two children together. I think I would know if he was a homosexual. Ed was a *friend*, nothing more." The speech had a practiced, pious efficiency about it, like the Pledge of Allegiance. But she'd knocked the bottom out of *friend* this time, erasing any doubt she was lying. I couldn't help but notice how Jim had been promoted to her husband again at the mere suggestion he might've been gay. Murphy and I traded a glance. He caught it too.

"We don't want to leave you with the impression we suspect your husband of any wrongdoing," Murphy assured her, meaning he did suspect—he just didn't want her to know. "But we are trying to locate him. He was under treatment for memory loss. He might be disori-

THE BRIGHT SPOT

ented, confused. Possibly in great danger. Anything that you could tell us to narrow our search could prove invaluable."

If the image of the poor lost Jim doddering around tugged at her heartstrings, it certainly didn't show.

I cut in. "You were with him when he did all his important work, weren't you? During the war?"

"Why, yes," she said, holding her head a little higher in spite of the brace. "Jim was once a brilliant, brilliant man."

"I'm trying to find out about some of his associates, but all I have are their first names." I rattled off the list of suspected other men from the diner scene. I never forget a line—a phone number or a bill, yes, but never a line. Not a single one of the names meant a thing to her.

"Lots of people came and went during the war," she said.

"But you were the one constant. It must've been hard on you to see him embroiled in controversy after the war."

"I told him to stay out of it, but he wouldn't listen to me. Ed got him into it—Ed and his precious *ethics*."

"Into what?"

"You know, the whole anti-'ware nonsense, as if what had saved the world from the extremists all of a sudden wasn't good enough for the common man. It lifted them up out of poverty is what it did, gave them hope, a new life, a purpose, a way to feed their ever growing families."

I'd heard this line before, but I didn't know there was still anyone around who had the gall to say it anymore. Jean and Jim must've had some interesting political discussions of an evening when they weren't avoiding the subject of sex. I decided this was a good time to lead trumps. "Is that where he met Galatea Ritsa? In the anti-'ware movement?"

If the silence before was a chord on the piano, this one was hoisting the piano to the ceiling and dropping it on the marble hearth. "I-I don't know *where* he met her exactly. I never actually met the woman. Now, if you'll excuse me, I'm really quite tired. At my age, I'm not used to so much excitement."

Murphy moved in. "Galatea Ritsa was hit by an SUV while jogging and killed not too far away from here forty years ago. Do you recall that incident, Ms. Brand?"

"I-I seem to recall something like that, yes. My husband was terribly upset."

"Were they close, Ms. Brand—Galatea Ritsa and your husband—or were they just friends as well?" Murphy's little cop smile was a beaut. He just kept it trained on her, the question hanging in the air.

Jean Brand's eyes narrowed. She would've gladly strangled Murphy, I'm sure. Exactly the result he'd been hoping for. "Don't think I don't see what you're doing," she seethed. "You're trying to imply Jim killed that woman in some crime of passion. Nothing's changed after all these years. You're still all determined, aren't you, to rake up some dirt on him? Well, you've got the wrong man for that one. I kept quiet all those years because he wanted me to, but I don't see how it matters in the least now. You want me to say it? Okay, I'll say it: Jim was gay. He told me, told himself I suppose, that he was bisexual. I bore him two children. He wanted children. He was bisexual enough for that. But there was no passion there.

THE BRIGHT SPOT

He fucked Ed Kennemeyer more than he ever fucked me. He tried to make it work with me, but Ed wouldn't leave him alone. Ed never understood that Jim *needed* me. Me! Not some philosopher with his head in the clouds. No one believed in him like I did. He said so. He *said* so! You happy now? My husband was a *faggot*. He married me, but he loved another man. Now, why don't you get the hell out of my house!"

HERE THEY COME

12

ESTRAGON: *We've lost our rights?*
VLADIMIR: (distinctly) *We got rid of them.*

—SAMUEL BECKETT, *Waiting for Godot*

"I THOUGHT THAT WENT WELL," MURPHY SAID AS WE got back into the cruiser. "This Galatea Ritsa just stirs things up wherever she goes, doesn't she? I almost hate to see her go."

He punched us on our way, leaned back in his seat, loosened his tie. He didn't look so good. He closed his eyes, and pinched the bridge of his nose. We were moving past any crimes way too fast to see them. The cruiser was almost silent inside. His voice came out heavy, pissed, and weary.

"You want to know how I spent my afternoon? I asked the feds for their files on Dumfries and Kennemeyer from forty years ago to see if there was anything there for the current investigation. They told me they were still classified. I tried to give them an argument, but they weren't having any of it. An hour later, maybe less,

THE BRIGHT SPOT

my chief calls me in, tells me the case is closed, just like that, and I should drop my investigation into classified matters that don't concern me—specifically any link between Dumfries' and Kennemeyer's past activities and the current murder investigation. 'We still got a dead guy,' I said. 'Is he down with that?'

"He told me to watch myself." Murphy pondered the irony of the moment. Any cop who starts pondering irony should consider a career change. Maybe they all should. He sat up, fixed me with his deep brown eyes. "Here's their story: The three pool guys confessed. They said they never loaded their 'ware up Sunday morning when they got the call, that they used their jobs as cover to attack Kennemeyer to steal from him, and because they have a deep-seated hatred of homosexuals."

"Deep-seated."

"That's what the man said."

I didn't know what to say. Three guys who only got up one morning and went to work just had the rest of their lives stolen from them. All they were good for now was suffering. That was five lives and counting. "You don't believe any of that shit, do you?"

"Course not. I *saw* the damn visuals from those three. They were running 'ware or there wouldn't *be* any visuals. But it doesn't matter. It's over for me. Nobody can even tell me who they did all this confessing *to*. They've been transferred to an undisclosed location for their own safety, standard procedure in hate-crime cases."

We reached our destination, and the cruiser bleeped softly in case we hadn't noticed.

"What about Salvador?" I asked.

"Who? The Maryland officer I talked to about that case is now on unspecified leave. Hell, maybe he's in Sri Lanka. They never heard of a Jesse Salvador murder case or a James Dumfries disappearance, and if I have the intelligence God gave a flea, I never have either."

"Is that why we went out and talked to the old lady?"

"No. We did that because I'm a stubborn son of a bitch who doesn't like being told what to do, and I thought we might get lucky, get some answers."

"We didn't do so badly."

"We got confirmation that Galatea Ritsa was real, an associate of Kennemeyer and Dumfries, who, as it so happens, liked to fuck each other. That might be good material for you, but it doesn't exactly solve any crimes in the here and now. This is as far as I go unless I got something real to go on. You're in this, Nick, you and Lu both, someway, somehow. Cover your ass, fine. But don't ask me to come clean it up for you. If in your *research* for this bullshit *role* you're playing, you find something I can use, you let me know. Otherwise, you're on your own."

"Just like that?"

"Just like that."

"And people think the government's inefficient."

"Listen here. I'm good at what I do. But I can't make bullshit smell like anything else. Those names you gave me, the ones you were supposedly having the little meetings with? Seems they conspired to launder the wrong money, the kind that rats you out when it gets caught. They've been living in a minimum security prison in Arizona for the past two years. It's a much nicer place than they're going to put you before this thing is over, if

THE BRIGHT SPOT

you don't fade away while you still can. Let me connect the dots for you—if the pool guys didn't do it, you're next in line."

I didn't see any reason to hang around after a line like that. I got out of the cruiser. He hadn't come to the logical place next to Murphy's this time, but at the other end of the street where the bus stops. The cruiser sat like a big shiny boulder in a rushing torrent of high-speed traffic. Murphy's window slid down.

"I couldn't help noticing you didn't drop in on your folks," I said, pointing my thumb down the street.

"Is it somebody's birthday? Somebody file a complaint? Nobody wants me around there. I was doing you a favor. If you want to be seen with a cop, that's your business, but it won't exactly help your standing in the community. Leave this whole thing alone, Nick. It's a dead end. Folks want it that way. Understand?"

"It must be hard, doing your job."

"Only when you try. Save your empathy for your characters." His window started up.

"Wait." The window stopped where it was. I stepped up, leaned on the roof of the cruiser. "Lu and I were doing a job with Salvador, scamming Dumfries out of his fortune, at least that's what we thought we were doing. It was a phony time-travel number with me as the young Dumfries and Lu as Galatea. Salvador had recordings—a Dear John scene in a diner—though I'm thinking there was more going on there. The old guy flipped out and came up to me while Lu's in the john. He tells me about Galatea getting killed the next day, says I've got to stop it. Tells me to find Kennemeyer. After Salvador stiffed us, I finally did. That's how the whole thing got rolling. Salvador took him to an old diner in DC, probably by limo. I can send you some photos. I don't know where we played our scene—a set in a warehouse somewhere. A limo ride. I can give you a description of the driver and the vehicle."

The window went up, the door opened, and Murphy emerged. "Why in the fuck did you have to tell me all that?"

"I didn't have to. I could've just let it alone, kept it under my hat, wherever I'm supposed to put it. You just said you're good at what you do. Well, *do* it. But don't give me this it's-what-folks-want routine when you fade. What folks *want* is for you to be good at what you do, to do the right thing instead of what you're told to do. Then they might get an even break for a change. If you don't like me telling you the truth, you can ignore it, like cops usually do. Let the pool guys do some hard time. After all, it's what folks want—the good folks at the top who decide which laws you're enforcing this week and which lives matter."

He didn't say anything for a moment. He might slug me, haul me in—I had no idea. But I didn't care. He'd pushed a button, I guess. Don't give me the will of the people when the fix is in. I took my chances.

"Lu ever say you remind her of her mother?" he asked.

"Never."

"Ask her sometime. One tough lady. When I was ten years old and giving my mother some grief, Bea says to me, since I was so righteous maybe I should become a cop. She meant it as a putdown. I showed her." He laughed, shaking his head, pondering irony again. "All

THE BRIGHT SPOT

right. We'll play it your way. I'll see what I can do with this better-late-than-never information without getting us both busted or killed. In the meantime, don't share it with anybody else."

"Even Jackson?"

"*Especially* Jackson. He doesn't like you one little bit."

"I'm hurt." I gave him a description of the driver and the limo, and he wrote all that down.

"You got a script for the diner scene?"

I tapped my head. "It's all up here. I'm a pro. I never forget a line."

"Write it up and send it to me. Maybe it means something."

"Lu and I will record you a command performance. Is it safe to be sending you something like that?"

"Anything incriminating in it?"

"Not that I can tell. It's all 'Please give me one more chance' and lines like that. It sure sounds like the guy was in love with her, no matter what the former Mrs. Dumfries thought."

"Maybe they were acting. The woman said he had a passion for the theater. Besides, everyone can act a little." He wrote down an address and phone number, tore it out, and gave it to me. "Send everything here—that address is only remotely connected to me, so it should be okay. Use this number to call me if you need to, but don't call just to chat. I'll contact you when I know something. If you haven't heard from me in a couple of days, or anybody else starts sniffing around, I'd suggest you and Lu leave town."

He got back in the cruiser and the window zipped

open. "I'd shake your hand but you'd have to move to another neighborhood. Second thought, maybe I should do just that." He smiled and gave me a little wave. "Be careful," he added as the window zipped up, and he was gone. I'd finally graduated from "Watch yourself."

I looked around my neighborhood and felt good, lighter for my confession. I knew I'd probably just let Lu and me in for a world of trouble, but I felt the same giddiness I felt coming here with her the first time. This being Nicholas Bainbridge was all right. He had good instincts, did Nick, and he'd had one helluva Monday—rubbing elbows with the rich and lustful—engaged to be married—so upstanding, policemen wanted to shake his hand—and not just to plant evidence.

I imagined our house down at the end of the street, all lit up, waiting for the bridegroom's return. That's a scene I could definitely play. The night was young, and so was I—a lot younger than when I decided to become Nicholas Bainbridge. A dry west wind blew talk and laughter up the street from Murphy's three blocks away. It sounded like so much mush up here—warm, pleasant mush. I started home.

There was also a faint, persistent buzz off to my left, and I looked that way. The road crew was at work on the next street parallel to ours, where the latest well-dressed dogs had started moving in. The sound came from the big lights. The workers were strictly mime.

I looked between the narrow houses as I passed. Each gap offered a brightly lit scene of the 'ware workers' wild, inhuman dance. I couldn't take my eyes off them, like

THE BRIGHT SPOT

watching cannibals dancing around a cauldron of flesh. Only these people weren't dancing around it. They were in it. The lives devoured here filled overfed guts who didn't live around here, people like Trey Kennemeyer, wherever he was. Guys who never had—and never would—given the 'ware a try, would never make something of themselves.

The closer I got to home, the more the vague Murphy's noise on the wind resolved into Dell's lamentations, Sylvia's laugh, Clinton and Lyndon arguing and speechifying, Vincente screeching a falsetto punch line. Behind all that, *Big* played for the umpteenth time. They all became soundtrack for the workers dancing in the lights, saying nothing, understanding nothing, remembering nothing, making something of themselves. The system worked, the politicians were always saying. Worked like a fucking charm.

Maybe I'd listened to too many of Kennemeyer's speeches, the poor old bastard, but I couldn't look at the workers anymore without a slow rage rising up inside me. How did things get to be like this? How were we ever going to find our way back?

Laughter erupted from another Vincente punch line, and I tore my eyes away from the workers and looked toward home.

I stopped.

There, under the streetlight halfway down my block, four members of the road crew stood shoulder to shoulder in the middle of the street, facing me. Their dead eyes, all eight of them, were trained on me.

I took a step back, and they started walking briskly and purposefully up the middle of the street toward me.

I looked left at the work site, where all the workers were rising from putting down their hoses, their picks, their lasers, to face me, like a cast rising from their final bow. Then they started walking, climbing over fences, knocking obstacles out of their way with an indifferent sweep of their hands, all headed my way.

I turned on my heel and ran back the way I came, hollering my head off. It took them a couple of beats to react, then they all started jogging at once, at the most efficient pace for moving the human resource from one site to another quickly without undue wear and with maximum endurance. They could keep it up for miles, hours. Me, I was doing the hundred-yard dash. There wouldn't be much left after that. I was an adrenaline rocket. No one seemed to hear my hollering but the dogs, who quickly drowned me out. I saved my breath. When that gave out, I was done for.

The first workers I'd passed now emerged from between the houses ahead of me, and I veered left. I scooped up an abandoned baby doll from the front yard and heaved it in a high arc, stripped off my jacket, and ran between two strategically chosen houses. Wrapping the jacket around my fist, I vaulted the fence just as baby doll bought the farm on the other side of the yard, and—relying on sheer surprise, sheer audacity that anyone would be suicidal enough to cut through *this* yard, of all yards—made it to the back fence before the resident dogs got it together and managed to kill me. I gave up the jacket to a pair of flying jaws and vaulted into the alley on a dead run, as the pack slammed into the chain link with furiously gnashing teeth, and the whole fence swayed. I fell, rolled, and kept on running. There were

THE BRIGHT SPOT

five of them—a pit bull bitch and her three sons, plus a rottweiler male as big as a pony. Buck, whose faith in fences was unshakeable, liked to linger behind their yard to work them into a killing frenzy, but that was nothing compared to the fury I heard behind me as they lit into the waves of workers trespassing through their territory.

None of the workers appeared in the alley in front of me to cut me off. I'd funneled them all into a game of follow the leader. Their tactical skills were clearly limited. They had no strategy but relentless pursuit of the victim. Maybe, I thought, I can get out of this alive.

I looked over my shoulder, and there were about a dozen of them back there, all jogging steadily. One of the guys out front had a pit bull hanging off his right arm. He didn't let it bother him any. Who needed a strategy? The boom of shotgun fire filled the night, as Mr. Lester, the owner of the dogs, opened fire on the stragglers. A dark shape fell from the fence into the alley.

A dozen pairs of eyes were still trained on me. No one had looked back but me. I tried, someway, somehow, to find more speed in my limbs.

I was almost to the road. Cars shot by in either direction. Somebody would see this bizarre scene, I was hoping, call the police, call the news, call on somebody besides God. My own prayers had Him covered for half an eternity already, and I wasn't even a believer.

By the time I stood tottering on the curb, my lead was less than twenty yards. Cars swept by in an instant. I did a wild, gyrating, arm-waving dance of my own. Before anyone saw me—if anyone was even looking out at the blur—they were gone. I could hear the workers behind me as steady as a marching band.

Down the road, lumbering northbound, the driverless bus approached, all lit up and nearly empty and across eight lanes of high-speed traffic. It was a chance. I focused on the first lane and waited for as close to a break as I was going to get.

I plunged into the road, dashing for the first lane markers, remembering the drill—keep your eyes on that fucking mark, land *on* it, become the thinnest, straightest, most vertical person imaginable, ready to face down the next lane of lethal machines, like charging bulls with jet packs. They sucked the air out of my lungs and tried to tear the clothes from my body, but each miss was a victory deeply cherished. The Bright Spot had done this before, in his misspent youth.

I made two lanes and was waiting for a break across the third, gathering my strength and nerve—I only had to do the impossible six more times—when the workers followed me into the traffic. Their skills didn't cover jaywalking on high-speed roads. They had no strategy, no luck, no moves. I looked back in time to see a heavyset man hit head-on. His upper torso soared into the air, bounced off the roof of another vehicle, and slid to the road in a heap. At least a couple of other workers were down, but I hadn't seen how. One was crawling toward me on his elbows. The others jogged around the fallen.

With the first impact, a siren began to wail, and the southbound lanes came to a complete stop. I'd lost my strategic advantage. I kept running between the cars, against the stopped traffic, staying low. The surviving workers kept coming, eight or nine of them. They were gaining on me, with the same steady, upright jog-along. Their skill set likely didn't include cops either, and neglected to instruct them to scuttle low, like a rat.

"Remain in your vehicles," a voice from above instructed. "Remain in your vehicles."

The workers were right on top of me. I watched for a break and plunged into the still-moving northbound lanes. One of the workers, an unnaturally tall, bald woman, obviously an altered veteran, stepped into the traffic after me and was torn apart, shattered. The northbound traffic stopped before the last of her hit the ground. I crouched down and slunk between the cars. I didn't even think about asking one of these nice machine-encased people to open up and help a fellow out. They didn't know me from Adam, never had, never would. *How do you do? Glad to meet you. I'm the Bright Spot, don't mind me, just slinking through.*

Riot cops started dropping out of the sky and shot the remaining workers dead in a matter of seconds. I crawled into the bus and huddled between the seats. A woman across the aisle slipped off her coat and threw it at me. "Here they come," she said.

I covered myself and went limp, just as the cops did their dash through. They expected anyone they were looking for to be running like hell or squealing like a cornered rat. Cops are looking to sniff out your guilt and your fear—any guilt and fear will do. It doesn't even have to have anything to do with them or the law. The only way to escape is not to have either one—or at least to act like you don't. They let my shameless, senseless, drooling wino under the coat sleep, and the bus started moving in no time. My rescuer snatched back her coat and got off at the next stop. I rode out the route. It was about an hour by the time I made it back around to my stop, where not a trace of what had happened remained, and traffic flowed as usual.

THE BRIDEGROOM'S RETURN

13

> *"We may not part until you have promised to comply with my requisition. I am alone and miserable; man will not associate with me; but one as deformed and horrible as myself would not deny herself to me. My companion must be of the same species and have the same defects. This being you must create."*
>
> —MARY SHELLEY, *Frankenstein*

I crept in through the back door in case anyone was watching the house, careful not to rouse Buck, easing the door silently closed behind me. I was hoping Lu would be asleep, hoping to clean up before she had a look at me, but every light in the house was on.

My right pant leg had torn from knee to cuff when I vaulted the second fence. There was a matching tear in my flesh, wrapped tight in what remained of the blood-soaked pant leg. The bleeding had mostly stopped, but I was still discovering lesser cuts and bruises. My shirt was filthy, soaked with sweat, torn in several places. The sole of my left shoe had developed a terminal flop.

I'd pissed myself too. I'm not sure when that happened. Early on, certainly. It was cold by the time I noticed it on the bus ride home. The stench of urine must've added just that extra touch of authenticity to my wino—might've saved my life.

The cops would've shot me for sure, just another fleeing suspect. We were all fleeing suspects. Can't have good people thinking the workers laying their roads or wiping their butts for them might get it in their heads to kill them. Might seriously hurt the economy.

But if the cops had known the truth, that I was no innocent bystander, but the *cause* of all this trouble, things would've gone worse. Any fool can get himself shot. They would've arrested me. Questioned me. I was obviously a high-level operative. They'd want some answers. Since I didn't have any except that twenty or thirty strangers had just died for no reason because someone, somewhere wanted me dead, they'd have to script a confession for me, and in the end, I'd believe it. I could make one now: *I* killed all those people—me, the Bright Spot.

I steadied myself on the kitchen counter, fighting another wave of nausea, remembering the tall woman's shattered body raining out of the sky. The man heaving his way along the pavement on his elbows, his eyes inalterably fixed on *me*...

I needed a drink. I focused.

There was an empty champagne bottle on the counter. Another bottle on the table, about three-quarters empty. The bong sat beside it. Some clippings from Kennemeyer's shoe box were laid out in front of the photo of old Dumfries, propped up against a bottle of

THE BRIGHT SPOT

Jamaican rum, also empty. Blender mess filled the sink. Something pink and clinging that really should soak. The air smelled like strawberries, pot, patchouli, and alcohol.

And me. Even I could smell me.

The bridegroom returns—not exactly the way I'd expected the scene to play. I'd assumed I was too late for any celebration, but one had started without me, and still seemed to be going on. Voices, music, and laughter were coming from the front room. Lu and... No, couldn't be.

Another cop copter roared overhead, and I ducked instinctively. The alley briefly flooded with light. They were everywhere. I should be grateful. It wasn't the cops trying to kill me, not these cops anyway. As long as they were around, I was guessing, whoever it was would lay low. Mr. Lester probably still had the reporters queued up in his front lawn, lit up like a work site.

I remembered the boom of his shotgun, not a single face turning back to see their comrade fall dead, the back of his head blown off. *No comrades here, Boss, just us workers.*

I must've made a sound, stumbled, sobbed perhaps, setting off the dog alarm. Buck burst into the kitchen, completely off his rocker, slipping and sliding and colliding with my bloody leg, snorting and snuffling and yelping. I scooped him up into my arms and discovered several new pains. He gleefully licked my salty neck and face.

Then I saw what had him all excited. I was speechless.

There, in the doorway to the front room, stood Dee

and Lu, side by side, very happy and a bit glassy-eyed, on the decaying side of an exceedingly high orbit. Sheryl Crow singing "If It Makes You Happy"—a Lu favorite from Bea's old tunes—was cranked behind them.

"*Nick*, guess what?" Lu said. "Dee and I've figured out where James Dumfries is in that picture!"

Dee and I? Picture? Is? "That . . . That's swell."

"Congratulations," Dee slurred, hoisting her champagne mug. "Lu tole me you guys just got engaged." The soft *g* was almost too much for her. She was wearing my clothes, an old sweater and khakis. My mukluks. This was beginning to feel a little too David Lynch for me. Put Buck in a tux, and he could play the dwarf. He kept lapping the rich salt vein of my throat, grunting softly.

"Buck," Lu said, "give it a rest." Then she focused on me clearly for the first time. "Oh my God, Nick, what happened to you?" She grabbed Buck out of my arms, thrust him into Dee's, took me into hers, and held me tight. Everyone seemed happy with that arrangement—I certainly was—but it didn't last long. Lu caught sight of the bloody leg, or maybe she smelled the piss and vomit, and the next thing I knew, the two women dragged me into the bathroom, stripped me, scrubbed me, and tortured me until I told them everything I knew, lying in the tub, drinking the rest of the champagne from the bottle.

Lu sat on the side of the tub with my wounded leg in her lap and her feet in the tub. She was quite the seamstress, a skill her mother had taught her—anything to avoid a trip to the emergency room. People died waiting down there. Why wait? Lu's mom, I was told, did gunshot wounds as well, a store of knowledge I hoped to leave untapped. Since there weren't any bullets to bite, Lu gave me a joint to work on while she picked tiny shards of glass and gravel out of my wound with tweezers.

Dee sat on the toilet seat, leaning back against the tank, her right arm draped over the sink. Her legs, propped up on the radiator, took up the rest of the room like a khaki pretzel. It struck me we were posed about the same, only she was roughly two feet higher than me and was wearing my clothes. She did what she could to help—holding the first-aid kit open in her lap without sliding to the floor. The effort of getting me in here and into the tub had nudged her into an alternate reality. Her eyes gazed on other worlds. She'd been into Lu's pills, I was guessing. Lu was a generous hostess.

If Lu herself had indulged, it certainly didn't show. She was like that. Sober and competent in a crisis, by all accounts her mother's daughter. "I'm glad you leveled with Murphy," she said. "He must've shit. He had you figured completely different."

"Yeah, me too. He said I reminded him of your mother. Ouch, watch it, will you?"

"Bea? He said that?" She laughed. "I can see it. She used to give Murph shit all the time." She bit the tip of her tongue as she tweezed a sliver of metal. I yelped again. "'Don't be such a baby'—that's what Bea would say if she was doing this. 'Don't be such a baby.' To me anyway. You'd probably be her sweet darlin'."

She shone a flashlight on my wound, looking for anything else that wasn't me. She did this several times, and I quickly ran out of flashlight jokes, tweezers jokes, any kind of jokes. It's amazing what an open wound will pick up when you roll around in an alley. She tweezed and searched, while I tried to follow Bea's advice.

When the tweezing was done, Lu held up a bottle of antiseptic and spoke prophetically: "This will sting like ungodly hell at first."

In the long first moments of hell, my leg bathed in liquid fire, I gazed up tearfully at Dee to distract myself from my leg, which I never wanted anything to do with ever again. She was rounding up the pixies on the ceiling for a dance around the Maypole, and I finally thought to ask the obvious, though I didn't get around to it until we were past the stinging and into sticking and hurting territory.

"Dee, I've got to ask—what are you doing here?" I didn't mean it to sound rude, but needle and thread were passing through my flesh at the time.

She started like she'd just fallen out of bed, rolled her head toward the sound of my voice, and eventually her gaze fell on me. Her pupils were twin black holes; her irises, green, mere crescents. It took her a moment to sort out whether I was real or chemical and how she should react.

"Yeah," she laughed. "It's *weird*, isn't it?" She rubbed her eyes and sat up a few degrees. She turned on the faucet at her elbow and unceremoniously splashed her face with cold water, rubbing vigorously. Then slapped herself a couple of times for good measure. I had a feeling she'd done this before. She gave her head one final shake, and there she was, almost all there. She started telling her story in fits and starts.

"The cop? The black one? Not the weasely one. He said nobody on 'ware for a while. But I didn't *think*. I never think." She roughly wiped her face dry with the sleeves of my sweater. The eye treatment was permanent. Her makeup never smeared, never went away. Her complexion never chafed, chapped, cracked, or reddened, no matter how many miles she ran, tears she cried, bottles she killed. So even now, her life falling apart and barely conscious, she still looked marvelous—one of the perks of marrying a rich man willing to invest in his assets. Must make the undertaker's job a breeze. I wondered how old she was, but it would be rude to ask.

Her gaze fell on the thread Lu was pulling taut, and froze there. She plucked the joint from my hand, took a hit, and handed it back. She grimaced, but watched, as the needle slid into me again, exhaled as the thread emerged from my flesh. "After the cops just all of a sudden cleared out, I called the guys to fix the security—all scared somebody was going to get me—then just let them walk right in like an idiot. They had, the what—the dispatcher guy—who wasn't on 'ware, but they killed him first. He was lying by the front door with his neck broke when I came running downstairs. They snuck up on me after I'd been running an hour. Maybe they thought I'd be tired or something. God knows. I saw them in my mirror and kicked a couple of them pretty good. High kicks." Her right leg kicked impressively at the ceiling, nearly taking out the light fixture. She lowered it slowly. "Then I ran downstairs, jumped in the car, and got my ass *out* of there. The car went to its last destination, and the nice guys on the corner brought me here. This nice old man gave me a rum and Coke. Lu was totally sweet—let me take a shower and everything. I never been so scared in my whole life."

"Let me make sure I get this straight," I said. "You showed up at Murphy's naked?"

She shrugged. "I was running. I always run naked. It's a discipline."

"A discipline?"

"A practice. A thing you do. I read about it in a magazine once, got the virtuals, did the course. There are special exercises and stuff. If you don't do it right, it hurts like hell. It improves my stamina—my respiration. I could only find a little towel in the car. Usually I got stuff in there, but I'd just cleaned up. I wanted to make sure there wasn't anything I didn't want the cops to find. I hope you don't mind me borrowing your clothes. I couldn't fit into Lu's."

"It's fine, really. And what—you asked for me, Nicholas Bainbridge?"

"Yeah, was that okay?"

"Okay?" Lu said dryly. "He's loving what this will do for his standing among the males in the neighborhood."

"The thought had crossed my mind. And who brought you down here?"

Lu answered for her. "Vincente and Dell's boy."

Too perfect. "What time was that, Dee?"

"What was that, Lu, nine o'clock?" Telling her story had sobered her a bit, or maybe it was watching Lu work. She couldn't take her eyes off the wound, the needle, the thread.

"Around then," Lu agreed, biting off the thread with her teeth.

"Murphy dropped me off around nine-thirty," I said. "So probably whoever set the security workers onto Dee came here and set the street workers onto me.

THE BRIGHT SPOT

Weren't you guys worried about me when I didn't show up?"

"You were with Murph," Lu said. "I figured you were okay. You didn't say when you'd be home."

"You didn't hear shotgun fire? Dogs going crazy?"

"Sure, we heard—and didn't go rushing out the door. I called down to Mr. Lester, who said somebody'd been messing with his dogs, and the dogs tore them up pretty good. He shot one going over the fence, he said. Killed him. I sure didn't want a look at anything like that. And I certainly didn't connect it with you—you'd be the last person to go messing with somebody's dogs. Right after, there were cops shooting up on the road, and they did a flyover, telling people to stay inside. They've been flying around ever since. The news is saying they flushed a sleeper cell. There's talk Mr. Lester might be this week's Hero of the Homeland."

"Jesus. Sleeper cell. *I* did all that," I said, tapping my chest. "Me. I killed all those people—set dogs on them, ran them into traffic, shot them. I'm the fucking Hero of the Homeland!" My voice rang from the tile. I realized I'd been shouting. There wasn't enough champagne in the bottle.

Lu's voice was measured and reasonable. "Nick, they were trying to kill you."

"No, *they* weren't. Somebody was using them to kill me. They were just along for the ride. A handy blunt instrument. It was just their tough luck to get too close to me."

"Why would anyone want to kill you?"

"How the fuck should I know? I just know I have to stay clear of anyone on 'ware."

"How are we going to do that?"

"I have a car," Dee said. "We could go somewhere—in the country or something."

"We have jobs," I reminded her.

To be honest, that's all I really wanted to do—go back to work and forget I'd ever heard of James Dumfries and Galatea Ritsa. But now all these people had died. I was supposed to want to do something, to save the day, to be the Hero of the Homeland, to atone. Not my usual role. I just wanted to run and hide. Preferably someplace imaginary. I always felt more at home with make-believe. That's why I was in the business.

Lu, who was wrapping my leg in gauze, suddenly broke into a smile. "*We have jobs.* That's it," she said. "Sometimes I'm so brilliant I can't stand myself. We not only take our jobs with us, our jobs pay the way. We talk Wally and Gary into going on location."

"How are you going to do that?"

"Nothing could be easier: Dee and I talk to Wally and sell him on a new story line."

I tried to imagine such a thing. He wouldn't stand a chance. "Dee?"

"We were going to talk to him anyway. He asked me if I knew anybody for the role of Galatea Ritsa. He thinks Brenda's too short. Dee would be perfect. She's a regular Amazon. Wally's got tall on the brain for this part. What do you think?"

I started to point out Dee couldn't act a lick, but didn't want to go into how I knew that. It wasn't a deal breaker anyway. "What about Gary? He hates to spend a nickel."

"He'll go for it. An old-fashioned location shoot in a

small town, just the thing that *BBG* needs to get a little notice and break into the big time. We're *poised*, haven't you heard? That's what Gary's been saying for weeks—*poised*. We rah-rah enough, he'll go for it. Besides, he does whatever Wally wants."

"But what kind of location do we need for a cop story? We've got mean streets enough around here."

"He only switched to cops because he talked to Murph. We get him to change it back to war—the *Revolutionary* War—and we all go to Colonial Williamsburg."

"*Virginia?* You're fucking kidding me. You've been working with Wally too long. Why in the *hell* would we want to go down there?"

"You don't sound very patriotic. No 'ware, for one thing, but that's not why. Why is because that's where James Dumfries is." The two women traded a smug look. I'd almost forgotten their claims of tracking him down. In the process, they seemed to have really talked, really bonded. I wasn't so sure how I felt about that.

"And how do you know this?" I asked, the question they'd been waiting for.

"I'll get it," Dee said, unfolding herself and loping to the kitchen, surprisingly steady on her feet. Must've been all that discipline. She returned with the photo, one of the clippings, and a magnifying glass. The clipping concerned the gazillionth performance of some patriotism-on-a-platter virtual they put on at Colonial Williamsburg rain or shine every day the planet turns. Before that, according to the article, there was a cheesy movie that'd finally been put out of its misery after its ten-gazillionth showing. Cheese endures. It might stink up the place, but it endures. There was a cast reunion shot for the virtual in a theater lobby. A fortyish Kennemeyer was there. Dumfries wasn't.

"I don't get it," I said.

"Look at the photos on the wall with the magnifying glass," Lu directed. "They show up in several of the clippings. This one's the clearest. Dee noticed it."

They were stills from the interminably running virtual. And there it was, the photo Salvador had given us—old man Dumfries in his rocker. Only it wasn't really the old man—couldn't be, Lu pointed out—but the young man made up to look old and frail. He played Grandpa Somebody-or-Other, the dying patriarch in a new land on the eve of war, never getting to cross over into the promised land of freedom, or some such drivel, and when Salvador wanted to give us broken-down wretch, he pulled this out of his files. Dumfries, apparently, was one of those guys like Walter Brennan who played old guys when they were young. We all play old when we're old if we've got any sense. The woman's mysterious headgear was exactly what it looked like, an out-of-focus rag hat, standard colonial attire.

"Kennemeyer must be saying Dumfries would go there, to where this theater is. Maybe he still owns a place in town or something. Dee and I checked. Dumfries and his wife lived in Williamsburg during the war. They were married there. And there won't be anyone on 'ware inside the colonial section—it's part of their authentic shtick. They don't even allow cars."

"Just what we need—another authentic phony past. But slow down, will you? Why is it we want to find Dumfries instead of running the other way?"

THE BRIGHT SPOT

"So he can tell us who's trying to kill us and why. This doesn't seem like the kind of thing you can run and hide from."

"What if he's already dead?"

"Then we won't find him, and we'll still be out of here."

"What if he's the one trying to kill us?" I wasn't sure why he was my leading suspect. I guess because he invented 'ware. Whenever Frankenstein's monster walked again, Victor always topped the list of suspects, unless he was already dead.

Lu didn't seem to think it mattered one way or the other. "If he's trying to kill us, then we'll find him and stop him. Whoever it is knows where to find us here. I say we send word to Murph and head south. We can spend the night at ReCreation in Dee's car, talk to Wally when he comes in. By this time tomorrow we can be in the eighteenth century without a 'ware worker in sight. Like Bea used to say, 'It's like chess—you can make a move, or you lose, but you can't get off the board.' What do you say?"

What could I say? When she started quoting her mother, she was unstoppable. And besides, this way I got to run away and still play the hero. That was more my kind of role. One of the guys still standing when the curtain drops.

"Why not? I'm sure you and Dee can talk Wally into just about anything. You through with my leg?"

"For now."

"Thanks, Lu."

She gave me a kiss. "You're welcome, sweet darlin'."

WHERE'S THE ART? 14

That the future may learn from the past.

—JOHN D. ROCKEFELLER JR.'S MOTTO FOR COLONIAL
 WILLIAMSBURG

I DRESSED WHILE LU HEATED UP SOME BEANS.
Every few minutes, I checked out the front window. The big lights still burned, all their equipment was lying where they'd set it down, but there wasn't anyone working under the lights, not yet. It would take time to round up a new crew, roust them out of bed, and haul them over here. The cops were still flying around shining their lights up and down the alleys. The crowd at Murphy's liked to get flashlights and shine them at the cops, just to fuck with them. Whenever the copter noise waned, you could hear there was quite a party going on four doors down.

I tried calling Murphy, but he didn't answer, and a message seemed risky. I sent him the photos and an account of the attacks on me and Dee to the address he gave me, which turned out to be a hobbyists' site for vin-

THE BRIGHT SPOT

tage remote-control toy boats. I also threw in the clipping, along with a blowup of the relevant portion of the photo. He was a trained detective. He could figure it out. I signed it Gilligan.

The easiest way to send him the diner scene was for me and Lu to play it at the kitchen table with Dee sitting cross-legged on the counter as audience and technician. We used the cam on the terminal, so the quality wouldn't be that great, but it would be better than those old videotapes. When we finished our lines, Dee was snuffling and dabbing at her eyes.

Lu returned from her tearful exit, and I took her arm in character, then signaled cut. No sense walking out the door. There wasn't a whole lot of nothing out there. Our recording would be full of cop noise as it was. If any of us on the ground made that much racket, they'd throw us all in jail.

Dee turned off the cam and burst into applause. "You guys are really, really terrific."

"Thanks," we said, and took a little bow, or two, as Dee continued to gush. We couldn't help ourselves. We had absolutely nailed the scene, even better than the first time. Something about the evening we'd spent had perfectly prepared us to play Jim and Galatea. She'd really sobbed. My lips were still wet with her tears, and I felt blessed. I sent the scene to Murphy and burned a copy.

But something about holding it in my hand in a little disk, all final and complete, made me question the whole scene again. Something about it just didn't ring true.

So I asked Dee to play critic—and the worst sort at that—a literary critic: "If Lu and I *weren't* so good," I suggested, "if you just had the script, the lines, is there anything that doesn't seem right, that doesn't seem like it belongs?"

She didn't hesitate. "When he starts naming all those guys? That was really cold. It seemed... too mean. It gave me the creeps. He didn't seem like the type for that."

Lu nodded her agreement. "Yeah. That's always struck me as a little out there."

"Me too," I said. "His wife never heard of any of them—not a one. How many guys could the two of them know his wife wouldn't know too? Or at least heard mentioned. And does it strike anyone as odd that he's married, and they're supposedly discussing *her* lovers?"

"Guys'll do that," Dee said.

Lu nodded her agreement again.

"Okay, so they will. But I still think this whole thing's about something else—Dumfries told me as much—and most of it's smoke, like you said, Lu—except the names. He's got to get the names said."

"You think it's a code?"

"It has to be. They must've known they were being watched, recorded. The scene was just cover. So what do you think?"

"It might be a code, but a code for what?"

"Judging by what's been going on, maybe a code to mess with 'ware workers. Maybe that's what Salvador figured he would have to sell."

"But Salvador had the recordings. If the conversation *is* a code, he's already got it. What did he need to go through all this for?"

THE BRIGHT SPOT

"He might need Dumfries to break the code, or use it, or say it, or whatever. Doesn't matter."

"Certainly not for Salvador, since he ended up dead. So you think Dumfries killed him?"

"Maybe. Especially if he found out Salvador was trying to screw him. But like Dee just said, he didn't seem like the type."

"You never know with some guys," Dee said.

I don't know why I felt like defending the old guy—sticking up for my character's character, I guess—but I pointed out we didn't need to pin anything on a broken-down old man just yet. He was the leading suspect, but there must be plenty of bad guys willing to kill Salvador to get their hands on something like that. "Like Salvador said, he was taking all the risks."

"Salvador was an asshole," Lu said.

Dee nodded her agreement, and she didn't even know the guy.

On that note, we started packing. Lu called into the bedroom, where I was stuffing dirty clothes into a heavy-duty plastic bag, the good luggage. "I almost forgot. Dell's boy left you something when they brought Dee over. It's on the bed."

"His name's Clinton," I called back. How old did you have to be around here to get your own name? There was a big envelope on the bed with *Nick* written on it. I could see how it'd been forgotten in the excitement. It looked like homework—the smart kid turns in another A+ assignment. Big deal. I had a look.

He'd found out everything I'd found out about

Dumfries and Kennemeyer at William and Mary—with all the details filled in—dorm room numbers, cast lists of productions they were in together, clubs they belonged to, but nothing after the war. The kid certainly knew how to sift the bones of the Web.

And then he outdid himself. Attached was a page of explanatory text and some photos, copies of a death certificate and a military ID. Clinton had a hunch about the way Galatea sat at that diner table and, given the dates, thought to check military sites, particularly war casualties. Not by name, but by face, using the photos to look for a match. At first, he'd demanded high confidence and found nothing. When he lowered his standards, he got an eighty percent match with a Marine in special ops named Lenore Chapell, missing in action during the siege of Cairo. Presumed dead, likely loaded with heavy-duty covert operations 'ware, and all the dates fit. She disappeared a year before Galatea turned up dead. Could be just another coincidence, a near miss, except for one thing.

I was staring at Lenore Chapell's photo when Lu appeared in the bedroom door. "Nick, what is it?"

I compared Lu to the forty-year-old photo. I wasn't search software, but I knew Lu's face with the highest confidence. Her match to Lenore was in the high nineties at least. Genes will tell. Lu looked more like Lenore Chapell than Galatea Ritsa did. Lenore might've had an injury that altered her appearance a little—she *was* a soldier—or cosmetic surgery when she took the name of Galatea. Lenore and Galatea were the same person with slightly different faces. Lenore and Lu were born forty years apart and looked like identical twins.

THE BRIGHT SPOT

"Lu, how come you never talk about your father?"

"Don't we need to hurry?"

"This is important."

"Is this still part of our truth telling?"

"Absolutely."

"Okay. I don't have one. When I kept nagging Bea about my father, she finally told me the truth. I'm not her child. She broke her arm and couldn't work. She was desperate for money. She carried me as a surrogate mother. The couple who hired her gave her this house and some money, set her up with a doctor, then disappeared during her last trimester. She never could find them, though they'd made arrangements for all the medical bills to be paid, and she still had the house. She assumed they must've died in a plane crash or something. She raised me as her daughter."

"I think you need to take a look at this." I handed her the envelope Dell's boy had dropped off, and she sat down beside me on the bed.

Lu read everything twice, looked at the photo of Lenore Chapell for a long while—she would look at it often in the weeks to come—and slid it back into the envelope and closed the little brass clasps. One of them was already about to break off. I took her hand, and we sat there on the bed, waiting for a cue, too stunned to speak.

Just me looking exactly like the young James Dumfries might be a coincidence. Both of us looking exactly like Jim and Lenore could only mean one thing, as far as I could see. At least I didn't have to ask myself anymore why the Bright Spot grew up in a home for boys, wondering who his parents were and why they didn't want him. Lu and I didn't have any parents, not really.

We were clones. Copycats. Born actors. I had no doubt it wasn't just fate that had thrown us together. It looked like we were made for each other. Now appearing in a life near you. *Jim and Galatea II*. We were a fucking sequel.

We were the secret weapon people would kill for, and we didn't even know how we worked. Whatever Jim and Galatea were up to then, I was guessing, we were supposed to be up to now. They should've known better. Sequels always have plot problems. I looked up over my head. There was silence. The cops had flown away. It was time to get the hell out of here.

With nothing to pack, Dee had taken my place at the front window, working on her third cup of coffee. She called back to us. "Hey, guys, there's workers showing up. Maybe we should go."

Lu looked around the room. "I was born here," she said. "Bea died here. Time to move on, wouldn't you say?"

We hurried down the alley to Dee's car and loaded up, with plenty of help from the crowd at Murphy's. The place was packed with folks, buzzing with what had happened right here in our neighborhood. The party had spilled into the alley, and we were caught up in the swirl of it even as we were throwing things into the car. I took the offered Icehouse.

Nobody bought the sleeper cell story. No conscious human being, terrorist or not, would line up to climb into a backyard with Mr. Lester's dogs to get their asses chewed off. They had to be running 'ware. Lyndon, one of the first on the scene, claimed to recognize the one

THE BRIGHT SPOT

Mr. Lester shot from the crew the other night. Nobody knew any of them personally. They'd been subcontracted from a paver out of Michigan. The guy who was shot was from Ypsilanti. But if it could happen to those guys, it could happen to them, far away from home and dead, with the last thing they remembered, just going to work, doing the 'ware.

There was lots of talk of not going to work in the morning. Those who did would be pretty hungover, not that they'd notice until after their shifts, when they came here to Murphy's to drink a few beers and talk about not going in to work in the morning. But where else were they going to go?

I took Clinton aside and gave him a copy of everything I'd sent Murphy.

"Was the stuff I dropped off helpful?" he asked.

I wasn't sure how to answer that one. If ignorance was bliss, this kid was no help at all. "Yeah. It was great. I'd especially like to know *anything* at all you can find out about Lenore Chapell. We're not exactly sure where we're going to be. I'll call you." I got his phone number.

"I'm pretty sure it's bugged," he said.

"I think you can count on it. Just don't use my real name."

We made some quick goodbyes all around. Nobody wanted to admit we might not see each other again. Nobody asked where we were going. They knew we were on the run. We asked Sylvia to keep an eye on the place and piled into Dee's car. Everybody called out, "Good luck." When the cops came around, they'd all sing the same tune for us. *L'il Lu who? Nicholas Bainbridge? Never heard of the fucker.* I knew just how they felt—or at least how they would pretend to feel. I had a growing list of questions for whenever I met my maker, an event, in my case, not necessarily supernatural.

We spent the night in Dee's car, parked around the corner from ReCreation with the security set on its most lethal, paranoid settings. Woe to the bird who flew too close, the cat hoping to nap on the warm hood. We were comfy, however. The inside was configurable to a room about the size of our bedroom, but plusher, with all the amenities. I listened to the two women snoring in the dark, sleeping it off, and entertained myself with the 360-degree night-vision display and weapons options menu. I was a man. I didn't need any fucking sleep. I had firepower. Hell. I was too scared to sleep.

I was surprised to find out there was a raccoon living in the neighborhood, but he didn't seem to be packing any heat. If he knew how close he came to being blown away, he might start, or swear off city trashcans forever.

Wally pulled into the ReCreation lot at six in the morning, and I shook Lu and Dee awake. "It's showtime," I said.

Wally was delighted to see us, especially Dee. "I write in the mornings," he told her, as if he were giving her a fascinating glimpse into the writer's life. Dee and Lu both were enthralled with the writing process and begged him for more. They laid it on so thick, I thought surely he'd see through it, but Wally never saw through bullshit. He just dove right in. It took them maybe fifteen minutes for him to have the great idea of shooting on location in Williamsburg with Dee in the role of Galatea Ritsa! That Wally was *so* clever!

Buck, meanwhile, had been lapping the loft with a

THE BRIGHT SPOT

fit of the zooms, until I finally tackled him and demonstrated the lapdog gene.

"Let me hold him," Wally pleaded, and made a big fuss over what a wonderful dog he was. In no time Wally had dreamed up a role for Buck as well—Patriot, a clever Revolutionary War spy dog, who, to help him in his work, had acquired the ability to speak English. "I'll do his voice!" he announced gleefully. I feared for poor Buck having to sit still for some long-winded Wallyisms, but as long as he was in a lap it shouldn't be a problem.

We offered to go to Williamsburg immediately and get the ball rolling, and Wally set about booking us rooms on his terminal, with ReCreation picking up the tab.

Stan was the next to show up, and he and Dee hit it off immediately. They seemed to enjoy being tall together, and they knew all their bones, muscles, tendons, and ligaments by name, which gave them plenty to talk about. To my surprise, the usually diffident Stan volunteered to join us.

"I could help you find your way around," he said. "I used to wrestle in Hampton Roads. I know the area pretty well. Around the college there." He ducked his head with a slight touch of embarrassment. I gathered the wrestler had dated college girls. If Mom and Dad only knew. Dee thought Stan joining us was a terrific idea.

So it was agreed, the five of us (counting Buck) were riding down to Virginia in Dee's car to make the arrangements for *Billy and the Big Guy* to shoot the eighteenth century on location. By the time Gary showed up, we were already booked in at the Liberty Lodge—

the cheapest place Wally could find close to the colonial section—and packed to go. Once Gary saw Dee and Stan together, he was all for it. He poked Wally in the ribs and pointed at the two of them. "Chemistry," he said, slapping the back of his right hand against his open left palm. "Chemistry."

Our feedback had shown a growing desire to tempt the Big Guy. Already, in response to ever-increasing numbers for "Would like to see more of BG?" Stan routinely had his shirt torn from him in the early stages of the mayhem, and in a recent episode, most of his pants as well. He took more showers. He worked out. The plot twiddled its thumbs during these peep shows, however, and now the adolescent girls who constituted most of this feedback weren't content just to ogle and twiddle. They wanted some action. They complained there was no chemistry between BG and the various villainesses Brenda and her bad-wig collection played, and Gary often spoke of the need for *chemistry*—with no biology, of course. Nobody screws was still the rule. Unsatisfied lust prompted ratings to swell, the theory went; satisfaction soon led to detumescence. It was chemistry, Gary maintained, that would get us past this *poised* patch into *pounce* or whatever it was that came next.

Wally was certain he'd found the catalyst for this chemistry in Galatea Ritsa—Dee's character, that is. She was no ordinary evildoer bent on corrupting Young William. Oh no. She was after Big Guy as surely and relentlessly as Delilah went after Samson. And without BG to come to the rescue, Billy would be as helpless as the jerk who played him, standing outside ReCreation, screaming after us as we drove away, while Wally excit-

THE BRIGHT SPOT

edly explained he'd soon be riding to Virginia for a whole new story about Freedom! You could see the excitement in William's eyes, the curses on his lips. Soon, very soon, if not already, he would start talking about his sacrifices. I was definitely in the right car.

We were on the road in time for the dawn's early light. Well, the dawn's late light maybe, but still plenty early. The eastern sky was a red smear. I closed my eyes, but there was carnage still playing there, innocent people torn apart by dogs and cars. How did sleeper cells ever get any sleep?

Dee had to be tall to play opposite Stan—so they could see eye to eye, at least when she was standing on tiptoe and he slumped a little. He'd slump a lot if necessary, pick her up if she asked him. They had no trouble seeing eye to eye lounging in Dee's car, chatting all the way to Virginia. Lu and I were pretty quiet. We had a lot to think about.

Nobody seemed to be following us, but how could we tell? This vehicle had a number; each point on this road, a numerical identity. The road knew exactly where we were. Any cop could ask the road. If someone was looking for us, we'd likely be found. Like Bea said, you can't leave the board. Might as well head for the king in his castle.

When Stan and Dee ran out of muscles, diets, disciplines, and breathing (miles and miles of breathing), they talked wrestling—she was a fan in her youth—and Stan said one reason he quit was because of the 'ware.

"You hurt yourself, and you don't even know it. You

just keep on with the routine. The other guy could be really hurt, and you're still whaling away on him, the crowd booing you. The 'ware ruins it. No spontaneity. Where's the art?"

Dee, whose husband's outfit wrote the wrestling 'ware—they wrote all the sportsware and most everything else one way or another—couldn't agree more.

"I like acting a lot better," he said. "You'll like it too," he assured her. Stan wanted everyone to be happy. I wondered idly if someone could find happiness doing something they had no talent for, but hadn't found the answer before I finally drifted off to sleep. Lu woke me when we got close, and I took in my new home. Or hideout, I guess you might say.

The war had done all right by Williamsburg. The war was practically a Norfolk export, and Williamsburg offered the closest decent round of golf. The money boys and generals who hung around to make sure the whole business ran smoothly lived here in communities so much like The Lakes at Llewellyn you'd think they were the same place, and you'd be right. I wondered if the developers ran a toy-cop academy somewhere to staff the gates, though there didn't seem to be too much riffraff around here to keep out. Maybe the rich people didn't trust each other not to steal their putters.

Golf courses were everywhere. Except for the difficulty of getting past those pesky suburban gates and the military installations lurking down at the end of every lonely road, you could play one continuous round of golf around the town, 450 holes or so, and counting.

THE BRIGHT SPOT

And that didn't count the miniature-golf courses in town. Sod farming was clearly a key support industry. Somewhere they dedicated themselves to growing perfect grass—perfect fairway grass, perfect putting grass, perfect grass to park your cart on. Grass so perfect it could make you weep, the way it had those sprinklers sobbing every morning, pumping the wetlands dry, filling them up with perfect grass food. Maybe that's where they recruited the toy cops—from the young sod farmers, longing for the exciting life of gatekeeper.

In the heart of this affluent husk, the patriotic tourist attraction, Colonial Williamsburg—along with its attendant pancake houses, motels, shoppes, and B & B's—soldiered on. It was originally bankrolled by John D. Rockefeller Jr. during the Depression, when the past—at least the version served here—definitely looked better than the future. It was a "living-history museum," a few square blocks where actors and history buffs were paid a pittance to pretend it was 1775 for the edification and inspiration of ticket holders. Catering as it did to the dwindling middle class, times had been tough for years. Patriotism hadn't sold like it used to. People asked embarrassing questions about slavery and Indians and poor people that were generally depressing to answer, and the place had been in danger of becoming out-of-date.

But then, early in the war, the President made a speech here—with the fife-and-drum boys warming up the crowd—that attempted to equate his war with the reputed virtues of the American Revolution—the famous (or infamous, depending on your politics)— "Exporters of Freedom" speech—and the financially troubled place got a healthy infusion of cash. Suddenly all its languishing grant requests were golden, and they couldn't ask for too much. That's what bankrolled the virtual that Dumfries and Kennemeyer were in, among other enhancements. The Prez outspent John D. Jr. to insure that freedom didn't go bankrupt on his watch and hurt his chances for reelection. After all, he had an export business to run. Bang, bang. You're free.

The town had long been a crossroads, where the rich planters came to wrangle over land, slaves, and tobacco. No fewer than a half-dozen roads converged on the place and pumped it with cars. I wouldn't be doing my jaywalking trick around here. If there was a break in the traffic larger than a few centimeters, I'm sure somebody somewhere lost his job over it.

Colonial Williamsburg itself was a carless, 'wareless oasis smack-dab in the middle, and that's where we were staying, or as close as we could get, at the Liberty Lodge, a place that claimed to be "Family Owned and Operated Since 1963." Unless the family had always been Egyptian refugees, they weren't talking the *same* family, but they didn't have anybody on 'ware, and they allowed pets. The woman who checked us in took one look at Buck and said, "Chow-Peke mix. Good dog. Very smart." And pleasant too, I told her. I liked the place just fine.

Lu and I formally blew off our halfhearted attempt to conceal our relationship from our coworkers and got a room together. We hadn't been alone since we'd become engaged. Maybe the news flash of where our genetic material came from should've "changed everything," as characters in crisis are fond of saying. But when you came right down to it, what would we do differently?

THE BRIGHT SPOT

What difference did it make? Call us shallow, but we didn't want to talk about it. We had one thing on our minds and set ourselves to reassuring each other that nothing had changed that mattered.

Meanwhile, Dee said she'd feel safer if Stan roomed with her, and they took the room next to ours. The four of us played honeymoon for a couple of days, emerging occasionally to try a different stack of pancakes. I never realized the founding fathers were such big fans of white flour and corn syrup.

Nobody tried to kill us. We decided we'd given trouble the slip, or it'd run the other way in the confusion.

When we got around to asking, it was easy securing permission to use Colonial Williamsburg for *Billy and the Big Guy*. They seemed thrilled to have us. I considered the possibility that there might be something to this Southern hospitality thing I'd heard so much about, or maybe they were just desperate.

We started working as soon as the rest of the company showed up, and it was great, getting back to work, back in character. Victor liked the eighteenth century. He felt right at home in the Enlightenment. We established a routine that kept us away from 'ware workers and kept us in a crowd. It wasn't hard. The 'ware workers mostly labored out in the communities and couldn't afford to live anywhere closer than Newport News. You could see them queued up each morning at the gates, ready to clean, to serve, to fix, to labor, and leave when the job was done.

The cooks who flipped our pancakes were mostly illegals or felons who couldn't get a 'ware job, burned-out 'ware workers, and allergics, the unfortunates blessed with an immune system that took exception to 'ware, setting up shop in the heart of downtown. They were cheaper than 'ware workers, and we favored businesses where profit margins were slim to anorexic.

Billy and the Big Guy even got the hoped-for publicity, and the increasing numbers of tourists who hung around while we recorded gave us an audience to play to. Even William was happy, despite the fact that in a few short weeks a talking Buck had totally eclipsed his cuteness numbers. As the man-boy pointed out, he managed to bang a different patriotic tourist's lonely wife practically every night—while the dog, who was fixed, got zip. William was an actor after Vincente's heart.

But if James Dumfries was around, we found little evidence of him, except in the rather dull theater lobby where his picture hung. The virtual it came from, never updated since the war, still creaked along, one of the most dreadful things I've ever seen in my life. But if bad art was the worst that was going to happen around here, I wasn't about to complain.

Maybe we'd actually been clever, given the bad guys the slip. Maybe someone was just trying to scare us off, and it'd worked. Weeks went by and nothing happened. Pretty soon it felt like we were just here to work, and that was fine with me.

But we never could make contact with Murphy, and we couldn't stop looking over our shoulders. The news kept playing along with the frame being built around Ed Kennemeyer's killers, as well as the sleeper cell story. Mr. Lester was indeed named Hero of the Homeland.

Lu and I talked a lot about our mysterious origins,

THE BRIGHT SPOT

but what was there to say? We were orphans who now had each other. We certainly didn't want to change that. We were used to the idea of not having parents. However we were conceived or why, we'd lived our lives. They were ours now. At least that was our stated position: *Free will now! Free will forever!* I'm sure the cosmos was shaking in its boots.

We decided to marry in the spring. We'd heard it was pretty here. Wally said we'd be staying awhile. The going-back-to-the-American-Revolution angle was prompting an incredible spike in our numbers. After World War II, it was our most popular war. If we didn't stop ourselves, we'd soon be famous, just like I'd always wanted. I hoped that would make it more difficult for whoever was trying to kill us.

All the time, deep down, I knew I was kidding myself. This thing wasn't over yet. But, call it denial if you like, I didn't see any reason to rush to the tragic conclusion. This wasn't *Hamlet*. Nobody was going to jump up and applaud when it was over. Nobody was going to take any bows. They'd just haul the bodies to the boneyard and lower them into the earth.

Curtain.

TOO LATE

15

I think we agree, the past is over.

—George Walker Bush

Every day, rain or shine, morning and night, Buck needed his constitutional. The two of us explored the motel grounds in the mornings. But Lu and I made a habit of walking him together in the evenings. It was a great walking town, and it gave us a chance to unwind at the end of the day. This cold night, however, Gary called in a panic about something just as we were out the door, and Lu waved me and Buck on.

I took him to his favorite place this time of night. It had everything—other dogs, lots of people to make a fuss over him, and the smell of roasting flesh in the air. While Lu and I preferred the woods and gardens, Buck fancied a promenade of an evening down Duke of Gloucester Street with his nose held high. In this place forever poised on the eve of the Revolution, the question on every tongue wasn't "What price freedom?" but "How long is the wait for a table?"

THE BRIGHT SPOT

Customers huddled around campfires outside the pricey taverns—part of that colonial fleecing experience—wondering if the food could possibly be worth the money and the wait. What the hell—they were on vacation. We weren't. Judging from these prices, the colonists must've been richer than the history books let on. There were no bread-and-cheese joints around here, no places that served a decent bowl of porridge with a side of jerky. These places were more nouveau olde by way of the Culinary Institute of Taos, with lots of cloned-grown venison and pheasant thrown in to give it the gamey tang of the colonies.

For the price of four entrées and drinks you could set yourself up with a nice hot-dog cart for a season and make a fortune. Not that they'd let you. I asked in city hall. "What if I had the really good sauerkraut, and hot mustard?" The answer was still no, but with a laugh that friendlied up the clerk. She helped me track down James Dumfries' substantial real estate holdings in town, even printed up a list for me.

They were mostly in the commercial shell around the colonial center. It took weeks to check them all out, handing out cards everywhere I went—might as well advertise while I was at it. But Dumfries wasn't living on any of it as far as I could tell, unless he was hiding in the back booth at Mama Don's Pancake Plantation.

I tried following the money. I've never been good at that. It always eludes me. I didn't get far. Mama Don sent me to the smarmy realtor who took care of business for Dumfries, keeping the properties leased and more or less repaired, collecting and depositing rents. It seemed like he would tell me anything in hopes of selling me a timeshare—a deal that sounded to me like a recurring motel reservation, but I'm no better with property than I am with money. Wherever James Dumfries was, Timeshare assured me, the man wasn't hard up for cash, as long as he remembered his PIN numbers.

Timeshare had never actually met Dumfries. If something came up he couldn't handle on his own, he dealt with a lawyer in DC. He gave me the number. The lawyer had had the same gone-travelin' message on his phone for the last month. The last time Timeshare actually talked to the lawyer, he said, was three winters ago when a pipe froze at Putts Mountain after the tenants-before-last skipped the lease without draining the pipes. "Busted all the waterfalls. The place is nothing without the waterfalls." I quite agreed.

I'd hit a dead end and couldn't afford a timeshare. To tell you the truth, I was glad. I was sick to death of James Allen Dumfries, and as long as no one was trying to kill me, I had my heart set on forgetting him. Pros were looking for him, I reassured myself. They'd find him and lock him up long before he found me or I found him.

Buck and I turned up toward the Governor's Palace, trying to avoid the groups wandering around in the darkness with various guides lecturing away, doing a pretty good imitation of school. I'd had too many opportunities to eavesdrop already. They were everywhere, in tight little lantern-lit packs of about twenty or thirty, shuffling along, learning up a storm. *The colonists would have called this a lanthorn!* Simply fascinating. Gripping. Whenever I got too close, some hapless kid would spot Buck and yell, "Doggie!" upsetting the educational flow.

I tugged him away, deeper into the darkness, before somebody called the principal on us.

It was a busy night. There was a big veterans' gathering in town. Some of the guys Lu met in Philly came by to watch us shoot. They brought along their grandkids, who got everybody's autograph, even Wally's. There seemed to be no shortage of grandkids on hand tonight, along with their dazed parents. It was like night school for zombies.

Didn't seem like much of a vacation to me. I hated school, but at least we had lights and heat and a place to sit most of the time. I figured it must be a puritan trade-off for the town's other big attraction: shopping. For every spun factoid you swallowed, you allowed yourself a purchase. Whatever you had your heart set on, always wanted, deserved to give yourself after what you'd been through, whatever bit of junk might cheer you up, make you feel sexy, remind you of your vacation someday under a heavy coat of dust—what*ever*—you could buy it around here, and *so much cheaper*. But I've never been much of a shopper.

Don't get the wrong idea. I liked the place just fine. I liked working on location with an audience. We were a tighter, better cast and crew. Lu and I enjoyed our time off rambling in the woods with Buck, who figured he'd died and gone to doggy heaven. So what was my problem? Wasn't I happy?

That was the problem. I was plenty happy.

I was put on this earth for a reason, one of the Bright Spot's characters said once—a cracker fundie I had trouble taking seriously when I played him—and now here I was: *I was put on this earth for a reason*. I didn't even want to think about what this reason had to do with the course of my life so far. I'd get too pissed off, and I had a lot more life to live. I was willing to let bygones be bygones. But from here on out, I'd work out my own reasons, thank you very much.

Lu was in the same boat. Or maybe we were rowing in the same galley. How many of us were there, we wondered—redundant Jims and Galateas set upon some mysterious errand we didn't understand? We could have a reunion like the vets. *Say, don't you look familiar!*

I preferred my previous assumption—that I had begun as the random coupling of the usual stereotypes abusing the usual drugs, resulting in me—a good old-fashioned burden to society who should be grateful I wasn't dead.

Lu preferred her romantic story of rich parents who perished in a fiery plane crash. Now those people who hired Bea to carry her looked like spooks deploying a future resource instead of rich people longing to spawn an heiress. She dealt with it better than I did: She cursed the whole business a few times, then seemed to let it go.

I was still working on it, and it was still working on me.

The last time my identity changed, I did it myself, or at least paid to have it done. I paid a couple thousand bucks—I'm sure I was overcharged—and considered it a bargain. But there wasn't any part of this life I wanted to chuck into the river. There wasn't anything I wouldn't do to hang on to it. It was *my* DNA now, goddammit.

Meanwhile, it was authentically dark on the football-field-size green fronting the Governor's Palace, and I had to keep a sharp eye out to make sure I saw

THE BRIGHT SPOT

where Buck did his business. I'd never find it in the dark. My plastic bag was conspicuously at the ready, sticking out of my back pocket like Buck and I were playing flag football.

I watched him snuffle in an endless state of hesitation, and listened to the snatches of passing tours. This close to the Palace, most were telling Lord Dunmore stories. Seems like every time he got in a sticky situation with the patriots, he threatened to free their slaves—two-fifths of the colony's population and climbing. That must've put a chill into the freedom fighters.

"Mr. Bainbridge," a voice came out of the darkness. There was a man sitting on a hitching post, little more than a shadowy blob. The flicker of torchlight from the Palace played across his face, but not so much you could tell what he looked like.

"Good evening," I said, thinking he might be a fan.

"Since you have disabled our surveillance, perhaps it is time for your rendezvous? Fortunately, you took out his surveillance as well. Gives us the opportunity to talk. Dumfries can't be trusted, you know. He's completely insane. You're much safer if we're involved, if we cooperate with one another. What is it the two of you hope to accomplish here, Mr. Bainbridge?"

Dumfries can't be trusted. Who the hell are *you*? I smelled cop, seriously bad cop. To go along with their *surveillance*. And I'd hoped I was just being paranoid. Now it'd broken down, and I was getting all the credit. Isn't that always the way? I decided to play stupid. I was a natural, though there was something familiar about the guy I couldn't quite place. "Buck and I? We're making a virtual," I said cheerily. "Right here in Colonial

Williamsburg—you should come by tomorrow, when the sun's up. You could meet everyone. We'll be at the jail again, I believe. I'll be the fellow in the stocks."

He chuckled badly. Dryly? "I see. Have it your way. Perhaps you think you can double-cross him on your own. That's been tried. It's my understanding you once worked with Jesse Salvador? He was a highly skilled professional. Now he's dead."

"I heard that. I'm sure he'll be missed. No. This is ReCreation Productions. We're highly skilled professionals ourselves. We do *Billy and the Big Guy*. You know—Billy, BG, the She-Creature. I play Victor Frankenstein. Buck here plays—"

"*No,* Mr. Bainbridge. I'm not the least bit interested in your ridiculous virtual. We don't have much time. If you'll take us into your confidence, we might prove useful to you. You need protection. What is your purpose here?"

"That's a bit of a philosophical question, isn't it? Entertain the audience? Express yourself? Enlighten somebody or other? Deceive them? All of the above? Certainly not get rich in this case, I can assure you. Though I must say it seems awfully rude to insult what a man does for a living. What is it you do, besides lurk in the dark, tossing out insults, knowing people's names and dropping them? I missed yours, by the way."

I knew who it was now. It was the limo driver. He'd traded in the Moose Malloy routine in favor of *it's my understanding* and *take us into your confidence*. Now he was Agent Limo, Mr. Casual's cop brother, a post-doc from the gatekeeper academy, who might call himself an operative, agent, dominion, multinational man of

THE BRIGHT SPOT

intrigue, nothing so tacky as *cop*. But it was the same guy, all right. I never forget an oink.

"My name doesn't matter," he said.

"If you say so. It's your name. I didn't hear what it was I could do for you."

"You can tell us James Dumfries' intentions." He was losing his patience, his smooth. He'd blown the scene. He was a bumbling amateur.

"Oh, I can? Wouldn't that be nice of me? Why should I help you bozos? Aren't you the guys who lost him? You had him safely stashed in a total living facility, and one of your own helped him get out. What was that helpful thing my mother used to tell me when I lost something of mine—'Where do you last remember seeing it, Nicky?'"

"Very funny. It was a meticulously planned operation, but Salvador turned. Dumfries killed him. We didn't plan on that. We didn't plan on Dumfries being criminally insane. But don't worry. We know where he is." A beat. "Don't you?"

Ouch. He could've been bluffing, but I didn't think so. I finally got it. As a spy, I was the bumbling amateur. They weren't *after* Dumfries. They were watching him, watching me, hoping to observe whatever clever thing he intended for me. Agent Limo and his pals were the jackals hoping to steal the carcass, the nature photographers who stake out a wounded goat to get some good predator shots. Dumfries probably knew they were watching and couldn't make a move until they blinked. Mutual Assured Distraction. This is what I'd mistaken for safety.

"Well, obviously, he's wherever you are, watching you, watching me. Isn't that how this thing works? Why don't you just leave me out of it and watch each other? Why should I tell you anything? Is it supposed to make me feel *safer*? If you want to learn something, buy a ticket. Why, did you know they used to clean type down at the print shop with *mule* piss? It's true. It's a fact. Whatever meticulous plan you guys had, it clearly flopped, and lots of people are dead. *Bust* Dumfries if you know where he is. Leave me the fuck alone."

"Don't underestimate us, Mr. Bainbridge."

I started to voice my doubts such a thing was possible when Buck launched into his victory dance, and I whirled around, instinctively whipping out my plastic bag, trying to spot where he'd done the deed. "Shit!" I exclaimed appropriately. This raised a disapproving mutter from the last of the passing tours. "Ye olde shitte," I hissed softly, searching the ground in vain, hoping not to step in it trying to track it down.

Too late.

"I tell you what," I said over my shoulder, trying to scuff my shoe clean in the dirt. "You tell me where Dumfries is, and I'll tell you what he's up to. Fair enough?" Most of the lanterns—excuse me, *lanthorns*—were past us now, swarming at the Palace gates like fireflies, filing en masse into the Palace to witness some sort of powdered-wig hoedown just tuning up.

Limo didn't answer me, so I turned around. He was on his feet. Something glittered and wagged back and forth in front of him. A half-dozen stragglers from the peripatetic classrooms were gathered around us. Then I realized what was going on. Agent Limo had a gun drawn and was trying to decide which truant to shoot

THE BRIGHT SPOT

first as they closed in on us. They looked old even in the dark. Probably some of the vets. With new orders.

"Don't!" I shouted at Limo. "They don't know what they're doing."

"I could give a fuck," he said, taking aim, as the one neither one of us had seen standing directly behind him wrapped an arm around his forehead and gave his head a quick, wrenching, final twist. The gun clattered on the brick walk. Agent Limo slid slowly to the ground. His killer's white hair shone in the dark. Once a 'ware soldier, always a 'ware soldier, apparently.

A wrinkled hand closed around my left arm, above the elbow. It belonged to an ordinary-looking tourist, seventyish, paunchy, frail. Only he was running 'ware. His grip was strong, like rope pulled tight, bringing back memories. *Don't struggle, boy. You'll hurt yourself.* Use the rage, I directed myself, and kneed the old guy hard in the crotch. He doubled over but didn't loosen his grip in the least. By this time, another hand gripped my right arm, a woman forced open my mouth and shoved a heavily perfumed handkerchief inside, cradled my fragile head in her arms, and two others took hold of my legs. They started up their little jog-trot, headed north down the middle of the green, away from the Palace.

Everyone seemed to have been sucked inside. Even as we crossed Duke of Gloucester, no one thought it odd to see an actor hauled bodily into the woods by a half-dozen old soldiers. Maybe they thought we were part of the show. *Is this where they tar and feather that guy?* Who would suspect this geriatric crew of foul play? Without the 'ware, half of them could barely walk, much less jog.

Their movements were perfectly coordinated, so

that my ride was unnaturally smooth, the ideal gait for crossing a battlefield with explosives. They didn't want to kill me, I kept telling myself, or I'd already be dead. They were kidnapping me, taking me to meet my maker. I wasn't so sure I was ready. There was a parking lot on the other side of these woods, or a trail down to the Colonial Parkway before that. I would be miles away from here in no time.

So Dell was right all along: *They say it shut down at the end of your shift, but it don't.* Not for these old soldiers anyway. It moved in and made itself at home, ready to be called up for active duty at any time. I could struggle, try to throw them off balance, but if we all took a bad fall, their old bones would crack, 'ware or no 'ware, and I'd have someone's shattered hip on my conscience. I was fucked, and they were too. I should just let it happen, I told myself. Once he had me, maybe all the craziness would end.

And then, behind us, as we started down the hill toward the woods, I heard the jingle of Buck's tags as he trotted along after us. He hadn't watched enough *Lassie*. He didn't know he was supposed to run the other way and fetch some help, preferably the kind with a gun and a badge. But he finally did the next best thing. He started barking, nipping, making a nuisance of himself. I caught a glimpse of him leading Agent Limo's assassin on a merry chase up and down and around the hill. My money was on Buck.

Then I heard a woman's voice, calling, "Daddy! What are you doing with that dog? Daddy! What's wrong with you?"

"Doggie!" a young voice declared from Duke of

THE BRIGHT SPOT

Gloucester as the next wave of lanthorn-led scholars approached the green.

By this time we'd attracted the attention of other dogs and their walkers. I recognized the baying of Gulliver, a full-throated bassett of Buck's acquaintance, who happened to be passing and joined in the alarm.

"Bertie! Dammit! Where *are* you?" a querulous voice called sternly. It sounded like Bertie had wandered off a time or two before, and the caller had simply run out of patience.

"Mother, you're going to miss the Palace!" another voice cried out anxiously.

The kidnapping was apparently abandoned as a botched job, as my abductors shut down as quickly as they'd ramped up, and let me go. I found myself airborne, landing on my back on the trail, the breath momentarily knocked out of me, but otherwise okay. In seconds, Buck was all over my face, licking furiously, with a growing crowd around us, tending to their relatives-turned-criminal and phoning up a storm. My abductors had fallen like sacks of potatoes, but they all looked like they were breathing, and the ground was thick with pine needles that'd served to soften our falls. I wondered whether that was mere chance or consideration.

"Are you all right, young man?" Bertie's daughter thought to ask me.

"Fine, fine."

"An ambulance is on the way."

"No, really. I-I'm fine." I sat up to prove it. "Who are you folks anyway?"

"They," she said—meaning my abductors, propping themselves up, looking around, wondering what in the *fuck* they were doing in these woods—"they're the last surviving members of their outfit. They haven't seen each other in over forty-five years. I can't imagine what got into them."

"Nothing really. Just a little reenacting. Fascinating place, don't you think? I never knew history could be so interesting." I got to my feet and took Buck's leash in hand. Bertie's daughter was summoned by her mother, and Buck and I took off at a brisk walk back up the hill. No one tried to stop us. Gulliver, who had given his walker the slip, continued to orbit the growing crowd, baying furiously. The ambulances showed up and emergency personnel came racing down the hill past me. I'm sure everyone was in good hands.

I borrowed a phone from one of the gawkers on Duke of Gloucester and called Lu to make sure she was all right. Stan picked up.

"Hey, Nick. Lu was starting to worry about you. We're all here talking about the show. You want to talk to her?" He sounded more depressed than scared. I could hear Wally and Dee talking in the background, Gary cursing about something. Everything was perfectly normal.

"No need. Just tell her I'll be right there. I just got hung up for a bit."

About the time I cleared the colonial section, I heard a woman screaming about a dead man and figured she must've fallen over Agent Limo in the dark. Those lanthorns weren't worth a damn on a dark night. You

THE BRIGHT SPOT

needed night-vision equipment for work like this. That or lightning or the full moon.

So much for my fantasy of simple, small-town living in the Enlightenment. I was back in the twenty-first century again, where clearly it wasn't enough to avoid anyone running 'ware, but potentially anyone who ever had.

All the way to the Liberty Lodge, I began to add it up. The night the road crew came after me, they were probably like these guys—trying to collect me, not kill me. And just me. I was the sought-after specimen.

The only thing I'd done differently tonight was head out on my own, without Lu. I remembered Dumfries leaning across the table, intense, scared: *She mustn't know we've spoken. She must never know.* Why? Why shouldn't she know everything? Lu, Galatea, Lenore, whatever you wanted to call her, she was clearly in it up to her ears. Why didn't Dumfries want her to know? Didn't he trust her?

JUST DOWN THE ROAD

16

> *"I swear to you, by the earth which I inhabit, and by you that made me, that with the companion you bestow I will quit the neighbourhood of man and dwell, as it may chance, in the most savage of places. My evil passions will have fled, for I shall meet with sympathy! My life will flow quietly away, and in my dying moments I shall not curse my maker."*
>
> —Mary Shelley, *Frankenstein*

Buck and I arrived at the Liberty Lodge breathless. Mr. Henry, the patriarch of the place, was out front smoking a cigarette in the glow of the sign. Pictured there was slaveholder Patrick Henry, the embodiment of Liberty, the man from whom Mr. Henry had taken his last name when he bought the motel. He thought it essential, he explained to me once, to change his name to something American to prosper in his new home. "When I bought this place, I asked, 'Who is that man on the sign?' and the real estate man told me about

THE BRIGHT SPOT

'Give me Liberty or give me Death,' and I decide to become Mr. Henry."

He blew his cigarette smoke into the air in huge clouds. This was Virginia. It was still legal here to smoke outside without trapping it—liberty and death as a twofer. He beckoned me over.

I liked Mr. Henry, even though he mostly brooded, wandering the Liberty Lodge grounds while his daughters made the beds and his sons complained and his wife dealt with the guests. I always imagined he was looking for the path back to Egypt, but I only knew him from moments like this when he smoked and I walked the dog.

"They are all meeting in your cottage," he said in his precise voice. "Your friends. I have not told them. I wished to speak with you personally, Mr. Bainbridge. I have always found you a reasonable man." Given the choices, I could see what he meant, but I had no idea what he was talking about. He reached in behind his cigarettes, took out a small plastic bag, zipped it open, pulled out a fly-size drone, and dropped it on his open palm to show me, then closed his fist around it. He zipped the bag shut and gave it a shake. It rustled like seeds. "I take precautions. I want no trouble. I detected some unusual activity near your cottage, so I cleaned the entire area this morning."

His eyes darted to the little satellite tower atop the office. Somewhere in that thicket was something illegal that brought down this little bag of spies with an unauthorized electromagnetic burst. The feds must've thought I did it, that I was on to them, Dumfries too, if

I could believe the deceased Limo. I couldn't mention any of this to Mr. Henry, so I tried a neutral smile.

"I found many of these devices," he continued. "They watch you and your friends. They like your cottage particularly. They follow you everywhere, even when you walk the little guy."

He smiled at Buck, who swished his tail. He and Mr. Henry had a thing going. I smiled at their moment, and Mr. Henry grew somber. He was afraid I wasn't taking this seriously enough. I was past serious into deadly serious, but I had to stick with the smile.

"You people do not understand how such things work. They watch you all. Then they watch the people you meet. Innocent people. But they are not innocent anymore because they know you. You think if you pretend they are not there, that it is just life as usual. No, my friend, this is the eye of your enemy—*always*." He gave the bag a shake. "You say, 'I have done nothing wrong,' as if your enemy cares about that." He held up his fist with the drone inside. "He doesn't care." He opened his palm and let the drone drop to the sidewalk, ground it with his heel. He bent over, crushed his cigarette on it, and straightened up. "It is easy to disrupt their flight. They still see everything, hear everything." He kicked the butt into the rush of traffic, tossed the bag after it. He spat on the scorched spot on the sidewalk. "Such devices are very expensive. Someone goes to a great deal of trouble to watch you. I very much regret that I must ask you and your friends to leave, Mr. Bainbridge. I am not your enemy, but I can't afford to be your friend. I hope you understand."

"I understand perfectly."

THE BRIGHT SPOT

He smiled, surprised at my ready understanding. He appreciated it so much, he did something stupid and stuck out his hand. I did him a favor and didn't take it. I probably shouldn't have said anything, but I spoke quietly, hoping the traffic would muffle the sound. "They're probably watching even harder now, Mr. Henry. Trust me."

They were probably watching just now when one of their own was murdered, watching when I was being kidnapped, watching when Ed drowned. They watch. They wait. They prey. Mr. Henry was right. They were my enemy.

He froze there for a moment. He nodded almost imperceptibly, thanking me for the warning. He bent over and scratched Buck's head. "Take care of yourself, little guy," he said.

Buck snorted a reply in Ipso Facto. Something along the lines of, *Talk to this idiot—I've already saved his sorry ass once tonight!*

"Good night, Mr. Bainbridge."

"Good night, Mr. Henry. Thanks."

Mr. Bainbridge, Mr. Henry—good strong American names, names you can trust.

Everyone was crammed into our tiny cottage. I took my time getting out of my coat, greeting everybody, thinking how to break it to them that we had to move—tonight. The kidnapping, the murder, the spies—all that would have to wait until Lu and I were alone—if such a thing was possible anymore.

Buck made a beeline for Wally, who put him on his

lap. "Greetings, honorable canine companion," Wally said in Patriot's voice, which was, in honor of Buck's Asian roots, a Mr. Moto/Charlie Chan article-dropping fortune-cookie-ese sure to insult more than half the world's population. Wally had cultivated the annoying habit of speaking in it whenever Buck was in his lap, which he arranged as often as possible.

Dee and Stan dwarfed the drop-leaf table in the kitchenette. Their four huge hands were laced together on the table like a big bunch of bananas. They looked even worse than Stan had sounded over the phone, like newlyweds whose honeymoon cruise just sank.

They all looked unhappy—Lu stretched out on the bed, Gary scowling in the other chair. Even Brenda, sitting on the air conditioner, usually as emotive as Mount Rushmore, looked... *heartbroken?* I remained standing, my mind racing. How to put this? *Oh, by the way, we've been evicted.* Only William was missing. Just as well. Somebody else could break it to him.

But my audience already looked deep into tragedy. This dark mood couldn't be about the surveillance, since Mr. Henry had told only me. Even if they knew, it shouldn't come as too big a shock to anyone. This was America. Spying on each other was practically a patriotic duty. We should be proud we were serving our country by offering up our lives for the cause—whatever abstraction we were taking on this week: *the War on Cynicism!* No. Something worse than a few drones had them looking like this. I decided my news should wait until I found out what was going on.

Maybe something had happened to the crew. Better paid than the talent, they lived at a nicer place out on the

THE BRIGHT SPOT

loop. They'd been having such a high old time on location, they didn't know where they were half the time. Their latest toy was a bit of recreational nonsense called Déjàviewer that gave the user déjà vu experiences every ten minutes or so. They could easily have gotten into some kind of trouble.

Then I realized what the trouble was—or who.

"Where's the asshole?" I asked.

"Ah, Nick," Stan said, as he usually did when I said anything disparaging about our costar. He never disagreed. He just didn't think I should say it.

"He's in the hospital," Gary said. "Somebody's husband finally beat the holy crap out of him. Knocked all his teeth out. Unfortunately, he'll live. But there goes the fucking show."

"It was somebody's *son*," Brenda quietly corrected. "Her thirteen-year-old son." Her terminal sat beside her on the AC, I noticed, in case we needed any additional information in our grief.

"Jesus fucking Christ!" Gary said.

"Most unfortunate occurrence," Wally/Patriot concurred.

"And our numbers were doing so *well*—up another sixteen percent last week," Brenda said sadly, with finality, a statistician's postmortem. She held her hand at a tilt to demonstrate the hopeful graph cut off in its prime, let it fall to her lap like Icarus.

You take your dog for a walk, and look what happens. They already had the show on a slab, and I was just in time for the wake. Not so fast. Kill a still-had-a-shot-at-being-successful show for *this*? This was nothing. I'd seen a whole lot worse than this. Hell, Lu and I were in way worse trouble than *this*! We needed this show.

"I don't see the problem," I said. "Write around him. Shift the focus to Stan and Dee. How are those numbers doing, Brenda?"

"They're strong," she said noncommittally. Was that a snuffle? She liked to remain a neutral source of information, part of some sort of number crunchers' Hippocratic oath. "Growing," she added. From Brenda that amounted to editorializing.

Everybody liked watching Stan and Dee.

Dee's Galatea, as her character had evolved, was an Indian Princess who oozed pouty-lipped great-cheekbones nobility. She'd gone to the same language school the Asian Patriot had, apparently, and spoke fluent Tonto, but in spite of that handicap, immediately became a popular character, and not just for the reasons you might think. She consistently "contributed to feelings of empowerment" in the high eighties among our cornerstone female adolescent audience. But she also did surprisingly well with adult women, who responded to her self-confidence and sexual aggressiveness. And males, well, there'd never been any question about those numbers.

Not that any of that mattered so much as that Dee and Stan had chemistry to burn. Everybody wanted to see them together. It didn't matter if she could act, or if her lines sounded like Yoda on the reservation. She just had to put her lips together and say "How." Stan had always been the most popular character in the show, and even his numbers went up when he smiled at Dee. Smiling wasn't something he got to do a whole lot of rescuing

Billy from fanged groundhogs or alien sportscasters—whatever wacky adversary Wally had dreamed up for the week.

It was a turn-on watching Dee and Stan together, no doubt about it, but it wasn't just that. The two of them getting together, doing the ancient dance, made you feel something like hope. And who didn't want that?

Lately Galatea had been attempting to woo BG away from the cause of Revolution as a bad deal for the Indians, poised as they were to cut a pretty good treaty with the British Crown. When last we saw them, Stan and Dee shared one hot kiss that left the Big Guy reeling. Thus far, naturally, both Billy and the Big Guy had been solidly in the patriot camp. Washington, Jefferson, Henry—that crowd. It was time to shake things up. Might as well go all the way.

"How about BG goes to Galatea's village for a pow-wow?" I suggested. "Get the Native American angle on the Revolution. Then let BG and the Princess explore her world for a while, do what comes naturally."

Everyone looked at me like I was crazy, and then, naturally enough, at Wally. Crazy was his department.

"What befalls most unfortunate Billy while BG in teepee?" he asked.

"I don't know. Kidnapped by wolves, cabin boy for Captain Hook, real live boy turns into wooden android—you'll think of something. Let *him* deal with it for a change. Just write him out, once and for all. Brenda, how have Billy's numbers been lately?"

"They have been slipping," she said judiciously.

"Slipping like an avalanche. Any lower and 'see more of Billy' will be a negative number. Put Dee and

Stan in a wigwam, and nobody's going to be asking 'Where's Billy?'"

"I think it was the Algonquins who had wigwams," Brenda said.

"A motel, then. This is *Billy and the Big Guy*. We're not known for our attention to realistic detail. Come on, guys, you know I'm right."

"What about Victor and the She-Creature?" Gary asked. "What are they supposed to be doing all this time with no Billy? They're supposed to be his... his what do you call it... *nemesis*, right? Don't they need him?"

"Don't worry about them. Villains can always find plenty to do. Right, Wally?"

Wally nodded sagely, nodding Buck's head in sync. "Villains wait for good men passing. Wise men go other way."

"Wally, could you *please* put a lid on the mysterious-Orient crap for a minute?" Gary said. "You're starting to make sense, and I'm trying to *think* here. What about the *nice* angle?" he asked me. "Remember what happened to that *Heart of the Congo* thing."

"*Darkness*, and trust me, I'll never forget. But it's time to dump *nice*. I turned to Brenda. "At this point, how dependent are we on the educational feeds anyway?"

"Under thirty and falling."

I spread my palms. "Look at *Lucky*. Do you think they were doing the edgy stuff they're doing now way back when they were a lowly edvirt? It's time to kill the kid. Besides, if you want to talk educational, that *is* what happens in the novel."

"He's right," Brenda said. "That could help bolster

THE BRIGHT SPOT

the ed numbers. They usually get a positive nudge from upping the FLS—sorry, Fidelity to Literary Source—rating."

"And with Buck, we've got cute covered," I pointed out. "The kid's just taking up space. What is it now? Five tedious minutes an episode? He has maybe ten lines—not counting 'Help, BG! Help!'—when he bothers to learn them."

"But his name's in the fucking *title*," Gary objected. "We can't change it?"

There was no chorus of dissent. Everyone imagined *Billy* banished. A few eyebrows went up. Lips pursed.

"Okay. So what's the gimmick?" Gary finally asked. It was an important question. He wouldn't ask it unless he was ready to let go of the old gimmick. What choice did he have, really? Where would he find another William, and why would he want to?

I said it slow and hammy the way they like, my hands in the air to evoke a marquee, though none of us was old enough to remember seeing a real movie marquee: "*BG and the Indian Nation.*"

"That's what the creature in the novel wanted," Brenda said enthusiastically. "To go live like an Indian in America—with a mate." Everyone looked at her, and she scrunched up a shoulder, embarrassed. Damn, she had read the whole novel, or Cliffs Notes at least. That explained her uncharacteristic lack of impartiality. I had at least one ally.

"And remember how this thing got started," I said, pressing my advantage. "Kids wanted the creature to get an even break, a *life*. What do we do? We stick him with Mr. Nice and his endless sacrifices—some helpless kid who needs saving week in and week out and has the emotional range of a daisy. What kind of life is that? We can get beyond that. We're just starting to get somewhere. Why quit now? What have we got to lose?"

Not a thing, they all agreed. The more they talked about it, losing Billy sounded truly swell, as Billy himself might say.

Wally could hardly wait to start writing now that we had a new gimmick. He'd brought his card table down to Virginia. He set it up wherever the fancy struck and weather and cops permitted. He was a regular by the women's tennis courts at William and Mary until asked to move along. "Let's go to Jamestown," he said. "They have Indian stuff down there."

"That's over a century and a half earlier," Brenda pointed out.

"No it's not. I saw it on a map. It's just down the road."

Who could argue with logic like that? Wally and Brenda traded a look of affectionate annoyance that for the first time made it plausible to me they'd once been lovers. In the celebratory mood of the moment, they might even be contemplating a revival.

Everyone simmered with enthusiasm. Dee and Stan—all of us, in fact—were delighted Dee's fledgling career and their hot romance would continue.

Gary was sold the minute I reminded him *Lucky* had dumped the ed feeds long ago. It was time to take it to the next level, he said, to take a decisive step. Enough of this *poised* crap.

Brenda suggested that—with the FLS up and the Native American cultural studies tie-in—we might even

THE BRIGHT SPOT

boost our ed numbers at the same time that we achieved greater mainstreaming.

"Main stream run deep," Wally observed.

With a name change, I pointed out, we might get some fresh reviews—certain to be kinder without the insufferable Billy in the cast.

Meanwhile, Lu watched the whole thing, never saying a word, smiling like the sphinx. She knew something was up. She figured I'd tell her everything when we were alone.

Everyone was so pleased a new plotline awaited us in the morning instead of unemployment, they hardly minded when I broke the news we had to move to another motel tonight. I explained quietly that William had made a pass at one of Mr. Henry's daughters, and he had asked us to leave.

After an awkward moment of silence, Stan said, "There's a Venezuelan place on Second, the other side of CW, that's got king-size beds for the same price." Gary called and secured rooms. He even talked the guy into a group discount once he heard we were with the virtual company in town doing *BG*. We had at least achieved local fame.

Everyone scattered to pack, and Lu and I were finally alone. As I closed the door, she smiled at me from the bed and clapped. "Another amazing performance by my favorite actor."

"Another interesting facet?"

"No, I've seen it before. I just forget it's there until it wakes up and springs into action. When you say the show must go on, you're not just fucking around. We were this close to looking for work. Even Wally was ready to pack it in. Your pitch was a thing of beauty, worthy of You-Know-Who."

That's what she'd taken to calling the Bright Spot. She knew better than to say Bright Spot—that was strictly for my use—so now it was You-Know-Who. She'd rented every turkey he'd ever been in—the ones you could still find. She couldn't resist telling me how good he was. Last week he was even brilliant. The bastard was like that guy in *Halloween*—he wouldn't just lie down and die.

"Why, thank you, ma'am." I lay down on the bed beside her.

"So, what's really going on?" she asked. "You walked in the door with the troubles of the world on your shoulders, not to mention pine needles all over your back. You been rolling around in the woods with someone?" She touched my cheek where the gag stuffer had scratched me with her nails, an accident I'm sure. Nobody wanted to hurt me—just spirit me away. I reeked of perfume my grandmother might've worn if I'd had one. "So, what's the real story, Nick? Mr. Henry's daughters are too young for William. He doesn't look twice at women under thirty."

Lucky for me I had no plans to lie to her. "Mr. Henry has some experience with being watched, apparently, and doesn't like it. This morning he zapped a bunch of drones that have been following us around, probably since we've been here. He figures he'll be safer if we stay somewhere else. He's probably right."

"Oh my God," she said.

"It gets worse. When he zapped the drones, the feds thought *we* did it and were about to make a big move—

THE BRIGHT SPOT

meet up with Dumfries for whatever—so they sent an agent round to recruit me to their cause and see what he could get out of me. It was the limo driver when we did the diner scene, all dressed up and talking proper. He thought I knew more than I do, and I was trying to parlay that into getting out of him where Dumfries is, when a half-dozen old vets—tourists on their way to the Palace—showed up running 'ware, broke his neck, killed him. Then they grabbed me and tried to carry me off. They were doing a pretty good job of it. If it hadn't been for Buck raising a ruckus and drawing a crowd, I'd be gone."

It took her a beat or two. It was a lot to process. "Jesus." She wrapped her arms around me and held me close. "Are you all right?"

"I'm fine. A tiny scratch."

She rocked me like a baby. "We've got to get you out of here."

I imagined myself bundled up in the chenille bedspread, whisked away from danger, safe in her arms, laid in the bulrushes.... No. I didn't like the end of that story.

"I thought you couldn't leave the board," I said.

She drew back and looked at me. "You can't, but you can make a tactical retreat. You don't hang around and get yourself killed."

"Retreat to where? You think we're going to give the slip to guys with billion-dollar flies? Find someplace where no one's ever run 'ware? Besides, those old vets weren't trying to kill me. They had every chance to kill me and didn't. They were *collecting* me. They were all in the same unit in the war. They were reactivated somehow, given new orders."

"They killed the limo driver."

"Exactly. In seconds. Because he stood in the way of taking me, or he was about to start shooting them, or because he was a cop. But they didn't kill me."

"They may try again."

"He. He may try again. I'm sure it's Dumfries. Agent Limo as much as said he's around here. Isn't that why we came down here, to find Dumfries?"

"Yes, but... What does he want with you?"

"I don't know, but as long as everybody's watching everybody, we'll be okay. We're safer in the spotlight, until we can figure this thing out."

Bad choice of metaphors. She tilted her head to the left, narrowed her eyes suspiciously. "This isn't about the *show*, is it?"

"What do you mean?"

"Jesus! It *is*! It's about the show. You can't quit it as long as it's got a shot. No matter what. You won't run for your life as long as the numbers are on the way up. You'd rather stay put and die than miss a shot."

W-e-e-e-ll... I wouldn't put it quite *that* way. "What if it *is* about the show? Does that surprise you? It's my dominant facet, you might say. It's billboard-size: *CAREER OBSESSED*. That's how I got to be so fucking brilliant. It's who I am. Am I not supposed to have a life so I can *save* it? For what? What do I trade in next—you and me?"

Her eyes met mine. "Never," she said quietly, and I pulled her into my arms. "I worry all the time," she said, kissing my cheek as she spoke. "They're not coming after

THE BRIGHT SPOT

me. They're coming after *you*, Nick. I'm so afraid of losing you."

Her body shook with crying as I held her, rocking her in my arms now. "We'll be okay," I assured her. "I promise you. Besides, you heard the man, we're doing a whole new thing. We're going to Jamestown. They'll look for us here, but we'll be a century and a half down the road. 'Which when did they go, George? Which when did they go?'"

I got a laugh mixed with the tears, but I didn't push my luck. After a while, she said, "I guess we need to pack, huh?"

"I'm going to call Clinton real quick, see if he's found out anything for me. I'll use the phone at the Dunkin' Donuts. Mr. Henry's got enough trouble as it is."

"I'll pack. It shouldn't take long. Everything's dirty. And baby? Promise me you'll be careful."

I kissed her and promised her I would. For now anyway. I had a feeling I was running low on careful time.

Clinton picked up immediately. I made a little small talk, invited him to the wedding in the spring, gave whoever was listening time to wake up and pay attention, before settling down to business. "What else did you find out about Lenore Chapell?" I asked.

He sighed with frustration. "Not much really. She was probably the best they had, top of her class everywhere she went. Everything else is just rumor. Her name has been suggested as one of the possible members of an ultrasecret unit field-testing experimental 'ware in the

Sinai. It crashed and left a dozen soldiers wandering around the desert with total amnesia. Some of them were supposedly never found. First the military denied it ever happened, then said that everyone involved was accounted for, so you figure it out. One version of the story has her surfacing in the underground, real pissed off, offering her services to bringing down the 'ware. Some say she was part of a plot to infect workware with a fatal virus. This would've been when Edmund Kennemeyer was getting a lot of press. Only problem is, those plots were rumored every other week back then, and nothing ever came of them. Whether Lenore Chapell was involved in any of them is pure speculation. Her official death is certainly vague enough to be a phony, but that doesn't mean it is. It just makes her a rumor magnet."

I tried to understand how a good student like Clinton felt about rumor and gossip without footnotes, but I was an actor and wasn't so particular. "Listen to me. It's a phony, all right, and her involvement's no mere speculation. Question is, who's doing the rumoring? Cover stories get to be rumors fast, helps spread them around. She's the best they had, huh? If you ran special ops, and you wanted someone to steal the most valuable secret in the world, who would you use?"

"The best I had."

"That's what I'm thinking. And she would be damn near irresistible—running the latest 'ware, willing to let Dumfries rewrite it, then report back to duty... a mole made to order."

"Should we be talking about this over the phone?"

"About Lenore? Sure. She's been dead for forty years. Besides, as you say, it's all speculation. More important,

THE BRIGHT SPOT

for the people listening on your phone to hear, is that I know what James Dumfries is up to in the here and now, so they better keep a sharp eye on me and keep me safe, because—and I'll only say this once—I'm the only one who can stop him."

"Uh," Clinton said.

"Oh, I almost forgot, I had one more question. You said Dumfries favored more-localized control and the brass overruled him. How was that going to work?"

Poor Clinton was still rattled at my willful indiscretion. "Uh... Voice command, I think. Ordinary language."

"With some kind of password or access code?"

"Or several. They could make it voice-print specific, for example, but the army said it could never be secure enough."

"They were afraid of mimics?"

"No. That's easily detectable. Good-enough recordings might not be. A captured commander might be compromised."

"What about twins?"

"That might work, but that doesn't sound very likely."

"Yeah. You have to work at it. And if this rumor was true and Lenore had herself infected with some virus to crash 'ware, how long would that take?"

"All her 'ware would have to be redone, especially if she crashed and the old installation was corrupted. You have to do it step by step, in layers of code. A series of installations. Several weeks, I would think."

"Installation. They use suppositories for that, right?"

"Usually."

"How fitting. Say hey to everybody at Murphy's for us, Clinton. Thanks a lot."

I hung up, leaving him with a thousand questions, just what every bright kid needs. I bought a half-dozen buttermilk donuts, Lu's favorite, as a peace offering.

I didn't plan on telling her I'd already broken my promise to be careful, but I had to make a move, at least act like I knew what I was doing, like I was solving the crimes, catching the bad guys. If I was good enough, I could even fool myself. That's where all the best acting begins. Fool yourself, and the rest of the world's a pushover.

DRINKS ON TREY

17

Twinkle, twinkle, little bat!
How I wonder what you're at!
Up above the world you fly,
Like a tea-tray in the sky.

—LEWIS CARROLL, *Alice in Wonderland*

THE NEW PLACE, THE PATRIOTEL, WAS LIVELIER than the Liberty. They had their own pancake house on the premises, doubling as a cocktail lounge at night. Nothing like a Black Russian and flapjacks to finish off the day. According to the sign out front, there was even a band. Los Refugios would be playing tonight well past my usual bedtime.

Since Wally had all this outdoors to work with, he'd grown fond of sunrise shots. This morning's sunrise, what seemed like days ago now, found me in the stocks, with the resourceful She-Creature picking the lock with her talons. I felt a good deal freer then. Good and stupid. We were on tap for another dawn shoot tomorrow, Wally informed me, on the island that once upon a time had been Jamestown and more recently had been another roadside attraction. I hoped to turn in early. It'd been a busy day.

But it wasn't over yet. Lu suggested if we were going to hang around and endanger our lives for a fucking *show*, maybe we should come clean with the others, in case they had more sense than I did. Since she put it so nicely, how could I disagree? It was one thing when we naively thought we'd given our pursuers the slip, but now that we knew we hadn't, we had to let them know.

After we moved, which took all of fifteen minutes, I called everybody. Gary, Wally, and Brenda were settled in for the night, so I arranged to meet them for an early breakfast, Wally's favorite kind. Lu and I met Stan and Dee in the bar for a drink. Feeling homesick, I ordered an Icehouse.

Maybe it was the big TV over the bar that had me thinking of Murphy's. Only this one didn't run movies. It was stuck on the news, and I made the mistake of sitting down facing it. Jury selection for the trial of the men accused of killing Edmund Kennemeyer had just gotten under way, and the hard-hitting, live, late-breaking newsies couldn't get enough of it. Ed, to hear them tell it, had done nothing else in life but be queer; his killers, nothing else but hate queers. Ed's murder was, they kept saying, "seemingly inevitable." They didn't even mention the 'ware controversy or run clips from Ed's speeches. What did that have to do with anything? Instead they talked to the killers' old schoolteachers, who thought they'd seen the early signs of hate and violence in their young charges, even though they were all basically good boys, and to Ed's teachers, who confirmed

THE BRIGHT SPOT

he was a good boy too, even though he'd always been basically queer. The graphic was a body floating in bloody water. *Pool of Hate,* it said. I tried to ignore it. The truth was bad enough. Why did we have to be subjected to the news too?

When they got around to Agent Limo at the bottom of the local news, he was a Colonial Williamsburg tourist—name withheld pending notification of relatives—who died of an apparent heart attack, the first such incident at CW—a perfectly safe tourist attraction—in a really, really, really long time. In an unrelated incident, a group of "elderly citizens" wandered away from their group and inadvertently raised a ruckus. There was footage of Gulliver racing around my geriatric abductors to great comic effect, and a newscaster yukking it up. Commercial: *Virginia Is for Lovers!* Jesus H. Christ.

"Nick?" It was Lu, reeling me in. I was supposed to do the talking, fill Stan and Dee in. Tell them everything. We'd never shared Clinton's little bombshell, never mentioned we were clones. We didn't know how they'd feel about it. Hell, we didn't know how *we* felt about it. Dee had a theory Trey was the root cause of anything gone wrong. As long as nothing was happening, that had been close enough. Now I was going to crank up their paranoia several notches. Just looking over your shoulder for the husband wouldn't get the job done anymore.

I put it all together as a narrative, starting with Lenore, then Galatea, and finally Luella. I filled in Ed, James, and Nicholas along the way, but I left out the Bright Spot. He'd just muddy the waters. Unlike

Clinton, I wasn't too particular about the footnotes. It went something like this:

"Lenore Chapell was a soldier in special ops who crashed and burned on 'ware and joined the underground, or pretended to, eventually finding Ed, who hooked her up with Dumfries. He rewrote her as Galatea Ritsa, loading her with a virus to mess with 'ware when she reported back to duty. Jim and Galatea probably suspected they were being watched and pretended to be lovers to explain their clandestine meetings, or maybe they didn't have to pretend. Either way, their tearful public breakup in the diner neatly served to activate the virus and explain her departure in one short scene.

"But something went wrong, somebody was on to them, and Galatea was killed before she could deliver the virus. Nobody got what they wanted, least of all Dumfries. I still think his grief in the diner was genuine, that they became lovers for real. I guess in the end it doesn't matter whether he loved her or not. She was dead, and their plan had failed.

"But they had made backups, cloned embryos of them both—meaning they both must've been necessary to the process, and whatever they were running was specific to their DNA—so it couldn't be stolen or messed with. Our DNA now—me and Lu. Lu and I are the clones. Dumfries arranged for our births, set us up in life, but somewhere along the way the feds took over, and he got himself warehoused in an old folks' prison. But the feds didn't know what he intended to do with us and were aching to know in the worst way. For over forty years now. When Dumfries' memory started failing, or he pretended it was, they sent in Salvador to pose as

THE BRIGHT SPOT

a shrink and see what he could get out of the failing old man.

"My guess is Dumfries dreamed up the diner gag and persuaded Salvador it was his idea as a means of finding us and springing himself. He offered to cut Salvador in, and once he got loose, he killed him. He sent me looking for Kennemeyer, and the next thing you know he's dead at the hands of a 'ware crew and 'ware workers are coming after me. I think Dumfries can tell any 'ware crew to do whatever he wants by voice command—including murder and kidnapping. This may be what the feds are after—the secret of how he does that.

"He did it again tonight while I was walking Buck down at CW. A half-dozen old vets came after me. They killed an agent who's been following us. One of the sweet old geezers snapped his neck. They wanted me intact, apparently, but once we drew a crowd, they shut down, and I took off.

"Meanwhile, Dumfries is still on the loose, still hoping to put us to the use for which we're intended, whatever it is. The only thing that's stopping him, I figure, is that the feds haven't given him room to maneuver. They've been watching all of us, Dumfries included, with tiny surveillance drones. Mr. Henry spotted them and zapped them temporarily. That's why he asked us to leave. But I'm sure they're up and running again. I don't think I can elude them, so my best move is to stay put, out in the open."

"And the show can go on," Lu added wryly.

"And the show can go on," I acknowledged. "We... Lu thought I should tell you, give you the chance to decide for yourselves whether you want to stick around."

Dee and Stan traded a look. "We're not going anywhere," Stan said.

"I don't understand why Jimmy killed Ed," Dee said. "Ed loved him."

"Somebody betrayed Jim and Galatea. That's why Galatea died. I think Dumfries thought that somebody was Ed."

"If she was special ops, like you say," Stan said, "I think she betrayed them herself. I know those guys. I don't buy the lost-in-the-desert story. That was just to get her close to people in the underground. She was following orders from beginning to end—steal his secrets. If the thing in the diner was a code, she probably had his secrets already installed. He switched her on; next stop, debriefing and download. Doesn't sound like he thought he was being played from the way he talked to you. Only somebody killed her."

"But why come after me?" Dee asked.

"Because I told you the code without knowing it," I said. "The names."

"That doesn't seem like enough reason. Like *I* would know they were a code."

"Maybe he's a nutcase," Stan said. "Cloning himself and his lover—I mean, you gotta admit that's pretty extreme. I was thinking, when you guys do the scene in the diner? Maybe it activated you guys too. Right? You must be running something. Just like *they* had to be running something."

"Right," I said.

Lu and I had worked our way through not having any parents, and now one of our progenitors betrayed the other? Perhaps was even programmed to betray the

THE BRIGHT SPOT

other? I liked them better as beleaguered freedom fighters with a tumultuous love life.

Stan saw the look on our faces. "Wait a minute. You aren't them. You shouldn't think you're the same people. Everybody's got their own soul. You have free will."

I recalled Stan expressing vaguely religious sentiments on occasion. Apparently they weren't so vague. "Along with genes, cops, spooks, and 'ware, we do indeed have free will, Stan. We'll keep that in mind. Certain inalienable rights too. I'm sure they're around here somewhere." I looked under the salt shaker.

"Aw, Nick."

"So who killed Galatea?" Lu asked. "Who *would* kill her? If she was a spook successfully completing her mission, the feds wouldn't kill her, even if they doubted her loyalty—the 'ware, whatever it was, died with her. There's no evidence Dumfries and Kennemeyer suspected her. Both sides wanted her alive."

"Can't help you there," Stan said. "You're right. She'd only be valuable alive—to either side. Once she's dead, the 'ware's gone."

I could think of more than one person who might've taken aim at Galatea and a tree for reasons that had nothing to do with 'ware, but that was all speculation too. "Dumfries told me they planned to meet, but that it wouldn't work out. He thought she was going to live. He wanted her to live...."

"Oh shit," Dee said.

I followed her gaze over my shoulder. Trey Kennemeyer had just walked into the place. I recognized him from the news, where he showed up often. The waitress was pointing us out. He looked fifty, which meant he was probably older. He mugged importance in case anyone cared to recognize him. It made me wish I hadn't.

He walked up to the table, grinning like we'd all planned to meet here. He had a couple of goons with him, bulging with weapons under their nice suits. "Hello, Dee," he said.

"Hello, Trey," she said icily. "How did you find me?"

"You forget. The car is mine. I know where it is at all times. Everything that goes on inside of it as well."

Trey and Dee glared at each other for a moment, broadband malevolence—fifty-seven channels of fuck you. Stan and Dee liked to take long rides in the country in that car, alone, or so they'd thought. "You only *think* you know," she said. "You don't know anything about anything."

He didn't argue the point. It was beneath him. He smiled past her at me and Lu and Stan. Nobody smiled back. "Introduce me to your friends," he said, pulling up a chair and sitting down. The goons remained standing, as goons will.

"Lu, Nick, Stan," Dee said. "This is Trey. We were all just leaving, Trey."

"No. Stay. I told the girl to come over. I'd like to buy everyone a drink. I could use one myself."

Drinks on Trey, just to show there were no hard feelings. How nice. I nodded my approval. I was part of the reason he wanted a drink, even though he seemed to have already had more than a couple. When he got a good look at me, his smooth had definitely hit a wrinkle, and I had a hunch I knew why. When the thirtyish "girl" came around, I ordered a single malt, a double, the best they had, with lots of ice. Stan and Dee abstained, of course, and Lu tried to, but I suggested *sotto voce* she order what I was having and pass hers to me. Trey liked my spirit and even though he had a substantial head start on the rest of us, ordered himself a double as well. The goons weren't invited to partake. They had to remain alert to laugh at Trey's jokes, smile at his wit, shoot his enemies.

He must've thought this a good time to crawl out of whatever hole he'd been living in since his uncle's lamentable death—to show the world he had nothing to hide, even if his queer uncle had gone and gotten himself killed. Now that he was back, he'd come to reclaim his wife and car, not necessarily in that order.

When Trey and I had our Scotches, he made a little idle chatter about the virtual business, just to show he knew a thing or two. He had interests, he said. He told us what each one of them grossed last year. A real art lover. "I hope your little company will struggle along without Dee's talents," he said. He took a big gulp of his Scotch.

"I'm not going anywhere," Dee said.

He smirked. "Sure you are."

"No, Trey. I've left you. For good. I'm divorcing you."

He laughed loud and long, a bit of a ham. "Please. Don't embarrass yourself, Dee. I don't intend to finance this nonsense indefinitely. The car fees alone are more than you make. It's gone far enough. You've had your fun. You're my wife, and you're coming home. Let me remind you that divorce would mean you'd be cut off *completely*—that's all the houses, the cars, *everything*. You signed a pre-nup, remember? You own zip."

Having seen one of his houses and too much of his art collection, I didn't see where he got off getting so picky all of a sudden about the kind of nonsense he financed, but I kept my opinion to myself. Besides, she didn't need his money. Dee was doing well enough, even on what ReCreation paid her, to live in a cheap motel with an ex-wrestler, if that's what she wanted to do with her life.

Trey was certain his single threat would do the trick, certain he knew how she was wired. She'd start bargaining for some little million-dollar shack somewhere and last year's car. And once she did, she'd be acknowledging her life was on loan, and he was calling it in. She'd plead awhile. He'd stand firm. And then she'd walk out the door on his arm, just another repo, her big stud watching with his jaw hanging out. Trey downed the rest of his drink and set it on the table with a bang, so confident how the scene would play, he hadn't left a single drop of single malt for another single take.

"Fine," she said calmly. "Go ahead. Keep your stuff. I don't want it." Stick that in your pre-nup.

He snorted. "I'm not joking, Dee."

"And neither am I, Trey. And don't embarrass *your*self by asking me why. Come on, Stan." She stood, and Stan stood beside her. The goons shifted to high alert, their hands inside their jackets, looking up at Stan, who wisely acted like Dee was doing just fine without his help.

This wasn't going quite as Trey had planned. Now she'd challenged him, openly mocked him, in front of all these loser friends of hers, with his goons right there, poised at the first opportunity to tell any and all how the boss' wife had not only dumped him, but chopped it off right there in front of God and everybody, proving him to be the rich, dickless wonder they always figured him to be. He only had the one move. He had to say, "No, I insist, Dee. Tell me why. Enlighten us all."

Playing Princess Galatea hadn't hurt Dee's "feelings of empowerment" either. She took on a royal bearing and gave Trey a look like the pity of the executioner, and he must've known he was done for. Her rage was perfectly under control, like her breathing. A discipline. A practice. "Okay, Trey. You asked for it. I'll en*light*en you. If you've been watching me and Stan together, as I'm sure you have, then you must be completely blind to think there's any way I would leave *him* for *you*—not for any amount of money or *stuff*. I'd have to be out of my fucking mind, wouldn't you say? I mean—you've watched us more than once, right? Watched the recordings over and over? I know how you like to watch. Have you *ever*, in your whole life, *ever* seen a woman have a better time? Not *me*, I can tell you. You never saw *me* have a better time. And here's the part you *really* won't get—we love each other like crazy. We're *friends*, you miserable prick. So go fuck yourself, Trey. You can use my big mirror."

Dee turned and left the bar, doing her best Indian Princess stately stride, Stan beside her like a walking hemlock from the forest primeval. The goons were at a loss. Their boss was going down ugly, but there was nobody to shoot. He spotted them looking embarrassed and barked at them to get the hell out to the car and wait. They scurried out, and Lu stood.

I stayed seated. "I'll just finish my drinks," I said with a lopsided grin, like a true lush.

"Not *again*," she said with a roll of her eyes, a whine in her voice. "Don't expect me to wait up for you this time." Then she left too, in a convincing huff.

Bless her, she always picked up a cue.

I wanted to talk to Trey Kennemeyer—asshole, 'ware tycoon, and murder suspect. I thought he knew things. Rich people usually do. That's how they got to be rich. Once they're rich, they buy more information to keep them that way. Maybe after the recent unpleasantness with Dee he wouldn't mind knocking back a few with a harmless, whipped lush like me, for a little misogynistic man talk. It was no surprise I'd tactlessly remained behind. After all, I was the guy who ordered two doubles. I had them sitting before me. I took my first sip, and it was good. "Tough break," I said.

He took a tug at his, but there was nothing left but ice. "She didn't have to do that," he said.

I nodded. What he said was undoubtedly true. As much as I personally enjoyed it, she didn't *have* to do it. It was classier she hadn't gotten physical, though I regretted not seeing her actually spit in his eye.

"When I met her, she was just a fucking *dancer*," he said.

"Vegas?"

"Yes. I have interests there."

"I *thought* so when I met her—about her being a Vegas dancer, I mean. She's got the moves. She's tall. Beautiful, of course. And those legs. She must look great with

THE BRIGHT SPOT

the high headdresses and everything. I'm curious. If you think so little of dancers, how come you married one?"

"You're awfully smart on my Scotch."

"It was a gift, remember? It's mine now. You wouldn't want to be an Indian giver, would you? I believe the term was coined around here somewhere by white men selling Indian land to each other. But I can't drink two at once. I can afford to be generous."

I slid my second drink to him, and he took it, took a proprietary belt. I sipped. We talked. He gulped, and ordered more. It wasn't so hard to bring the conversation staggering around to Uncle Ed and his old pal Jimmy Dumfries. After all, Trey was practically looking at him. James Dumfries was clearly one of his ghosts, and here I was showing up to haunt him, Ed barely in the ground. The news loop had rolled around, and we watched the "Pool of Hate" story together.

He didn't look like he believed it any more than I did. He looked at me, took a pull at a fresh Scotch, double number three. "You know, when I saw who you look like, I figured you did it. A love nest gone bad deal. Something like that. What did Ed pay you to make yourself look like the 'love of his life'?"

"You've got it wrong, I'm afraid. This is how I look. I'm an actor. I was tapped to play James Allen Dumfries in a postwar bio, and I talked to Ed about him, the one and only time we met. Then someone murdered him."

"Uh-huh. What did he tell you?"

"Nothing. Nobody will talk to me about Jimmy Dumfries. Everyone's too scared. What about you, Trey? You scared?"

Trey rose to the bait like those cloned marlins you

can pay to catch in the Keys, if it's too much trouble to open a can of tuna and you have a few thousand bucks to blow on some Hemingwayish manhood. And all he had to do was talk. He was pretty drunk, but he could still talk okay. He'd been loaded at some fine schools where one learned to keep talking in more or less complete sentences, practically until one passed out. Trey had whole paragraphs left in him yet.

"I can tell you *plenty* about James Dumfries," he said. "Him and Ed. My parents'd leave me with Ed when they traveled, which they did a *lot*, spending my inheritance." He chuckled. I was supposed to chuckle too. I did, though I'm not much on parent jokes. "Jimmy showed up at Ed's every other night for a quick boink before hurrying home to the wife. Ed always lived as close as he could to the guy. It was pathetic, really. Jimmy was never going to divorce his wife and make an honest queen of him. I made myself scarce when Jimmy showed, and they'd be at it in no time. They thought I didn't know what was going on, that I was just a dumb kid. They even took me sailing on Jimmy's boat once. They were down below for like an hour." He smirked. "Making sandwiches."

His smug, drunken smile hinted at a story that might be coaxed out of him. He'd shown the old fags he wasn't so dumb in the end—watched them too, I wagered. He liked to watch.

"That must've been some interesting pillow talk," I said. "Inventor of the 'ware and its most outspoken critic—two of the most brilliant men of the time."

Trey snorted. A good, manly, drunken snort. "Those two? They were idiots. Smart, but idiots. Dumfries in-

THE BRIGHT SPOT

vents this incredible thing and thinks he can just put it back in the box? 'Sorry, I didn't mean to'? Come on! Ed thinks people's *consciences* are going to stop them when there are *trillions* to be made off of it? This is Planet fucking Earth here. They were so smart a thirteen-year-old *kid* could outsmart them is how smart they were." He took another gulp, though he didn't need it. This chemical imbalance registered on his face almost immediately, and he took a moment to pull himself and the room together. It looked like he might have a few pieces left over. He was telling a story, he recalled. He took on a conspiratorial air, leaned across the table. One false move and his face would fall on it. "Wanna know how stupid the great James Dumfries was?"

I noted the past tense, but didn't make anything of it. Trey was doing his own time-traveling, and he was as close to thirteen as downing three double Scotches could get him. The James Dumfries he was talking about was about my age, long, long ago. The three of me nodded our encouragement. He wasn't sure which one to focus on. He leaned in closer. I slid his glass out of his way, so he wouldn't knock it over. "I'll *tell* you how stupid: He had this ancient *laptop* he'd had since college or something, lugged it with him everywhere. It had everything on it, all his research, his notes, tons of 'ware code. Unsecured. Pretty stupid, huh? I mean, *anyone* could come along while they were *fucking*, steal his hard drive, swap it out with a busted one—takes *five* minutes." He held up five fingers even if he couldn't have counted them himself. "He wouldn't suspect a thing! They'd jus' think Jimmy's old *laptop* had finally crashed! Time to get a new one! Too bad they don't make them anymore!" He sputtered laughter. "It didn't even *occur* to them how much the fucking thing was worth. You might say I owe my substantial wealth to James Dumfries, a fucking idiot." He found his drink—I hadn't moved it far enough—and toasted James with the last of it, probably not a good idea. He swallowed and blinked. He didn't have much longer.

"What about Galatea Ritsa? Did she help you out too?"

"Who's that?"

"A woman James Dumfries had an affair with after the war, also went by the name of Lenore Chapell."

Trey smirked, wagged his finger at me. "I *knew* you were a spook! Showing up looking like Jimmy right after Uncle Ed gets killed. Actor! You had me going for a minute. If you weren't fucking him, you were playing him, right? I told you guys already I don't know anything about it, have no idea who did it. Fucking crazy is what it was. The guy was totally on ice. A fucking philosophy professor. Didn't know a goddamn thing except he missed his sweet Jimmy. Poor sick fuck. Now we got this shit to deal with." He waved a hand at the television.

"How do you know Galatea Ritsa?"

"Hadn't heard the name before. Didn't know I'd need it. She must be the babe in the video some of your buddies played for Ed back then to show him what his true love was up to, am I right? Jimmy and this woman fucking like rabbits. I couldn't get a good look at her face, but she had a body on her." His hands held air tits. The memory seemed to revive him. His eyes gleamed with lust.

"What did they say about her back then?"

THE BRIGHT SPOT

"I couldn't hear, but it looked like they had Ed right where they wanted him, crying like a baby. He would've given up his own mother, looked like. That was the last time I saw the great James Dumfries—in that recording, banging away. Ed watching."

"I'm curious. How did you see it? Were you in the room?"

"Oh *hell* no. You could see into Ed's office out my bathroom window. With good binoculars."

I'm sure he had the best. He liked to watch. The whole country did, apparently. Behind him on the TV, the news loop had rolled around to the damn *Pool of Hate* logo again. The top story of the hour here in the homeland. There must've been a hero shortage that day. Maybe they could do another of their "Richest Men in America" stories. Those were always good on a slow day. Gave the little people something to aspire to. He might even buy them some of the good Scotch, share some of the secrets of his success.

"Tell me something, Trey, you ever stand outside and watch your wife running naked?"

"Outside? No. The cameras pick her up from three different angles."

"I hope you saved the recordings. I don't think you'll be seeing her again—except in virtuals, like everyone else. She's going to be a star, Trey. You just wait and see. Losing you could be the best thing ever happened to her. She's already made the adjustment to running outside in the real world with clothes on. You should see her and Stan together—like a couple of gazelles. It's a shame about your wife, Trey, but now that you've had your answer, I suggest you back off. You've stumbled onto something out of your league here. National security interests are at stake. You wouldn't want to compromise the good relationship you have with the Administration, would you, Trey? You're crowding us here. It's time for you and your boys to move on down the road. Thanks for the Scotch."

I finished my drink, though it'd gotten pretty watery by then, and left before I saw whether he bought it or not. He was just drunk enough. I'd be lucky if he remembered any of it. By the time I hit the door, he was headed for the bathroom.

I found the goons shivering outside by Dee's car. I told them to give their boss a couple of minutes, then find a bucket to carry him back to The Lakes at Llewellyn and toss him in. They smiled.

"Tonight ain't over," one of them said.

The other one nodded his agreement, then wagged his big head back and forth. "Dee shouldn't've shot off her mouth like that. It's gonna be ugly. Does he have another clean suit?"

"Shut up," the other one said. "Here he comes."

When I turned and saw him, I knew I'd overplayed it, not hard to do with a cliché. I let my dislike of the guy push me too far. He came lurching out the door, made a little gesture with his fingers. The goons took a step closer to me and lost their friendly way. I thought it prudent not to do anything to annoy them, like move a muscle or take a breath until their boss arrived, swaying back and forth in front of me, his frosty breath smelling like Scotch and vomit. He wiped his mouth on his jacket sleeve. "The current *Administration*, Nick, are a bunch of fucking weenies, and you can tell them I said so, if you ever meet any of them. We haven't had a decent President since the war. You're not a spook, or you'd know there's *nothing* out of my league. You're the help. Galatea Ritsa, huh? Must be more there than I thought.

"When I saw you, after I threw out the toy-boy idea, I said to myself, I just bet he knows Jesse Salvador. Excuse me. *Knew* Jesse Salvador. Ed couldn't afford a toy boy. He didn't have a dime. Jesse, however, had vast resources at his disposal. He approached me a while back with an offer concerning some very interesting technology. Most of my interests are in technology. Would you know anything about that, Nick?"

"I have no interests, interesting or otherwise, that would interest you. I'm just an actor in a small-time virtual."

"Cute. And I'm a successful businessman. God, I'm starved. Aren't you? Let's go for a ride, have some dinner, refresh your memory. I understand old Jimmy's had some memory problems lately too. But I haven't had the opportunity to speak with him yet." He grinned like a shark. He might be drunk, but he was a drunk shark, and there was blood in the water. "Let's take Dee's little pussy palace here, shall we? Step right in, Nick."

One of the goons opened the door to Dee's car. The other one put his hand inside his jacket.

"I really need to be turning in. Lu's waiting up for me. She'll be worried."

"She said she wouldn't this time, remember? She can come along if you like, keep us all company—so she won't have to worry about you. Or she can stay here, so you won't have to worry about her. Which will it be?"

I got in the car.

A FINAL MESSAGE

18

When you are entertaining, try not to feel that something unusual is expected of you as a hostess. It isn't. Just be yourself.

—Irma S. Rombauer, *Joy of Cooking*

ONE OF THE GOONS WENT RIGHT FOR THE SECURITY panel and started playing with it. The other was assigned to the fridge. "There's nothing here but plain yogurt and wheat germ."

"Stupid bitch," Trey said. "Find us a decent restaurant around here," he said to the one at the security panel. "What's the wrestler's name?"

"Stanton Wetherell," the goon said, restaurants scrolling before his eyes. They had star ratings. He tapped the screen, the riffraff vanished, so only the four-stars remained.

"Arrange to send him a message, will you?" Trey said.

"Is this a final message?"

Trey thought a moment. "No. I think a *clear* mes-

THE BRIGHT SPOT

sage will do for now." All this time, he'd been changing out of his funky suit into a clean one just like it, like a snake shedding its skin. He popped a couple of capsules, took a deep breath. Good as new. "So. Mr. Nicholas Bainbridge. Talk to me."

I shrugged. "Salvador hired me to scam Dumfries with a phony time-travel number. I never got paid. End of story."

"No. Beginning of story. Otherwise you wouldn't be so closely watched." He smiled the shark smile again. He was having a good time. He was in his element. "We clean yet?" he asked the security goon.

"Yeah. All clean."

"Restaurants?"

"The closest is a World Palate at the next exit."

"Perfect. I have an interest in those places, never tried one. We'll see what my money's up to these days. And you, Nick, you can tell me why your DNA is identical to Jimmy Dumfries'. I find that very, very interesting."

I didn't ask him how he knew that. I'd been leaving my DNA carelessly strewn about all evening. "This would be Jimmy Dumfries the fucking idiot?"

"Yeah. Exactly."

The World Palate was for gourmets on the move who liked to watch their food prepared by expert chefs with an extra dollop of flashy in their style. Anyone could do it, with the help of Trey's latest 'ware. They might not be able to boil a hot dog when they got home, but here they could do it all—chop, flame, knead, toss, fondue, flip, fillet—without the temperament or the salary, preparing any cuisine you could imagine or sell. There was a whole platoon of them in trim white outfits throughout the dining room; tiny spotlights would find them at the climactic moments of their culinary performances. It was like a mass audition for a food movie. *Mostly Babette's Tortilla Soup* or something. Dough soared and thumped. Knives slithered, chopped, sliced, and clanked. Woks sizzled and sighed clouds of garlic steam. Flames shot into the air from mesquite fires and flaming desserts. Diners oohed, ahed, ate, and paid. A lot.

My dinner with Trey.

The surveillance system pegged Trey Kennemeyer on the premises, and the manager, one of the few employees not running 'ware, was all over us in an instant. Loaded up to his eyeballs with obsequious toady, he didn't need 'ware. He couldn't do enough to ensure Trey's happiness now and forevermore. He would be *honored*, his very verb, to make a selection of their finest dishes for Trey and his guest. I considered telling him I was no guest, but a kidnap victim, then thought better of it. As Trey most charmingly put it, this was Planet fucking Earth here. This guy would gladly serve me for dinner if Trey asked him to.

In no time we had a corner of the dining room to ourselves, Trey and I, with the goons flanking it like lawn lions. He watched the show for a while. "Kind of tacky, isn't it? Incredibly profitable, though. Labor costs are nothing, but people still pay for the show. Not unlike what you do, huh?"

"Not unlike."

"What's the old guy up to?"

THE BRIGHT SPOT

"I don't know."

"Like fuck you don't know. But we'll have something to eat first. I want to get the taste of that shitbag motel out of my mouth. How do you live like that?"

"It's only temporary. The rock I was living under is being remodeled."

The wine steward had personally selected a trio of wines for our dinner from the database of Trey's preferences and was pouring the first. He didn't spill a drop. The towel over his arm probably lasted him a whole week. He only had one expression. Pleasant. They could've given him a range, but the fixed expression reassured the diner this wasn't a person standing here so close, but service, distilled down to its essence and planted in his soul, up his ass. He filled my glass and withdrew as if he were on wires. Trey offered a toast.

"To life," he said.

The wine was perfect.

"I'm being watched by the feds," I offered. "We are now, I imagine."

He wasn't impressed. "They watch everybody, that's why they never see anything. By the time they figure out what they're looking at, it's over. Information goes astray. They really should be better paid, don't you think? Public servants, elected officials? Working for the good of us all?"

"Presidents?"

"That dumb fuck would be overpaid at half the price. What do you make, Nick?"

"Less than the President."

"Maybe you'd like to make more."

One of the spotlights seemed to miss its mark,

illuminating an empty patch of floor. Then I realized it was the 'ware chef who was out of place, off his mark. Several were. They were shifting our way, repositioning themselves closer and closer. The goons looked past them like they were invisible.

"I don't care about money," I said, keeping the conversation going.

"Everybody cares about money," Trey said. "Unless they're a fucking idiot. You want work, is that it? That's not a problem. I have interests."

"What's the part?"

"It doesn't fucking matter what the *part* is, Nick. We agree in principle, am I right? Big part, big money, big name. That's what all you guys want, right? Fine, you got it. So speak to me."

The 'ware chefs were arrayed in a crescent around us. One of them started toward the table with his little cart. The goons didn't even give him a glance. He rolled the cart up next to us and fired up a burner. He peeled bananas, sliced them lengthwise, making a big show of it, then started sautéing them in a copper pan.

Trey followed my gaze. "Bananas? What is this shit? We starting with dessert? Where is that idiot manager?"

With an expert flick of the chef's wrist, the bananas did a somersault in the air and landed back in the pan. A pinch of this, a pinch of that. He was quite a showman—or whoever wrote the routine was. Trey missed the whole performance, searching the dining room for the manager. He still didn't get it. The chef picked up a bottle of brandy and splashed it into the pan, then lit a spoon full of the stuff with an old-fashioned Bic and let the blue flame cascade into the pool below, poofing into

THE BRIGHT SPOT

an eyelash-singeing ball of blue flame. The oohs and ahs sounded even without a spotlight on us. Trey gave the whole performance a bored roll of his eyes. Then the chef brought his arms up like a conductor, the pan and bottle still in his hands, and dumped the flaming bananas onto Trey's lap.

"What the fuck!" he said, as a stream of brandy from the upended bottle hit the flame and doused his clothes, enveloping him completely in flames. He jumped to his feet, and the chef brought his arms down as abruptly as they'd gone up, smashing the empty bottle over Trey's head and smacking him a good one upside the head with the skillet.

The goons took their first clear shots, and the dessert chef did a jerky dance and fell, taking his still-lit cooking cart with him, blocking the goons' way as they tried to reach their boss, who was careening through the empty tables. He finally crashed to the floor, still burning and screaming, a trail of burning tablecloths behind him. The sprinkler system kicked on, but it was too late for Trey.

I was still sitting at the table alone, like I was at a sidewalk cafe waiting for the check in the rain. The goons stood over Trey behind me. The chefs surrounded us. "Guys," I said over my shoulder, and the goons turned around.

All the chefs raised their right arms and brought them down. I dove under the table as a squadron of knives passed overhead. I grabbed a couple of table legs and started chugging toward the exit as fast as I could chug. I looked back, and the goons weren't going down easy. They both had knives sticking out of them every which way, most of them stuck in body armor, but not all, and they were losing a lot of blood. Their boss lay in a smoldering heap behind them, but they were leaning up against each other, guns blazing, chewing up the place and everybody in it with bullets for as long as they could stand and fire.

They finally dropped dead, but the bullets kept up until the guns were out of ammunition or jammed, leaving a couple of gaping holes in the dining room floor, where the water gathered and cascaded into the basement. All the chefs, easy targets, lay dead. They literally never knew what hit them. It was the surviving customers who were screaming, crying, cradling their dead and dying in their arms. Blood was everywhere, though somehow I'd managed to make it to the exit without a drop on me.

I crawled out from under the table. I looked around the dining room just above the suffering, the likely angle for the surveillance system to be looking back, and made sure it had a good look at me. With shaking fingers I took out a card and laid it on the table, Mr. Kennemeyer's table, where it might easily be found. With any luck, the locals would find me first. Best they came looking for me. Here I might get lost in this crowd of innocents. I walked out to Dee's car and went back to the Patriotel.

It was late, Lu was asleep. The band over at the lounge covered my noise as I slipped out of my wet clothes and stashed them out of sight. I slid quietly under the covers

THE BRIGHT SPOT

beside her, and she came half awake. "Find out anything?" she murmured.

A sob was trying to escape my throat, but I couldn't let it. It wasn't in the script I was playing. The mole. The ram in the thicket. "Not really," I said. "Nothing new." And I guess in a way that was true. I'd already figured out James Dumfries was insane. I just hadn't wanted to believe it. I lay awake a long time in the dark, considering my options. *What price freedom? How long a wait for a table?*

I eventually drifted off to sleep to the sounds of a familiar guitar riff out front of a decidedly Latin rhythm section, as Los Refugios over at the pancake lounge made the Patriotel windows rattle with a festive yet plaintive rendition of "Tierra Dulce Alabama" (where the *cielo* is so *azul*).

Sometimes I was proud to be an American, like all the signs said—not very often, and for all the wrong reasons, I'm sure—even if the signs had taken on an increasingly commanding tone since the war. But pride was a deadly sin, I'd been told, and was inclined to believe it. Maybe it was pride that got us into this mess, lulled us into letting things go to hell while we looked the other way. And now it was all of us humans, American or not, wired to the same madness, running the same 'ware. But it didn't work perfectly. Not yet. Los Refugios slipped through. That was the part that made me proud, proud to be human.

Morning came too early. Lu reminded me I had an early breakfast with Wally and Gary and Brenda. She declined to join me, as I knew she would. She couldn't stand to watch Wally eat.

I found Gary and Wally sitting at the same pancake lounge table where Trey and I had spent the evening. The TV was shut off, so I didn't know whether the dead Trey had made the news yet. We were way early—it was still dark out—and our hosts were busy cleaning. The lights were up. The bar was stacked with dirty dishes. Stray swizzle sticks were everywhere. From behind the swinging door to the back came the steady clatter of dishwashing. In the far corner of the room, an ancient Hoover roared.

I sat down in the same chair I'd had last night. The table topper with the drink list and band schedule had been replaced with a lazy Susan sporting six kinds of syrup. The waitress fixed us up with coffee and took our orders.

"Brenda's still in my room," Wally said, stirring his three-sugar, three-cream coffee. "She's real tired."

"Don't gloat," Gary said. "It's gross."

"I'm not gloating," Wally said. "I'm just explaining to Nick."

"You and Brenda are back together again?" I asked Wally.

The question seemed to catch him off base, not that Wally was ever entirely on base. "I guess you could say that. I'm not really sure. We haven't discussed it."

He seemed on the verge of discussing it with me, and it was way too early for that. So I launched into my story while I had the chance. I started with the diner scam, making my way through murder and attempted kidnapping. I left out my dinner with Trey and Trey's murder. The less they knew about that, the better—later on, when they were questioned.

When I was done with the tale—Ed and dozens of innocent workers dead, the feds constantly watching, one of their number murdered, and a madman attempting to kidnap me—Wally said, "These are some great ideas, Nick. I'd like to work them in somehow." He smiled at me and Gary, dancing his eyebrows.

I couldn't speak. I considered screaming. Fortunately, Gary broke in. "I don't think Nick's pitching an *idea* here, Wally. You're not? Right? You're serious, aren't you, Nick?"

"I don't see what difference that makes," Wally said. "If it's a good idea, it's a good idea. Whether he's pitching it or not, whether he's serious or not. It can still be a good idea, can't it?"

"That's ridiculous. Of course it *matters*. He's saying someone's trying to kidnap him, maybe trying to kill him. Feds are spying on us, Wally. Don't you even care?"

"Of course I *care*." He smiled around the restaurant. He looked dangerously close to having another idea. "It's just like being in a virtual, isn't it?" he asked me.

I didn't know whether Wally was incapable of understanding what was going on in the real world, or I was just incapable of explaining it. But there was one thing I did know, whether I could explain it or not. It was an essential bit of knowledge in my line of work, and with illusionists generally: "No, Wally. They most definitely are *not* the same. The whole point of make-believe—the stuff we do—is that it's *not* real, even when it seems real, *especially* when it seems real, it's not."

"Oh," he said. This seemed to come as something of a blow.

Fortunately, the waitress showed up with our food, and Wally gleefully laid into something called the Plantation Breakfast and cured his sorrow with a medley of cured meat, flanked by the obligatory pancakes, eggs, and grits.

"These people wouldn't know a bagel if it bit them on the ass," Gary said. "What should we do here?" he asked. I knew he wasn't talking about his bagel.

"I think we need to go about our business, stick together, stay visible. I hope things will come to a head very soon, Dumfries will be arrested, and we can all just go back to work."

That's what I was always telling Gary in one form or another: The show must go on. And he always listened. That was my role. If it weren't for me, we would've packed and split when William got his teeth knocked out.

"Are you listening to the man, Wally?" Gary asked. "We have to stick together."

Wally, chewing thoughtfully on a slab of ham, was peering furtively around the room, busily pursuing his own thoughts. "How many people do they use, do you think, to listen to us and watch us? I mean, do they work in eight-hour shifts? What if one of us goes back to our room or goes to the bathroom? What if one of *them* has to go to the bathroom? Seems like it would be awful hard to work out. What do you think?"

"I think we should talk about something else," Gary said. "This shit's depressing."

"No it's not," Wally said. "It's interesting. What do you think, Nick? How many people are listening to us?"

THE BRIGHT SPOT

"Why don't you ask them?" I said, being cute. Sometimes I'm too smart for my own good.

He looked puzzled for a moment. "Oh, I get it." He spoke to the air in the voice he might use for a bad phone connection or a non–English speaker. "How many of you are there? Want some ham?" He held up a forkful. That cracked him up. The piece of ham wriggled on the end of his fork like a speared fish, while Wally himself jiggled all over with laughter.

What had I started? I tried to talk him down. "Wally, they might not be literally listening and watching all the time. They probably let machines do that, using software looking for key phrases, face recognition, stuff like that."

"You mean like, like... *Blow up the President! Overthrow the world! Conquer Cleveland!*" He laughed uproariously. "*Ass-ass-ass-assinate Wa-wa-washington!*" He flung his arms wide, and the piece of ham arced across the dining room.

"Wally, would you *please* keep your voice down?" Gary implored. Other customers were definitely starting to notice. It was mostly an older crowd who'd been drifting in couple by couple, looking for bran muffins and decaf. I worried that among them a retired general contemplated caning Wally for his insolence.

He was oblivious. The only thing slowing him down was he was laughing too hard to speak, but he managed to pull himself together for another whooping fusillade: "*Fuck you, Attorney General! Bite me, sp-spooks! Doo-doo! Caca! Ch-child p-p-pornograph-y!*" At least that's what I think he said. He was laughing so hard it was hard to tell, punctuating his laughter with dish-bouncing thumps to the table. I was tempted to join in.

The waitress came over, and I thought she was sure to toss us, but she righted and refilled our tumbled coffee cups, smiling sympathetically at Wally, his face buried in his arms, his shoulders still heaving with laughter. "Is okay," she said. "My brother in Caracas, he have the exact same thing, only in Spanish. Sugar help him sometime."

I dumped a half-dozen sugars in Wally's coffee and stirred the sludge well. It took the rest of the meat and half the coffee to get him to the point where he quit making random faces at the air and giggling. I encouraged him to try all the syrups, and he did, finding the strawberry-and-ham combo to be particularly delectable. By the time the kind waitress cleared his plates away, he was eager to discuss my ideas, a smile of satisfaction on his face. I understood why so many Buddhas were fat.

"I like the part where you figure out they're trying to kidnap you instead of kill you," he said. "Kidnapping's more interesting, more complicated. You have more options. You kill somebody, and they're just dead, and ghosts are stupid. Did you know the English kidnapped Pocahontas?"

Gary had his eyes closed and was pinching the bridge of his nose.

"I'd heard that," I said.

"True story. She was just a young teenager. Can you imagine if that happened now? Then she married the tobacco guy, Rolfe. I like that name. Rolfe! Rolfe!—like a dog barking, isn't it?—then she became a Christian

THE BRIGHT SPOT

somewhere in there, went to England, met the king, and died of tuberculosis. Brenda told me that story last night."

"Is that all you can think about?" Gary demanded. "Some stupid story Brenda told you in bed? Have you been listening to a *single* word this man's been saying?"

"Keep your voice down," Wally said. "People are looking at you. Besides, it's not a stupid story. It's history."

Gary did a slow burn, and I took the opportunity to excuse myself. I figured I had a big day ahead of me, a lot more explaining to do before it was over. Wally was better off with his own reality anyway. Why should I deprive him of it when I should be trying to work a trade? Syrup, sex, exciting stories—Wally's life had it all.

THE SNOWMAN RULE

19

Where are the Snowdens of yesteryear?

—Joseph Heller, *Catch-22*

Back in the room, munching the empanadas I'd brought her, Lu asked, "Did you explain to them what was going on?"

"Hmmm...I'm not sure, exactly. Let's just say I made a full-faith effort. Wally had his own take on things. He and Brenda spent the night together last night, and he was feeling frisky. Gary told him not to gloat."

I did a little Wally-Gary scene, got a good laugh, and left it at that. Everybody was happy this morning, ready to ride out to where the nation was born to watch the sun come up, and do some ReCreating. Why bring up my dinner with Trey and spoil it for everyone? Hadn't I shared enough already?

"You coming?" Lu asked, standing in the open doorway all bundled up in the hooded fake leopard-skin coat that was the She-Creature's cold-weather gear. The sky

THE BRIGHT SPOT

behind her looked like steel wool. Snowflakes swirled in the air. Wally might have to rethink shooting the sunrise. It looked dead already. But the smiling face ringed with leopard spots made my heart swell, and I smiled bravely back. The show must go on.

Everybody accepted my story that Trey decided to leave the car behind. A drowsy Dee rested her head contentedly on Stan's shoulder, his arm wrapped around her. Last night she'd walked away from a few billion dollars to be with him, and he didn't mind a thing. I was glad to know Trey wouldn't be bothering them again.

Lu and I held hands and watched the snow transform the woods. Where I grew up, *winter wonderland* was an oxymoron and the name of a bad acid that made the rounds one spring. This was the real deal, like a Currier and Ives print. We all seemed to float down the Colonial Parkway through the swirling snow. Ahead of us in Wally's boxy Mercedes, Wally chattered at Brenda, hatching the day's plot, as Gary scowled, at the plot or the crew or both. Just as we were leaving, the crew called to say they'd gotten lost (code for just crawled out of bed) and Gary liked to fume about such things, though he never fired anybody.

The road was a strictly tourist thoroughfare from Yorktown to Jamestown, with CW in the middle. Cluster marketing, I think it's called. Today we had it to ourselves. The route was laid out to be pretty, and it was, skirting the broad James River, where almost five hundred years ago the English showed up in three dinky wooden ships to permanently alter the planet.

They'd been a business enterprise like we were, here to strike it rich like that Spaniard Cortéz who'd done so well for himself down Mexico way. They came with the blessing of King James of Holy Bible fame, armed with muskets and their own secret weapon—viral disease.

We, however, hadn't even called ahead. It hadn't occurred to Wally that the National Park folks who ran Historic Jamestowne might want to be consulted before ReCreation just showed up and started rewriting history. You needed permits for that. The island didn't have much to offer as a location anyway. There were few ruins, and the old woods were long gone. They had something called an archaearium, but even Wally couldn't figure out a way to fit that in.

The ranger, a very pleasant archaeologist who offered to show us any number of interesting holes in the ground, suggested the folks Wally was looking for would be Jamestown *Settlement*, a little ways down the road, another living-history museum. They had a fort, an Indian village, boats, whatever we might need—all first-class phonies. They were a public/private Commonwealth of Virginia something-or-other, and would be glad to do business, he was sure.

But when we got there, the boss wasn't in yet, and Martha the cashier, an earnest woman in her early twenties, wouldn't let us look around unless we bought tickets. Except for the interpreters, loitering somewhere offstage, she was the only one there.

Gary started to give her an argument, but she wouldn't be deterred from her recitation of the various ticket options. Then one of the seventeenth-century boats went gliding by outside the window, surprisingly

THE BRIGHT SPOT

close, and we all stopped and gaped. It was a lovely thing, gaily painted like something from a Gilbert and Sullivan set, made all the more enchanting by the snowstorm. I'd expected something more rugged, weatherbeaten. It wasn't much bigger than a city bus. What kind of nuts sailed across the Atlantic in winter in that thing? A seventeenth-century sailor ran up the rigging to the crow's nest like a toy monkey on sticks. Another on deck hauled away at something. We were all impressed. This was more like it. The ship completed its transit across the window and was gone.

"Wow!" Wally said, speaking for us all.

Martha pointed out that the admission price now included a ride on one of the three boats. They used to just sit by the dock, she explained, but competition for the tourist dollar was stiff these days, and people expected more. "That's why we are constantly upgrading our attractions to better serve the public." I didn't know why they always had to split that infinitive while they were at it, but we all wanted to ride on that boat.

I told Martha we'd take the deal that included the T-shirt and the coin purse (or coffee cup) for all seven of us, plus the crew whenever they showed up.

Martha was delighted. "The hats are on sale this week," she said.

"Yes, definitely. They come with the feathers?"

"Yes, goose. You can upgrade to turkey for two dollars more."

"Turkeys all around."

Martha gave us a great big smile, Wally handed over the ReCreation credit card, and we'd done our good deed for the day. As we waited for the boss, she got all our autographs in a Jamestown Settlement autograph book. I asked her if she had John Smith or Pocahontas in there, and she giggled. Making her happy had already made my day, but then, I had the lowest of expectations.

Boss arrived and introduced himself as Lofton Wilcox. He was only a couple of years older than Martha, but he'd grown up with more pretentious vowels and probably had a degree in history. I don't think he liked me much. Gary made all the arrangements, which went quite smoothly once Lofton saw the bill we'd tallied up already.

We had the complete use of *Susan Constant* with sailors, the use of the Indian village (including the use of both a *yehakin*—neither teepee nor wigwam—and a dance circle), and the run of the fort (including the interiors of the guardhouse and the church) for a period of three days, to commence once the crew arrived. We were all set.

I drifted outside to wait for the crew and watch the snow come down. It made even the empty parking lot look pretty. Lu came up behind me and wrapped her arms around my waist.

"What you thinking?" she asked. "You seem awful sad this morning."

"I was thinking about snowmen."

"Really? That's a great idea. I love making snowmen."

I raised my right arm, and she came around under it, her arms still wrapped around me. "I've never made one," I confessed.

She moved around in front of me, found my eyes. "You're kidding. I had the idea it was cold where you

THE BRIGHT SPOT

grew up. Didn't it snow?" She asked cautiously. She knew I didn't like to talk about my childhood.

"There was plenty of snow. No snowmen, no snow angels, no snowballs. We had rules for everything. There was a kid once who'd gotten frostbite in his hands making a snowman and lost some fingers, so they made it a rule after that, no snowmen. We called it the Snowman Rule. The only way they could enforce it was to lock us down whenever it snowed. Once, some of us got caught sneaking out. We hadn't even picked out a place yet. As punishment they made us stick our hands in the snow for five minutes, while they timed it, or pretended to. They actually took longer, someone told me, waited until we begged their forgiveness." I looked back to the snow, the flat white plain. The crew might not be here for another hour, I thought. We could make a snowman now. My first.

"They?" Lu asked softly. In my childhood narratives, that pronoun often went begging for a clear antecedent. She had a pretty good sense of the *we*—a bunch of homeless kids warehoused in an institution. She had less sense of the *they*, the keepers. The blessed fathers.

"Here they come now," I said, pointing. Coming across the causeway, their lights flashing red, making the winter wonderland look more like the bad acid than the old song—a half-dozen white James City County police cruisers headed our way like polar bears driving in a snowstorm. It took them long enough. It's too bad they showed up now, just as I was warming to the snowman idea.

They pulled up around us, showing badges and

great teeth. Very well-mannered cops. You never knew who might be rich. They asked if we knew Trey Kennemeyer, and, of course, we did. Once they got a good look at me, they rounded us up and loaded us into the cruisers in no time. I had the back of a cruiser to myself, where an earnest-cop recording explained my rights to me in a loop. He didn't stop for questions.

I felt bad for the disillusioned Martha standing behind the plate glass with Lofton watching the actors getting busted. We'd seemed so nice.

It was a first-class jail, brand new. They still had the architectural model of the place sitting under a plastic bubble by the elevators, as if they had trouble letting go of the concept now that the reality had arrived. Under the bubble, little cruisers were parked under little trees. It was spring under the bubble, with a few cobwebs hanging from the trees like Spanish moss. Somebody needed to collar a spider or stick this thing in the attic.

JAMES CITY COUNTY—OPEN FOR BUSINESS SINCE 1607 in highly polished brass was bolted to the wall behind the bubble in case the spiffy new place misled you into thinking you were dealing with some upstart. This was Uncle Sam's eldest. *1607* it said right there on the seal. What looked like the *Susan Constant* floated above the date, which I took as a good omen, since we had the boat booked.

Here's how I thought things would go down: The cops would let Gary and Wally and Brenda go right away—there was nothing to connect them to any crimes. The cops would have some questions for Dee

THE BRIGHT SPOT

and Stan and Lu, since they had recently talked to the deceased, and Stan and Dee might be said to have a motive. But they also had an alibi, asleep in their rooms miles away from the scene of the crime. Unlike yours truly, who was, let the records clearly show, the last man standing at what appeared to be a gangland hit or a terrorist attack, a man who then fled the scene of the crime in a vehicle belonging to one of the victims. They couldn't possibly let me go. They *had* to listen to me, lock me up at the very least. Then maybe Dumfries and the feds would have to give it up as another draw and drop the rope. They could bust him, throw him back in another facility. And then maybe people would quit dying everywhere I went.

I was mostly right, except for the most important parts. I must've had spiders in my brain.

They installed me in an interrogation room. They let you sit awhile, getting you in focus, analyzing your breath for controlled substances, giving you a moment in a featureless box to contemplate your future. I tried to get myself into the right frame of mind. *Guilty, Your Honor. Forgive me, Father, for I have sinned.* I was eager to tell what I knew and when I knew it. I wanted the knowing to be somebody else's problem.

I learned as a kid, if you can't disappear, make yourself bigger. A high, preferably loud, profile sometimes deterred predators if there was no place to hide. I could vanish in a cloakroom in summer without a trace, but my true calling was getting everyone's attention. No doubt a factor in my career choice. It was a strategy, of course, that depended on someone, once you had everyone's attention, caring.

My cop came in, pulled out the chair opposite, sat down. Suzanne Feldman, her nametag said. She had a solid, professional look. Black blazer, touch of gray at the temples, probably grew up on *CSI: Virtual!*

"Do you know why you're here, Mr. Bainbridge?"

I didn't waste any time on cute. I was lucky the locals had nabbed me first. That didn't mean the feds weren't far behind. "I was present at the World Palate last night when Trey Kennemeyer was murdered along with dozens of other innocent people. I fled the scene and did not contact the authorities."

This wasn't quite the reaction she'd been expecting. She glanced down at her notes, probably to double-check whether I was high on anything or not. "Have you been advised of your rights?"

"Oh yeah, they took care of that. I'd rather not have an attorney present, if it's all the same to you. It would just slow things down."

"What do you know about these murders, Mr. Bainbridge?"

"Everything."

I did what I could to make good on that claim, once she'd assured me every word I said was being recorded as evidence. Wally had inspired me. My story was full of great ideas. I pitched my heart out.

Maybe I pitched a little too hard. She wasn't entirely convinced I wasn't delusional. Spies, clones, double crosses, mad scientists, dutiful zombies run amok—what was not to believe? But she'd also seen the surveillance recordings from the World Palate and knew whatever was going on was no ordinary crime. It took her a moment to figure out what to ask me first. "So if what you're saying is true, Mr. Bainbridge, agents of the federal government likely monitored the events at the World Palate last night and did absolutely nothing to stop them?"

"Trey was about to take me out of circulation, fuck up Dumfries' plan. The feds couldn't let that happen. Did any of the 'ware chefs survive?"

She thought about not answering. "No. They were all dead on the scene."

"What are you telling their families, that they were murderers? Kennemeyer's goons could take the fall, I suppose, but the recordings must be pretty clear as to what happened."

"That's none of your concern, Mr. Bainbridge. Do you have any proof of these claims you're making?"

"Check out my DNA. Dumfries must be in the database."

I could see by her expression this was already in the works. "If what you're saying is true—that you're so closely watched—how did we manage to arrest you?"

"You've got me there. They've had a lot of fires to put out lately. Losing an agent last night might've slowed them down. Trey was probably screwing with their surveillance too. Maybe your own chain of command—"

There was a knock at the door, and it came open a crack. "Suze," a male voice said. Suze excused herself, went out in the hall, and came back. She looked at me differently now. Nobody was taking in this stray, I was fucked. I couldn't even get myself arrested, not here, not anywhere.

"You're free to go," she said. "We're dropping all charges and deferring all further investigation in this matter to other law enforcement agencies better equipped to deal with the complexities of the case. Thank you for your time, Mr. Bainbridge."

I stayed in my chair. "Fuck you and your time. You're my one chance. Don't you get it? They'll play this murder like Ed Kennemeyer's—another talkathon. Like *life* was a living-history museum. 'What turned these boys into killers? What does it mean for America?' I know the answer. *Not a fucking thing*. Because it's a crock. They didn't *hate* Ed. They don't even remember him. This thing will be even worse. They'll invent new kinds of experts to talk about it. The Prez will have to weigh in—Trey Kennemeyer being such a friend to America and all—blaming it on 'certain malcontents who wish to destroy our way of life.' Our way of life. That's a good one. Nobody will know what really happened. The evidence will evaporate. Already, I bet, God himself couldn't lay hands on the recording of the conversation we just had. Only you know what I said, and now you know it's true, because you've been ordered to release me when you've got a dozen reasons to hold me. You can't let me go out there."

"I can't help you."

"'To protect and serve up,' huh?"

"Mr. Bainbridge..."

"Nick. You've already checked, I'm sure. And you know that's not my real name. Doesn't that bother you? A bad phony like that? You're thinking I have to be a spook to walk away from something like this, some serious badass trying to play you. But if I were a real spook,

THE BRIGHT SPOT

I'd be better at it. I don't want to be involved in this any more than you do. I'm just looking for a way out, shelter from the storm. You're saying there's no room at the inn, fair enough. But if you're going to throw me back out there, you can at least remember what I said, watch out for me and those around me."

"I'm *sorry*. I can't help you. I can't even talk to you."

Oh, Suzanne, you shouldn't have let that slip. She *was* sorry. You could hear it in her voice. She'd clearly lost sight of her job description. Being a cop meant never having to say you're sorry. "Sure you can. You're doing fine. I've played a few cops, but it's nothing like real life, is it? When real lives are at stake. If you can't protect me, maybe it's time I met my maker on my own for the good of everyone. Mr. Henry gave me the opportunity, but I blew it. Maybe you could help me—"

"*Mr.* Bainbridge, we have been instructed by an unimpeachable authority that this matter is no longer in our jurisdiction. I—"

"Ever do the 'ware yourself, Suzanne?"

She held my gaze for a long moment. "Yes."

"What about the others? Is anyone building a frame around them?"

"We were told to let you go. They didn't say anything about the others."

"Not even Luella Anthony?"

"No. Only you. I've said too much already, Mr. Bainbridge. Now, would you please leave?"

"Yes, certainly. I've never had a cop say 'please' before." I stood and took my exit. "By the way, there's no such thing as an unimpeachable authority. Look at these guys. They don't even seem to realize Galatea and Lu are the key to the whole thing."

Lu was waiting by the bubble downstairs. When I came out of the elevator, she threw her arms around me, and I held her close. She felt so good. It was all I could do to let her go.

"What took you so long?" she said. "I was starting to worry they were going to hold you, afraid maybe you'd pissed somebody off again." She gave me a quick but passionate kiss. If she knew I should be behind bars, she gave no sign of it. She thought it was just routine questioning.

"Me? Where do you get these ideas about me? I'm a sweet guy. Everybody loves me. What about the others? Are they out?"

"They let Wally, Gary, and Brenda go right away. Wally's disappointed he didn't get arrested. They asked the rest of us a few questions about our run-in with Trey, if he said anything about his plans for later, that sort of thing, then let us go. The cop who talked to me was more interested in you, where you were last night. I just told him you had drinks. That's right, isn't it?"

It's true I never had dinner. "That's right. One drink. I gave him yours."

She shuddered. "There must be lots of people who would like to see that creep dead. Stan and Dee are seeing about the car. I said we'd meet them out front. We all got out twenty minutes ago. What made you so popular?"

"They were interested in the story Trey told me last

THE BRIGHT SPOT

night—that he stole the basis of his fortune from his uncle's friend James Dumfries when he was just a thirteen-year-old kid."

"You think Dumfries killed him?"

"I'm certain of it."

"But why?"

"Trey stole his life's work and turned it to shit. That's reason enough. But I don't think that's why he killed him. Trey was about to get in Dumfries' way, interfere with his plans."

"I can see where you two share the same DNA."

"That's not funny."

"I didn't mean it to be. But don't be so sensitive. You didn't kill him, did you?"

Him him? No, not him specifically. Death just follows me around. "No," I said, way too seriously.

"You look awful. Maybe you should get some sleep. We can turn in early tonight."

"No way. I want to build my first snowman tonight." It may be my last.

She smiled her approval.

Back at the Patriotel, the ReCreation crew had shown up and were waiting in their bullet-shaped bus. They were all wearing hats with turkey feathers and Jamestown Settlement T-shirts pulled on over whatever else they had on. They had Martha with them as well, sitting in Mike's lap, déjàviewing like crazy. When she spotted me, she experienced a vivid déjà vu of having just met me. She seemed disappointed when she realized she actually had just met me. I didn't take it personally. She was undergoing a life-changing experience. Good for her. We all need those every couple of years or so, even if we can't remember them any too well later on.

"Whatawe doin'?" Keith, half-deaf soundman, hollered across ten yards of parking lot like we were at opposite ends of a football field.

"Building a snowman," I hollered back, and everybody piled out into the snow. The racket soon brought Gary, Wally, and Brenda out of the pancake lounge, and the rest of the guests out of their rooms.

Half of them turned out to be members of Los Refugios, several of whom had never made snowmen either. So we made a snow band in the front of the parking lot under the sign. The crew made snow roadies to go with them. Our hosts didn't mind. We ended up shoveling all the walks and most of the parking lot, with the occasional pancake break. Stan, who said "I like to shovel" with conviction, did half of it himself.

When the whole snow crowd was made, including several buxom snow sunbathers by the pool that were Wally's doing, we saw them, and they were good. Lu and I had even made Parson Brown from the song and armed him with the Gideon from our room. I fed him his lines—"Do you, Lu, take this actor to be the spouse in your house?" To which she replied, "This louse? I'd take him anywhere—in a motel or in a cell." To which I didn't say anything, which I suppose is just as well. Parson Brown pronounced us "seriously involved in a long-term, committed relationship."

Lu suggested a word change. "'Lifetime,'" she said. "'Long-term' is too..."

"I agree. Absolutely. 'Lifetime' it is." It was a script

we could play beautifully if given the chance. I was sure of it. Parson Brown advised me I could now kiss the bride, and I did. Our guests insisted we dance. Lu asked Marco, the leader of Los Refugios, for something old-fashioned and romantic, and we danced to "The Way You Look Tonight" in Spanish. And even though we were both bundled up in down coats, beneath the fluff she felt like Señorita Rogers in my arms. I felt like Señor Astaire. A feather broke free from her lining as she twirled, and floated in the air. *Bailando.*

Some hours later, when the snow had finally stopped and the stars came out, I asked the lead player if I could borrow his guitar and amp and attempted what I could remember of Jimi Hendrix's rendition of "Star-Spangled Banner" in honor of I wasn't sure what. It was traditional to fuck up the groom, and between the crew and the band, the party had been well provisioned, and I was blitzed. The amp was cranked. Syrups for miles around must have rattled on their lazy Susans. By the time I got to the "home of the brave" line, there were three cruisers full of pissed-off cops just listening and watching and staying up late. What did I care? Until the feds gave up on me, I could piss on the mayor's lawn in any municipality in the country and *still* not get to spend the night in jail.

Eventually, Suzanne came out of the shadows. She'd changed the black blazer for a black bomber jacket and a black beret.

"Nice hat," I said.

"Thanks. Mr. Bainbridge, we know there's nothing

we can do to you, but do you think you could quiet down? Folks are trying to sleep."

That did sound like a good idea. Sleep all around. Only a few dollars extra. "Undoubtably-dubitably-dutedly. Whatever. How thoughtless of me. I'm too loaded to play anyway." Untangling myself from the guitar strap was proving more difficult than usual. Suzanne lent a discreet hand, and I came loose. She deftly plucked the guitar from my hands and returned it to its rightful owner, who wasn't nearly as concerned as he should've been. "Thanks," I said, when I was more or less steady on my feet again. "We thought we might make some snow cops later to keep all the snowfolks in line. Wanna help?"

"No thanks, Mr. Bainbridge."

"Nick."

"Nick."

I leaned forward confidentially. "Sh-sh-sh!" I said. "Don't tell the cops, but not a bit of the shit I'm on is legal." I took a step sideways and stepped into a hole. I struggled to maintain my balance.

"Let me give you a hand," Suzanne said. She took my hand, and I immediately sobered up, or at least stumbled in that direction. For inside her cop hand was a small plastic gizmo she smacked up against my palm like she meant me to keep it.

"Sometimes people require a certain amount of *silence*, Nick. So they can think their own private thoughts, have a little *space*. I'm sure you, always in the public eye, can appreciate that. We're just trying to do our jobs. You can always count on us to be on the job 24/7."

THE BRIGHT SPOT

"I guess my test results came back positive."

She nodded and left me holding the bag, or the heavy little thing, whatever it was, a flattened cylinder with a button on one end. I was guessing it made silences, banished listeners from the forest so trees could fall in peace. It was a portable version of Mr. Henry's bug zapper. I'd said I wanted to meet my maker. She was handing me the means, and with her "always on the job" line, offering to watch my back.

I dropped it into my coat pocket, and I felt it there, like someone tugging at my hem, hand thrust out, *Help me, please, mister. Help me, please.*

Don't beg, I learned early. Sing, dance, lie, juggle, do magic tricks. Act. But don't beg. It never worked out.

Buck's hysterical barking interrupted my thoughts. His belly heavily encrusted with icicles, he stood atop a snow mountain and yapped with wild-eyed delight. Lu and Dee and Stan had taught him the joys of belly sledding, had even built him a ramp that wound around the mountain. Buck threw himself onto it once again, slid down like the stripe on a barber's pole, gurgling and snorting with joy. He was my hero. He was my role model. A happy Sisyphus. He raced back up the mountain. Like Jack, like Jill.

I stood there awhile, just watching him, then Lu—watching her laugh, listening to the sound, remembering the way she looked tonight. *No hay nada para mí, sino amarte.* There is nothing for me but to love you. I wished I could tell her what I was going to do, but I couldn't. I couldn't tell her a thing.

I turned to Wally, working on his fourth or fifth

Irish coffee with extra whipped cream and cherries and chocolate sprinkles. "Tomorrow. Leave Buck out of it."

"But we need Patriot, for when Galatea is kidnapped, and—"

"No, Wally. You don't understand. No Buck tomorrow."

"Okay, Nick. If you say so."

"I say so."

I wandered over to the crew's bus. Inside, Martha was either having or remembering really great sex with... Keith, it sounded like. No one noticed or cared I got another device out of the prop chest for my other coat pocket, to balance the weight. Its purpose was less mysterious. You pointed the barrel and pulled the trigger. People died. Or in this case, one particular person. Once I was alone, I figured he'd find me soon enough. Then all I had to do was point and shoot.

THE RiME OF THE ALDEBRIAN MARiNER

20

> *"Why don't you pass the time by playing a little solitaire?"*
>
> —ANGELA LANSBURY IN *The Manchurian Candidate*

It was a beautiful morning for a sail—snow and sun and bright blue sky and water—and I was wishing I'd worn my sunglasses, when I realized I had them on and cranked to near opacity. They just weren't up to the task. All the way to Jamestown Settlement, we seemed to be heading ever deeper into the heart of an incredible brightness. It was enough to make you miss the Congo.

Now we were gathered around Wally and Brenda in the empty white parking lot, in the midst of the great white world. I stared into my black coffee, and gave my eyes a rest.

There would be a wait before we could get started. For some reason, Lofton hadn't expected us to show, and wasn't quite prepared. Maybe he wanted to talk to a lawyer. He had it in his head I was the one not to be trusted and eyed me with special suspicion. The troublemaker. He knew the type. He was sure I had something to do with Martha calling in sick this morning. (She was actually asleep in the back of the crew's bus, due to show up anytime now.) But Lofton was Gary's problem.

While they sorted things out, Brenda and Wally filled the rest of us in on their *vision* for *BG*. They actually said "vision." I swear I did not groan audibly. I tried to make allowances. They were excited, they were giggly even. I didn't know how they did it. Not after all that whipped cream, not after all those maraschino cherries. But there you had it, the magic of love or art or both. They thought they had a great idea—call it *Pocahontas Meets Frankenstein*—and maybe they did. I wasn't the one to ask this morning. I kept a stoic silence. I wasn't up for any loud noises.

They told the story in a happy tag-team singsong I won't try to duplicate. Here it is, more or less untangled:

Victor and the She-Creature—noting Billy's departure on a walking tour of the Alps (where he'll soon be buried beneath an avalanche)—kidnap Galatea in hopes of luring BG into some as-yet-unwritten trap. But the ship becomes icebound, and BG catches them unawares on a dogsled pulled by a pack of local dogs recruited by Patriot, who, after an effects-laden sweat-lodge peyote vision sure to make him sick as a dog, has switched his allegiance to the Indians. BG sleds home with Galatea in his arms, and they pledge their eternal love and have great sex in the *yehakin*. Impressed with BG's daring rescue of his daughter, Chief Seems-to-Have-Several-Names-Because-Wally-and-Brenda-Can't-Decide—played by the Los Refugios lead singer, Marco, even though he's about five-six and five years *younger* than

Dee, his daughter—gives his blessing to their union, and asks BG to act as his representative to form a coalition among all the Indian tribes to run the English out before those greedy land-grabbing developers Washington and Jefferson carve up the Kentucky hunting grounds and put their slaves to work turning it all into tobacco fields, golf courses, and outlet malls—

"Whoa! Whoa! Whoa!" I said. (I wasn't *that* hungover.) "I sense us headed over the falls in a barrel here. The Washington, Jefferson thing might be... unwise."

"You think so?" Brenda asked guiltily. Knocking Saints Tom and George had clearly been her idea. She had hidden depths, did Brenda—perhaps a degree in social theory or some equally dark secret—before she discovered her gift for herding data and shepherding feedback beside the still but shallow waters of commerce. Maybe that explained her attraction to Wally, though I didn't see how anything explained that. But I liked the direction their collaboration was taking them. I just wasn't crazy about doing a cannonball for our first dive off the high board.

"Go easy on any presidents with their own monuments *and* coins," I suggested as a rule of thumb.

"What about folding money, tombs, and libraries?" Wally inquired earnestly.

Sometimes Wally was quick, I'll give him that. "No problem. Libraries are practically an invitation to work them over."

"Anything else?" Brenda asked anxiously.

This was beginning to feel like a workshop. Death by comment. *Nick, perhaps you'd like to comment on Patrick's performance?* Perhaps I wouldn't. I'd heard enough of me. I was ready to move on. "Otherwise, it sounds great, better than great. Goofy and heartwarming and edgy and whatever. If Lucky Lucifer's the biggest star in the country, I don't see why BG and the Indian Nation can't win the war."

I had to bite my tongue on the sweat-lodge business. I've always hated those vision things. But it was a break for Buck, so I let it pass. Still. I got to say, watching someone else's enlightenment is like watching humor dry. Give me a pratfall anytime. Hold the special effects, please. I imagined Buck in a spacesuit like Keir Dullea in *2001*, whizzing through psychedelic tedium until he finally morphs into a space puppy. That made me smile. Smiling didn't come so easy this morning.

"There's more," Wally said. "The first slaves come in 1609, and there's bunches by the Revolution. I say they rise up too!" He made it sound like they just showed up to party. He danced his fingers as if slaves revolting were just so many champagne bubbles.

I could feel them bubbling up through my aching sinuses. I imagined Charlie Chan, Tonto, and Amos and Andy, armed with lead pipes, following Wally down a long, dark alley. "We're doing all this *today?*"

"Oh no. Just some of the boat stuff. We wanted to give you the big concept first."

"The big concept. Jesus. What about *lines*, Wally? Have you got any of those yet?"

"You don't have to be such a grouch," Wally said.

He smelled faintly of boysenberry syrup and sex. Like Tom Hanks in *Big* had finally scored. Of course he was happy. Why shouldn't he be? "You're right. I'm sorry.

THE BRIGHT SPOT

Too many snowpeople last night. We done here until the boat's ready? I need some aspirin. This sun's killing me."

"Sure, Nick, sure. You just take it easy. We'll blow a whistle or something." He giggled again. "That's what you use with boats, isn't it? A little whistle?"

"A boatswain's pipe," Brenda informed him affectionately.

"Aye, aye," I said.

I headed toward the gift shop without a word. I'd been such an asshole all morning, they must've been glad to see me go. I didn't want anyone following me. My plan consisted almost entirely of making myself truly *alone*. If I survived, we could all make up later. For now, I had to focus on getting myself abducted.

There was a kid I grew up with who read Whitley Streiber's *Communion*, an alleged first-person account of alien abduction, and it changed his life. It was a jacketless copy donated to the school library and mistakenly shelved in Religion by a librarian who would've burned the book if he'd known what it was really about. My friend saved him the trouble by stealing it, hiding it under his mattress. He underlined passages, read them to me after lights-out. He read that book until it crumbled, basing his whole life on his longing to be abducted by aliens.

I understood. Anyplace was better than where we were.

He had all sorts of theories about what would attract them. Mushrooms, he decided once. They liked mushrooms. He ate them out of the yard, threw them up on the front steps. Purging impurities, he said. He adamantly refused to have his hair cut, and had his rebellious head shaved for his insolence—his secret intention all along, he confided in me. Hair, hats, hoods blocked the signal. No matter how cold it was, his hairless head was always bare, always waiting, hoping. Praying. I don't know what else to call it. He carried dead batteries in his pockets, claimed they would heat up if aliens were close and act as a beacon for their tractor beams. I carried them too, in solidarity with my friend.

But most important, he said, if you hoped to be abducted by aliens, was you had to be *alone*. It was more than a mere physical fact, a matter between you and other creatures, but a matter between you and yourself—like one of Dee's disciplines. The alone inside the loneliest aloneness. The Honeymoon Suite in the Heartbreak Hotel. The vast prairie of the Lone Ranger's soul. He tried to explain it to me repeatedly, though words always failed him. I confess I resisted the idea. If I was *alone*, who would be my audience? Who would laugh at my jokes? Who would applaud? Not that dopey one-hand clapping, I hoped. I tried to kid him out of it, but the older I got, the more I understood what he meant.

And then my friend was abducted by something, his mind at least, and he passed from weird to crazy. He frequently broke into gibberish he claimed was Aldebrian, a language, as he rendered it, sounding like a cross between African Bushman and Portuguese. The effect was mesmerizing and utterly convincing. You believed it was a language. You believed he was fluent. He became increasingly bolder in these outbursts, until he was regularly disrupting meals, and then one Sunday, before us all, during the blessing of the sacrament. The translation he offered up when the fathers demanded one was thrillingly blasphemous and obscene. These episodes soon earned him the change of residence he longed for.

Years later, the Bright Spot borrowed his Aldebrian dialect to play an alien in a stinker sci-fi saga, radical only in that the universe didn't speak English. The Bright Spot's linguistic turn was the sole subject of praise in the scathing reviews, so maybe my friend knew what he was talking about. Last I heard he was running serious antipsychotic 'ware so he'd be no harm to self or others and said nothing, not a word—the same in every language—to anyone, ever.

I always liked his name, thought it made the perfect actor's name. He wasn't making much use of it, so the Bright Spot abducted it, took it as his own, my own, when I needed a new one. It was cheaper and easier, I was told, to steal someone else's languishing identity instead of whipping up one from scratch. So that's where my name came from. Who my name came from: Nicholas Bainbridge, Aldebrian abductee.

I told myself, when I took it, that I'd do the name proud. Today might be my chance. I hoped I didn't blow it.

I veered away from the gift shop and headed into the museum hall, a gauntlet of display cases to prep you for the fun stuff outside. I was ticketless, but nobody was at the entrance to stop me, and I plunged into the artifacts. The roof leaked, and the place smelled like colonial-era mildew, given fresh life by the thawing snow. From somewhere behind the scenes came the familiar plunk of water in bucket. Several buckets. Most folks would be wearing an interpretive headset to tell them what to think and wouldn't hear it. In this place, the thing should hold your nose too.

I turned the first bend and stopped, taking a few deep breaths in spite of the mold, searching out *alone*. I was surrounded by the personal effects of people who'd been dead for four hundred years. I had no parents. My childhood gave me nightmares. I'd discarded one phony identity for another stolen from a madman. I was, by conviction, a devout nothing, dedicated to a dying craft. I confessed to the cops and lied to those I loved. I had a loaded gun in my pocket. After today, I might be dead. After today, I might never work again. I could feel it creeping over me, like the shadow of Poe's raven croaking "Nevermore."

Alone.

I was almost there.

Showtime.

I slipped my left hand into my coat pocket and wrapped it around the device Suzanne had given me, firmly pushed the button with my thumb. The displaycase lights flickered, brightened, buzzed, then returned to normal.

There was a noise like a handful of sand hitting glass, and I knelt to see the carpet littered with little drones. They'd crashed into a display case of diaries and letters. If Mr. Henry was right, and they could still see, they'd have something to read until the vacuum cleaner or the mold got them. Their favorite too. Other people's business. I saluted the fallen soldiers with my middle finger and rose to meet my maker.

Just then, from behind me, came a girlish voice.

"You can't enter the exhibits without a ticket, sir." It came from the entrance. I peeked around the case of diaries, thinking she must be speaking to me. She wasn't, but to Stan, who bore down on her with the slightly stiff-legged gait he used for BG. At first, I thought he was just kidding around. She was even younger than Martha. Tiny. I don't know why she hadn't been there before. Maybe she stepped away from her post to go to the bathroom, maybe she was late. Too bad she wasn't later.

"Sir?" she squeaked one last time, as Stan's arm swung from the shoulder in a classic Karloff move and sent her flying into a glass case of flintlocks.

Dumfries didn't waste any time. *You asked for this*, I reminded myself. *Everything that happens is your responsibility.* I told myself to shut the fuck up. Stan bore down on me, his big shoulders grazing the cases and setting them teetering. My right hand, wrapped tight around the pistol grip, my thumb on the safety, loosened, and I let the gun fall into my pocket, raised my hands in the air. I didn't say anything. It only looked like Stan. He couldn't hear me, see me, tell me all about the fucking *soul*, the goddamn *free will*. He was the monster. And me, I was fearless, a regular Gunga Din, a fucking R2D2. Take me to your leader.

Stan bent at the waist and hit my gut with his shoulder, hoisting me onto his back in a fireman's carry without missing a step. I saw stars, but I'd ridden elevators that were a rougher ride. His wrestling 'ware was still humming, apparently.

He hit an emergency exit, and the door slammed open into a blinding white world. Everything was turned upside down. Snow-covered trees, a line of blue water, gaily painted boats. An alarm blared.

"BG! Jesus! Quit clowning around. You scared the crap outa me and Lofton here." It was Gary. I didn't even have time to warn him before Stan flattened him with a backhand. He looked up at me as I passed over, bleary-eyed and squinting in the glare. "Nick?" His mouth was full of blood.

Lofton ran screaming back into the building. He'd have the cops here in no time, for all the good they'd do. Agents were probably already on their way to tell them to back off.

Stan took the gangplank onto the *Susan Constant* in two strides, dumped me on deck beneath the mainmast, and joined the rest of the crew, working with unnatural speed and singleness of purpose to get under way, slipping the lines, pushing us off with poles, synchronized like fingers on a hand. Not the usual crew of reenactors, this was Dumfries' handpicked 'ware crew. No period costumes for these guys except the here and now. Their clothes, filthy from weeks of wear, gave clues to where Dumfries had conscripted them in the name of his cause—collecting garbage, paving a road, guarding a military installation, lying in bed, slaughtering chickens. I hoped the regular crew were safely reenacting some coffee and donuts somewhere and weren't drowned in the James.

The sails billowed and snapped, and we headed downstream toward the bay at a terrific clip. I had no idea a sailboat could move so fast—or that I wanted it to. The dock was soon well out of sight behind us.

The wind cut through my coat and stung my face.

THE BRIGHT SPOT

Several of the crew, their duties completed for the moment, gathered around me, sitting on the deck like Cub Scouts on a field trip to hell. Several wore uniforms. Some still had equipment hanging off them like they were sales racks in a hardware aisle. Some were themselves the equipment, sex workers dressed in tattered kinky. None of them was dressed for the cold, their flesh tinged gray, their eyes sunken. Half-starved. Above us, framed by blue sky, Stan manned the tiller, staring indifferently into the chill wind.

I stood, and nobody seemed to mind except me and my gut. I'd worked pitched stages, whirling stages, gyrating stages, pretending to be everything from earthquakes to storms at sea to a plummet into the pit of hell (the fundie had a nightmare)—all a lot less steady than this deck. So why should it be so hard to walk the length of this boat? Its creaks and groans sounded like gruesome laughter as I staggered from face to face, eyes to eyes, searching for someone, anyone, whose eyes looked back at me. There was no one.

Then I found Murphy, slumped against the bulkhead, still in his wrinkle-free suit, split open and torn in several places, but still not a wrinkle. Nor a glimmer in his dark eyes. He'd lost at least fifty pounds. He must've caught up with Dumfries months ago and found himself shanghaied. Good Citizen Nick had given him the clues. The Bright Spot had shown up in his life with a little ray of sunshine to light the way. *Leave this whole thing alone, Nick. It's a dead end. Folks want it that way. Understand?* No. I didn't. It wasn't a dead end yet. I had a final message for Massuh Dumfries.

I took the gun out of my pocket and crept below.

There were no lights, but shafts of sunlight snuck in here and there and diffused through the musty gloom. Motes floated in the beams. I peered into the dark, musty recesses, giving my eyes a moment to adjust to the light, relieved to be out of the relentless wind. I was reminded of my childhood room. I had the old man to thank for that too.

It was fifteen by eighteen, six beds. Nicholas' had been next to mine. There was a chalice-shaped light fixture, milk-white glass hanging from a trio of brass chains dead center of the ceiling, the bottom dark with the shadows of moth carcasses. Or maybe they were angels. They cast a shadow on my bed like a big fingerprint. I was tiny, almost nothing, a doll in a dollhouse. Soon the roof would come off, a big face would appear, big hands reach inside to find me, to take me out to play. I'd wake up screaming. When I was fifteen, they made the mistake of moving me to a room with an exterior window. Life on the street proved comparatively easy. I never looked back. I wondered if Dumfries lost track of me then or whether he knew where I was all along.

Dumfries wasn't here. Nobody down here but us ghosts. I reemerged on deck to find the whole crew looking at me. Then they all swung their right arms and pointed into the sky. I looked up, half expecting to see an albatross banking overhead. The only thing in the sky was the speck of a cop copter shadowing us at an unchanging distance. I assumed Suzanne was up there with a good pair of binoculars.

My eyes came to rest on the crow's nest. The only place I hadn't looked. Way up there. My heart froze. Yo, ho, ho, you're fucking kidding me. I had a fear of falling.

THE BRIGHT SPOT

The boat was pitched over so far, I'd miss the deck altogether if I fell. No broken bones, just freezing water and hypothermia. "This is nothing," I whispered to myself. "I've been through worse shit than this." You and the Bright Spot both, Nick. Don't forget him. He played a pirate once or twice, counting that one from *Penzance*. He could do this. He still had another scene in him.

We were heading out into the bay, no land on the horizon. How long had it been since we left the dock? How much time did I have to stand here and find my nerve? If I had all day, I might never find it, and I knew I didn't have all day.

I ran at the mast and threw myself onto the rigging, scrambling before I could think about it, as if I were on the clock and we were going for a take before we lost the light, this blue sky, this deep blue sea. I tried to remember the sailor's moves yesterday, but I couldn't find the rhythm. I felt like a turtle climbing a ladder. But by the time I reached the top, numb with cold, gasping for breath, my chest aching, I was terrified not only by how far down it was, but also by the vastness of everything all around.

I pulled out the gun, slipped off the safety, clambered up the ropes into the crow's nest, my heart racing, but there was no one there. Just something that looked like a harness for a very large dog. I held it up. *Rolfe! Rolfe!* I thought, and managed a grim smile.

I looked up. The cop copter was louder and closer and closing fast. A line trailed from the copter's belly like an umbilical cord. I got the gag. I dropped the gun in my pocket and stepped into the harness. The line had a hook on the end to match the ring that nestled up against my breastbone when I cinched the harness tight. The hook swayed ever closer, like a hypnotist's watch.

I'd never played Peter Pan or an astronaut or one of those silly flying kung fu masters. The closest I'd come to flying was auditioning for a musical *Superman* that never got off the ground—and they only asked me to sing a song. I thought it just as well until I stood there watching the mother ship coming for to carry me home, and I wished I'd had a chance to get the flying thing down when no place more important than Neverland or Metropolis was at stake.

I couldn't think about it. I just had to do it. I grabbed the line on my second lunge and fastened it with a clink. *"Man of Steel," key of D, please*. I was abruptly yanked into the sky, swinging around like a botched yo-yo trick, more slapstick than superhero. No one bothered to reel me in as we banked wide and low and sped across the water toward the sun.

COMMUNION

21

Batter my heart, three-personed God, for you
As yet but knock, breathe, shine, and seek to mend;
That I may rise, and stand, o'erthrow me, and bend
Your force to break, blow, burn, and make me new.
I, like an usurped town, to another due,
Labour to admit you, but Oh, to no end.
Reason, your viceroy in me, me should defend,
But is captived, and proves weak or untrue.
Yet dearly I love you, and would be loved fain,
But am betrothed unto your enemy:
Divorce me, untie or break that knot again,
Take me to you, imprison me, for I,
Except you enthrall me, never shall be free,
Nor ever chaste, except you ravish me.

—John Donne, *Holy Sonnet XIV*

The best thing you could say for flying was that it beat falling, the only thing I had to compare it to. Don't look down was all I knew going in, and about all I took away. I learned more about cold. If you're cold enough, nothing else matters. If you're cold enough, it quickly becomes obvious, you're dead. With the windchill deep into the negative numbers, hatless, gloveless, witless, I lost all fear of falling. I would've gladly fallen if it'd been any warmer down below. It was probably only five minutes or so before I spotted his smallish vintage yacht bobbing on the horizon, another five before the copter set me on deck and a couple of 'ware hands took me below. I couldn't have taken another ten. Fortunately, one thing Jimmy and I didn't have a whole lot of was time. Time alone, just the two of us. Pete and Repete.

My host, my captain, my creator, once again sat across a table from me, looking just as I remembered him months ago when he claimed I must recognize him, know him, do his bidding, change the fucking world. He was wrong. I still didn't know him.

"I'm sorry I had to put you through all that," he muttered, meaning merely the last half hour or so. "We must have privacy."

He tried to look patient as I recovered from the cold, but he wasn't doing a very good job of it. He kept glancing over my shoulder out the porthole. Probably sooner than later, there'd be boats and planes on the horizon headed our way any direction you looked. Already, I'm sure, satellites gazed down fondly upon us and chanted our coordinates to the faithful who sought to witness such a momentous reunion. The madman meets his twin forty years later. Our devoted audience might be disappointed. I planned something short and violent.

He'd given me a thin blanket to wrap around my shoulders, hot cider to drink. I hate hot cider. I warmed my hands on it. I shrugged off the blanket. "How am I doing?" I croaked. I begrudgingly sipped at the hot cloying sweetness to clear my throat.

He tilted his head, furrowed his brow, me playing an old, old man, politely befuddled. "Doing?"

Part of me just wanted to shoot him and be done with it, but then me being me, I had to say a few words first. "When I met you, you said it was my job to *change things*. Well, how am I doing? Have I fucked things up enough for you yet? Have I killed enough innocent people? Sufficient property damage to suit you?"

He compressed his lips. I'd hurt his feelings. The ungrateful child. "I understand your anger."

Don't you have to have a counseling diploma on your wall to get away with saying shit like that? Especially when it wasn't true. "No. I don't think so. You don't understand shit. You think I owe you something, or you wouldn't be dragging me here. You're going to tell me how I *work* now—give me my operating instructions. Isn't that it? And then I'm just supposed to do it. Right? Isn't that what you've got in mind? You stick me in hell for fifteen years and forget about me. Then—after I somehow manage to bust out and get a life, a wonderful fucking life, mind you—you show up to give me my *mission?* Fuck you, Jimmy! I don't think you understand my anger at all." My hands were warm now, most of the stiffness gone from my fingers. I wanted them in good enough shape to do what I told them to do.

I reached into my pocket and took out the gun, slipped the safety off, pointed it between his eyes. I couldn't miss. "Not that it matters. I'm not killing you because I'm angry, though that should make it easier. I'm doing it because, no matter how many people die, it seems nobody else is even trying to stop you. Even worse, they blame your crimes on innocent people, like Ed's hate killers, just to let you off the hook, so you can keep fucking things up, and you stand by and let it happen. All because you've got a plan, a vision, something they want. I don't know. I don't care. This is where I get off. I've seen enough of your handiwork. I don't want any job you'd give me. Understand *that*? I'm tired, Jimmy. I only plan to witness *one* more violent death. Yours." I raised the gun.

I wanted him to cower, break down, plead for his life, beg my forgiveness. The prick reasoned with me. "Please listen to me. You can't kill me. Not yet. Not until I've told you why you were made, what you, and only you, can do to change things, to right a terrible wrong. Then you may kill me, if you like, once you know the truth. I'm ready to die."

Know the truth. You and only you. My finger tightened around the trigger. The barrel shook. "Get this straight: You're not ready to die until I say so. And here's the *truth:* If I even *think* you're going to tell me what more I can *do* for you, I'll blow your fucking head off. Understood?"

Dumfries nodded, looking as calm as a glacier. He might've been sitting in the park feeding the pigeons, the nice old man with the slaves. Maybe he *was* ready to die, like he said. I wasn't sure why, but that made it harder to kill him.

He said, "I'm sorry for everything you've had to endure, Nick."

I winced as if he'd prodded an open wound. I didn't

THE BRIGHT SPOT

care one way or the other if he was sorry, but he didn't actually call me Nick. He used the name I once thought of as my real name, and sitting there, hearing him say it, I had a revelation.

"I don't use that name anymore," I said. "Ever. I just realized something: You must've given it to me when you dumped me in my childhood home. Is that right? Did you *christen* me, Jimmy? When you stuck me in that shithole?"

He grimaced, filled with guilt, sympathy, excuses. "Yes, I did. I know your time there wasn't pleasant. I'm terribly sorry. There were limited choices, and once you were there, I couldn't get you out without drawing attention to us both. I was so closely watched, I couldn't interfere. And then, well... you managed to get out on your own. If it's any comfort, they all went to jail not long after you left."

I heard. Word traveled in my circles when somebody who actually deserved it did time—like an urban legend or something. "Jail didn't seem like enough to me. I wasn't looking to be comforted. I wanted them to go straight to hell for eternity."

"You believe in hell, Nick?"

This time he got the name right. "Yeah. Of course I *believe* in it. Like you say, it wasn't pleasant. But it doesn't matter what I believe. They were the ones who believed in hell and all the rest of it. Seems only right they should be judged by their own rules."

An ironic smile blossomed and faded on his sad, wrinkled face. My smile. Another reminder we were playing from the same genetic script. But we weren't the same. He'd done things I'd never do. At least I didn't think I'd do. God, how I hated him. "You played me, used me to lead you to Ed, so you could murder him. Why? He adored you. He was a harmless old man. Why did you kill him?"

He scowled. He didn't look particularly penitent. "He was no harmless old man. He deserved to die for what he did. I used you, yes. You have a tracking program, part of your original installation. I realized I could use you to lead me to Ed, if I could trick you into seeking him out. I hadn't planned on doing it, but when I saw you and Luella pretending to be...her and me..." He choked up. It took him a second to get a grip. "I felt everything all over again. I *knew* it wasn't real, but it didn't matter. It was as if I was sitting there again hoping our great plans would work, terrified something would go wrong. But I also knew what I didn't know then— that Ed had already betrayed us and would murder her within hours, run her down like a dog, because he couldn't bear the thought that I was going away with her, that I loved her. It was like going back in time. In here." He tapped his chest hard. He looked like something awful lived in there. "I decided to do what I should've done back then. I'd imagined it often enough." His boney hands clenched on the tabletop, strangling ghosts.

"Did you *see* Ed kill her, or are you just playing the scene in your head?"

Dumfries shook his white head dismissively. Who needs to see when you have the truth? "No one saw it. But he did it, all right. Agents showed him recordings of Galatea and me together. He went crazy. He hadn't known how we felt. I intended to tell him, but... You never could reason with him. He steadfastly refused over

THE BRIGHT SPOT

the years to understand our relationship was impossible. He would never leave me alone. That night, he showed up at the house, completely hysterical. Fortunately, my wife wasn't home. He and I had words. He said awful things."

"Imagine that. I can't figure out why he gave a damn about you. Sure he was pissed. That doesn't mean he *killed* her. He knew she was essential to your plan to end 'ware, right? Whether you loved her or not wouldn't matter. Ever listen to his speeches? I think he would've done anything to end 'ware. Giving *you* up would be the least of it. He must've been longing to be free of you for years anyway. I met your ex-wife, by the way. Do you know what she said about you?"

He flinched at the question as if I'd slapped him. He did know. Exactly. "I knew you called on her," he admitted.

He knew more than that. "She called you a *faggot*, not a term I approve of. What did you think of it?"

He was pale, the lines around his eyes and mouth giving away his pain. "She was angry, provoked. I understand her feelings."

"You're a real understanding guy. This tracking program. What else does it do besides track?"

He hesitated a moment, glanced nervously at the gun barrel. "I can listen, hear what you hear."

"Any time, any place, if you wanted."

"Yes."

"What do you need to access it?"

"Any terminal, the address and password."

"Vision?"

"The data stream's too wide."

"Pity. Here I didn't think you cared, and all along you've been listening to my prayers all these years. Ignoring them, maybe even fucking with them, but listening just the same. I'm touched. You're wrong, by the way. About Ed. But maybe you know that already."

He looked out the porthole, his eyes pinched, his old lips trembling, no longer looking for what was coming but at what had been. He was walking a thin line. I wanted him to fall.

"Who tipped you, Jimmy? Who told you the truth? Salvador?"

"That disgusting pig!" he snarled. Jim was a fierce old dog when you kicked him in the right place.

"What did he tell you about Galatea?"

He avoided my eyes. He tried to sound dismissive, but he knew he wasn't fooling anybody. "He thought I was a gullible old fool. He showed me what he claimed were Galatea's original orders as Lenore Chapell, laying out everything she did, making it seem she never intended to bring down 'ware, never intended to go away with me, never loved me, that it was all just a charade to trick me into giving up my secrets. It was a cheap trick. They were clearly forgeries after the fact to knock me off balance, to... to break me down."

It didn't look like it would take much to accomplish that. He stared into space, remembering, then made the mistake of looking at me. Maybe I looked a little doubtful about his take on Galatea. He leaned forward, determined to persuade me, beseeching me with my hand gestures. "She was shattered when she came to me. Do you understand? She scarcely knew who she was. I put her back together again. I *made* her. I *named* her. She would do anything for me without question. I loved her. She adored me, looked up to me. And Salvador expected me to believe she was deceiving me the whole time because of some scraps of paper he fabricated? He...he clearly wasn't trustworthy."

Ah, but Jimmy could believe it, even coming from the untrustworthy Salvador, couldn't *stop* believing it, even after he'd murdered the messenger and stuffed him in a garbage truck. "Maybe he was right," I said. "Maybe they weren't forgeries. Maybe she played you from the beginning, understood what made you tick and ran you like the little windup tin god you are, running you like you were one of your own soldiers. How fitting. What goes around comes around. You know what they say, Jimmy, the power of pride goeth before the fall."

His eyes burned into mine. "You think you're so smart. So smug. Freedomware saved the world, preserved our way of life. It was necessary. Its original purpose was noble. It was going to make us free—free of want, free of limitations, free to pursue our dreams. But it was stolen, cheapened...."

"Corrupted?" I suggested. This guy wouldn't know freedom if it was staring him in the face. So that was his story: I gave humanity this wonderful gift, they just weren't worthy. *Exterminate the brutes!*

"Face it, Jimmy. Galatea was on their side."

"What about you? You're a fool if you think you can trust that bitch Luella. She was fucking Salvador, you know. He told me about it, said she was like an animal, couldn't get enough. She doesn't care about you. She's working for them. They're all the same, the—"

I pressed the barrel against his forehead, shoved

until the back of his head hit the bulkhead, and he shut up. There was a moment there I didn't know whether I was going to shoot him or not, until it was over and his sorry head was still in one piece and there'd been no big bang, no expanding universe of Dumfries' brains splattered all over the cabin. I pulled the barrel away from his forehead. It left a small purple O. I didn't like the feeling of having almost killed a man. Even him.

"Galatea's been dead a long time, and Lu's a subject I suggest you avoid altogether. We're talking about *your* crimes for the moment. You killed Salvador because he told you the truth and you couldn't handle it. Then you killed Ed because blaming everything on him helped keep the lie alive. Trey had lots of reasons to end up dead, and none of them interest me, since the world's probably better off without him. But what I don't understand is how you can kill all these innocent people along the way in the name of ending 'ware. Innocent people who never heard of you and Galatea. People you don't even know. You don't sound too trustworthy yourself, Jimmy."

"Look at me. I'm an old man, watched constantly. How long would I last on my own? I had to use those people. Do you think we could be having this conversation any other way? Can I pilot a helicopter? Sail this boat? Take on armed professional killers? I had to use the only means at my disposal. This is too important not to. I regret the loss of innocent lives. I didn't intend they should die."

"You didn't *intend*? You thought Trey Kennemeyer would just go up in flames and no one else would get hurt? You might be a fucking idiot like he said, but you're not that stupid."

"He would've ruined everything. He suspected your importance and wasn't about to let you go until he'd figured it out. He would've murdered you when he was done with you if he didn't kill you in the process."

"I'm supposed to thank you—swapping all these lives for mine?"

"Of course not. But how can you condemn my actions when you don't even know why you're so important?"

That line almost earned him a bullet. "Listen to me, old man: I'm important because I'm alive. I'm important because I'm a superb actor. I'm important because Lu loves me. I'm important because I fucking say so and I'm good to my dog. Any ideas you have on the subject don't interest me."

He looked at the barrel again, deciding he'd take his chances that what he had to say didn't interest me like Moses didn't care about the Commandments, like Sleeping Beauty didn't want to be kissed. He was going to tell me anyway. It was good for me, it was good for everyone. He thought he knew things like that. That's what made him so dangerous. "I wrote the original Freedomware with voice command, but the generals told me to take it out. I didn't, but said I did. Access was limited to my voice, which you've shown you can emulate, and my genotype. *Our* genotype." He eyed me significantly to make sure I'd been awake that day in biology class. "I left it that way. They never knew. When Freedomware was stolen for commercial purposes, they just wrote routines on top of my code, so it's still there beneath all their crap...."

Commercial purposes. All their crap. How tacky. The poor guy. Enough to make you want to go out and murder a few dozen people. He was going to make supermen, Jedi knights, and all he got was pool guys and garbage men, and now the Homeland would never be the same.

"As you've guessed, our dialogue in the diner was a code. The question 'There's someone else, isn't there?' initiates the sequence, signaled by the response 'Yes, there is someone else.' The names are a code string that activates the switch to voice command, pending verification of genotype."

"Kissing the tears."

"Exactly."

"So that's why you wanted Dee. She heard the names, she kissed me. You thought she was working for Trey."

"How do you know she wasn't?"

At least he was consistent. "Doesn't matter. She's certainly not working for him anymore. Trey's dead thanks to you."

He'd drawn me in. He'd told me my trick. I could instruct a workware crew to do my bidding with a string of names and a kiss because I had the right voice and DNA. I knew half of the routine. And I still hadn't killed him yet. I might as well hear the rest of it. "So what was Galatea running, a virus?"

"That's what I told her. For her own protection I thought she should know as little as possible. Viruses are slow and ineffective, a mere annoyance. Voice command

THE BRIGHT SPOT

gives you and me the ability to control any single crew. She carried a simple instruction set permanently making *everyone* in the system, everyone running 'ware throughout the world, once she entered the system, a single crew for purposes of voice command only, regardless of whatever conventional command hierarchy they might be running under. She needn't stay. Her mere presence would permanently alter the operating system. Afterward, the workers would go about their usual businesses, follow their transmitted work orders, with no change at all until they receive a voice command—which can only come from you or me—then they all act as a single crew. What you say to one will be heard by all, and obeyed regardless of any other instructions. By all of them. Unfortunately, it's very rudimentary. They all obey any command simultaneously."

"How long are they one crew?"

"Under voice command, permanently, once the instruction's given. It can't be rescinded without crashing the system."

"And that's what Lu's running now. Once she runs 'ware, all the workers in the world would be one crew ready to follow my orders. That's how you and Galatea set it up. She would link them into one crew, then you give the order."

"That's right."

"And what instructions did you intend to give them, the workers of the world, when Galatea logged in and made them one crew, forever subject to your command?"

He looked back at me calmly. I don't know what I'd expected him to say, but there was a moment before he spoke when I knew he was going to surprise me, knew that perhaps I shouldn't have asked. I felt a chill go up my spine, raise the hairs on my neck, tingle like a halo around my head. He spoke clearly, with absolute conviction. "What you must say when the time comes: Quit. Shut down."

I tried to imagine it, everyone throughout the world running 'ware shutting down, planes falling out of the sky, fires raging, workers dropping dead in the street from the air they could no longer breathe. "Thousands would die."

"Many thousands, I should think. But then it would be over."

"What makes you so sure they wouldn't just start it all up again?"

"I can't be sure, but not without a great deal of opposition. Ever flown in a zeppelin?"

"This is a pretty big *Hindenburg*."

"It has to be. The whole species is at stake." He smiled his sad smile again. This time I could see it wasn't quite like mine. He was insane, and I wasn't. Not yet anyway. I was still young.

"And what happens to Lu if she ever runs 'ware and delivers this simple instruction set?"

He shook his head at my foolishness. "What do you care what happens to her? Do you think—"

I shouted him down. "What happens to Lu, you sick, fucking old man?"

He could've lied to me. I've often wondered why he didn't. I like to think it was because he knew how much I would've hated him if he had, and he couldn't bear the thought. But knowing him, it was probably just the principle of the thing.

"She dies if she runs 'ware," he said. "Salvador told me. It will look like a violent allergic reaction. The agents who were watching us planned to grab Galatea before she could affect the system, but they laid a lethal trap for her genotype, in case she eluded them. Insurance, they thought. It's still in place. It will kill her when she runs 'ware, shut down her autonomic nervous system. Her heart will stop. But the damage will have been done, the instructions given, the system permanently changed. They won't even know what's happened until you act, and then it will be too late. Do you understand what you must do?"

I looked back at him a moment. I wasn't going to shoot him after all. It was too late. I'd listened. "I understand what you want me to do. But I don't think you understand me too well. I can't let Lu run 'ware, knowing she'd die. Even if you could convince me she's the deceitful monster you've got in your head, the answer's still no. Because you know what? If that were true, then workware can have the fucking planet anyway, because I won't give a damn. Either way you lose."

I expected him to give me an argument, but he didn't. He seemed to understand, and maybe he did.

"I've told you," he said. "That's all I can do. The choice is yours."

Some choice. I laid the gun on the table in front of me. We both knew I wasn't going to kill him. Moments later jets crisscrossed overhead. We looked toward the porthole simultaneously, mirror images, like an old vaudeville routine. It was supposed to be funny when one person pretended to be the reflection of another, especially in all the little ways it could go wrong. "Shall we wait on deck?" he said. "They'll be concerned for your safety if they can't see you."

I doubted that, but I let him lead me up the companionway. It was still brutally cold on deck. We were holding our position in a tight circle. The jets were a lingering echo, off to round up the rest of the gang. There was nothing visible yet on the horizon, but they'd be here soon enough. The gun was in my pocket. I didn't see any more use for it. I pulled my coat tightly around me.

"I can't let them question me." He smiled apologetically. "I know things." He actually waved goodbye before he broke into a passable run for a man his age. I don't know how I could've stopped him short of fumbling for the gun and shooting him in the back, and what would've been the point in that? He dove over the rail and plummeted toward the icy water. I reached the rail just as he hit the surface and went under.

In seconds a Klaxon blared, and his 'ware crew automatically launched into their rescue routine, diving into the water after him, their bodies tuned to handle the cold, racing through the water. Even so, he must've been dead before they reached him. He was certainly dead when they laid him out on the deck and checked his vital signs, tried to revive him. Nothing. Then they bagged him, left him lying there, and returned to their positions. Mourning wasn't part of the routine.

I followed the helmsman up to the bridge. He shut off the Klaxon and parked himself by the wheel. He was lean, with big hollow eyes. Who knows how long he'd been on this boat, carrying the old man around.

"Is there someone else?" I asked him.

His eyes met mine. "Yes, there is someone else."

"GusCarlTerryArthurAlanGeorge..." By the time I was done, his eyes were gushing tears, and I kissed them. "What is your name?" I asked.

"Blaine Causwell," he said.

"Take us home, will you, Blaine?"

He took the wheel and gave it a turn, and we headed west, toward the mouth of the James. I sat on the deck, beside the body, shivering in the cold. About the time I spotted land, agents dropped out of the sky and boarded us, whisked Blaine and the others away as evidence.

"What did he say?" one of the agents asked me urgently when they found me by the body.

"What did who say?"

"Dumfries! Who do you think?"

"Nothing," I said. "Paranoid delusional nonsense. He was completely out of his mind." That was my story, and I stuck to it. I passed out before they even got me off the boat. I woke up a few days later, a new man.

STEER CLEAR OF THE CONGO

22

"Mistuh Kurtz, he dead."

—Joseph Conrad, *Heart of Darkness*

The only thing I saw when I opened my eyes was Lu looking back at me. "Nick? Are you awake?"

I was, but I didn't speak right away, basking in the tender concern in her voice and expression. Either she was the greatest actress who ever lived, or she adored me. Either one suited me just fine.

"Nick?" she whispered.

"Who you calling Ted?" I croaked.

"I didn't call you Ted."

"Well, why don't you?"

She smiled like a dirty-minded angel. "Because you're in the hospital."

"That must be why the sheets are so clean. Ted can't come to the hospital?"

"No. The man in the next bed might mind."

THE BRIGHT SPOT

I doubted that, but I could understand how Lu might. "When do I get out of here?"

"I'll see if I can find out. There are lots of people who want to talk to you."

She didn't exaggerate. Some of them were even doctors. "Hypothermia is no joke," one of them told me. That little gem cost me a week's salary. There wasn't much wrong with me other than a lot of stress, a touch of pneumonia, and a little exposure.

But I never wanted for visitors. I talked to shrinks, cops, cop-shrinks, and several agency officials whose precise agency and title could not be divulged to me without an extensive background check I'm sure I wouldn't pass. If they asked me a question, I answered it.

"Mother's maiden name?" one badly briefed fellow asked me.

"Garbo," I said.

He wrote it down. "First name?"

"Greta."

He wrote that down too. "Sounds foreign," he suggested.

"She was from the Aldebrian Emirates," I said.

"Never heard of those."

"They're new."

I could say anything, apparently, and he would write it down. Okay. I'll play. It beat watching television, where the latest news was the recent terrorist attack at the World Palate. It only has to get on the news to be the truth. No arrests had yet been made of those ever elusive terrorists, though there was no shortage of file footage of suspects from yesteryear to blame it on even though most of them would be pushing ninety by now and were probably dreaming the big sleep.

With Dumfries dead, at least the feds quietly let the case against the pool guys fall apart and tossed them back into their shattered lives. They would've been better off convicted. They could've written a book. Now they were just bums.

Once my keepers figured out I wasn't going to change my story, recruit 'ware workers to murder diners in posh restaurants, or talk to the press, they just let me go. They continued to watch me, I'm sure, probably kept us all under permanent surveillance to see what might turn up. Wally would have someone to talk to over breakfast for the rest of his life.

Murphy, looking pretty good with the weight he'd lost, was in a room just down the hall. He told me how he used the clues I gave him to get himself kidnapped by Dumfries: "The feds left an easy trail. I figured the limo for a rental. No agency's going to own something like that. There's only a handful of high-end limo rentals. It was a slow weekend. A guy answering Salvador's description rented two limos for that morning using the name of Robert Zork."

"Zork?"

"Zork. The guy with him fit the description of your limo driver. He later returned one of the vehicles, saying the other one had crashed. He flashed a badge and told the limo's owner the feds would make good, which they hadn't, of course, so he was more than glad to cooperate with me. He showed me his GPS records on the allegedly crashed limo. Its location when the GPS quit working turned out to be the old diner, where it used to

THE BRIGHT SPOT 311

be anyway. The whole building's empty, has been for a while. I figured Dumfries had to be using the car. About then I got your message about Williamsburg and asked the locals there to keep an eye out. He hadn't even changed the tags. I collared him down at the marina. I was reading him his rights when he asked me some weird question or other. Next thing I know I'm waking up in the hospital."

I told Lu if she ever did 'ware she would die, and made her promise she never would—a promise she'd already made to Bea. I didn't tell her the rest of it. I couldn't take the chance she might want to break her promises and save the world. I knew that was wrong, but it was an easy decision. Could I live without her? No. Next question? It didn't matter.

I told Lu the same story I told everyone else. The man was looney tunes. You can forget all about James Allen Dumfries.

His funeral in the rain on the news looked like a spook convention; Jean Brand, bereaved widow in the foreground, was the only one crying. The son and daughter flanking her were absolutely stone-faced. It was like I could hear her, insisting, *No one believed in him like I did. He said so. He* said *so!*

Must be true, then.

Me, I believed in him like I believed in hell. He was what he was.

Meanwhile, we'd missed at least three weeks' work on *BG and the Indian Nation*. Fortunately, Suzanne slipped us the surveillance video from the *Susan Constant* abduction as her way of apologizing for failing to protect me—Dumfries had her piloting the helicopter, actually. It was great stuff. With BG at the tiller and a ghost crew stolen from the future (you had to hand it to Wally), we were able to milk that for half a dozen episodes, while we played catch-up with the rest of the plot.

The *yehakin* just didn't feel right, according to Wally, so we produced Buck's sweat-lodge scene in the crew's bus with the help of The Ironoclastic Hysterians (the band after Los Refugios), a few pounds of hamburger, various flashlights, and bonfires of cheap incense. It took all day, but Buck was a real trouper, and somehow the scene worked. Even I liked it. The crew was now thinking about redoing the bus's interior in rattan since they couldn't get the incense smell out.

The switch to *BG and the Indian Nation* hadn't hurt our numbers, but hadn't helped them either. They were doing just okay, maybe good enough to stick around, maybe not—we'd flattened, as Brenda put it.

Then we got the kind of break you wait a whole lifetime for.

An outfit called the Christian Soldiers, based in Chesterfield County, Virginia, and headed up by a nutcase calling himself Gabriel, as in blows his horn, denounced *BG and the Indian Nation* as immoral, unpatriotic, satanic, the list goes on and on—all leading up to the conclusion Gabriel always reached: The End of Days is at hand; better send money, honey, or meet me down at the motel.

At the height of his tirade against *BG,* he got particularly cranked up over the depravity of Buck's sweat-lodge scene and ran a clip from it glossed with liberal

THE BRIGHT SPOT

doses of Revelations and his own wacko tracts. Gabriel had a big fringy audience—everybody from the psychotically devout paramilitary types, to college kids who liked to make fun of him, to lonely women who found his muscular certainty sexy and longed to be filled with celestial fire. Enough people, in other words, so that what he denounced was news, especially if it came with good visuals. And Buck was the best. The newsies loved the sweat-lodge scene. For a while there, you saw more of Buck's mug than the President's. Every comedian needed a few Buck jokes. By the end of the month, Buck's bug-eyed communion with the Great Earth Spirit was the cover of *Time*. The headline read "The Numbers of the Beast!" Brenda's terminal practically fried itself crunching them.

Buck was a star.

This changed things.

Unfortunately for me and Lu, our characters quickly faded to the periphery, like those older-generation Vulcans on *Star Trek* or the first-season succubae on *Lucky Lucifer*, on call but forgotten. The show was getting too serious for our slapstick ways. Satire was out; wisdom was in. Before you knew it, Buck had a book coming out, a compilation of Wally's fortune cookie aphorisms called *Patriot-isms* that was destined to become an instant classic, with a promotional budget big enough to get him elected President, if only he met the age requirements. Success didn't go to his head, however. He was still the same old Buck, only busier, jetting around the world. We walked down some mighty fine alleys, he and I, security lurking at a discreet distance. I still picked up after him myself. It was a matter of principle.

Without anybody ever asking us, Lu and I soon found our names in the show's credits under "Buck's Handlers." Our salaries rose accordingly. I later wrote a book about our experiences called *Ipso Factoids,* but nobody bought it, in spite of a glowing blurb on the jacket from Patriot himself.

Stan and Dee fared better. BG and Princess Galatea were given a wisdom makeover as well. With an Eastern dog, a Western princess, and a guy who'd been dug up out of the churchyard, esoterica was pretty well covered on all fronts. The show was essentially *Lassie, Come Om:*

Come quick, Patriot! Timmy's chi just fell down the well!

Perhaps that is his journey, Squashblossom.

You can see where Victor and the She-Creature didn't exactly blend.

We would've looked for other work, but being Buck's handlers was pretty much a full-time job. In addition to keeping him healthy and happy and on time, we personally answered all his correspondence. Lu made me answer all the ones asking for advice. You'd be amazed at the things people will ask a talking dog. I made him a witty correspondent, had him explain that his phony accent on the show was only a role, that actually he spoke in a French baritone. His advice was always the same: Be yourself, and if that doesn't work, act like somebody better. No one sued.

There was one last bit of unfinished business that nagged at me ever since I saw Jean Brand crying at her husband's funeral. We were on Buck's book tour and calling it a honeymoon when we passed through the city.

THE BRIGHT SPOT

I called her up and told her I was the last person to see Jim alive, and I had a matter I wished to discuss with her.

It took her a moment to get over hearing my voice—his voice. "I've been expecting your call," she said softly. Maybe she had, which was all the more reason we should talk. I didn't want her looking over her shoulder for the rest of her life. With all that yoga she might live forever. I took along a copy of *Patriot-isms* as a peace offering. It's small enough to fit in a coat pocket or on a toilet tank.

Bus connections were better to the old money, some of whom still preferred to employ the old-fashioned servants who could think and talk and steal and gossip and ride the bus. I could afford to take a cab, a limo if I wanted, but I spent too much time riding around in cars these days, so I took the bus. If anybody knew or minded I was a famous dog handler, they didn't let on.

After our last gloomy conversation, I'd pressed for a daytime meeting. Otherwise I would've brought along a miner's helmet or a candelabra. She suggested the library. She looked good, in a smart white suit—what people wore on ocean cruises, she informed me, modeling, flirting, actually. She didn't look a day over seventy.

She accepted the book graciously. She insisted I select a volume from her excellent selection of drama. She planned to sell it off, she claimed, when she returned from her cruise. I chose a vintage paperback of *You Can't Take It with You* in a collector's plastic bag and thanked her profusely. By this time we'd avoided the subject of her husband for about as long as either one of us could stand.

"I understand that you had an encounter with Jim," she said.

"That I did."

"And was he mad as a hatter?"

"Yes, I believe so."

"As I suspected."

"All along?"

She shook her head, a little scared of that idea. I wasn't crazy about it myself. "No, it was all the pressures after the war. All the demands made upon him. His senseless, relentless guilt."

"His heartbreak?" I suggested.

She laughed her Hepburn laugh again. That's where I'd seen the suit before, *The Philadelphia Story*. "You would be very much mistaken, Mr. Bainbridge, if you think he suffered greatly over the end of our marriage."

"Nick, please. That's not what I was referring to."

Our eyes met. Now she knew why I'd come. Maybe she was wondering how much it would cost her, but I don't think so. She liked me. If only Jim had been more like me.

"Would you like some sherry?" she asked. "And almonds. I love the two together, don't you? They're behind you." She pointed to a small table where a crystal decanter of sherry and a dish of almonds waited. Sure, why not? I poured and spooned and dished and fussed. And we sipped and nibbled and chitted and chatted. Any moment we would start talking about T. S. Eliot or Bob Dylan. Stalling until she had enough sherry in her to say, "When you say 'heartbreak,' you mean that woman, don't you?"

"Galatea Ritsa."

THE BRIGHT SPOT

"That wasn't her real name, you know. She didn't even know her own name. I was here the night they dreamed it up, when he brought her here. For Edmund it was a great moral crusade, but for Jim it seemed just another puzzle he could solve brilliantly. She would be the medium, the clay to be molded and fired. She sat over there, read books all night, hardly said a word. She was a beautiful thing. He couldn't take his eyes off her. I suppose I knew then that he would fall in love with her. That was the only time I ever saw her."

Not quite, but I didn't quibble. I knew what she meant. "You never drove an SUV, did you?"

"I didn't care for them."

"That's why Ed told the cops that the car that hit Galatea was an SUV."

Our eyes met. "Yes."

"How did that happen?"

"I had come home from a meeting with government agents. They had shown me images of Jim with that woman. I don't suppose I have to tell you what sort of images. They thought I would tell them things, betray him. I didn't. But that didn't mean I was...unaffected. I was sitting in the car outside, gathering my nerve to go in, when Ed came running out of the house, completely hysterical, and saw me there. He told me Jim planned to run off with her, that he was leaving us both. It was the only time we ever openly acknowledged the state of affairs that existed between us.

"I took off. I had previously followed them to their assignations, followed her to the apartment where he put her up, always remaining at some distance. I don't know what I thought I was accomplishing. Until I saw those images, I'd managed to convince myself my jealous fears were just that, and not to be acted upon.

"I pulled into the parking lot for her apartment, the motor still running, it was only moments, and there she was. She'd come out to jog along the road overlooking the river. I let her get out of sight around the bend, counted to ten, and stepped on the gas." She relived the moment, flinched when machine hit flesh. She'd relived the moment many times. She took a deep breath.

"Ed had followed me, afraid of what I might do. He got me away when he was too late to stop it, went back and called the police, claimed to be a witness, told them it was a man in an SUV. He did it for Jim, I suppose. To protect him. He did everything for Jim."

There'd been entirely too much of that going around. "That's pretty much the way I had it figured. There was no real investigation at the time. Officially, she was already dead before you met her. I came out here to tell you I don't plan to set the record straight. I don't see what purpose it would serve."

"Did Jim know who did it?"

She was desperate for me to say yes. That would be her small vindication. He knew. He spoke her name. But I hadn't played Marlow for nothing. The truth might be too terrible altogether, but hey, it's all you've got. "He thought Ed did it. That's why he killed him."

"Of course. Ed would be the passionate one, wouldn't he? Since Jim never felt any passion for me, he couldn't imagine I would be the one to fly into a jealous rage. You should've seen his grief afterwards. He was inconsolable. All those years, I told myself his lack of passion had nothing to do with me, then to see..." Her

THE BRIGHT SPOT

voice trailed off as we drifted around the bend, and the past finally seemed to be behind us.

"I understand," I said. "But I don't think his feelings had anything to do with *her* either, no matter how beautiful she was. Want to know what he told me? 'I *made* her.' The only thing James Dumfries was ever passionate about was himself."

"You're wrong about him."

"I *knew* you'd say that. But you know I'm right. You'll come around. Have a great cruise, Ms. Brand. And be sure to steer clear of the Congo. You look great, by the way."

"Jean, please."

I kissed her cheek. "*Bon voyage,* Jean."

RISE AND SHINE

23

And now, once again, I bid my hideous progeny go forth and prosper. I have an affection for it, for it was the offspring of happy days, when death and grief were but words which found no true echo in my heart. Its several pages speak of many a walk, many a drive, and many a conversation, when I was not alone; and my companion was one who, in this world, I shall never see more. But this is for myself; my readers have nothing to do with these associations.

—MARY SHELLEY, INTRODUCTION TO 1831 EDITION OF
  Frankenstein

NOBODY LIVES FOREVER. DOGS ESPECIALLY. BUCK caught a respiratory ailment at the height of his career that took him out in a matter of days. He was twelve, which I guess is a respectable run for a dog, but it didn't seem near long enough for such a good-hearted creature. Lu and I were devastated. I had no idea you could grieve so hard for a dog. ReCreation had cloned Bucks, a whole stable of them, which they promptly deployed, but we never had anything to do with them. Buck was Buck. There will never be another. Even if Ipso Factos are now a registered breed with the AKC. "Exceptionally intelligent," I read of them recently, "prone to respiratory infections, should avoid air travel." They didn't even mention the lapdog gene.

As much as we missed Buck, Lu and I were glad to get back into acting. Lu found a niche as a rich bitch (as she herself liked to put it) in any number of guises, from sci-fi aristocrat of the Aldebrian Empire (one of Wally's) to a cattle baron's shrewish widow in the Western revival that finally rode into town. She did a great turn as Miss Havisham in an uneven remake of *Great Expectations* that got lousy distribution. She did drug commercials, joking she'd finally given in and started dealing. They never liked me for those things. I could gaze hopefully at the horizon as well as the next guy, but my heart wasn't in it.

I had other work, though. I did a little bit of everything, but not much of anything worthwhile except a cheating gambler who gets shot between the eyes fourteen minutes in. It opens with me shuffling the cards, talking fast. They're *my* fourteen minutes, best thing in the virtual. I expected a flood of calls from other directors dying to bump off Bainbridge in their own distinctive styles, but none ever came.

Then I did a town drunk who witnesses a murder and inexplicably drops out of the plot, a couple of kindly interchangeable grandfathers (Gramps and Popsy), a lifer in the laundry giving the young hothead who didn't do it a little advice on getting along in the big house that's laughably out-of-date, and a stupid centurion arresting

Our Lord, the idea being, the youthful director explained, that if he busted God, he must be a *real* dummy. I'd read for Judas, but they thought I was too old. You're only as old as you feel, I said, but they weren't going for it. I would've pointed out their Jesus was well into his fifties, not counting the face work, but I needed the money too badly. "How stupid do you want this centurion?" I asked. Very stupid. You got it. The old Jesus worked out okay, by the way. It made sense that a thirty-three-year-old messiah might put on a few extra decades before all was said and done.

I looked for smarter roles and ended up getting typed as the explainy scientist, like a particularly painful stretch of Jeff Goldblum's career, but I resisted that undertow, even if it meant doing instructional virtuals for power tools, where at least the lines made sense. A router didn't have to go faster than light. Sci-fi bullshit generally *did* have to go by at least that fast to make it sound even vaguely plausible. When we reach Alpha Centauri, we can talk. Till then, spare me the starships.

Listen to me. I'd jump on any one of those roles now, of course. Beggars can't be choosers. Pleaders either. I prayed a couple of times, though I never liked it. I couldn't find my audience. It didn't work. Because pretty soon *all* the work started drying up. You could watch it happening, but you couldn't stop it, like all those swamps shriveling up in Florida, leaving the bleached bones of golf communities like balls buried in the sand.

First, *all* the crews went 'ware in just a couple of years. Nowadays, people who actually know how to make a virtual are as common as typewriters, and just about in the same demand. Though, come to think of it, there *are* people who collect old typewriters, but no one wants to keep an old soundman around the house.

Then, just like Lu predicted, came Trouperware. You load the 'ware, enter the script, and the workers perform it, simple as paving a road or disemboweling a chicken. So even the instructional work dried up. Every factory or restaurant could take workers off the line and make whatever virtuals they needed.

Live theater was almost immediately dead and buried, though it'd been on rich-people life support for forever. But now the same crew that cleaned your house, for a few dollars extra, could put on a decent-enough performance of almost any length from skit to five-act tragedy. They could perform *while* they were cleaning if you preferred. You could pause them if you got bored or busy and have them come back the next time the toilet backed up to finish off *Lear* or do the time warp again. There were all sorts of packages available.

For a few seasons there, at The Lakes at Llewellyn everywhere, backyard opera was all the rage. Three tenors? That's nothing. Try a dozen. They go great with the fajitas. The workers did everything from build the set to mix the drinks and never missed a note.

But most (poorer) people still preferred their culture served up in commercially produced virtuals for the home-box market. Trouperware immediately sucked up every bit part and most of the supporting roles. Any fantasies I had of fading quietly away playing the folksy janitor or the nosy neighbor ended abruptly. Soon there were no more than three or four non-'ware parts in any dramatic project, and those were strictly for stars or those in the running to become stars—not old warhorses like me and Lu.

People still liked stars, the wisdom went, and a star couldn't be using 'ware. Stars, of course, advanced this wisdom, and it still seems to be limping along—a star holding it up under each arm—though I don't give it much longer. Who needs them, right? They're hopelessly inbred. Most new stars are to stardom born. Reviews typically begin with the lineage of the stars and stars-to-be, like nobility, like a dog show. You don't need Déjàviewer to get the feeling you've seen these people before. Most aren't any better than the Trouperware supporting cast, and some aren't half as good.

And don't get me wrong. Trouperware is good, even very good. I've studied up on the stuff. Professional curiosity, you might say. Workers on Trouperware will consistently deliver a three-out-of-four-star performance. They never blow a line. They do their own stunts—the stunt package is included, along with every other damn thing imaginable—accents, martial arts, dance steps, weathering, impressions, birdcalls, whatever. If you want a sunburned Astaire as an Aussie pilot shot down in the desert who gets the sudden urge to yodel, just punch it in.

But if that's all they could do, they'd be useless. Where they truly excel is in expressing human emotion, arguably better than most humans do. They can blush like a sunrise, tear up like a tidal wave, but that's the least of it. Workers on Trouperware emote based on the extensive mapping and analysis of thousands of expressive markers in the face, in the voice, in the smell even. So that when these guys follow a direction—using the

THE BRIGHT SPOT

Directorware that comes with the package—they're not just fooling around. You direct a Trouperware worker to do abject terror, you'd better stand back and be ready to clean up after.

Not that they can't do subtle. They can do the little twitch that breaks your heart acting's been all about since the close-up was invented, and they can do just the right timbre in the voice you can't hear in an amphitheater to go along with it. I can watch them and tell you the code you enter to get the precise expression that wrings a poignant tear from your eye. But you know what? You'll cry anyway, and probably won't even have noticed that all *tenderness* now looks and sounds the same. All *dismay,* all *wonder,* all *curiosity.* All *I'm-totally-fucked.* All *sincerity.*

All acting.

There aren't any actors anymore. There are only menus. Extensive menus. And I'm not on any of them.

It used to matter if you knew how to do something. It's not so hard, I suppose, to read and emulate other people. It used to take practice, study, maybe a certain sensitivity, though that may be pushing it. I've known plenty of excellent actors who were assholes, including yours truly on many occasions. That's the beauty of it. It's not about whether I'm a good guy, but whether I'm a good actor, then I can be any guy in the world, any world you like. But now all it takes is the money for the 'ware, like everything else.

It used to be fun. For the actors, for the audience. At least I always hoped so. Doesn't it *matter* that I was here hoping, even if it all ends up as digital soup? Maybe not. Now it's just something else the lucky worker can make of himself for shit wages, something else the hungry consumer can swallow. I read the other day that "since the introduction of Trouperware, consumption of the dramatic arts is actually up." I wonder how they measured that—dollar volume or meals served? I got out just in time, before I lost any fingers or toes, heart or soul.

Bon appétit.

Fortunately, Lu and I aged gracefully enough to get steady work modeling sportswear for seniors. We were essentially mannequins who could take direction but were cheaper than using licensed 'ware. We were getting by okay. But you know how it goes. First it was impossible to get ahead, then hard to keep up, and then before you know it, we were falling behind, just as employers started telling us we were too old. Eventually we couldn't afford to fix the roof or pay the taxes, and we had to sell the old place before the city just took it off our hands and sent us packing.

We wouldn't be missed. Murphy's was long gone. Everything around us had been scraped off and upgraded. Our new neighbors glowered at us with open hostility. Mr. Casual was now president of the local civic association, an organization whose sole purpose, it seemed to me, was having us scraped off as well. They were hoping for scraped off the planet but would settle for just the neighborhood. Property values were suffering. The city heard their pitiful cries.

Yeah, it was time to move.

Then Lu got sick, or discovered she was. She'd apparently been sick for a long time. The limited-assistance

THE BRIGHT SPOT

living facility we were trying to move into required a health screening to make sure we wouldn't be too much trouble. Lu's tests had revealed "something"—the limited-assistance health technician who broke this news said—something *serious*, something, well, *fatal*.

As we sat there in stunned silence, he went on to scold Lu for not being tested earlier. "Now you have severely restricted your treatment options," he said.

I told him he had the option to severely fuck himself, and that made Lu laugh out loud. It was the strain of the moment, I guess. But still, it beat the alternative. I tried to make her laugh as long and as often as I possibly could. It must've worn her out, but she never complained. I wish she'd been more of a complainer—she confessed to the health technician an impressive list of symptoms I'd never heard anything about before. But I wasn't about to scold her. Broke and sick isn't a role anyone's eager to play. Besides, there wasn't time for scolding. The long and short of it was the limited-assistance facility wouldn't let her in, since they weren't set up for someone with such limited options, and by the time such a caring facility was located (with a waiting list longer than Lu's life expectancy), there were no options left.

But one. *Home Death Alternative*. The latest thing. Popularly known as the Double-D, for *Drop Dead*. You agreed to keep your hopeless self at home and spared the public health-care system—an imaginary creature if there ever was one—the expense of attending to your demise. In return for your pledge, they gave you a booklet and some good drugs and a hotline staffed by dedicated volunteers. You even got a grief counselor with that at no expense. Three sessions. One before, two after.

Best of all, if you were accepted into this program, the city wouldn't forcibly remove you from your home for nonpayment of taxes. Required were forms waiving all rights of any sort and proper medical documentation of the certainty and proximity of your approaching death. Lu's prognosis of "a matter of weeks" qualified her for the city's benevolence with perhaps days to spare. The cutoff line on the upper end was shadowy. It probably depended on the real estate market. The city didn't have a program to fix the roof, of course. That would've been socialism, and I understand that's some terrible stuff. I wouldn't know. I'm just an actor. With any luck, the place would fall on us to spare the city the cost of our burial. But for the time being, we got to keep our house.

We celebrated our reprieve from homelessness with a candlelit dinner. I cooked—a cup of the good lentils and a half cup of basmati—put on some music—a compilation of the depressed turn-of-the-century women singers who were Lu's faves Bea played for her when she was a kid—Aimee Mann, Sheryl Crow, Lucinda Williams. She talked about Bea a lot, remembering. I'd splurged on a box of wine. It should last a matter of weeks, I thought in the store, and got my crying out of the way before I came home. It's hard to take a stand, Sheryl reminded me. Maybe the music wasn't such a good idea.

It started raining, a real summer downpour, and we shut off the music and just listened to the rain falling inside and out. She tired easily. She tried to put on a front,

THE BRIGHT SPOT

but she drank her wine in exhausted little sips and had to concentrate when setting the glass on the table. This wasn't any Hollywood disease. She was in pain pretty much all the time. The painkillers would be kicking in soon. They "managed" her pain by knocking her out cold. I couldn't put off telling her any longer. I'd been stalling until the house business was settled. I didn't know when I could work up my nerve again, and no time was a good time.

She nestled up against me, sipping her wine, and I finally told her everything Dumfries had told me, over thirty years ago now, boiled down to its essentials: How the two of us together could bring down 'ware, probably for good. Still could, if we wanted. I thought I should tell her. I knew how she felt about the 'ware—the same as I did.

"What do you want me to do?" she asked. "Do you want me to do it?"

"It's completely your choice," I said. I sounded so severe. I feared becoming my fathers. "I mean...I don't want to influence you. I don't know what to say."

She searched my eyes. She was the calm one, as usual. Though maybe this time it was the drugs. The grief counselor had suggested some for me as well, a different flavor from Lu's, but I'd turned them down. "I know it's my choice, Nick. But you've had so much more time to think about it than I have."

Many long years. "I know. I'm sorry...."

"No, I don't mean that. I'm glad you didn't tell me before. But you must've thought about it. What will you do, if I...you know."

She'd gone to the heart of the matter, teetering right

on the brink anyway. "I'm not sure. Sometimes one thing seems right, sometimes the other. I don't think I can really know unless I actually have the choice."

She nods, imagining, pondering. "Does 'ware ever seem right?"

"Never."

"Just the ending of it?"

"But at what cost? Is it right to cause a horrible cataclysm in order to save the world?"

"Isn't that what all those wars were supposed to be about?"

"And look how well they turned out."

She had a dreamy look. The painkillers were coming on. I plucked her wineglass from her hand and put it on the table. "It's not the *world*, though, is it?" she mused. "Just us humans. Do you think we're worth saving?"

"Yes, absolutely."

As usual my certainty surprised and pleased her, and she managed a weak smile. "Why's that?"

"Because you're one."

"You're sweet," she murmured. "Why else?"

She was drifting off, her eyes were fluttery. She was right. I had thought about it. "Because we pretend to be better than we are, and sometimes we pretend so well, we actually become better."

She curled up in my arms. "Mmm. I like that. I can't decide." She fell fast asleep.

Look at me, I would've added if she'd been awake. *I pretended I was someone lucky enough to spend my life with you, and that's who I've become.*

• • •

THE BRIGHT SPOT

In the morning, through a fog of sleep, I heard the front door open and close. In one of those tricks of sleep, I thought it was years and years ago, and Lu was just going out to take Buck on his morning walk up and down the fashionable alleys, and they'd be coming home any moment now and get back into bed with me. It was a delicious feeling. So vivid was this illusion, I half expected, when I opened my eyes, to see a cup of coffee on the bedside table, covered by its saucer.

Instead, there was an envelope propped against the lamp. It took me a moment to focus on it, to realize what it was. *Nick,* it said in the wobbly scrawl that had become Lu's handwriting.

I leaped out of bed and ran outside. Down the block a Maid-To-Order van was pulling away, loaded up with 'ware maids making their appointed rounds. I knew a woman who did Maid-To-Order, her hands calloused halfway up her forearms. When she cooked spaghetti, she scooped it out of the boiling water with her hands. "I don't feel a thing," she said to impress me. I hadn't thought of her in years. The van had brought her to mind.

I didn't see Lu anywhere. I had no idea how much time had passed since I heard the door, how long I lay there dreaming. It could be minutes or hours.

One of my neighbors was gaping at me like he'd never seen an old man in his underwear before. "Have you seen my wife?" I demanded before he had the chance to give me any shit. "She's not well. She shouldn't be out."

"She just left," he said, pointing after the Maid-To-

Order van as it inserted itself into the torrent of traffic at the end of the block. I ran back inside and called them. They passed me from one idiot to another.

Meanwhile I read Lu's note through my tears. She said she loved me. She said she was ready to die. She said whatever I decided was all right with her. She said goodbye.

By the time I finally got off the phone with the assurance a company representative would give the matter his utmost attention and get back to me immediately, no more than an hour had passed since my dream.

I barely had time to pee before the phone started ringing. I ran to the phone and grabbed it.

"This is Melanie Tidewater from Maid-To-Order Customer Relations. May I speak with... Nicholas Bainbridge?"

"That was fast. What did you find out? Did you locate her?"

"Is this Nicholas Bainbridge?"

"I've been talking to you people all morning."

"I... I wouldn't know anything about that, sir. You are Nicholas Bainbridge?"

There was a touch of panic in her voice, fear. She had to make sure it was me, but sure as hell didn't want to be the one to tell me why. "Yes," I said softly.

"Would you hold for my supervisor, please? Her name is—"

I hung up the phone. I never learned her supervisor's name. I knew what she was going to tell me, and I didn't want to hear it like that. I didn't want to hear it at all.

THE BRIGHT SPOT

Lu was dead. She'd run the 'ware. Her heart had stopped.

It wasn't hard to scrape me off after that. I didn't put up any fight. The limited-assistance facility that wouldn't take Lu took me—a room and a bath. I'm healthy as a horse, apparently. I cook in the cafeteria to earn my keep. I give acting classes. I think too much. I grieve.

My young grief counselor suggested I choose a pet from the facility's acceptable-companions list. She suggested a lot of things, actually, but that was the only one I took. I hope she never took any of my suggestions. After all, she was only trying to do her job or get her degree. I have anger issues, was her stated opinion, and I'd give her an A+ on that diagnosis.

The acceptable-companions list wasn't much of a list. No dogs, cats, anything you could warm up to. Then I noticed *chameleon* and thought we might have something in common.

He came in his own habitat. That's what they call it. Looks like a cage to me. I named him Spot. We don't have much of a relationship, but he puts up with my humor. "Feeling blue?" I greet him when he's perched on my jeans. "Seeing red?" I ask him on the fire extinguisher. He's always got the hint of green no matter what color he turns. I've come to think he likes some colors more than others. He looks really good on golds and oranges and seems to know it. Lizards might be cold-blooded, but they have a quiet dignity. I'm supposed to keep him in his habitat at all times, but I don't. Locking him up is supposed to be for his own safety. He might get lost—sucked up by the vacuum cleaner is the favorite scare story. But he's easy enough to find if I need to get him out of harm's way. The only window's in the bathroom. I just open the shutter a crack so that the sun hits the tile, and in no time, there he'll be—on the bright spot.

So there I was, me and Spot, feeling too pathetic and fragile to actually *do* anything, though all I ever did was think about what I should do. I was drifting, an albatross hanging around my neck. I needed a miracle. Then Cassie Rockworth happened. I tell you, life's a hell of a story.

I'd just made tofu stroganoff for 150, who all complained there weren't enough mushrooms or there were too many, and I was in no mood to be trifled with, when somebody came to tell me I had a phone call. I was sitting on the front porch, glaring at the spring, listening to the click of dominoes and dentures all around me.

"Who the hell is it?" I inquired of the messenger.

I was given the phone and the finger. Fair enough. I pushed the button.

"Hello?" I said cautiously. I hadn't received a phone call since I'd been here.

"Nicholas Bainbridge? Is it actually you?" Female. Fortyish, near breathless with excitement and emotion. She was almost certainly trembling. I suspected a practical joke, but nobody liked me that much.

"Yes. This is Nicholas Bainbridge. How may I help you?"

"Oh my God! It's actually you! You haven't exactly

THE BRIGHT SPOT

been easy to find. There were times... Oh God, I'm so sorry." She snuffled noisily, blew her nose. "You'll have to give me a minute."

She was actually crying. Hell, I was crying too, and I didn't have any idea what the hell was going on. It was certainly intense.

"You must think I'm crazy. My name is Cassie Rockworth and we met years and years ago. I was just a little girl. You probably don't remember me. We were riding on a bus, and I was very rude, and you gave me your card...." She got choked up again. No, *couldn't* be, I'm thinking.... "I became a terrific fan of *BG* after that. And then *all* your work, and that started a lifelong interest in the dramatic arts and your work in particular. I did my dissertation on your work and have published about it extensively. I've tried to track you down many times before, but always failed, but with the festival coming up and everything, well, I bribed someone I met who works for the government, and he gave me this phone number. You are Nicholas Bainbridge the actor, aren't you?" You've never heard so much hope packed into one plaintive little voice in your life.

I'm your man, little lady. You just dry the tears from your eyes. I still have skills in spite of my advancing years, so I offered my credentials in the form of a long and bloodcurdling maniacal laugh that stunned the limited-assistance porch into silence and thrilled Cassie no end. "Oh my God! It's you! It's really you! This is the happiest day of my life!"

I didn't know how I felt about her going quite that far, but I appreciated the sentiment. "Festival?" I got around to inquiring when she'd calmed down a bit.

"Yes," she said excitedly, "a celebration of and symposium on your work. We're calling it the Bright Spot!"

A cold wind blew through my heart, and I almost dropped the phone. "The... the what?"

"The Bright Spot. It was my idea. You know, from the mid-career nickname. It's the pivotal chapter in my dissertation on the connection between your early work, and your later work as Nicholas Bainbridge. It was quite a breakthrough when I demonstrated you were the same person. It sort of put us both on the map. I'm at the University of Arizona now, and we were hoping we could fly you out for the festival, and... and maybe you could say a few words?"

Can I say a few words? I can say plenty, actually. I'll try not to embarrass you. "Certainly. I can do that. I'd be delighted. The Bright Spot. You came up with that? I... I like that. That's... me."

Tucson's pretty. I brought Spot along in his habitat and turned him loose in what they call an *arroyo* around here. I figured he'd like it out west with all this sun, all these different golds and oranges to be.

The festival concluded last night. It was quite a week. The highlight was a series of virtuals in which my old performances were mounted in new settings with doctored scripts and volunteer actors and crew, all dedicated, it seemed, to making me look good. It was really quite embarrassing. Almost as embarrassing as Cassie telling me I'd changed her life on the Llewellyn Connector over thirty years ago, or telling the packed auditorium of scholars I was "immortal."

THE BRIGHT SPOT

A coalition of scholars—that's what they call themselves, a coalition—are furiously pulling strings to have my copyright-infringing masterpiece restored and distributed in time for next year's festival. They hope I will attend. At least they hope that for now. They may feel differently after what I'm about to do.

Cassie's supposed to pick me up to take me to the airport, but there won't be any planes flying today, and she'll find me gone. I've left her a note thanking her for everything and explaining something has come up and I'll make my own way home.

I found a pancake house just down from where I've been staying. I've finished my short stack, and I've just been sitting here, watching the sky slowly brighten behind the lights of a road crew working, dancing in the dawn. There's about a dozen of them.

The booklet Lu got with her drugs was called *Happily Ever After: The Art of Facing Death*. "Everyone dies," it begins. Fair enough, if everyone gets the chance to live first, if there's at least one open window, one shaft of light on the tile, one bright spot in the sun. Otherwise, it's all a lie, isn't it?

I pay my check, step out into the cool morning air, and head toward the lights and the workers, hoping to have a word with them.

About the Author

Robert Sydney is the author of several critically acclaimed works of fiction under another name. He lives, under another name, in Richmond, Virginia.

DON'T MISS

SPECTRA PULSE

A World Apart

the free monthly electronic newsletter that delivers direct to you...

- < Interviews with favorite authors
- < Profiles of the hottest new writers
- < Insider essays from Spectra's editorial team
- < Chances to win free early copies of Spectra's new releases
- < A peek at what's coming soon

...and so much more

SUBSCRIBE FREE TODAY AT

www.bantamdell.com

SF 7/05